Promise Me

The Promise Me Series
Book 1

Tara Fox Hall

Published by
Melange Books, LLC
White Bear Lake, MN 55110
www.melange-books.com

To Tammy, the first friend to encourage me to live my dream of writing.

To my mother for all her encouragement, such as the statement, "If you don't make this more exciting, I'm not reading more than the first chapter."

To my husband Eric; my anchor, my oak and my rock.

To Eve M., who remained patient with me even when I was cranky and bitchy. To Nancy S., for taking a chance on a new author, and Caroline A, for a stunning cover.

Lastly, to my beloved Ghost and Darkness: I miss you every day.

Prologue

Danial was dying.

He could feel it in his blood, the burning in his flesh. He pulled the truck onto a side road and accelerated. His pursuer couldn't be far behind. He glanced at his arm, at the small gash that was even now healing. It might be better for him if he opened it up again. He'd cleaned it the best he could, but it wasn't like he'd had time to do more than pour water on it. It felt as though a razor had cut him and was working its way deeper into his flesh.

Had to be poison. And no run of the mill arsenic or derivative.

His mind worked frantically. What poison had been on the tip of that arrow? Who had that been in the shadows? Who'd known he'd been working on the Donaldson contract, that he'd be there tonight, watching? And most importantly, who had dared attack him?

It was possible the attacker hadn't known his name. But whoever had done this knew the breed of man he hunted and had prepared a special end for him. He'd gotten a glimpse in the shadows of what had hunted him; red eyes and a masculine form moving at supernatural speed. In his world, that still left a long list of possible suspects. For certain, it had been another of his kind.

He came to a crossroads and went west, then to another and headed south. There were no headlights behind him, at least so far. Best to leave the most complicated trail he could.

With some bitterness, he wondered why he was fighting so hard to survive. His life had been pointless for the last half century. Modern books and novels talked about how fun it was being a creature of the night; so romantic and glamorous. What a crock of shit. If he hadn't had

1

his business, he'd have gone crazy. And as for there being so many women who wanted to be with…someone like him…for the most part, it was a phase girls in their twenties went through. Looking for a bad boy to titillate and seduce them. Not one had been anything of substance. It never lasted very long. But the ones who wanted in for the long haul were worse. There was always the vow of doing anything for him and the promise of eternal devotion. Until they found out that he couldn't give them what they wanted. Then it was wheedling and hints of what he would do if he really cared for them. He'd stayed away from any serious commitments lately, say the last thirty years. Why bother, when they were doomed to fail?

Enough of depressing thoughts! God, wasn't death at the end of the night depressing enough? He smiled at that and checked the rearview mirror. Still no lights. His attacker was either a master tracker or an amateur.

Maybe his life wasn't everything he'd hoped for when he was young. But he'd be damned if he'd give it up without a fight.

He felt a wave of nausea, and swallowed. If there was going to be a fight, it had better be quick. He could already feel himself getting lightheaded, and it was getting worse by the second. He had to pull in somewhere and get out of the open. The night was more than half over. He'd never make it to the campsite he'd planned on, not how he felt.

* * * *

Terian paused, full of righteous triumph, a wide smile on his face. This was going perfectly. He'd hit his target, and it would all be over in a matter of hours. If he was lucky and had gotten the arrow deep enough, it might be only one hour. That poison was damn effective. Better yet, fate had done him a favor. The killer had been calling on his cell when he'd been hit, and in his shock and rush to get away, he'd dropped it.

Slowly, red eyes gleaming, Terian held the phone in a taloned hand and crushed it to pieces. No help coming tonight.

He still had to be careful. After all, he'd never done anything like this before. This was no time to get cocky. It wouldn't be over until he'd either seen a body or a nice mound of ashes bathed in daylight.

Better get a move on. The night was already half over and his prey had a big head start.

* * * *

Where the hell was he?

Danial looked around and saw only cornfields and wooded areas. Small houses were interspersed here and there, some with barns or paddocks. Livestock were in some of the pens; if only that would work tonight.

The muscles in his arm suddenly contracted. He swerved, barely missing a truck coming the other way. He overcorrected, sending his truck almost into the ditch. But then he saw a turnoff. At least, he hoped it was. His eyesight was going dim, and he knew his time had run out.

He swung the truck into the opening among the trees, evoking a loud clank from the front fender. Nothing like a metal chain to scratch paint, not to mention leave evidence of a trail. The road seemed little more than a path, and he maneuvered as best he could; but his strength was failing fast. He slumped over the wheel, and the car rolled to a stop.

He had to get to safety. At least, in the trees there'd be darkness and shadows, where he might be able to find shelter.

Exhausted, he pushed against the door, momentarily forgetting how to work it. He fell against the passenger side door, disengaging the lock, and opening the door. In slow motion, he fell, the ground rushing up to meet him.

The door, at an angle, remained open for a moment, illuminating his body in a pale glow. Then the door succumbed to gravity and swung slowly shut with a soft click, leaving the vehicle and Danial's still body in darkness.

Chapter One

Yawning, I saw it was close to eleven p.m. It was Monday night, and I was curled up on my couch, cats sharing my lap. Sipping a glass of wine, I read the latest DeMille thriller. Jessica, my male cat with gender-identity issues, and my black cat Cavity had persuaded me to stay up past my self-appointed bedtime in order to provide some warmth and company. My slightly feral cat, Asher, was also there, hiding beneath the sofa, while two dogs, Ghost and Darkness, slept at my feet.

It had been a long day, but I was used to that. Living alone at thirty on fifty-plus acres of both forest and rich-yet-rocky soil with pets and a job, even a part-time one like mine, meant long hours. And the work could be brutal. Today, coupled with visits to both Flora, my pseudo-grandmother, and my best friend, Kat, I was exhausted. But chain sawing and wood splitting tended to do that to me. Worse, this would be an extra busy week for me. That dentist appointment today had upset my work schedule, meaning I'd need to go in on Wednesday this week to make up the time.

I probably shouldn't have bought those flowers for Flora, I thought sheepishly. But she loved them, and she was only going to turn ninety-eight once. I could get by with waiting another month to make my first foray back into the dating world. What would it hurt, to wait another month?

Flora, of course, had taken the opportunity to remind me to get on with my life in her usual fashion: "People come in and out of your life. It's the time you have here with them that matters, not that they may not be around forever."

To make matters worse, Kat had then reminded me that we were both getting older. *I'm worried about you*, she'd said, taking my hand.

Promise Me

You need to let go, Sar.

I'm okay, I'd replied a trifle coolly. *I feel good.*

We aren't getting any younger, she'd replied, her tone a little sad. *It slips away so fast.*

It matters how you feel. I feel young, and good. I'm okay.

But the truth was I'd lied. I did feel good most of the time. But I wasn't okay. When I was twenty-something, I'd thought of thirty as "old." I'd been sure that by the time I was thirty, I'd be married, with two cats, and maybe even a kid or two. At the least, I'd figured on knowing who I'd be with the rest of my life. I'd found out too late that even the best laid plans could fall in on me like a house of cards with one fateful gust.

Maybe that was a good sign, that I knew I was missing something, unhappy living alone. I missed having a man around, both in my life and in my bed. I'd lost someone I loved. But I wasn't dead, and maybe it was time to stop acting like I was. There was that singles thing coming up in town...

Suddenly, my comfortable and reflective mood was interrupted by distant snapping and crunching sounds. They were faint enough to register with my challenged brain that all wasn't as it should be. The cats didn't act as if anything was wrong, but they were unreliable. If the house was burning, they might only move when the heat became unbearable. But the dogs at my feet were motionless, their heads raised. Dogs have ears that don't fail.

I stepped to the window just in time to see headlights slowly following the road. That was the sound I heard: a car driving on the property edge, along my neighbor's access road. Whoever was out there at this time of night was most likely not traveling the road to inspect the gravel pit at the end for safety violations.

Some jackasses were out looking to have some fun. My neighbors would have no idea that anyone was there, their home being a good ten minutes by foot through the trees, not to mention roughly a hundred feet higher in elevation. Many a truck load of raw earth and gravel had been dug out of the hillside, providing a perfect depression in the land to conceal any telltale lights from anyone's view but my own. No one else could see them from the road, and even if they could, no one would care.

5

Most people minded their own business out here, unless you wanted to make trouble and were prepared to deal with the business end of a shotgun.

The decision was now mine: did I want to involve myself with this? Whoever was up there was just going to smoke a little grass or drink a little, or have the kind of fun that involves little plastic square wrappers. But it might well be something worse they were doing, like crack or meth, and that could be dangerous for me to interrupt.

I cursed aloud and decided I'd better take a look. Whoever had decided to take a little side route to adventure had first gotten through the heavy steel chain that blocked the access road. Bolt cutters would have been needed to cut through that thing, and who carries bolt cutters in their car? Someone had planned this, and if they were willing to cut a chain, they might be planning worse than some drinking and partying.

Throwing on some clothes and collecting my waist-length hair in a plastic clip, I gathered a flashlight and my keys. I debated taking a weapon, but I talked myself out of it. Then, on the way to the door, I talked myself back into it, and got my .38 Special revolver. It was loaded. Depending on the size of the car, there could be six people at the most. Six bullets were enough.

I buckled on my gun belt and knife and went out the front door. Walking to the barn, it occurred to me that I might be overreacting. But I wasn't one for hiding in the house, waiting to see if someone would leave me alone. It wasn't my way and had never been.

The first fall I'd owned the farm I'd seen a hunter parked by my barn during deer season. I hadn't called the police, hoping they would show up before he either left or put a bullet through one of my windows. I'd loaded my shotgun and walked over to his truck. I'd racked the weapon within hearing range, and when his head had whipped around, I'd asked him what the hell he thought he was doing. He'd been properly apologetic and left. More importantly, he'd spread the word, and I didn't get many trespassing hunters anymore. People who wanted to hunt on my land respected me enough to ask me, and if I thought they hunted with care, I let them. That was that.

Tonight, I hoped I could just ask them to leave nicely and have them agree. Most times, despite my worries, that's exactly what happened. But

I didn't hear the usual sounds I expected: loud talking, music, the sort of giggling that meant sex was a definite possibility but not a surety. Odd that whoever was in the quarry wasn't laughing it up.

I got to the barn. Its outside light was on and welcoming. I slid the door open and walked into the darkness inside. I knew the barn in and out, and I wasn't afraid. There was nothing that was going to hurt me in there. I'd never been afraid of ghosts. I believed in God, and I had faith. And what my faith couldn't handle, my .38 Special was sure to be able to take care of.

I cranked the key to my 5310 tractor, and the fifty-five horsepower diesel engine roared to life. I raised the front-end loader and backed out, swung around, and headed in low gear up to the quarry. I hoped to give them enough time to realize I was coming right for them and to clear out. The access road led up to the quarry directly from the southernmost edge of my property. I wouldn't cut them off. Instead, I'd come in directly in front of them, leaving them the option to back out, or turn around and go out the way they came in.

The stars were out, and the wind brought me the smell of rain. It would be here before the night was through. I was remarkably awake for this close to midnight, which was a good thing. It's bad to operate heavy machinery when you're impaired. OSHA said so, and that was a large part of what I adhered to in my job, so I was familiar with the rules. The tractor had enough power to drive though a house wall, so it was good that I'd had only one glass of wine.

I navigated the access road with my headlights, and sure enough, there was a car in the quarry. Rather, it was a convertible truck, one that switches to a SUV. Its headlights were still on, the engine idling. There was no one in the driver's seat; and from what I could see, no one in the vehicle at all.

What to do next? I hadn't anticipated this.

Time to bluff. "This is private property. I've called the police, and am going to get your plate number before I go. So you'd better clear out!"

There was no reply, or sounds of running feet. Where were they? I checked for footprints or signs that someone had been outside the car, but other than some leftover prints from my neighbor's ATV in the muddy spots, there was nothing. How was that possible? Someone had to have driven the car, so there had to be footprints.

I turned around and walked back towards the truck. This time I approached in the shadow of the car instead of the tractor headlights. It was then that I discovered that I hadn't been as alert as I'd thought. Blending with the shadows was a large man lying on his back beneath some hawthorn bushes, his legs twisted. He'd tumbled out of the truck once it had stopped.

He was attractive, thick dark hair to his shoulders. I would have thought Native American, but he was pale in the extreme, at least in the headlights. His build reminded me of a professional athlete. Not a bodybuilder with steroid-inflated muscles, but more like someone who did marathon running or ice skating. There was a solidness to him that spoke of strength and power with a purpose. His clothes, which I'd taken for gray, were actually dust-covered.

I never assumed he was dead, lying there, but I finally thought perhaps I should stop admiring his physique and check him for injuries. I hesitated a few seconds, worried maybe he was waiting for me to get closer, so he could grab me. Then I told myself I was just being stupid. Hell, if he'd wanted to rush me, he could have done so easily when I was distracted. I touched him. He was cool, but not cold. He wasn't dead, not with a pulse. It was sluggish, but he was definitely alive. I couldn't see if he had any injuries. I thought about trying to move him, but I couldn't budge him. He had to weigh about two-twenty at least, all of it lean muscle. I was pretty strong, but I wasn't able to move him, not alone anyway.

I climbed back up on the tractor and slowly inched it closer to him, levering the bucket down. Stopping the tractor, I pushed him into position and carefully got him in without causing further injury. I looked him over under the spill of the tractor lights, but I could see no blood or wounds. He was covered in dust himself, and the light was bad, so my inspection went no further than determining there were no gaping holes. I used my shirt as a makeshift pillow, so his head wouldn't bang on the metal when I drove went over bumps. Either he was going to thank me or think I was crazy.

I went as slow as possible down the access road and opened the door to the garage. Slowly lowering the bucket to the ground, I considered the second problem: how to get him to the basement guest bedroom, twenty feet away.

As much as he might thank me for getting him out of the coming rain, he was *not* going to thank me for strapping him to a dolly to wheel him to bed. Easier to bring the bed to him—at least, the part I could carry.

I laid a plastic tarp down and dragged the mattress out from the bedroom onto it. Draping a blanket over that, I climbed back onto the tractor. Positioning the bucket over the mattress, I slowly rolled him out onto it, then maneuvered him onto his back. I tried to be as gentle as possible, while also ignoring the thoughts in my mind that were telling me what I was doing was not only irresponsible, but potentially dangerous.

Satisfied that he was comfortable for the moment, I backed the tractor up and shut the garage door. I swung her around and headed back to the barn. The night was hardly over and I had to finish this up fast. It was after midnight by now, and I was losing steam and reasoning powers.

I left the tractor at the barn, still rumbling, though the thunder from above my head was so loud it nearly drowned out the tractor. Lightning flashed over the velvet black tree line, and I thought, shit, I'd better hurry, unless I wanted to be soaked! I walked quickly back to the quarry, praying the truck was an automatic. It was still idling with over half a tank of gas left. I checked the backseat, but there was no one hiding in it. I got in, closed the door, and drove the truck down the access road, to my barn. After parking it on one side, I maneuvered the tractor in behind it.

I wasn't an idiot. I knew what I was doing was irrational and probably dangerous. I had just taken a man I didn't know into my house. He could be dying. I checked the glove box for a hint of his identity or a way to contact his loved ones. My reasoning told me to call 911, but something stopped me. Something told me not to call anyone.

There were a few things I knew for sure. First, he was unconscious. He might have a concussion, or worse. But I hadn't found a mark on him. Secondly, the truck wasn't damaged to explain his condition. Something or someone had driven him unconscious. Lastly, I had to get to bed. And before I left, I had to check the truck's custom-built carrying box in the cargo space. It was unlikely but possible someone else might be hurt and lying unconscious in there, and if I found someone in there, I was calling 911.

I opened the truck box, hoping with sick humor there wouldn't be a body there, now that I'd put the tractor away. A dead body was only marginally better than what I found. It was full of gear, some for camping and cooking outside, and bottled water, although I didn't see any actual food. The rest were guns. A couple handguns—a .44 semiautomatic and a .38 revolver, like the one on my hip, and a Glock 9 millimeter. I'd never seen a silencer outside of the movies, but I thought I was looking at one now on the end of the Glock. There was a double-barrel sawed-off shotgun and a sniper rifle, complete with scope and tripod. And boxes of ammunition—a lot of boxes. I didn't see any phone or personal gear, though there was a sleeping bag. Everything was broken in, though not worn out, and appeared to be top of the line. This guy must spend a good bit of time outside.

There was no paperwork of any kind, not even a list of groceries or people to kill. I'd have to wait for answers until my guest recovered enough to tell me, if he was so inclined. But I wasn't going to call the cops, or anyone, not yet. If I did, the poor guy would be arrested as soon as he woke up, just for having the guns and the ammo not separate in his truck. And he'd lose his handgun license for sure, too, permanently. Sure, he had guns, but I knew people who lived on my very street who had more. Most of all, I wanted to know who he was, beside an avid gun aficionado.

I grabbed the sleeping bag and left the rest. Everything would be safe enough, locked up here in the barn.

I locked the door and returned to the house, getting soaked in the process. My guest was still where I'd left him. I examined him again for any signs of injuries, but other than some dried blood on one arm and a scratch that looked a couple of days old, there wasn't anything I could find without removing his clothes. As much as the idea suited me, getting dry and going to bed was even more seductive. I covered him up and left him a note telling him that he was safe and to please stay where he was until I was up; there were vicious dogs roaming upstairs. I also locked both the garage door, and the cellar door, engaging the deadbolt on the latter. Without his guns, even if he woke up angry, he wouldn't be much of a threat. Any noise he made getting those doors open would wake the dogs, and they would wake me. And I was armed not only with my handgun, but also with a shotgun.

Deciding I'd done all I could to prepare for the Worst Case Scenario, I went to bed. My pajamas had never felt so good. The rain had arrived and the initial shower had turned to a drenching full-force rain that pounded on the roof. My last waking thought was: *What had I done? And why?*

Those concerns woke me to ponder a few more late-night thoughts, like why I hadn't called the cops? While it was true that I'd been known to risk life and limb to save an animal from certain death on the local roads, I'd never been accused of this degree of kindness toward my fellow human beings. I liked animals better.

He might really need a doctor, but I kept coming back to the fact that he didn't look injured other than being unconscious. How could he have been hit hard enough to knock him out and not have a bruise? He could have been on the edge of exhaustion when he'd pulled into the quarry to sleep. He might have fallen from the car if the door hadn't been properly closed. Maybe the chain had already been down. I would check it in the morning.

I resolved to call the police in the morning if he didn't regain consciousness. Rationally, I was feeling more and more like I should have contacted the police, or at least, one of my neighbors. But something, some inner knowledge, still told me not to call anyone. I'd trusted this intuition all my life. I would trust it at least for now and reevaluate the situation in the morning. By then, hopefully, my guest would be awake. If he found himself supremely grateful that I'd saved him from a mud nap, he might be persuaded to take me to a nice breakfast, or perhaps dinner. With that thought, I fell asleep.

My dreams were dark and confusing. I kept walking, knowing something was just out of sight, keeping pace with me; but I couldn't see it, nor could I escape. I woke up in the night and brought one of the dogs into bed with me. My .38 hung in its holster within reach. Comforted that I'd be alerted to any danger, I went back to sleep.

It was late when I awoke, about ten or so, but I didn't look at the clock. I remembered my guest downstairs and knew I had to check on him as soon as possible. But I also knew better than to go downstairs without waking up enough to handle what might be down there. So I showered, and took care of the animals. I was still groggy from lack of sleep, but I made myself hurry as fast as I could.

By the time I'd gotten everyone settled and dressed myself, I felt awake enough that I headed down to see him. He seemed the same. My hope of a nice breakfast vanished with a sinking feeling. I resolved to check him over more carefully, and if I couldn't get him to wake, I would call 911. I was beginning to feel like I'd made a big mistake, and I kicked myself for not using better judgment last night. I mean, what had I been hoping for, some kind of fantasy? Idiot.

I headed back after breakfast with some soap and water, which I used to clean off his arm. Under the blood, a scratch had healed. I worked the shirt off him but I wasn't daring enough to take off his filthy jeans. I washed his face, which had been lying in the dirt, and revealed features that took my breath away. There was an elegant symmetry about him that made him look both younger that I originally thought and more vulnerable.

I heard myself saying, "What happened to you? Why would anyone want to hurt you?"

I stroked his smooth cheek. He moved suddenly, taking a breath, revealing incisors twice the length of my own. His eyes didn't open, but he settled back with a sigh.

Holy Shit! I snatched my hand back, both excited and a little scared. It was time to face the facts, principally being that my guest was not what I'd talked myself into believing last night. This was no over-armed hunter or Mafia hit man. I was harboring a vampire.

Chapter Two

A vampire. A real, honest-to-God vampire.

That must have been why there was water in the truck, but no actual food. It was a good thing I hadn't been able to lift him. I might have carried him in the front door, to the more comfortable extra bedroom upstairs, where the morning light would have reduced him to a nice pile of ash.

The guns hadn't really bothered me last night, but they bothered me now plenty. I had no way of knowing if he was a good vampire hunting bad people, or a bad vampire killing for blood, or just sport. Maybe the only good vampires were the make-believe ones from the Buffy Universe.

If the legends were true, someone might have tried to kill him last night. That someone had involved me by dumping him so close to my house. I'd done the last thing expected; sheltered a total stranger in a basement with no windows. If I'd left him outside, he'd be a pile of wet ash by now. The truck would be empty, and I'd have called the police when I went out this morning to check the quarry. They would have come and hauled it away, and that would have been the end of it.

My thoughts were manic, but nothing like this had ever happened to me before. I'd involved myself in something I had no experience to handle, and I wasn't used to the feeling. But I was confident that I'd work it out if I reasoned over it long enough. My more prevailing thought was curiosity. I wanted to know what was going on and why this guy had been dumped here, and who'd hurt him. His sexy appearance stirred things in me that hadn't been stirred in a while. Many a woman had been swayed by either curiosity or lust before. Together, my rationale plans to call the police didn't stand a chance.

So what if he was dangerous? I'd helped snapping turtles off the road that could have severed a few fingers. I'd risked my own to help them, despite that they would have hurt me if I'd given them half the chance. Of course, a vampire wasn't a turtle.

I looked at him lying there and made my decision. I would try to help him. If he was a vampire, then I knew what he needed to regain consciousness. Blood. And I wasn't going to offer up any of my animals for sacrifice, so that left only my own.

Ew. I wanted to help him, but I didn't want to give him my blood. What if he took too much? What if he hurt me? Hell, what if he killed me?

I sat down beside him and put my hand on his. He was cooler than he'd been earlier this morning. I guessed he was getting weaker. He was motionless beneath my fingers.

"Give me a sign," I said softly, almost whispering. "Give me something to show me you won't hurt me; that I'm not making the biggest mistake of my life."

I squeezed his hand gently. He squeezed back—almost imperceptibly—and I froze. I thought that was it, I was going to do it. It was probably a mistake, and I might very well die; but I knew if I didn't do it, I'd always regret it, and I knew if I didn't help, he'd surely die. I would always wonder what might have happened if I'd given him my blood; if I could have saved him.

I got up and went about preparing. I most likely was risking my life. I had no guarantee he wouldn't hurt me once he was conscious. My hope was that saving him from being dust would count for something. Then again, it might not .

I checked in with my parents and made arrangements to call them back later that night. I told them nothing of what I was planning to do. If I failed to call when I said I would, they'd come over to investigate. In that event, I left them a note on the kitchen counter explaining what had happened and told them to call the police. I did all the chores that were absolutely necessary, ate a large protein-filled meal, and then about five p.m., I threw my courage about my shoulders, and descended the stairs.

On the last step, I stopped. Was I really going to do this?

Yes, I was.

I went to the vampire's side and unwrapped my bandaged arm. I hadn't wanted to cut myself, so it was fortunate that while cutting wood the previous day, I had gouged my arm on a spear-like poplar branch. The wound wasn't large, but it was deep. With some quick courage and a healthy helping of pain, I reopened the wound with a sharp knife. A large drop of blood welled up... I said a quick prayer to God that I not die and traced some of the blood on his lips.

He stirred and moved his mouth, tasting the blood. I took a deep breath, and saying another quick prayer, put my arm to his lips. A few seconds passed, and I wondered if it was too late, maybe I'd waited too long.

Like a snake, he struck. Without sound or warning, an iron fist closed over my arm, while his other arm pulled me closer. He sucked at the wound, and though it was deep, it wasn't deep enough. I felt his teeth tear into my wrist, and I let out a shriek, trying to pull away. But he wouldn't let me go. His arm was like a steel band, pulling me close, and I struggled in his grip. He seemed to like that and held me tighter. I couldn't breathe, and I was losing consciousness. I wasn't sure how much blood I lost, but my arm seared. I passed out with his arms still around me, his throat working, swallowing.

I awoke some time later. My watch said two hours had passed. I checked my surroundings and realized with dread that I was still locked in the vampire's embrace, his mouth still pressed to my wrist. I tried to move away, but my blood began flowing again. His grip tightened, and he dug his fangs in, swallowing over and over again. His arms were like a vise, but they were warmer than before.

Wasn't this supposed to be enjoyable? Where was the pleasure, the so-called sexual thrill my vampire novels had always spoken of? I could tell from his body that he was enjoying this, but I felt fainter by the minute. More worrisome was that the pain in my arm didn't feel as bad as it had been. The wound had to be worse and should have hurt more, not less. Was this a sign that I was dying?

A burst of adrenaline rocked me. I put everything I had into pushing him away. I might as well have tried to throw a three-hundred pound boulder. He was partially on top of me, and the weight of him immobilized me. My struggling didn't faze him, and despite my best efforts, I passed out again.

I awoke at nine p.m. I felt as if I could barely raise my head. I felt lightheaded, and sick. But I was free. The vampire had released me, and I lay by his side, within easy reach. In my fogged brain, I noticed he looked much better, and there was a faint blush to his skin. Odds were, he was a lot warmer than he'd been earlier in the day, but I wasn't going to touch him to check. I knew I wouldn't wake up from a third round of being bitten.

I checked myself out. Despite my arm being ragged, the wound was clean, and there was no blood on the sheets. Nor was there any on him or me. I was surprised, but I felt better not knowing how much blood I had lost.

I had to get away while I could. I moved slowly, inching off the bed, and painfully walked upstairs. I locked the basement door behind me, though I guessed he was strong enough to break it open if he wanted. I wanted to make it hard for him, just in case he wanted more of my blood. I regretted what I'd done in a big way. I'd acted like a character in a vampire romance novel, thinking he was going to wake up and shower me with love, tell me I'd be his forever. I felt tears in my eyes for being such a fool.

"Feel sorry for yourself later," I hissed at myself. I needed to take care of things, before I could rest, and I had to hurry, while I still had the strength to do it.

I called my parents to tell them I was fine. Next stop was the animals, who I made sure were all alive, cared for, and safe. I staggered to bed and tried to treat my wound. It looked angry, even being scabbed over. The rips his teeth had made resembled a bad dog bite. My stomach turned just looking at it. It wasn't the two neat holes I'd been expecting. I put some Neosporin on it, and tried to wrap it, only to pass out again.

I woke up around nine in the morning, called in sick to work, and told them I'd be in the following day. I had a migraine headache and my arm ached. It looked much better, smaller, and scabbed over. There wasn't any pain like there'd been the day before, but my bone felt as if it had been gnawed on. Not knowing how much blood I'd lost, I was afraid to take any painkillers. It had to be a significant amount, and I spent most of the day on the couch, sleeping on and off, and eating as much as possible. I had no appetite, which was unusual, but I made myself eat lunch at noon and felt a lot better for it.

My thoughts were disjointed and didn't make a lot of sense. By what I remembered of the vampire's appearance, ingesting my blood had saved him like I'd hoped. Now I had another problem. He was now stronger than me. If he wanted to finish me off, he could, as soon as night fell.

I'd be damned if I was going to wait for him to come and get me. I staggered to my feet and grabbed a decorative cross, then went downstairs to check on him, wishing for the comforting weight of my gun instead.

He hadn't moved and his eyes were still closed. For all I knew, he hadn't opened them through the whole episode. I resolved that tonight he would open them for me.

Dusk was at seven. At six forty-five, I went downstairs and positioned myself with a book so I could watch him. I'd given a lot to find out what was going on with this man, and come hell or high water, I wanted to know the truth.

A little after seven, I finally saw him stir. He blinked his eyes, put his fingers to his face, and rubbed his neck and forehead. Then he slowly raised himself up on one arm. He knew I was here and what had happened between us. All the things I expected him to do or say didn't happen. He merely looked at me, as if taking in all that I was, maybe reading my mind. He didn't seem in any rush to talk, and I had no idea how to start the conversation. My normally verbose nature went silent. Since he didn't speak, I simply looked back at him, and noticed that sense of grace again just in the way he held his head. His eyes were the color of rich earth, a brown almost the color of gingerbread. Not what I'd call kind eyes, but they weren't cold either. Reserved maybe, and a little sad. He wasn't Indian, as I'd thought last night, but perhaps European. His shoulder-length hair was cut in a simple style. He was still covered in dust. He had a nice chest. I caught myself staring and looked away.

"Thank you," he said. His voice was softer than I'd expected, but its tone caressed me.

My breath stopped in mid-intake, but I made myself finish so I could speak. "You're welcome," I said, not meaning it. I might be the walking wounded, but I would be polite if it killed me. It just might.

"Why did you save me?" he asked, puzzled. "I can tell you gave me your blood, and most likely sheltered me during the day. You don't know me, though you must know what I am. Why would you risk your life?"

"Let's come back to that," I said, "as I'm not sure that I have an answer for you." I couldn't very well tell him that I thought he was hot. At least, not so soon. He would think I was some kind of groupie. Good thing I'd lost blood or my face would be scarlet. "What were you doing in the quarry?"

A look of introspection came over him, and I could see that he remembered the previous night. Something clicked in his mind. Alarm dashed his features. "The truck. Where is my—"

"It's stashed in the barn, out of sight. Keys are upstairs." And sarcastically, I added, "And I turned off the ignition for you, so you have some gas left."

He looked at me with something close to curiosity and calculation. "Why would you think to hide my truck?"

"It seemed like a good idea at the time," I said, a little defensively.

"Like taking an unconscious man into your house?" he returned, looking at me. He was looking at me all calm and sincere, but I could feel the mirth just beneath the surface. If he was going to be so blunt, two could play at that game.

"You wanted to die then?"

"No," he said, pausing to give me a thoughtful, yet more calculating, glance. "But something tells me that you didn't know what I was when you brought me here."

"True," I admitted. "I should have called the cops, but something told me not to, and I trusted my instincts. Then I saw your teeth, and I knew you were…something else."

He made a wry face, and then the obvious occurred to him. "How exactly did you get me down here, into your home? Does anyone else know I'm here? You must have had help."

I smiled. "No, just me."

"Pardon me, but although you might be strong for a woman, there's

18

no way you carried me here."

"I had help, but no one else knows you're here." I hoped that wouldn't come back to haunt me.

He smirked. "What did you do, get a wheelbarrow?"

"Front-end loader." I couldn't help grinning at that myself.

It took him a minute to register what I'd said, but then he roared with laughter and fell back on the bed. I shivered with the sound of his humor, and that feeling of being caressed came back. I was glad he couldn't read my mind.

"Thank you for hiding me." He again studied me, his dark eyes looking into my green ones. "I was in the quarry accidentally. I was exhausted and injured, and although I'd managed to heal myself, I was losing consciousness. I planned on parking the truck in the back of the quarry and walking into the woods to camp. Even though it wasn't state land, I didn't think anyone would be out this time of year. It's not hunting season, and with just camping the night, I didn't think anyone would notice. But I didn't make it." He paused, and then asked in a soft voice, "Please, tell me what happened?"

I related the story of rescuing him and hiding his truck. He considered me carefully. "What is your name?"

"Sarelle McGarran, but you can call me Sar. I think we can be on a first name basis here."

"I'm Danial, but you can call me Danial."

He winked at me. I didn't know whether to be annoyed or not. In any case, I was tired of sitting in the cellar. "Can I get you to help me with the bed?"

He looked around and finally noticed that he was lying on a mattress on a cement floor. "Okay."

We each took one end and carried it back to the extra bedroom, where we put the bed back together. I folded up the tarp and staggered a bit. His arms were around me before I knew it, catching me. He was a lot warmer than he'd been. If I hadn't known what I knew, I'd have thought he was human. His arms were strong, and I felt a chill at the memory of the last time I'd been in them.

"Thanks. I'm tired; it's the lack of sleep..."

"It's the blood loss," he said matter-of-factly. "You need to eat something and rest."

I steadied myself, and he let me go. He followed me upstairs, and I was a little unimpressed at my dogs' reaction. I thought they might attack him, but both sniffed him and wanted to be petted. The cats also liked him. Even Asher, the most skittish, came forward. He seemed to like them back.

"And what's that one's name?"

"Ash."

"Ashes?" he said, looking horrified and rolling his eyes.

"Short for Asher." I should be happy that I ended up with a vampire who had a sense of humor, and not some Bela Lugosi or Christopher Lee-type.

We went into the kitchen, where I heated up soup and made toast. He excused himself to slip out to the truck to bring in some extra clothes and take a quick shower. I devoured my food, thinking Danial was right. I did need to eat, and this tasted like the best food I'd eaten in a year. It was past dinnertime…

Dinnertime. Oiy. I didn't know how to ask if he was hungry without making it seem like I was offering to feed him. After all the blood he'd taken from me, I couldn't lose anymore—not if I wanted to wake up tomorrow.

"Are you feeling better?"

He stood in the doorway, fully dressed. He seemed to like denim, as he was wearing a denim shirt and jeans. His hair was wet from the shower, and he looked delightful. As in full of delights. I stomped on my desire again.

"Want to watch TV?"

"Okay." He clicked on the remote and selected LIST.

I was glad I hadn't saved any old episodes of vampire shows on my TiVo. He'd know for sure I was a vampire groupie who was tickled pink when a real one landed in her lap. Even if that was true to some extent, I didn't want him to think that.

"That new reality show on housewives is on," I said, sliding my eyes to his to gauge his reaction. He made a face, and I said, "Just kidding." I felt a little bad at this point, as I had only basic cable. But wait… "I have Supernatural, the second season, on DVD. Do you know the series?""

I was sure he probably didn't know what the hell I was talking about, but he surprised me. "Sure, I've seen some of it... I can identify with Dean." I tried to cover my surprise while he put the DVD on, and selected play.

While we watched, I tried to decide what to ask him next. If he knew the show, did he have a house where he sometimes watched this? Was someone waiting for him back at the ranch, so to speak? Was he some kind of demon-hunting vampire? Was that why he had the silencer and other weapons?

Ten minutes into it, I suddenly felt my eyes grow heavy and told him I was going to bed. I got up too fast, forgetting that I was the walking wounded, and collapsed onto him. He reacted in a second, catching and easing me onto his lap. I struggled a bit, but he wrapped his arms around me and tilted my head up to look into his eyes. They looked so intent I froze under his gaze.

"I won't hurt you like I did before," he whispered, tracing my jaw. "I promise."

"Promise?" My voice was breathy, and I gazed into his eyes, thinking how much I wanted him to kiss me and knowing it was too soon. But I didn't try to move back either.

"Yes," he said seriously, his fingers holding my face.

"You can't take any more. I'll—"

"I won't need blood for at least a week," he said." If I have to, I can survive on animal blood. That's what all my gear is for."

He was lying to me. No one killed deer with a silenced handgun. Most of that gear was for something darker. But I was caught up in the moment and said nothing.

"My baser instincts took over to keep me alive. I can't apologize for my nature, but I'm sorry it had to be so painful for you. It doesn't have to be painful, if I don't let it get out of hand."

Out of hand? You mean rip open the food instead of just drinking?

"Please forgive me."

I got to my feet, swaying a little, but I was determined to be dignified. "Look, it wasn't your fault you reacted the way you did. I'm not holding it against you."

Though I'd like to—
Stop thinking like that!

I tore my eyes away from his. "I've got to go to bed. I've got work in the morning."

"What do you do?"

"I work at a metal fabrication shop."

"What do they do there?"

"Fabricate metal. Really, just stay here and we'll talk more tomorrow night."

I turned to go, but he reached up and pulled me back into his lap. I thought briefly about struggling, but his lap was where I wanted to be, so what was the point?

He reached under my legs and shoulders, and in one fluid motion, stood. I had one arm across his shoulders, but he had me securely.

"I'm taking you to bed."

God, yes, please take me to bed.

Sar, get control of yourself. You barely know this guy. He's a vampire, for God's sake, and who knows what else.

He carried me into my bedroom, where he sat me down on the edge of the bed. I was embarrassed that I was breathing hard. At least, I hadn't nibbled his neck like I'd wanted to.

"Show me your arm," he said.

I unwrapped the bandage. The wound seemed mostly healed, but it ached fiercely.

"I was afraid of this," he said with regret.

"What?" I asked in alarm.

"Your arm healed on the outside, but the inside is still open."

"What?"

"I hoped I wouldn't have to do this, but I'm going to have to." He slipped his hand behind his waist and pulled out a small knife. "Relax, Sar."

He'd gotten more than clothes from his truck. I thought for a fleeting second that he'd brought a gun along as well.

"Ah," I said, trying to scuttle away from him on the bed. He grabbed me with ease and held me in place. He looked at me as if asking permission.

"What are you going to—"

"Save you from being crippled. Please, let me."

I took a shuddering breath and said, "Do whatever it is you're going to do, just make it as fast as possible and don't tell me about it."

I felt him slice my arm open. I recoiled with a hiss, but the pain abruptly faded. His lips were on my arm, but he wasn't sucking. He was holding his mouth over it. The relief was wonderful. I let out a deep breath I didn't remember holding and relaxed. He remained as he was for a few seconds, and then gave my arm a final lingering kiss. He released me and showed me the injury. It was completely healed.

I looked up at him worriedly. "Does this mean I'm a—"

"No," he said. "You're still you, but now you can go to work tomorrow without pain."

"How is—"

"I don't want to get into it now," he said tiredly. "Suffice it to say that my kiss heals. You'll be fine."

I saw that it had cost him to heal me. There was a weariness about him that hadn't been there a few moments ago. "You need blood," I said.

"I can get some easily enough. Get some sleep."

"You had better not even think about drinking my pets," I said heatedly.

He held up his hand to stop my concern. "I'm not going to hurt your animals. Must you be so feisty?" A wry corner of his mouth smiled. "I'll find some game."

"Oh…okay."

"I'll be in the basement after I get back. Call out if you need me." With those words, he was gone.

I got up to let the dogs out and went to bed right after. I was exhausted. Now that I wasn't in pain, I could barely keep my eyes open. I was in dreamland before I could wonder more about why Danial had lied to me.

Chapter Three

Morning dawned bright and early. Way too early. I laid there wondering if I should call in sick to work, but my better nature prevailed. I tried never to do a half-assed job, even when the job was only delivering a richly deserved verbal observation. So I got up and fed the dogs and cats, resisting the urge to go downstairs. I told myself to let Danial sleep, that he probably wouldn't be awake anyway.

My mind was uncooperative, whispering to me that I could just take a quick look at him. He'd be lying in bed, perhaps the covers pushed back to reveal—

I slammed the door on my desires. What was I thinking, acting like a high school girl with a crush on the quarterback? I didn't know him at all. I reminded myself that he'd refrained from telling me anything that I really hadn't already known or guessed at. Besides, I remembered the lie about his weapons. Together, that was sufficient to cool my lust, at least until I saw him again. In any case, I had real work to do.

I worked part time at a metal fabrication shop to supplement my small legal settlement. My boss was also my friend, but that just gave me more reason not to let him down. I would probably need to stay late to catch up from yesterday, but that was good; I'd have more time to decide how to approach the matter of the Big Lie. Not that Danial would necessarily be there when I got home...

Throwing aside that dismal thought, I drove into the parking lot, parked, and went inside. I was immediately engulfed in the comforting odor of burning metal and welding fumes. I scanned my badge in the time-clock computer and glanced through the open steel doorway, into the shop as I headed to the main office. Hard rock blasted at seventy-plus decibels from a huge boom box on top of one of the many Computer

24

Numerically Controlled machines. Under that was the shrill whine of metal edges grinding down and the cracking of acetylene welding torches. The shop had several sections where parts were welded, painted, ground, sawed, or milled. It was eight a.m., and most of the guys were at their stations. I went through the office door, and Mark said hello as he got a sandwich from the vending machine.

Breakfast, I thought. I greeted him and went in to face the work.

There was a pile on my desk, so I got to it. As I went from task to task, my mind kept returning to Danial, and not just for his looks. On the surface, I'd made myself act like I'd taken the events over the last two days in stride. But inside, I wondered if I'd done the right thing by involving myself in his problems. In books, any heroine who suddenly got involved in a vampire's problems was almost always doomed in the end, along with the relationship. Sure, maybe there were romance novels with a happy ending, but that wasn't reality; it was contrived. My experience saving Danial had been painfully real. I'd had enough heartache from mortal men. I sure as hell didn't need any from an immortal one.

* * * *

All went well at work and I left work only an hour later than usual. As I drove home, I debated what to say to Danial if he was there when I arrived. Should I call him on the lie? Demand he tell me what he'd been doing in the quarry? Ask him what was for dinner?

I decided to play it loose and see what he had to say. Hell, maybe he'd bring one of these topics up himself. But if he tried to pass off another lie I was going to call him on it, no matter how he thought to distract me. I wasn't hurt now, and my will wasn't completely under my hormones' control.

To my disappointment, when I got home, Danial wasn't there. I felt a pang of sadness at the idea that he'd gone to the trouble to leave before I got home. I went downstairs after calling down, to see that the bed was made and his sleeping bag was gone. I didn't have to go to the barn to know his truck was gone, too.

Let down—but also relieved I wouldn't have to confront him now—I took a shower, ate dinner, watched some non-vampire-related TV, tucked the animals in for the night, and went in to bed to discover a surprise. There on my bed, waiting for me, was the shirt Danial had worn the night before, after showering. There was a tiny speck of blood on the cuff—my blood or his?—and on it was a note.

Sar,
I have to leave now to take care of some things. I'll try to come back and see you before I leave town. I'm leaving you my shirt to let you know I'll come back, even if it's not for a while. You helped me when you didn't have to. I don't take that lightly.
Danial

I was simultaneously aroused and creeped out. A shirt with blood on it? Maybe he didn't know how to work the washer. Maybe he only had two shirts, and he didn't want to wear the bloody one out on whatever job he was on? If he was out killing someone, the one with blood might be more appropriate. But it was only a tiny spot, so I didn't really care. Maybe this was some kind of vampire foreplay?

I picked up the shirt and got the faintest whiff of something delectable. I brought it closer and inhaled deeply. Cloves? Cedar? Spices mixed with cedar? I couldn't tell for sure, but it was Good with a capital G. It smelled like lust, good sex, and dessert afterwards, all rolled into one. I realized with the scent lingering in my nose that I wanted Danial. Really wanted him. This was more than a crush. But it was way too soon to be love. It was infatuation and the danger of being intimate with a creature out of legend. I was glad he wasn't there. I didn't want to fall into bed with someone I couldn't trust. But I was alone tonight, so I was free to indulge myself, and I suddenly no longer felt any creepiness about the blood on the shirt. I thought briefly about putting it on my dresser so I could make that wonderful scent last, but I wore it to bed instead. I slipped into sleep quickly, immersed in the delectable scent.

I dreamed of Danial. He'd come back during the night, and even though I'd locked the doors, he'd somehow gotten into my room. He was beside me, reclining close, but not touching. His hair was glossy, a brown so dark it could be called black, and it fell unbound to his shoulders. He was dressed in denim jeans but had no shirt on. I opened my mouth to ask him where the hell he'd been and if he'd killed anybody, but he held a finger to my lips. I opened my mouth to protest but he covered it with his own. His lips were soft and eager for me. I would like to say I protested, but I gave in without a second thought.

He felt my surrender and gathered me to him. I was burning up from the inside. His kisses were warm and slow. He leaned over me and touched my cheek, stroking my hair back from my face. He leaned farther and moved his legs, and suddenly he was on top. He was careful not to crush me with his weight, holding himself up on his forearms. I reached up to pull him down and covered his mouth with mine. I ran my fingers through his hair and pulled him close. He felt so good, his weight, the softness of his hair, that amazing scent rolling off his body, intoxicating me. The scent I'd been smelling all along had been his, the way he'd smelled to me.

He smelled so good. I breathed deeply, over and over, and the more I breathed in, the more aroused I became. I brought my hands over his neck, down to his chest, and stroked his pale skin. His hands were busy themselves, sliding up my thighs, over my T-shirt, to my breasts. He cupped them gently through the thin material. Without a word, I pushed him back, sat up, and stripped it off, baring my body to him, my unbound hair falling over my breasts and shoulders, to my waist.

He gave me a long calculating look and stripped off his jeans. Before I could see what I'd been waiting to see, he returned to me, kissing me again. He stretched out and I felt the length of his body press against me. I wanted him so badly at that moment that I almost cried for him to stop the foreplay and get to the sex. But he stopped kissing me instead and drew back, raising his eyes to mine.

"I need you to know that I can't get you pregnant or give you any STDs. I can't catch anything you have either; my immune system would kill anything that tried to make a home in me. I want your consent for what's about to happen between us, that you really want me, knowing full well what I am."

I looked at him. I wanted him all right, but his talk had cooled my desire somewhat. Talk of STDs tended to do that, especially when a couple is about to commit the act that propagates them. But I appreciated that he cared enough about what I thought to stop and ask, knowing that

27

there was a fifty-percent chance that it would stop him from getting any. He waited for my answer, unmoving. I could still feel the length of him pressed against me. It was true I barely knew him. And I knew we shouldn't do this, not this fast. But I looked at him, breathed in that scent, and didn't care. Killer for sure, maybe murderer, probably assassin, liar at least a few times over, and vampire, I wanted him. Right now.

I looked at him and put all my lust into my voice. "Danial, I want you. Right here, and *right now.*" That last came out as a growl.

He replied by covering my mouth with his own and slipping into me with an ease that brought a gasp from my throat. He found his rhythm quick enough, and his hands and lips were everywhere. I was close, but I wanted more, so I leaned to the left and rolled him into the middle of the bed. He was surprised and broke his rhythm, stopping. He looked up at me, clearly wondering if I wasn't pleased with his performance. I began my own rhythm for us, taking his hands and placing them on my breasts. He held me as I moved above him, and then leaned my upper body down to embrace him. He locked me to him as if he would never let me go.

He was everything I wanted, and as I felt the orgasm begin to roll over me, I also felt his hand brush my neck, lifting away my hair. As I climaxed, he struck. A wave of pleasure washed over me as his fangs slid into me. There was pain, but it was small in comparison to the pleasure that washed over me in waves. I felt him climax within me, still drinking, still holding me tightly. Long before I would have weakened, he stopped drinking, pulling back with a sigh of contentment. He brought his lips to the wound and kissed it. There was no pain, and I lazily rolled off him, reaching up to feel my neck. The skin was warmer in that area than the rest of me, but I couldn't feel any marks. He watched me as if I'd shown him something he hadn't expected to see, and that amazed him. I snuggled close, and he put his arm around me, pulling me close again. He brushed the hair from my eyes and kissed me.

"I wanted to show you what it could be like between us," he whispered. "It doesn't have to be pain. It can be pleasure."

"It was that and more," I answered.

"You have to know I didn't want to stop, to make that speech, but I had to."

"I'm grateful you did, and that you cared enough to."

He tilted my head back so I was leaning with my head on his chest, looking up at him. "I do care." He kissed me again, slow and contentedly. "Remember that."

I awoke to find my bed a mess, but Danial's shirt still on. I had one thought, splayed there like a discarded rag doll: WOW.

And then I realized that I had to get up and go to work. It was Friday—payday—but how the hell was I going to do that when I still felt the aftershocks of the dream?

* * * *

Driving home that night, listening to the radio, I played back the previous night's dream in my head. It had felt so good to be intimate with someone again. It was also wonderful that it had been a dream. I had all the luscious scenes to display in a slide show and none of the guilt. Though really, why should there be any guilt? I was a single woman, who at this stage in her life was old enough to decide who was allowed in her bed. But I still believed in knowing a person before being intimate with them, and I didn't know Danial at all. Most of what he'd told me was questionable. Did I trust him? I wanted to, sure. He hadn't hurt me or my animals when he could have, but that wasn't enough. I wanted him to care about me.

Arriving home, I took the dogs out for a long walk. I was able to catch a brilliant watercolor sunset, but clouds were moving in, signaling a thunderstorm was on the way. The air smelled of fall, and the cornfield rustled in the wind. The corn stood unharvested, waiting for a hard freeze to be gathered for seed corn. A few bats swooped above my head, looking to help me with the year's last mosquito crop. By the time we were halfway home, thunder crashed faintly to the south. We hurried the rest of the way and managed to get in sight of the house before the first raindrops fell. By the time we'd got in the door, we were soaked. I dried the dogs off, gave them their nightly Cheweez, and stripped off my wet clothes to jump in the shower.

I usually didn't sing in the shower, but the past week had put me in a rather ribald and joyous mood. I belted out the beginning of "Iris." As I finished with, "I just don't want to miss you tonight," I heard a seductive voice say, "Missing me already?"

Danial stood outside the shower door. My breath came out as a screech.

"What are you doing in here? I locked all the doors!" In my indignation, I swallowed water. "Get out of here! I revoke my invitation!" I sputtered. I could hear him laughing, and that pissed me off.

"Ah, if only it were that easy. That old wives trick doesn't work."

Son of a bitch. I rinsed out the shampoo as fast as I could. "I'll show you a much better one shortly. It involves a cross and some holy water."

"Crosses, holy water, bibles, and all other symbols of man's religion only work if the vampire you're using them on believes they can hurt him. I happen to be agnostic. Try again," he laughed.

I grabbed my conditioner and began working it in. Damned long hair. "How about a nice stake?"

"That would work if you had the power to get it in my heart. But you don't, not by yourself, and certainly not at night." He was no longer laughing.

"A nice decapitation?" I offered, sarcasm threaded through my words.

"You are testing my patience," he said, and it came out as a growl.

Why was this conditioner taking so long to rinse out? Argh! "And you're testing mine! Go outside and wait for me. I'll be right out."

"Fine!" he said abruptly. I heard the bathroom door close with a slam.

I toweled off and threw on a long-sleeved T-shirt and jeans. I squished some leave-in conditioner in my hair and put some moisturizer on my face, all the while readying myself for what was probably going to be the Big Confrontation. I came out to the dining room to see him giving my dogs treats. Even the cats were around as he parceled out tidbits for them. It was odd the way they liked him so much, but I was reassured; they were usually a good judge of character. I may not have trusted Danial, but I trusted them.

"Tell me straight, why are you here?" I said bluntly, sitting on the couch.

"I came back to see you," he said sincerely, sitting down beside me.

"Cut the crap. You aren't dealing with some blonde bimbo who'll accept anything you tell her at face value." His eyes narrowed but I plowed on, before he could say anything. "First, you got into my house with all the doors locked, which means you either stole a key or had a copy made. Your truck is in my barn, so you must have a key for that too—"

"I took a key from the hook by the door, just in case. You told me it was okay to stay here as long as I needed to. I didn't want to leave everything unlocked while I was out. And I don't want to knock on your window at five in the morning if I've been out to make you get up so I can get in for the day."

"But why not just ask me for a key? Or why not just tell me you were taking one?"

"I apologize for that. I should have waited, but I expected you home before dark. Then you didn't show. I thought maybe you were hoping I'd leave before you got home."

"Look, I want to trust you, but you've got to tell me the truth. There's no way you need a silencer to hunt anything but people. Don't tell me it's for self-defense; you have an arsenal of guns that could be used. And your rifle with the scope, that's most likely for sniper work. So tell me what all of this means, or you have to leave."

"You won't believe that sometimes I use guns to take out prey?"

He meant animals, right? We'd go with that. "Why would you need to shoot them, when you can...um..."

"What, jump on them and tear their throats out?" he said loudly in disgust. "Why would I want to terrify them or make them suffer, when a well-placed bullet just ends their life? What kind of animal do you think I am?"

"Look, I just want to understand. I'm not judging you for what I consider to be your business. But I still don't buy the silencer for that. Tell me the truth."

He gave me his now customary calculating look. I watched him silently, waiting. "Fine," he said. He took a deep breath. "You are right. The guns aren't all for game. Most are for protection. Someone or something is hunting me. That's why I was worried that my truck was out in the open. I had to make sure I didn't lead anyone to you by

31

accident."

"Do you live around here?" I asked, watching him carefully.

"I've lived in New York for the past seven years," he continued. "I moved here originally from Colorado. I have a small business that makes decent money." Seeing my motion to interrupt, he said, "Yes, even vampires work. Most of us aren't so old that we have an endless reservoir of funds to draw on. And eternity can get boring if you don't have a reason to go on existing. Mine is my work. I built my business from the ground up, and it matters to me that it succeeds."

"What exactly do you do?"

"I help big businesses solve problems. You'd be surprised how inefficient some companies are. Sometimes the solution is simple, such as firing one person, or switching vendors for cost savings. Sometimes it's more drastic, like down-sizing or overhauling company procedures."

It was strange to hear this boardroom talk from someone with fangs, but maybe I needed to get with the program. America was equal opportunity. And there was a note in Danial's voice I hadn't heard before. He really was into this, and clearly proud of what he did. But before I started hailing him as the best supernatural entrepreneur, I thought I'd better clarify a few points. "Or like killing someone?"

He glared at me, exasperated. "Why would I kill someone? I give my recommendations to the CEOs, or when the CEO is the problem, to the board of directors. They can choose to take them or leave them. Either way, I get paid for consulting."

"And the silencer and the tripod?"

"The first is if whoever is pursuing me catches up with me while I'm in a hotel or a crowded campground. I'm hoping to get him before he gets me, and do it quietly enough where there isn't a panic." I must have looked as skeptical as I felt. He continued, irritated. "Have you ever fired a handgun in an enclosed place? It's so loud, you're deafened for a while. In a place filled with people, there's sure to be someone who hears." He looked at me intently. "Do you understand I can't afford to be noticed or investigated? How would I show up for a trial in the daylight?"

He continued his explanation. "The second is for the same reason, but used in a different location, alone, miles away from anyone. Again,

I'm hoping to get him before he gets me, and I want to have every advantage."

That sounded like good strategy, if a bit overkill, and I nodded in understanding.

"I don't want a shoot-out unless there's no choice. Frankly, there may be more than one bad guy on my tail. I can't be certain, but in my business, where I sometimes get people fired, there's more than one person who wouldn't hesitate to shoot if they had me in their sights."

He was right; it wasn't as if the cops could protect someone like him. He didn't fit in their world, especially as he seemed unwilling to follow basic gun laws. But I wanted proof that this was legit. "Can you show me some of this work you do?"

"Yes."

I followed him to the basement, where he'd set up a makeshift office, including a state of the art laptop and a small printer on the nightstand. A box of office supplies was on the floor beside it.

"Sit down. I'll open up some files for a company I just got some inquiries from."

I sat on the edge of the bed and tried not to appear too comfortable sitting on the bed beside him. He seemed totally oblivious about it, with his mind on his work.

He quickly powered up the laptop. It had a bunch of icons on it, and he went to one that was marked "Inquiries." He brought up a file dated a week ago and opened that so I could read it. It was an e-mail from a CEO of a prominent company that wanted him to investigate how the company could cut its losses in the coming quarter without letting any employees go. There was mention of a new software program with programming issues that needed to be fixed. The CEO also suspected one of his vice presidents of embezzling funds and wanted Danial to find out if it was true. Attached in the e-mail were all sorts of reports and information on the company, with the CEOs' statement to ask for any other information needed.

A wave of relief hit me. I'd been so wrong. He was legit. Once I'd learned he was a vampire and had weapons, I'd automatically assumed he was a killer, and not educated or intelligent. But Danial was computer savvy, much more than I was, and clearly a businessman. I'd underestimated him and I felt bad about that, because I wanted him to like me. I wanted there to come a time when we were together, like we'd been in my dream. I felt a rush of warmth, remembering how he'd felt to me…

Stop it. I let out a deep breath and pushed my memories of the dream away. "I'm sorry. I jumped to conclusions when I shouldn't have. I should have asked."

"Don't think any more on it. Events conspired against us. There wasn't a lot of time for talk, especially the night we met." He put his laptop down on the floor and pulled me to him. I looked up at him questioningly. He shifted me so I was sitting on his lap, and he put his arms around me. He felt so good, I didn't even try to fight how I felt. It felt right, and that was enough. He leaned in close and said, "I hope you don't mind if I stay here a few weeks. I can give you money. You can think of it as rent—"

"You don't need to pay me," I said quickly. "I said you could stay here and I meant it. Keep the key until you leave." Then it registered that he'd offered me money, and I felt it necessary to add, "I may not have a lot, but I have enough to be happy."

I was sensitive to him having more money than I did. I knew my home wasn't grand or even solid construction; it was a prefab home termed a doublewide, and I would be just as cold this winter in it as I had been last year. I wondered if Danial felt sorry for me and that was why he'd offered. I struggled to get off him, not wanting him to think he was my savior, or that I needed one.

He chuckled softly and pulled me in close. I felt the muscles of his chest and arms, and despite myself, I relaxed. "Fine then," he whispered. "Let me buy you something, and you can think of it as a present. How's that?"

I opened my mouth to protest, but he nuzzled my neck, so I just said, "That'd be fine."

Chapter Four

Danial left soon after our talk on Friday night, saying only that he had business to attend to and he'd be back soon. Despite that I wanted him to stay, I didn't ask him to, or when he'd be back. Instead, I spent all weekend catching up on chores and finishing last minute summer projects. I got everything done, running myself ragged in the process. It was time for a little relaxation and heady anticipation of returning home to possibly find him waiting for me there.

Sure, I'd fallen right into the role of a storybook heroine. But I was different. I was smart, and I kept my eyes open while going into it. Maybe nothing would come of us except a few passionate months together. It was true, I already hoped for that—and more—but I wasn't going to turn away if that was all he was willing to give. Chances like this didn't happen—not to me—and I'd never been the kind of girl who'd returned a gift. I would hold onto this one tightly and enjoy it like hell for as long as it lasted.

I got home from work Monday night, received a robust welcome from the dogs, and took them out for a walk. The farmer who'd sublet my land had mowed the seed corn. I didn't farm the land myself, except for a small garden, and I was happy someone could use it, in exchange for a little sweet corn and help keeping the fields mowed. The shorn field brought it home how quickly winter was coming. There was no snow in the forecast, and I wouldn't be building any snowmen soon, but the flowers were closing up and turning brown. It always made me sad, the passing of summer and the dying of everything green. Soon, I'd be walking the dogs in the dark.

I smiled, thinking maybe I could encourage Danial to join us. There was a plus side to winter after all.

I brought the dogs in as the sun was setting, and made myself some soup and a bagel. I was just finishing up when I felt Danial's hands on my shoulders, sliding down my arms, and heard that rich voice. "Hi, Sar."

He brushed his cheek against mine. I closed my eyes and reveled in his touch. Without letting go, he asked, "Want to watch something? I know you go to bed early, but I wanted to spend some time with you before you go to sleep."

"Sure," I said, "but you should know that I'm off Tuesdays and Wednesdays. We could spend the whole night together." As soon as I said that, I kicked myself. I thought about quickly adding on the words "watching movies", but I decided the least said, the better.

He seemed to have missed my Freudian slip. "I'd like to stay here with you, but I have to take care of some business this next week. I won't be able to stay all night."

I bit my lip, irritable. Frankly, I felt like we had gone from strangers to some kind of romantic friends, and gotten stuck on a plateau, missing the good clothes-tearing part of the relationship, before other priorities overshadowed love and lust. Then I decided I wasn't being fair. Hadn't I wanted Danial to be more than eye candy? Hadn't I wanted him to be more than a creature of the night? Maybe he just didn't want me like I wanted him. Or maybe I was just trying to push things too fast because of that dream. With a little shame, I reminded myself that it had been a dream and the real Danial standing behind me hadn't ever acted in any way but protective and friendly, much less admitted to caring for me. I felt downcast but held it in. "Okay."

"I can be back early Friday morning, sleep, and meet you when you get home from work. I'd like to take you out, if you'll permit me to."

I clamped down on the excitement flooding me, telling myself to play it cool. "What did you have in mind?"

"Why not some dancing and a movie? On the weekends, they have midnight showings. I used to go alone, but I'd like to take you out. If you want to go," he whispered as he kissed my neck.

"Sounds *great*," I said, putting an emphasis on the word. He laughed, a deep rolling sound. I laughed too, giving him a smile.

I gathered my plates and took them to the kitchen. "What's this business you have to do? I mean, I understand what you do, but it seems most of it can be done by e-mail. Is it to collect payment?"

He seemed to sense I wasn't prying, just curious. "Sometimes I have to make a report in person. Occasionally, the problem is caused by an employee who's more than just an employee." His voice was low, and I gave him a curious look. "Sometimes the saboteur is a relative of the person who runs the company. It happens far too often, and it's the only part of my job I hate. Most of the time, the employer doesn't want to believe it, even when I have proof." He seemed to look inside himself. I wasn't sure if he reflected on some bad event in his past or the worst possible scenario with the client he could imagine.

"Do you ever have problems with nonpayment? If they don't want to hear that in the first place, they probably don't want to pay to hear it."

Danial snapped out of it. He flashed his familiar rueful grin, his eyes laughing. "I've never had that problem, not with my reputation. But let's not talk about this. You like action movies, I see. Shall we watch one? HBO likely has one on tonight."

"I don't get that channel," I said, a little apologetically. "Sorry."

He clicked on the channel anyway. His face registered surprise when it gave him the message, *You are not subscribed to this channel, call your cable station for details.* Typical; you could take the vampire out of the man, but never the man out of the vampire.

"I can think of better ways to spend the evening," I said, gently taking the remote from his hand and laying it aside. I could see I had his full attention. Once again, typical, but this was the type of typical I liked.

"What did you have in mind?" he asked carefully, his eyes on mine.

"This." He'd been sitting at one end of the couch and I at the other, both of us with one foot up, sort of sprawled. I got up from the couch and turned to face him, standing in front of him. He straightened up so he was sitting upright, facing me, with his feet on the floor and his arms on the back of the couch. I slowly eased down onto his lap, straddling him. He seemed a little wary. I wondered if I had looked like that a few nights ago. Shit, what if he—

"What's the matter?" I asked, leaning back from him. "Was I reading the wrong signals?"

"No." He gave me a wry smile. "I've just never met anyone like you."

"I find that hard to believe," I answered, trying hard not to be offensive. "You have to be older than I am, at least by a decade. In all those years, there weren't any women who were confident enough to approach you? C'mon."

"Ah, but you aren't thinking. The world wasn't the place it is today. A woman's role was well defined by the men around her. A woman couldn't go where she chose without an escort, couldn't own property, and couldn't express herself because she didn't often have a good education. Men still ruled. There were strong women, but they operated in specific circles. Even a strong woman in those days could be toppled by a weak man."

He was talking about women at least fifty years ago, if not more, which made him definitely older than me. "In short, society at that time sucked."

"Yes" he said, looking amused. "You could say that."

"What about modern women?" I said, holding his eyes. "I can't be the first to approach you like this."

"The first one to save my life," he said softly, stroking my cheek. I went still under his hand. He smiled, and it was almost a smirk. "By the way," he added, "I'm not that old. Only about seventy-six or so."

I tried not to do a double-take. This guy could be my grandfather. There was an ick factor involved, and I had to talk my way through it before I embarrassed us both. "You mean you were turned, and then you're adding on the years you were a vampire?"

"Yes. I was turned at thirty-five, and I've been vampire for forty years or so."

Ah, thirty-five...I felt my desire flooding back.

"Women up until the sixties were so lackluster. You, on the other hand," he said as he reached around me so our faces were only a few inches apart, "are vivid and vibrant. You say what's on your mind and don't keep it hidden."

"That's true. I'm not one of those women who walks around when she's mad, saying over and over that nothing's wrong. If you piss me off, you'll hear about it loud and clear."

He grinned, baring his fangs, and then said in a sultry voice, "I think

38

I'd like to hear other sounds from you, Sar."

His arms tightened. He grabbed my hair and yanked it back, bearing my throat. I wasn't alarmed this time, though he was holding me with just enough force to make it uncomfortable. I froze motionless, knowing I couldn't move without pulling my hair. He placed his lips over my neck and began to kiss me, feather-light kisses trailing up and down my neck. I felt the brush of his fangs, but he made no attempt to bite. Just those light kisses.

God, it felt wonderful…I melted from the heat he stirred in me. All my reservations about moving too fast slipped away. Hey, I knew him pretty well. He said he wasn't a killer. We were officially dating now. He was to-die-for on the seductive scale; a twenty-five on a scale of one to ten. We were two consenting adults. I was single, and I was pretty sure he was. The fact that I hadn't asked and he hadn't said anything seemed unimportant. Maybe we could make that dream I'd had come true.

He ran the edge of one fang down from my chin to my throat. I let out a moan.

"Like that, did you?" The edge of his voice held a growl. I wasn't the only one being turned on. I could feel the bulge in his jeans. I looked into his eyes, which had gone dark with lust, and I rubbed against him with my hips. It was his turn to let out a moan.

He released my hair and reached up for my head, bringing my lips down to his. I'd wanted him to kiss me for days now, and this was everything I'd hoped it would be. His lips were cool against mine, and I felt the prick of his fangs. I wondered if he'd spent a good part of those forty years as a vampire learning how to kiss, because it felt like it. He moved his lips expertly over mine, tasting me gently. When he opened his mouth, I opened mine as well, so he could taste me with his tongue. He kissed me harder, his hand on the back of my neck going up and tangling in my hair, while the other hesitantly slid down, under my top. His fingers slid up underneath, caressing the skin of my back.

He expected me to stop him, to say no, that I wasn't ready for this, but I was more than ready for this. When he could tell I wasn't going to stop him, he slid his hand around to cup my breast through the fabric of my bra. I let out a shuddering breath, and he slipped his fingers under my bra. I let out a gasp, and my nipple tightened under his hand. I expected him to ask me if I wanted to move to the bedroom, but he said nothing, just kept kissing and stroking me. The longer it went on, the more I wanted relief. But I wasn't completely without decency; I wasn't going to be the first to initiate taking it any farther, no matter how much my body asked me to.

Just when I thought I was going to have to take the initiative because I couldn't stand it anymore, he stood with me in his arms and laid me on the couch in one fluid motion. I looked up at him, breathing hard. "Done for the night?"

"Not remotely."

He bared his teeth, growled a little, and lunged at me, settling his body atop mine. I shrieked in delight before he cut me off with another deep, lasting kiss, molding our bodies tightly so I could feel the length of him against me. It was so much like the dream that I gasped. He pulled back to give me a smoky look, lightly tracing my jaw with a finger before bringing my lips to his again. His hand traveled down to cup my buttocks, pulling one of my legs over him, holding me tight against his leg.

I could feel him ready against me. I knew if I wanted, I could make the dream real. He wouldn't turn me down. I ached with the need to feel him naked against me, moving in me. But, as good as it would feel, I didn't want our first time together to end as the dream had, with me waking up and him gone. He'd said he had to leave before dawn.

Danial suddenly stopped still, as if he sensed my reservations. "What's wrong?" he asked warily.

"I want you," I said, gazing at him with heat in my eyes.

"I don't see any problem with that." He smirked, running his hand along the outside of my breast.

I closed my eyes, shivering deliciously, and tried to keep my mind on the words coming out of my mouth. "I need you to know something, Danial. I know you might not believe this, but I've never done this before."

He pulled back from me. "I'm not sure what you mean."

"I was married, before," I said, raking my hand through my hair. "I'm not a virgin. But I've also never been so hot and heavy this soon with a man I only just met—"

"Sar, don't feel like I'm pressuring you, or anything—"

"I don't," I said quickly.

"You don't have to do anything you don't want to," he said seriously. "I can accept you saying no. I'm not going to be angry. It's true you don't know me well. I want you to know that I plan on getting to know you if you're interested in spending more time with me."

I swallowed hard. "Yes, I want to get to know you. Will you think badly of me if I'm honest with you?" I added in a small voice.

"If it's the truth, no," he replied, puzzled.

"I don't want to wait weeks or months," I said carefully. "Do you understand? I'm not saying no. I'm saying yes."

The lust in his eyes deepened, and he moved to take off my shirt. I stopped him, and he gave me a questioning look. "Didn't you just say—?"

"You said you had to leave soon. I want more than a few hours with you if it's going to be our first time. I don't want to wake up and find you gone."

I thought he would be mad, maybe suggest a quickie and we'd do a longer version later, when we had time. But he surprised me.

"Yes, I want that, too," he said, studying me. "I don't want to rush with you, or have to leave afterwards." He stood and helped me stand. "Go to bed. I'll see you on Friday. We'll go out and have a good time. Saturday—" He pulled me to him. "—we'll finish what we started here tonight." He put his lips against mine hard enough to feel the pressure of his fangs. He broke away and kissed me on the forehead. "Dream of me," he whispered, "and I'll dream of you."

I smiled. "Have a safe trip. Watch your back."

"I have extra incentive," he said, winking.

I turned to go but hesitated "Danial?"

"Yes?"

"I need to know. Is there anyone...else? Anyone waiting at home for you while you're here with me?" I felt a little strange asking now, when I'd pretty much already agreed to have a relationship with him. I tried to cover the awkwardness, looking down. "I should have asked before I even kissed you, but...."

He stopped me with a finger on my lips. "Shhh, you don't have to explain. I'm the one who suddenly feels awkward and cloddish." He paused. "Sarelle, look at me." I raised my head to meet his eyes. "There is no one but you. And I won't be returning to anyone else should I return to home. There's no one there, except security people."

A wave of relief hit me, and then joy.

"I thought you knew that, but it was my mistake if you suspected otherwise. I should have told you the first night. I don't have a wife or lover. I haven't for a long time."

I basked in the knowledge that he was all mine. But I had to ask "Why not?"

"My life isn't something most women would embrace. Packing work and *necessities* into eight to ten hours doesn't leave much time left to share with a friend or lover. The women I meet on the job are all career-oriented, with nine to five jobs. Trusting them with my life...I could never do it."

He had a point there. It was probably easier for him to meet a woman and seduce her than it was for him to walk, but to find someone to trust who cared for him was probably hard. There weren't a lot of options. The only reason he trusted me was because I'd saved his life when I could just as easily have taken it.

"I realize now that I should have asked you the same question. When I came into your life, did I interrupt anything? Did you have anyone?" He eyed me anxiously. "Do you have someone?"

"No. I've been alone for a year now."

He heard the sad note in my voice but didn't ask about it. "I'm glad. I dislike being the other man."

I gave him a quizzical look.

He sighed. "I shouldn't have said that. But I have trouble with women seeing me as more than a fantasy. I was a man before I became vampire. I want to be wanted for that person, not for being vampire." He gave me a reserved look. "Be honest with me, Sar, are you saying you'll sleep with me because I'm vampire? Is that the real reason you want to know me?"

I flushed. I tried to think of a good answer, but blurted out what I was thinking. "In part, yes, maybe. There's something I find irresistible about you, and some of it might be what you are. But mostly, I like that you're funny and intelligent. I find the real thing a little too real." I flushed as I spoke, but since he was going to be blunt, so was I. "I don't want you for your fangs. At least, not just your fangs."

I thought I might have offended him, but he smiled and hugged me. "Good, because I don't want you just for your blood. At least, not for that alone."

Chapter Five

After Danial left that night, I lay in bed and thought about whether it had been the right thing to admit so boldly that I wanted a sexual relationship with him so soon. I thought about it for a good hour and finally decided I'd done what I'd wanted. I had a vampire in my house as a part-time tenant, and down deep, I wanted him there. I wanted him in my life. I wanted him in my bed. I wanted to see where this was going, if we could make this work, and maybe, if I was still capable of loving someone, even someone who had fangs.

* * * *

The week passed. I had brunch with my mother, lunch with a friend, shopped for groceries, took the dogs to the vet, the usual things. But during one of those, it was harder to act as if everything was business as usual.

"Something happened," my mother said over dessert, grinning. "Or was it someone?"

I tried to remain impassive, but I'd gotten my body language from her.

"You met someone!" she crowed triumphantly.

Diners in the surrounding tables cast us a look. I felt the blush spread across my face. So much for not being embarrassed. But the worst was yet to come.

"When are we going to meet him?"

I thanked God that I'd swallowed water instead of food, or I would have choked. As it was, I coughed and spat out water. A passing waiter asked if I was all right.

"I'm fine," I gasped. "No problem."

"I asked when we were going to meet—"

"I heard you the first time." People watched us; some smiling, some frowning. "You aren't going to meet him for a while. I just met him. When I know him better, I'll bring him by one night—"

"Why don't we all meet for lunch this weekend?"

She was persistent, as always. "No, we're going to be busy." Because Danial would combust in the sun. And I doubted he would eat regular food, though I had yet to find out for sure.

"He's the first man you've mentioned since Brennen. Of course, I want to meet him. I want to know everything about him. Chris will want to take him fishing." She grasped my hand, her eyes moist. "I'm so happy for you."

Crap. I couldn't fault her for wanting me to be happy. So, of course, I put my foot in it and said, "We'll try to stop by Friday night."

She smiled happily, said that would be fine, and went back to her dessert. I thought to myself that I was grateful to have a mother like her, for her to care so much about my happiness, but I'd just added another problem for Danial and I to navigate.

Kat was easier. I spilled the story to her with relish, editing the parts where I'd rescued Daniel, him being a vampire, and the fact that someone wanted to kill him. In short, everything except that he was handsome, had a good job, and was taking me out on Friday. She was ecstatic for me and didn't add anything judgmental, such as: you're letting him live with you and you've known him only a week or you're going to sleep with him, and you've known him only a week?

When she asked how we'd met, I told her it was through a mutual friend at the friend's house, which was kind of true. I'd met Danial on my neighbor's property.

It was then that I remembered something I'd forgotten.

Right after lunch, I headed home. When I pulled up to the access road, much to my relief and consternation, I saw that the chain was up. On closer inspection, it clearly wasn't the same chain; it was newer and without rust. I got back in my car, mollified. Now I just had to make sure it had been Danial who'd replaced the broken chain, and not my neighbor.

* * * *

Thursday night, I did some housecleaning, which included Danial's room, though he kept it pretty neat. It gave me a charge being around his things, even if it was ridiculous

I walked the dogs. Ghost was a little antsy again, but Darkness was her usual self. I hadn't seen any signs of bear, but maybe the coyotes were around. The neighbors had sighted a pack of five, but I'd only ever seen one by itself. There used to be a few around, but as the farms in the county failed, forests replaced the fields. More animals used these "corridors" to make their way south from Canada. Hell, I'd seen a bobcat out my window one night.

I listened and looked as we walked, but I saw no sign of any predator.

* * * *

I opened my eyes and grinned. Friday. I'd waited all week, and it was finally here. I would see Danial tonight, and we'd have our first real date: dancing and a movie. I'd left all the details to him, so I wasn't sure where we were going. But I wasn't going to sweat it. I was a decent dancer and I could hold my own on the dance floor. I'd taken professional lessons when I was younger, which was about the only girlie thing I'd done. I had good movement and grace, though I was out of practice. Seeing the movie would be easier and would tell me more about him, at least from my point of view. One of my standing rules of dating was choosing a movie together and enjoying it. If a couple couldn't do that, they probably weren't compatible. We'd see if we could pass the test by what he suggested and how much he liked what I suggested.

I wanted to stay in bed and imagine being with him, but it was past time to get up. I wanted to be early to work to handle anything that came up and still be able to leave on time. The day went by in a blur, and I got home around five. I didn't expect Danial to be there until seven, so I had a little time. I walked the dogs, gave them their daily Cheweez, and showered. I initially wanted to dress up for him, but decided against it. He hadn't said to, and I felt more comfortable in casual clothes.

46

God, even in my mind, I felt like I was babbling.

I put on a long multicolored gypsy skirt with tiny beads, and a sexy but not too revealing white bustier for dancing. Over that, I put a loose white tunic sweater. This was for the movie, where I would probably be cold. I put on some simple gold hoops and looked in my jewelry chest for something else. I pulled out a bracelet but stopped. Sitting in the chest were my wedding rings. I hadn't worn them for almost a year. I remembered picking them out with Brennan and how happy I'd been. A tear formed in my eye, and I blinked it away.

Damn it, I didn't need to think about this now. I shut the chest and neatened up, picking up the few clothes I'd thrown here and there in my search for the perfect outfit.

When I made the bed, I found Danial's shirt. After my dream, I hadn't worn the shirt to bed again, afraid I'd lose the scent too fast. Instead, I'd draped it over the bedpost to make that wonderful scent last longer. I'd asked Danial what the fragrance was and he'd said it was a mixture of cedar and nutmeg, plus a few other "secret ingredients."

The shirt had fallen off the bedpost during the night. I picked it off the floor and hung it up again. It still smelled wonderful. I breathed in the fragrance, suddenly aroused.

Shit, I had to move it! I gave one last sniff, and then hurried to put on a little makeup. I wanted to look good. Screw that, I wanted to be breathtaking—or as breathtaking as I could be. I wasn't a supermodel, but I was striking. Or at least, I had been once.

I put on some foundation and a little blush and added eye shadow to enhance my green eyes. My hair had dried since the shower, and it tumbled down my back to my waist. It was various shades of blonde, both from the sun and the highlighting kits I used occasionally to streak it. It was almost all one length and moderately curly, so I fixed it to stay out of my eyes with a barrette. I had a hair appointment soon and debated cutting it off to send to a cancer charity. But I kind of liked it now and thought about putting off the appointment for another six months.

My eyelashes were so light that I needed a little mascara if I wanted anyone to know I had them, so I put that on, as well as lip liner and a touch of gloss. None of the makeup was stark or noticeable, but I wasn't going for the Victoria's Secret model look. Maybe I'd try that on Saturday.

I admired myself in the mirror. Pretty damn good.

I thought about wearing high heels, which would make the outfit *swish* better, but I hadn't worn any for a while. My standard work shoes these days had steel toes. I went to the closet and got some low-heeled slip-on sandals. These were nice enough to dance in, but not too high that I'd be hobbling by the time we got to the movie.

Oh shit, I hadn't painted my toenails. My fingernails I'd had to give a pass to. I never did much for them beyond making sure they were clean and filed. It was another brand of the life I lived; handling steel parts and firewood broke nails off in a nasty way if I didn't keep them short. But tonight was special, it was our first date. Even if Danial never saw me with painted toenails again in my life, I wanted to go all out tonight.

Did I have enough time? I checked the clock. Yes, if I hurried.

I put on two coats in record time and a top clear coat over that. Fortunately, my few bottles of polish were all of the fast-dry variety. Another fact of my life was that any pampering I did lasted a half hour at the most.

I double-checked that everything was set to go and that I had money in my purse, just in case. Just as I was closing it, I saw headlights out of the corner of my eye coming up the driveway.

Danial parked in the basement garage. I heard the sound of the garage door closing, his footsteps coming up the stairs, and then he was there. He set a package down and crossed the room to hug me. It was so good to feel him in my arms again. He was almost warm, and I leaned back to look up at him.

He'd been ash pale when I last saw him. Though he was pale now, it wasn't an abnormal pallor, and the luster to his skin was back in spades. His hair had been a dark brown, soft and shoulder length, with a slight curl. Now it was darker, a shade away from black, and curled only at the ends. It was also cut short and was feathered back on the sides. Had he done his hair for me?

He was dressed in jeans and an ivory linen shirt with an open collar. He had on leather boots that had to be handmade.

"Do you like what you see?" he said, tilting his head and looking at

48

me.

Was he kidding? I couldn't take my eyes off him.

"I take that as a yes?" There was satisfaction in his voice.

"Very much," I said huskily, "You seem to have recovered from your injury."

"Yes," he said sturdily, maybe to reassure me.

"You never told me, but what was it that hurt you so badly?"

He was silent for a moment. "Believe it or not, an arrow. Someone tipped it with a special mixture just for me. Vampire poison—lethal. The only cure is human blood, a lot of blood, which has to be taken within forty-eight hours of being poisoned. The toxin stops our systems from regenerating, and it takes the massive influx of blood to jump-start our system again."

"So if I'd waited much longer?" I murmured quietly.

"If you hadn't done what you did when you had, you wouldn't be talking to me now. That's why I reacted the way I did," he said uncomfortably. He grasped my hand, and brought it to his lips. "I'm sorry for that. Forgive me?"

"I thought you weren't going to apologize," I said teasingly.

"I changed my mind."

"I accept your apology. But it's okay; I knew when I gave you blood there was risk."

"Can't you ever just agree with me?" he asked sardonically.

"I promise to agree all night," I replied, smiling gently.

He pulled me closer. "I'll hold you to that," he whispered and kissed me. It was as good as I remembered, and I lost myself in him. I ran my hands up to his newly cut hair. He stopped kissing me long enough to say, "Do you like it?"

"I love it."

"Come," he said eagerly. "I have something for you."

"If you're the one who fixed the chain to the quarry that was all I needed."

"I had it fixed before I left the first time, but I got you something special, as I told you I would."

"You didn't have to," I said coquettishly.

"It would be rude of you not to accept it when you promised to agree with me only a minute ago."

Danial handed the package to me. It was wrapped in expensive gold paper with a huge bow. I unwrapped a blood-red velvet box and opened it. Inside was a necklace, but none like I'd seen before. It was a choker, but made entirely out of— "Is that *gold*?"

"Eighteen karats. Anything purer and it won't last."

"It's beautiful." And it was. The clasp wasn't like any I'd seen before and didn't even seem functional. I didn't have a lot of expensive jewelry so I couldn't say. The links were delicate, the filigree somehow twined together so it resembled cloth, like chain mail, but more delicate. It looked decidedly feminine. On the front, a tiny symbol hung.

"Is that a wolf?"

"A fox. That's my symbol—my family's symbol and my company logo." He raised his hand and showed me the heavy gold ring on his finger. It was old and bore the same figure. A fox with its head down, eyes staring up, baring no teeth. "This was my father's ring. The eyes on your necklace are small rubies, like the ones here."

"Thank you," I said appreciatively. "I love it." I was a little worried about the money he'd spent on me. It was hardly the kind of present to give me so early in our relationship. But I had saved his life and it felt wrong to make a comment that might make me sound ungrateful or rude.

He reached into the box and brought it out. It made a soft clinking sound as he fastened it around my neck. It fit perfectly, and I slid my hands over it.

"How did you get it the right size? *Where* did you even get something like this?" I faced the hall mirror to admire how I looked. The filigree banded my neck, while the fox hung in the hollow of my throat, the eyes winking softly in the overhead light.

"I had it custom made for you. I know a goldsmith who does excellent work, especially rush orders."

I grew uneasy. "You didn't have to pay extra to rush—"

"Sarelle," he interrupted, "this is more than a necklace. It's security for you."

"Why would I need security?"

"This identifies you as someone who means something to me. Vampires aren't very numerous, contrary to what all the books and shows say. There aren't many in the country, and most are familiar with my symbol. They would know what this choker signifies and leave you alone. I want you to wear it for me. When I'm not here with you, be sure to wear it, so you're safe."

"Why? No one knows you're here. No one knows about us."

"We can't keep our relationship a secret forever. That arrow was meant for me, and I've been able to track down the culprit. It wasn't just another mercenary. This was a vampire. Should he somehow track me to you, he'll see this and leave you alone, even if he attacks me. It's against vampire law to do otherwise."

I touched the necklace. "I don't like any of this, but I'll wear it."

A horn sounded, and Danial said, "He's waiting. We're going to be late." He noticed me picking up my purse. "Leave your purse; tonight's on me."

I set my purse down and grabbed my driver's license for ID, then hesitated. Wait a minute, He who?

I locked up and walked out with him. There was a black Expedition in the driveway, gleaming in the faint light from my porch. When we reached the SUV, I saw someone in the driver's seat. Danial opened the back door and followed me into the car.

"This is my most trusted employee, Theo."

Theo turned around, pulled down his sunglasses, and gave me a wink.

Sunglasses at night? I chalked it up to some supernatural ability and let it go. Theo was a little younger than Danial, maybe late twenties. He had sandy hair and blue eyes, a lean build, but also an ease of movement that told me he was strong and most likely fast.

"Hi, Sar." He spoke casually, with mirth. "It's good to meet you after hearing so much about you."

I could see he didn't have any fangs when he grinned. Then I realized what he'd said and was glad it was dark. What had Danial told him about me? "I hope it was all good things," I said gamely. "It's nice to meet you, too."

"I've checked the property and no one seems to be here," Theo said to Danial "But I left Aran on the access road to watch the house while we're gone."

51

"Good."

"You must be more worried about an attack than I thought to have set up all this security."

"There have been attempts on and off for as long as I've run my company. But recently, due to the past few jobs, I've added at least one more enemy who may be out for revenge. The security is just in case." He smiled faintly at me, his eyes troubled. "Don't worry. You're safe."

Why worry, just because I felt like I was living in one of the Godfather movies? Was it always like this around him?

Theo added his own assessment. "In any case, this vampire who tried once already thinks he's on some kind of mission. He'll attack again, and soon."

Danial gave him a dark look, then turned to me. "When he does, I'll handle him."

"We'll handle him," Theo said pointedly, not looking at Danial.

"We've been over this," Danial said icily. "The matter is closed, Theo."

I wisely said nothing.

"It's better if we—"

"Enough," Danial growled. "We are going to be late."

Theo wasn't intimidated. He just put the Expedition in gear and drove off.

"So," I said to fill the silence, "Where are we going?"

"To the college town a little north of here," Danial replied. "There's a club there called the Haunt."

That settled, I sat back and enjoyed the ride. It would be about thirty minutes.

Danial held my hand. His was a little cooler than mine, and I covered it with my other hand to warm it. When I remembered just what he was, I wondered what it would be like when we were together tomorrow. All of him was sure to be cool, not just his hands. I shivered a little. Danial mistook my apprehension for a chill and asked Theo to turn up the heater. I *was* a little cold, so I didn't correct him. I tried to get my mind off sex and started listening instead. When I resumed listening, I realized Danial and Theo were talking about business. From the way they shared and gave information, I deduced that Theo was something akin to head of security for Danial's company. More than that, they seemed to be good friends. Theo had a wicked sense of humor, but he was ruthless.

"We've got to take care of the Phoenix problem," Theo said, exasperated. "We can't just let it hang out there until it decides to bite us in the ass."

"We can't act right now, you know that. Not unless we're willing to kill the man pulling the strings."

"Then let's kill him and be done with it," Theo said. "Better one dead patriarch than a bunch of our guys wounded when Maximillian sends a bomb to your office."

I was shocked that he would talk so casually of killing, like ordering out for dinner. My feeling of unease came back, but I said nothing. Danial's company was a little larger than I'd envisioned. I'd thought it was a small business, just him and two others. Maybe he *was* Vampire Entrepreneur Extraordinaire.

"I'll think about it. I don't want to start something that's going to spiral out of control."

"Max threatened your life," Theo argued. "You have two choices: ignore him and brace for an indirect attack, or take him out before he attacks you—"

"Theo," Danial warned.

Theo noticed that I was still in the car and hastened to cover his words. "I meant objectively, not literally, Sarelle. We have to neutralize him before he can strike."

Right. Why didn't I believe him? I was getting those danger signals from him that told me he meant business. I was both alarmed and relieved that I could still tell when someone was bullshitting me.

We arrived at the Haunt. I could hear loud rock music even inside the car. Danial got out, and I followed him, holding his hand. There was a line, but Danial said something to the bouncer, and we bypassed it. I was impressed.

Inside, the Haunt was decorated for Halloween. With a start, I realized Halloween would be next weekend. The DJ was playing Starship's *We Built this City*. I saw that the couples around us were predominantly in their thirties and forties, though there was a few twenty-somethings here. The song ended and switched to the Pointer Sisters *Jump (For My Love)*.

"Do you like this?" Danial asked, his arm around me.

"Yes," I shouted over the din. "But do you? If you didn't grow up listening to these songs, they might seem a little...dated."

"Let's enjoy ourselves. Someday soon, I'll show you the kind of dancing I like."

I took that as a double entendre, but maybe it was just sincere sentiment. Or sincere lust.

"Do you want to dance or get a booth?"

I gave him a wide smile. "I don't need to work up to it. Let's go." I led him onto the dance floor and put my arms around his neck. "Show me what you've got."

Jump ended, and appropriately, Kenny Loggins's *Meet Me Halfway* came on. Danial showed me he did have skill. He hadn't spent those forty years just learning how to kiss; some of it had been spent learning how to dance. Even to this music, which was hard to move badly to, he showed me that he knew exactly how to move. All too soon the song was over. The next song that came on was Robert Palmer's *Addicted to Love*.

Here was the moment of truth. Could he dance to faster music? I'd never met a man who felt comfortable dancing to fast music, and the ones who did...well, they did it badly. Even men in movies seemed to do it half-assed, except Travolta. But Danial could have been Patrick Swayze in *Dirty Dancing*.

After a half hour, I was hot and wanted to take my sweater off. "Let's sit down for a bit," I said, breathing hard. "I need a drink."

We found a booth in the corner that said, "Reserved." Danial pushed the sign to the side. I looked at him questioningly. "It was reserved for us," he said.

Wow, this was nice.

A waitress materialized and took my order for a glass of wine. She came back fast for it being such a busy night, bringing both my glass of Shiraz, and a scotch glass for Danial. He read the little note attached to it and laughed. He downed the contents and gave it back to the waitress, saying, "Tell her thanks, and I'll be careful." He turned and said to me, "A friend of mine, Tatiana. She owns this place. She held this table for us." He laughed easily. "She's having some fun with me."

"That was blood, wasn't it?"

"Yes, and a note said to be careful, and don't drink too much."

"Does everyone know what you are?"

"If you mean Theo, Aran, and, Tatiana, yes, they know, along with a few others. It's just as much a mistake not to trust anyone as it is to be too trusting. Life is about being satisfied, both with yourself, and the path you're on. Otherwise, you may as well be dead."

"I agree. Life is for living."

Danial nodded once. "I'm glad you agree. Let's dance."

He reached for my hand, and I remembered I hadn't taken off my sweater. I stripped it off. Danial gave me the up and down look with his eyes, then a sexy smile as he led me out to the dance floor. We danced to several songs, took a break, and then danced some more. On the third break, I said, "I'm going to have to stop. I haven't danced in a long time, and my stamina's gone."

I worried that I let him down, but he flashed me a relieved smile. "We have to get going anyway if we're going to make the movie."

I checked my watch and realized it was eleven thirty. I finished my wine and grabbed my sweater. Danial hadn't acted tense in the club, but he visibly relaxed walking out with me. I hid my smile, thinking he'd been as nervous as I had been. Now I knew why he'd suggested going dancing first, instead of the movie Theo was in the parking lot with the SUV. He drove us to the theater and dropped us off, where we caught the latest revenge-action movie.

We enjoyed it, both of us glad to see true justice was done in the end. The theater was cold, and I was glad I'd brought my sweater. But I was happier that Danial and I had agreed so easily on a movie we both enjoyed. We'd passed the couples test I'd dreaded. Now, if I could just get past the violence that seemed such a big part of his life.

Theo picked us up after the movie ended. As we rode home, I fell asleep on Danial's lap. Drifting off, I heard Theo say, "You know this is a mistake."

I came alert at once. Danial answered more forcefully than I expected. "I'll have this one thing and it won't be sullied, not this time—"

"It's too late for that."

"You don't know that," Danial said angrily. "It might work."

"You're lying to yourself, Danial," Theo said grimly.

"Shut up and drive," Danial growled.

But Theo wasn't done. "I warned you. That's my job. My conscience is clear. This will not end well."

Chapter Six

Bright light hit me in the eyes. I blinked rapidly, looked over at the clock, and found out that it was two in the afternoon.

Oh shit...

I dashed from the bedroom to take care of the dogs, cursing myself for not remembering to set my alarm. They would need to go out, and the cats hadn't been fed.

I stopped short in the doorway to the wood stove room. There, I said a quick prayer of thanks for having worn full pajamas to bed and not just a T-shirt; or worse, nothing at all. Theopolis, a.k.a. Theo, waited for me in the recliner next to the wood stove, reading a book. A nice fire was going strong. My dogs bolted to their feet, panting, and came over eagerly.

Theo looked up and flashed a grin. "Good morning, Sar."

"Good morning, and what the hell are you doing here?" I asked as I walked past him toward the kitchen. The dogs followed beside me, their watchful eyes on him.

"I took care of the cats and let them outside. I tried feeding your dogs, but they didn't want to eat."

What he meant was that they wouldn't take food from him. They wouldn't go near him either, though they weren't growling. There wasn't a cat in sight, which was strange. Why would the animals behave this way? I remembered the sunglasses Theo had worn and wondered if there was something different about him, something animals found upsetting, maybe dangerous. Then I told myself I was being foolish. Danial must have told him to stay here for a reason, to guard the both of us. The animals were acting this way because he was a stranger.

With me standing next to them, Ghost and Darkness ate. Afterward, they did their business outside and came back in, taking up their positions between Theo and me. He was still sitting in the other room, reading his book or pretending to.

"Come and give them a treat," I said as nicely as I could manage

Theo got up. He went through the procedure of giving each dog a treat, which seemed to do the trick with easing their tension. Ghost visibly relaxed and laid down, going through his normal morning yawn. I could tell by her eyes that Darkness was still thinking about biting Theo, but she also lay down. One problem solved; on to the next.

"Why are you here?"

"Danial gave me instructions to help out this morning. If you didn't wake up on your own, I was to let you sleep and take care of the animals. I'm also supposed to help you today until sundown, and then I'm off duty. Help you with what, he didn't say."

"Don't you sleep?" Every human needed sleep, but maybe he wasn't human?

"I've been sleeping when I wasn't reading this book of yours. Aran is still outside on duty. Everything's been quiet." He handed me the book. "How can you read this stuff? It's just sex, page after page. No one could have this much sex and still function."

I saw what he was reading and flushed. I snatched it from him. "No one told you to pick *this* book."

"It said *Sleeping Beauty*—"

"Never mind! Next time you decide to grab a book, stay away from the shelf where you found this. That shelf is off limits. Pick one from any other shelf—"

In the midst of my tirade, I noticed his eyes sparkling with mirth. I started to smile but bit my lip to stop myself. "You knew what this was when you picked it up, didn't you?"

"I had to see what you'd say," he chortled. "Your face is so red—"

"I don't think joking about sex with me is appropriate, Theopolis." My voice was low and had an edge to it.

His smile faded. "How do you know my full name? You heard what I said to Danial. You weren't asleep—"

"No, I wasn't. Why were you warning him away from me?"

He said nothing, his eyes holding mine solidly.

58

Try another tactic. "Look, I care about him. I had a great time last—"

"It's not that, Sarelle. I don't doubt your intentions for each other."

"Then what? Spit it out."

"As you said, this isn't appropriate for me to talk about," he said coolly, looking at me with a smile that didn't reach his eyes. "You also shouldn't be strolling around in your pajamas either."

He was right. I had a lot to do, getting dressed being next on the list. I threw out my best argument. "Tell me, Theo, or I'll ask Danial about it when he gets up. And whether he answers me or not, you'll still get yelled at for saying what you said to him in front of me."

I had him and he knew it. He grimaced at me. "Okay. You two are from different worlds, with different expectations. Whatever life you had before you met him is sure to change just being with him. Are you ready for that? Is that what you really want?"

"I don't know," I said honestly. "But I want to be with him. I'm willing to try."

"You know what he is. There are many things he can't change, like what he needs to do to survive. And what he can and can't share with you, even if he wants to."

"There are some things I can't change, either, but I'll do my best to adjust. I mean that. I'm not just saying that to make you feel better."

"I hope so," he said softly, "for both your sakes."

I excused myself to take a shower, my good mood slightly soured by his gloom-and-doom outlook. Afterward, I got dressed and went out to get Theo, who was on the deck with the dogs.

"I'm making breakfast. Do you want anything to eat? Do you need to shower?"

He grinned. "Are you insinuating anything?"

He was bantering all the time. It was amusing, but also annoying.

"Yes or no?" I said, trying hard not to smile in spite of myself.

"No, Aran and I took turns showering last night when we got back here. I hope you don't mind that I used all your shampoo."

Ballsy, but I was beginning to think that was his middle name. "Don't worry; I keep a supply on hand. Breakfast?"

"No, we already ate."

Strange that he hadn't joked about that, when he had about almost everything else. "After breakfast, I need some help with the firewood and some cleaning."

"I don't do windows," he deadpanned.

"I hope you put up Halloween decorations, cause I need help with those, too."

* * * *

Theo did try hard; I gave him that. His wisecracks didn't stop, but we worked well together, me being witty myself. He was just full of keen observations, in fact he had one for every new room we worked in.

In the living room, he asked, "Why did you pick these curtains? No one has ladybug curtains."

"I like ladybugs. They eat garden pests. And they never ask questions."

In the woodstove room, he asked, "Is there any reason why you keep all your porn on a shelf where visitors can find it?"

"I like it accessible in case I need it in an emergency."

In the pet area, he stated, "There seems to be a large quantity of supplies on hand. I understand some, but are you expecting a shortage of cat litter this winter?"

"Anything forty pounds is easier to carry when you don't have to haul it through ice and snow. But you're right; those seven tubs should be in the cellar. Why don't you carry them all down there for me? Afterwards you can carry up the box of replacement bricks for the woodstove, the shovels, and the bags of rock salt, too."

In the dining room, he asked, "Why do you have so many weapons around? There's something in every room."

"You never know when a sword or ax might come in handy."

He laughed. "Did you ever think you might be more than a little strange?"

"No. I'm a lot strange. But don't worry; you have me beat hands down."

By the time we'd finished the dusting and winter reorganizing, we gotten relaxed around each other. Next was getting enough firewood from the woodshed. As we walked to the barn, he said, "Let me get this straight; you named your dogs after two African lions that killed over a hundred people?"

"That's right," I said, a little confrontationally.

"You're right. You're very strange."

"It would be worse to be utterly normal."

"That's true."

"I wouldn't get to meet people like you," I said, winking.

"True again," he said, returning the gesture.

I unlocked the barn and rolled back the door.

"So this is what you use to get firewood?" he said, looking at my tractor.

"You can hop on if you want a ride, but we aren't going far."

"Can I drive?" he asked hopefully.

"Sorry...no one drives my Deere but me."

I climbed up and cranked the engine. It roared to life. I reached down to help Theo up, but he climbed up agilely, holding onto the roll bar and side handle. I backed the tractor out and swung her around, then drove to the woodpile.

"Do you want gloves?" I pulled mine on to start loading wood.

He gave me a disdainful look and declined, then let out a yelp when he got a splinter on the next piece of wood. I stopped what I was doing and worked it out for him. His hand was warm in mine, and I was conscious of him standing next to me. I remembered his talk of killing the night before, but pushed it aside. My hands needed to be steady, and if I thought about what he'd done in life, they wouldn't be.

I got the splinter out and handed him a pair of men's gloves, saying nothing but smirking. He gave me a dark look and put them on. We loaded the rest of the wood, brought it to the house and unloaded it in the basement. I tried to be quiet, knowing Danial was trying to sleep close by.

"Don't worry about disturbing him," Theo said. "He already knows we're here. He's heard us by now, just like he heard us moving around upstairs earlier. But that alone won't wake him. He'll get the rest he needs."

I relaxed. The work went faster. We finished unloading the wood and drove back to the woodpile. Theo hopped down and brushed wood chips off. "Decorations now?"

"We aren't done. We need to get at least one more load into the basement."

He made a face. "What? I'm going to get all dirty again."

"That's right," I said smugly. "Grab some wood."

We finished moving the second load in record time, still trading insults and jokes. By that time, I'd completely relaxed, deciding Theo couldn't be the stone-cold killer I'd thought him to be. He was simply too warm and friendly, his laughter too contagious.

After storing the tractor and locking the barn, we walked back to the house. As Theo had predicted, we were filthy with dirt and sawdust. "Why don't you go in and take a shower?" I said. "I need to mow, at least the part by the house."

"No can do, Sar," he said seriously. "You should go inside and start getting ready. It's almost six. Danial will be up at seven. That gives you an hour." He gave a long-suffering sigh and said in a martyr's voice, "I'll mow around the house."

I envisioned him doing all sorts of horrible things to my mower blade in his urge to get it done. "Forget it. We'll take turns showering, and then put up the decorations."

Heading inside, I was abruptly hit with an attack of nerves. What did one wear for sex? What did Danial expect? What did I expect? Was I making a mistake doing this, especially so soon?

Theo stepped close to me. "Some words of advice, Sarelle?"

"As long as you're serious."

His eyes softened. They were a grey-blue color, like the sky before a storm. His expression was serious, neither joking nor dangerous. "Be yourself and dress how you want. Danial wants you, not an actress."

"Thanks," I said, feeling relieved and not knowing why. His advice wasn't exactly a revelation. "I know that, but I needed to hear it. I'm nervous."

"He probably is, too; just like he was the other night. Now make sure to leave some hot water for me."

I rolled my eyes at him. After I'd cleaned up, we began putting up decorations—all seven boxes of them. I hadn't put up any last year. This year, I was putting them all up to celebrate.

Promise Me

"Is there any particular place these should go?" he said, holding up a stuffed ghost and a skull candle.

"No. Be creative."

When I rejoined him a few minutes later and saw what he'd done with the giant spiders and a pose able Halloween King, I gave him precise directions on what exactly to put where. We finished at a quarter to seven.

Theo put on his jacket. "Aran and I are heading out now. We won't be back tonight, but two others will be here by seven."

"Will they be watching from outside, or—"

"No one will come in," he said quickly.

"Thanks for your help today. And please call me Sar."

"You're welcome, Sar. Have a *good* night." He shot me another grin as he left.

I had maybe ten minutes to change clothes and apply makeup. I decided on jeans and a sweatshirt, at least until I found out if I could convince Danial to go for a moonlit walk. After I'd dressed, I fluffed my hair and put on my usual makeup: lip-gloss.

I heard Danial enter the room just as I was smoothing it on my lips. A moment later, he put his arms around me. I relaxed back into him, and we studied our reflections.

"Why do they say no one can see a vampire in the mirror?"

"I'm not sure. I've never understood it. There was something about us being allergic to silver, but I think they got vampires confused with werewolves. And even that's not true."

"Do you know any werewolves?" I asked lightly. If one legend was true, were others?

"No," he said solemnly, his eyes sad.

"What's wrong?"

"There used to be a lot of werewolves in America, back when there were wolves here. There are some hiding around the large tracks of privately owned land, but that's it. The large packs were exterminated when the wolves were wiped out. Any who could leave did, but getting around back then wasn't like it is now, and most of them couldn't get away except for walking." He paused. "It was a slaughter. Most of the survivors never came back. Werewolves live predominantly in Canada,

63

Alaska, and Russia now, where they're safe." He grew even more somber. "They're shot sometimes on sight from planes even in the wilderness. A good friend of mine was killed that way years ago."

There was an awkward silence.

"I'm sorry." I put my hands on his, still around me, and squeezed lightly. I remembered Theo's message about the relief security showing up at seven and told him.

"Want to join the dogs and me for a walk when your people get here?" I asked.

"Let's go now. I want you all to myself later." He trailed a few kisses over my neck as he held my gaze in the mirror. "I admit, I spent a good portion of the past hour thinking of you. Was Theo a help? I heard you two moving around."

"Yes, he was. Thank you for that."

Any lingering doubts about the night faded away. I was happy being with Danial. After everything I'd been through, I deserved to be happy.

"Won't they worry if we aren't here when they get here?" I asked.

"Their job is to watch the house. If there's a lapse between when we leave and when they get here, they'll check the house from top to bottom before taking up their positions."

I called the dogs, locked the door, and joined Danial outside. The night was cool with a light wind. I wanted there to be romantic moonlight, but it was obscured by clouds. A few crickets sang happily in the dark beyond the barn lights. We walked into the field, through the woods, and out to a clearing, with the dogs staying close by. Both of us were waiting for the other to start talking first. I outlasted him.

"It's a beautiful night," he said, his voice drifting on the light wind, caressing me.

"It is," I said nervously.

"Why don't you tell me how you came to be here," he prompted.

I brushed the hair from my face and took a deep breath. "I grew up in the city. My dad died when I was less than a year old, and my mom and I were left to ourselves. She did the best she could, but we were poor. I didn't care because I was happy. My grandparents lavished me with attention. I have a lot of great memories of my grandmother's garden and fishing. By the time I was ten, we were able to buy a house, and we lived there for seven years. By the time I graduated from high school, my Mom had met the man who would be my stepfather. His name is Chris. They dated for several years, and eventually married. I went to a community college and graduated with a degree in chemistry. That's where I met my best friend, Katrina. I worked as a manager at my first job, overseeing a chemical sampling center." I took a deep breath. "And then I met the man who would become my husband."

I had dreaded this part the most. We walked in silence for a while.

"I'm not sure what to say," I finally said. "The condensed version is that I had the great fortune to marry a wonderful man I loved very much, and he died when he wasn't supposed to." I'd spoken slowly but the words came faster, just pouring out of me. "The life insurance and my part-time job are enough to keep me financially set, at least for now, while I'm young enough and strong enough to do most of the work without having to pay someone to help me. I try not to think about the future too much because I don't trust long-term plans anymore. We had a lot of plans for life, Brennan and I, and they never came true."

"What happened to him?"

"He died on the Infinite Spur of Mt. Foraker; retreat is difficult to impossible after about a day. There's nowhere to go but up. You have to leave some of your gear on the mountain for every hundred and fifty feet you descend. That's the maximum length of the rope used. You can only carry so much gear when you ascend, and that gear is used over and over. By the second day of the descent, after about fifty rappels, you don't have much equipment left, so you run out, and then you find yourself on the side of the mountain, unable to descend any farther. The climb has only been done less than five times." I sounded like I was babbling, but I couldn't stop; I had to get it all out. "If it sounds like I've studied it, I have. I wanted to believe it wasn't an accident. But his harness snapped when it should have held." I could feel tears in my eyes, and I wiped them away. "This is more than my home; it was our home. I've been here ever since. I didn't want to move back to the city, even though living in the country alone is hard. So I stayed."

"I'm sorry for your loss," Danial said, taking my hand. "It hurts to lose someone you love." He cleared his throat. "I've been in your shoes."

"Tell me," I said, and I felt his hand tighten on mine.

"I had a wife once," he said. "Before I was turned. We had a child, a son. His name was David, after my father. It was a simple life by most standards: getting enough to eat, keeping warm, and having a place to sleep. No one worried about retirement and redecorating the house, or vacationing abroad." He paused. I squeezed his hand to reassure him.

"I worked as a laborer most of my life, and the work was hard. When I was twenty-seven, I became a guard at the local prison. I got the job through an influential friend, and I was grateful. It was dangerous work, but it paid better than farming, and I wanted a good life for my family. When I'd been on the job a little more than three years, I was told I'd have to accompany a prisoner who was being transferred to another city for the death penalty. My wife didn't want me to go, but I told her the bonus for doing this would make it possible for David to go to a real school when he grew up. He could be more than a guard's son who'd be lucky to someday be a guard himself. If I refused, I'd probably have been fired." He paused again.

"Was this here, in America?"

"No," he replied. "In a rural section of Spain. But that's not important."

"Please go on."

"A hundred miles into our journey, we were attacked. I wasn't a fighter then, and I had little skill with weapons. The attacker killed all but me and one other, another guard. Both of us were wounded but we were able to get away. We had no horses, no supplies, and only the knives we'd been able to escape with. We didn't know what would happen to us when we returned and the magistrate learned that we'd lost our prisoner. We argued over what to do. I said I had to go back to my family, I couldn't run. He wanted us to disappear and take our chances elsewhere." He smiled wryly. "We didn't know that would be our last night as human."

"We woke up as vampires. The one who'd attacked us had been a vampire, though we didn't know. If we hadn't taken shelter in a cave we'd both have been dead when dawn came. As it was, I was partly exposed, and when the sunlight hit my skin, I screamed. I got out of the light, and the pain lessened. My companion reached into the sunlight and the same thing happened to him. He had fangs and I felt my own when I cut my tongue trying to speak. We'd changed, but we didn't know what we were or why the sun made our skin smoke, or why we suddenly had fangs. Neither of us had much education. We were both scared and just wanted to go home more than anything.

"We headed back the way we'd come. We had to travel by night, and it took a long time. A third of the way, we crossed paths with a traveling merchant. He didn't recognize us and mentioned our names in passing as gossip. The massacre of our party had been discovered, and it was believed that we'd done it. The law was looking to take us in dead or alive."

Danial took a deep breath. "My companion killed him as soon as he slept. I watched him drink his blood. When he offered me some, I drank the rest." He hesitated. "We parted company after that. He went north and I went back to my wife and son. I thought they loved me enough to accept me and I could find a way to deal with what I'd become." He was quiet for a time. "It went badly."

"What happened?"

"The moment she saw I had fangs, she recoiled. She was deeply religious and thought God had cursed me. She held a cross up to me as if I was a demon from Hell sent to steal her soul. She notified the priest, but I evaded him. I left to go south, and then west, trying to find out what had happened to me, if there was a cure. I encountered another vampire and learned how to survive. After a year with him, I went back to convince my wife to join me. Humans and vampires could sometimes have relationships if they were both willing to compromise. Disease had beaten me to them by three months. They were both dead."

I embraced him. We stood that way for a few minutes, giving each other comfort. Then, we drew back from one another.

"Neither one of us is unscarred," I said. "Sometimes I get overwhelmed by the past, and I feel as if I'm drowning in grief and misery. You sound like you've had more than your fair share. Together we can work through some of it. Once we have, maybe we can build something of our own."

"It's a deal," he said, touching my cheek.

We were almost to the welcoming light of the barn. I smiled, thinking to myself that I'd developed a fondness for ten thousand watts when I'd started living in a place where there were no streetlights.

As we rounded the corner to head into the light, Danial stopped suddenly.

"What is it?"

"Too many heartbeats... Down!"

He shoved me beneath him, and I heard the whine of bullets overhead. I saw a figure peek out near the woodshed and then a muzzle flash from the darkness to our left. A bullet thwacked the ground a few feet in front of me.

Chapter Seven

"Sar, get to the house. I'm going to be hit. When you hear it, keep going."

Danial kissed me quickly, and then hauled me to my feet, shielding me with his body as we ran away from the light, towards the tall grass of the corral. He was hit at least twice before we made it to cover, the bullets making him jerk as they impacted.

"Go!" he hissed painfully, giving me a push toward the house.

I didn't say a word. I just grabbed both dogs' collars and got moving. The dogs, well trained as they were, came with me without barking. Luckily, we were in weeds over waist high. They hid us from view and extended almost all the way to the house, and we were able to make it to the edge of the woodpile without incident.

I crouched there in the long grass with a hand on each of them, wondering what to do. Dare I cross the deck? The light would reveal us, and I'd have to stop to open the door. I'd be hit for sure, or they would. I needed another plan.

I heard more shots behind me and hoped Danial was killing some of them. Forget shoot to wound; they'd ambushed us. Those bullets hadn't been meant for him alone; they'd tried to hit me. Where in the hell was our security?

I decided to circle around the house and go through the basement door. There were no lights on now back there. The keypad would be able to open the overhead garage door faster than a key, and we could get in as soon as the door rose partway. The bad part was the noise; anyone nearby would hear it going up. But it was our best option.

We worked our way to the edge of the house, and then made a dash for the garage. As soon as the dogs and I were in, I shut the door. It had only opened a third of the way. Had anyone heard?

No one was in the cellar, neither the garage or the finished section, or so the dogs told me. I left them down in the basement, knowing the stairs were too steep for them to climb without help and a lot of cajoling. I wanted to hide down there with them, but who knew how many attackers there were? Danial's men had either still not arrived or been taken out. With there only being him and me, we needed to fight. I crept upstairs, kicking myself for not having my gun with me. And me being a card-carrying member of the NRA.

I eased up from the cellar stairs to the main floor. The lights were on, but none of the cats were around the cozy woodstove. Someone was in the house. Was it Danial's people, or the enemy?

I panicked and dashed for my bedroom door, shutting it behind me. In there, I grabbed my gun, giving thanks that I kept it loaded. I grabbed two speed loaders, too, thinking I might need them before this was over.

Thinking of how best to help Danial, I headed for the side door of the house, the one closest to the garage. The back fence would give me cover to reach the garage, and my SUV. I might be able to make it to the barn and Danial in that.

Before I got five steps, someone grabbed me from behind.

The attacker tried to pin my arms behind my back, but I was a lot stronger than he'd counted on. He wrestled with me, and I pitched to the side, throwing us to the floor. He got to his feet in one fluid motion, drawing a long knife. His eyes fixed me where I lay on my side, zeroing in on the dangling fox head. I bit into my lip to stop the shaking threatening to loosen the grip on my gun.

"Your lover's bound to break cover when you start screaming. But if he doesn't, it's okay, cause that means he's already dead. Just like you're going to be." He advanced, whistling some somber tune, the blade gleaming. "Let's get started."

Do it, Sar, just do it. Fucking shoot him or he's going to kill you! He's almost to you! I raised the gun in both hands.

"No," I said weakly, and fired, blowing a spray of blood out of his back after the hollow point punched out his left shoulder blade. He didn't make a sound, just gave me a shocked look as he went to his knees. He looked at the hole in his shirt, then crumpled, his knife clattering to the linoleum.

I thought about shooting him again. But he wasn't getting up again, not with that mess of meat the bullet had made of his back. I'd killed a man in my house. It was all I could do not to cry. I held the gun with both hands, the acrid smell of burnt gunpowder making my eyes water.

My ears were ringing, yet I heard another shot faintly from outside, then another. It brought me back to the present with a jolt. I had to get up and help Danial. He was still fighting, so some of the enemy must be alive yet.

I didn't move. I was afraid to go back out there. I wanted to stay here, where it was safe. For all my posturing, I'd never shot at anyone, much less killed them. And no one had ever shot at me before.

My conscience would have none of my cowardice. It told me to get the hell up and help Danial. Except I'd charged into this room, and that hadn't worked out so well. What if I went out the front door and got shot? Danial had told me to get to the house. I'd trust him, stay here, and wait for him.

I stayed there for I don't know how long. In retrospect, it was probably only a few minutes, but it felt like hours. The corpse didn't move, and from where I sat, a half-open eye glazed over. I smelled both blood and urine, and bit my lip to take my mind off my nausea. I didn't want to throw up. But I could cry, and I did, bawling at the unfairness of the world. It seemed like fate couldn't wait for me to hope again before it smashed that hope to pieces. I knew Danial would bring trouble, but why tonight? Couldn't I catch a break?

I heard voices, but they weren't any I recognized. I stayed quiet. Then I heard Danial calling me.

"I'm here," I whispered. I took a deep breath, got to my feet, and went to the door's window to look.

There was a veritable army walking toward the house. Danial was there, surrounded by at least ten people carrying weapons, mostly men. Behind them, animal shapes darted in the distant light of the barn, then disappeared into the dark. What had those shapes been? Some other kind of guardians?

"Sar!" Danial called. "Yell if you can hear me! It's safe to come out!"

71

I let out a gasp of relief, unlocked the door, and stepped out. Everyone, Danial included, immediately dropped and took aim.

"It's me!" I screamed. "Don't shoot!"

Danial raced toward me, vaulted the stairs, and hugged me. I sagged against him. "You're not hurt?"

"No."

He turned to his people. "Get inside and check the house."

"My dogs are in the basement. Don't hurt them," I stammered. "And I have three cats—"

An Asian woman with uneven black hair nodded to me. "I'll see to it," she said, her words clipped.

Danial held me as she and the group went inside. He murmured softly to me that I was safe. For a while, I didn't think about anything but being protected and that it was over. By the time his people assembled on the deck a few minutes later, I was able to deal with the world again.

"House is clear," the woman said. "One dead. Lander's taking care of him."

Danial moved back from me. "Go to your bedroom. I'll join you in a minute."

I nodded and went inside. To my relief, the body was gone, though the blood was evident. I saw a man, likely Lander, heading toward it with cleaning supplies. I hurried into my bedroom and shut the door.

Even my room smelled of gunpowder, and I opened the bathroom window. As I did, I caught sight of myself in the mirror and saw specks of blood on my face. I wiped them off.

Screw it; I was taking a bath. It would help me relax.

Through the open window, I could hear Danial's angry voice, cold as ice, demanding to know what had happened. I turned on the water, then turned it back off when I couldn't hear him anymore.

"Suri, call Theo for me. Demetri, set up a perimeter around the house. Ivan, go up in the barn and watch with the starlight scope. I don't want to be disturbed again tonight."

"Theo for you, sir."

"Give him what we learned. Janice, you monitor the police channels. If you hear anything, notify Demetri. Lander, you're in charge of the bodies. There are twelve more near the forest."

"Okay," I heard a voice in the woodstove room say. "Inside's almost done."

Danial was the leader I'd taken him for. He'd covered all the bases, making sure that I was safe and we wouldn't be spending a good portion of the night in a police station. Maybe it was illegal, but I told myself Danial didn't have a choice, being what he was.

I heard his voice again, this time sounding weary. "Theo, it's me...Yes, yes, you were right; I was wrong. We should have taken a stronger approach. What happened tonight was my fault. It was Max. We managed to capture one of his men. He gave us everything, the plan, how they found out where I was, and where Max and his family are hiding." A pause. "Yes. Do whatever you think is fitting. No, she wasn't hurt, but she had to kill someone to stay that way. There were about fifteen of them, not a lot for what Max has at his disposal. But we're set for tonight. And Theo, make sure that when you settle this, you add in the interest due to him and his kin. I want them dead before dawn."

I abruptly closed the window, chilled by his words. This was the man I was falling for? He'd just told his hit man to take care of a problem by killing an entire family. I shuddered as the hot water filled the tub. I stripped off my clothes and got in, hugging my legs against me.

Danial was as ruthless as Theo, maybe even more so. Could I live with that? Could I trust him enough to be intimate with him, now that I was learning more about what he was capable of? His business was more than I'd thought, and there was an ugly side to it. Thinking back to the e-mail he'd shown me, it made sense he'd have help, especially to watch over him in the daytime.

I took a hard look at the killings. The ones here had been in self-defense and didn't bother me, at least now that the bodies weren't in sight. Sending Theo after the man who'd caused the problem didn't bother me either. Killing Max's kin was the only thing that did, even if it was probably prudent to do. I'd heard stories where a child or woman had been spared because it was the moral thing to do. They always came back later for revenge. I didn't want this to happen again because someone wasn't ruthless enough tonight. Max, a man I'd never met, who knew nothing about me or my life, had ordered me to be tortured and killed just because I knew Danial. I wouldn't sit here and cry for him or his family.

That realization prompted another concern; would Danial ever hurt me? He'd been a little forceful when we kissed but he hadn't done anything I didn't like. I'd had a great time on our date, as well as tonight, up until almost getting killed. No, I didn't think he would. If I saw the signs, I'd break things off.

The tub was full and I felt much better. I relaxed back in the water. After another ten minutes, I began to wonder if Danial would make an appearance. As if on cue, the bedroom door opened. He came in, but not into the bathroom.

"Are you sure you're unharmed?" he said with concern.

"I'm doing okay." My voice wavered. "I'm not fine, but I'm dealing with what happened. Are my dogs okay?"

"Yes, they're still in the basement. My people left them there. The house is being watched, so you're safe."

"Thanks," I said uneasily.

"Would you prefer that I left?" he asked carefully. "I don't have to stay tonight, if you—"

"I want you to," I said, blushing. "Come in here with me."

He crossed to me and crouched beside the tub, wrapping me in his arms. I hugged him hard, then moved back, apologizing for getting him wet.

He didn't respond. He took all of me in with a faint smile. His eyes were a little wistful and very affectionate. I watched as his desire filled those dark eyes, turning them darker. He ran his hand down my arm, into the water. I was as tense as a coiled spring, motionless. His hand crossed my stomach, one finger tracing my skin. Our eyes locked. He ran his palm under my breast, around and over the top, to slide up to my neck. His eyes were almost black, and I suddenly wanted him with a longing that made me tremble.

I'd almost been killed. I was through being lady-like, through with waiting. But I still wanted to be somewhere more comfortable than the tile floor.

"Can we go downstairs now?" My words were rife with heat.

He gave me a slow smile, the same heat in his eyes. "Sure. Let me call Theo and tell him I'm staying." He got to his feet. "You go

74

downstairs. I'm sure the dogs are eager to see you."

I grabbed a towel and stood up, wrapping it around me as I went down to the cellar. Ghost and Darkness were fine. Someone had even given them a Cheweez treat and brought their beds down. I gave them each a hug and told them they'd been brave. I left them snoozing, went into what was Danial's room, and stopped. It had changed since I'd last been down here. He'd moved his equipment to a desk in the corner, creating a home office. The biggest change, though, was the bed. It had been a spare bed before, nothing elaborate. The sheets and comforter hadn't even matched. Someone had put on a new box spring and mattress. The sheets, pillows, and comforter were forest green. I thought initially that they were satin, but touching one to push it back, I realized they were cotton. The sheen came from a high thread count.

I admired the room as I dried off. It looked a lot nicer than I'd been able to manage with my limited means. I sprawled naked on the bed and waited for Danial.

The look on his face when he walked in and saw me waiting for him was priceless. He couldn't get to me fast enough.

He pressed the full length of himself against me, kissing me deeply. His tongue darted in, and I licked him in return. He tried to take off his shirt without disentangling himself from me, but it didn't work. He reared back on his knees and stripped it off in one fluid motion. He was breathtaking. A pearl-like luster against his now flushed skin outlined his muscles. He touched me everywhere, exploring my body, as I explored his. He felt so good, just like the dream. This made me remember something we'd both neglected to discuss before we'd started. I pushed him back from me, panting.

"What about safe sex?" I asked, breathing hard. "I don't want to—"

He put a finger to my lips. "I can't make a child within you. My body can only regenerate itself. It gave up the power to make life long ago, becoming sterile the moment I became vampire. So don't worry, okay? My immune system destroys anything that tries to make a home in me. You're safe."

This was hardly the moment, but I wondered aloud "Then why are you still able to...um...?"

"Have sex?" he laughed. "Magic, I guess." He nuzzled me.

"Sorry," I said in false apology. "I probably jinxed it." I smirked at him.

He gave me a libidinous smile. "Think so?"

He rolled off the bed and stripped off his jeans. I had three thoughts: Oh. My. God. He was perfection, from his muscular chest, down to his tight abs, to his well-formed masculinity. Clearly, everything was working as it should.

Danial dove back on the bed. I bounced when he hit, but his arms were already around me, pulling me to him. Then we were making love, and it was better than the dream. For each thrust, I was ready for him, meeting his body with mine. He felt so good inside me. Too quickly, I felt my climax building, and a moment later, we came together, clutching each other. The aftershocks lasted for the both of us as we writhed together on the bed, moaning our pleasure. Finally, he rolled off me, and we lay on our sides facing each other.

"That was wonderful," I said, deeply gratified.

He kissed me softly. "And for me," he said, satisfaction in his tone.

He gave me a lover's smile; one that said, *I've tasted your secrets, all of them, and there is no going back.* I gave him the same smile and stroked his chest. He turned me over to spoon against me. I felt the strength of his body holding mine and was completely content. I was half-asleep when he said, "I bet I know what you're thinking."

I wasn't thinking of anything except how good I felt, despite the FUBAR beginning to the night. But I did wonder what he thought I was thinking. "Tell me."

"You're wondering why I didn't bite you."

Now that he mentioned it, I was surprised he hadn't. "So why didn't you?"

He rolled me onto my back and raised himself up on one arm, so he was looking down at me. "If you give me your permission, I'd like to try it." He bared his fangs at me in a teasing way, and I laughed. "Until I know you've recovered from what I took from you before, I don't want to risk taking any more. And I won't do it then unless you want me to," he said tenderly.

He dipped his head, ran a fang down my breast, and suckled me, careful not to cut me. I reached down to feel him lengthening in my hand.

This time was slower. I got to examine every inch of him, and he did the same to me. I rode him as he rocked my hips astride his, caressing my breasts. Later, he entered me as he sat, forcing my hips down on his lap as he kissed my neck. I leaned back against him, reaching my arms up to twine them around his neck. I kissed him as he thrust into me. His hand deftly stroked me as I let out soft eager cries.

I couldn't get enough of him, not his body or his kisses. He was everything I'd ever wanted. Much as I didn't want it to stop, as the night wore on, my body told me it was time to. After the sixth time, I said, "I'm loving this, but I'm exhausted."

We kissed again, and he stroked my face. "Good, I'm getting tired, too."

We both laughed and snuggled closer. I fell asleep with his arms around me, my head on his chest.

* * * *

I woke in blackness. What time was it? I was missing my watch, but it had to be morning by now. I could feel Danial next to me, unmoving. I touched him, and he was cool, not cold. I put my hand over his chest, where his heart would be. I didn't feel anything for a moment. Then I did feel a slow beat. Ten seconds later, I felt it again. I'd have to check it when he was awake, to see if it sped up any. I kissed him lightly, but he didn't wake.

I grabbed his shirt, remembering I didn't have any of my own clothes down here. It covered me to my mid-thigh and would have to do. I had to go check on the dogs.

I opened the adjoining door and found them still in their beds. When they saw me, they bounded to their feet and whined. I helped them navigate the stairs with a lot of coaxing, pushing, and pulling. Once upstairs, I let them out. No one was around, at least not in the house. Someone had made a fire but it was going to go out soon, so I put a few more logs on it. I let the dogs in, fed them, and called the cats, most of which had spent the night outside. As I fed them, I noticed it was about ten a.m.

I sat down and turned on the TV. There was nothing about any Max on CNN. I checked the weather channel next, where reality sheared my fantasy morning. It said that a large thunderstorm was headed our way, coming up from the southwest—the remnants of a hurricane that had hit the Texas coast a few days ago. It would be there by that night. I had to get out there and mow the lawn.

I showered, put on my watch, and dressed in sweats. Cavity joined me on my way to the barn, heading upstairs to the loft when I started the mower. I looked for signs of last night's trouble but didn't see anything out of place, not even a brass casing.

As I mowed, I thought about the last things needing to be done before the first snow and made a mental list. I thought about Danial and how good sex had been. His coolness hadn't bothered me. If I'd not known he was a vampire, I'd have thought he was human.

Two hours passed before I was done. I cleaned the mower, put it away, and headed inside for lunch. I made myself a sandwich, treating myself to a soda. I decided to watch a movie, but the cats decided they'd been ignored for far too long and applied themselves to my lap. I only saw the beginning of the show before I fell asleep.

I woke up as it was ending and decided to take the dogs for a walk in case the storm arrived early. This time, though, I went armed. I checked the chamber and replaced the bullet I'd used last night. The gun didn't need cleaning, as I'd only fired it once. I buckled on my holster and went outside. Ghost and Darkness bounded all over in their exuberance.

We started toward the barn. It was a beautiful sunny day, so beautiful that I wondered if a storm was really coming. As we came up to the building, I saw a figure on the road. The dogs didn't bark. It was Theo.

"Good Morning," I said, flashing him a smile.

He looked down his nose at me. "Afternoon, you mean. Where do you think you're going?"

"For a walk," I said, petting the dogs. They again acted nervous around him. "Want to come?"

"You know you'd be safer if you stay around the house."

"I'd be safe enough if you came with me. Or don't you do walks?"

He rolled his eyes.

"C'mon," I coaxed. "There's no lifting involved."

His mock sigh turned into a laugh. He used his cell to tell someone that he was "accompanying me on a dog walk" and for them to take a break.

We began to walk. Theo let the silence last for only a few minutes. "So Sarelle, how'd *it* go?" His voice was filled with innuendo and lust.

"*It* went just fine. Thanks for asking," I said smoothly, not looking at him.

He flashed me a grin that I saw out of the corner of my eye. "No problem."

Bringing the topic back to safer ground, I asked, "Have you guys been out here all day watching me mow the lawn?"

He turned serious. "Yes. After last night's mess, I didn't want a repeat incident today."

"Weren't you ordered to take care of Max last night? You're here, so you must have. I'd think we'd be completely safe now."

Theo stopped walking, irritated. "Do you always listen in on conversations that aren't for you to hear?"

"Yes, when it's important, and they concern me. Look, I'm glad you're protecting us. I'm glad you're taking...um...precautions...so we aren't attacked again. But I need to know if it's always going to be this bad."

To his credit, there was no denial of any problems, no stupid comebacks such as "What do you mean?" or "Define bad." He just looked at me, sighed, and started to walk again. I followed.

"It's been worse than usual lately. We had the problem with Max and his vendetta even before Danial met you. There also a threatening email from a woman who swore she'd see Danial dead, but so far, she's done nothing. She's probably harmless. We're still keeping an eye on her, but for now, the worst is the vampire Danial claims is after him."

"Claims?"

"No one's seen him, only Danial. The only thing proving that there's someone after him is what brought him to your door."

"He said there was vampire poison on the arrow that struck him."

"Yes, there was. He sent samples to verify the type. It slows the body's ability to regenerate itself, until it stops it altogether."

Danial had mentioned that. "What can you do about this vampire?"

"Not much," he said grudgingly, obviously hating his helplessness. "We have to wait until he shows himself again. All the other vampires in the area say they're innocent. They usually get along fairly well with Danial."

My bullshit detector went off at that. At least one vampire around the area was Danial's enemy. But the confusion in Theo's voice was real enough. "So they're lying?"

He shifted his eyes to me. "I believe them. This vampire is a rogue, and that means he's a wild card." He turned to me and suddenly took me by the shoulders. He'd never touched me until now, and it startled me. His eyes bored into mine. "Listen when I tell you this. Danial believes all vampires will respect you as his...woman; that no one will bother you because they'll see the symbol and respect it. But this vampire wants to kill him, not get his attention. Get it?"

I got it all right, loud and clear.

"When Danial and I leave, I'm going to add extra guards here, so someone is always watching the house. And I'm going to leave this with you." He reached behind his back and withdrew a gun, which he handed to me. "You have revolvers, so you should be able to handle this one."

I examined the wicked semiautomatic. I hefted it and admired the sleek lines. It was a nice piece of work.

"Are you going to give me a holster, too?"

"Yes, but not now. This back holster was custom made for me. I'm having a smaller one rigged for you. It'll be ready by the time Danial and I leave."

"Thanks, but what good are bullets against vampires? At least two bullets hit Danial last night, and he was fine afterwards."

"Yeah, I'll bet he was," he laughed and smirked at me.

Always with the sex. Did he only think about sex and weapons? "He was more than fine last night. Now tell me why you think this gun will be of any use against a vampire when they're practically immune to bullets?"

"Danial wasn't hit with bullets like these. Max might have been out to kill him, but Danial's vampirism is a closely guarded secret. Max has no idea what he is and sent his men with regular bullets. That is the *only* reason the attempt failed."

I shivered. "I know they were planning to kill me, too—"

"They weren't expecting you to have a gun, much less to use it. They expected you to be a playmate." He grinned at me. "Maybe it was your long blond hair—"

"Tell me about the gun already, before I shoot you with it."

"The bullets in it are for vampires."

"That can't be. I thought only stakes could kill vampires."

"Sar, surely in a world that has vampires and...other creatures—"

I stopped and turned to him, enjoying his uneasiness.

"—you can allow for a gun that's a little out of the ordinary."

"Just tell me, Theo. Drop the weirdness and the cute words."

I thought that might piss him off, but he just nodded. "Okay, Sar. The bullets explode. Danial's heart does beat, despite all the folklore that says it shouldn't. Never could understand that idiocy, why a stake in the heart could matter if the heart didn't beat in the first place." He grimaced. "Anyway, a vampire's heart is a lot tougher than a human heart, and it heals a lot faster. A lot more force is required to rend it. We haven't tested it on any vampire yet, but in theory, it should work. The bullets are nonstandard; they have to be made to specs for the gun because they carry more than gunpowder. They have a pinhead's worth of C4 and a Nano computer chip to detonate it on impact."

C4? Nano computer chips? Fuck me, this was getting complex.

"Be sure you fire this gun only at a vampire," he continued. "I don't know what it would do to a human or animal, but it wouldn't be pretty."

That was grim. Hollow-point bullets made a mess of their targets as it was. Explosive bullets were sure to make more of one.

Theo turned and began to walk. "Come on, we should head back. I can smell rain coming."

I called the dogs, and we walked back in silence. I wanted to ask how he'd smelled rain when I hadn't, but I kept that question to myself.

Chapter Eight

Six twenty-one p.m. Three minutes since the last time I'd checked. I shook my head slightly, amused by my nervousness, and took another sip of wine. Near the woods, a flock of turkeys foraged the cut cornfield for missed ears. I couldn't see them very well in the fading light but I heard them calling to one another. A slight breeze blew. I felt a little self-conscious; knowing at least one pair of eyes watched me.

This would likely be the last time I used the deck this year. Snow was forecast for the next weekend, Halloween night to be exact. That was okay; I'd gotten everything prepped for winter.

My thoughts abruptly turned to the gun, holster, and box of exploding bullets stashed in my dresser drawer. Theo and I hadn't talked for the rest of our walk. When we'd gotten back, he'd excused himself to check with the other guards. The holster and bullets had been delivered an hour before by courier. I'd made sure the gun was loaded and ready to go, wanting to be prepared if I had to use it. The holster was a little big for me but I'd tightened it down enough to work. Test firing the gun in the quarry had been enough to get an idea of the damage it would do; it had left a ragged apple-sized hole in the hardwood stump I'd used it on. And the recoil wasn't too bad.

I checked my watch again to see it was six twenty-five. Hell, I was really out on the deck because I was nervous about seeing Danial. I knew neither of us regretted taking our relationship to the next level, but men sometimes acted differently after sex. He would wake soon, if he hadn't already. Would he be distant or loving?

I heard someone open the door behind me. It was Danial. He gave me an affectionate look and walked over to stand next to me. We both leaned against the railing, looking out into the black night. He slipped an arm around me.

"Good evening, Sarelle," he said in his best Dracula voice.

I cracked up, and the tension broke just like that.

"How did you sleep?" I asked.

"Deeply. You tired me right out. Did you get enough sleep?"

"I felt okay when I was mowing earlier." I leaned into him. "I wasn't tired. But I'll need to get some extra sleep tonight."

"Do that. I need to leave soon anyway. I've got some business to take care of tonight."

"When will I see you next?" I tried not to sound too eager.

"I'm really busy this week. I'll try to come back again this weekend. If I don't..."

If he didn't, I was cutting him off, but he could find that out for himself.

"Is something wrong?" I asked bluntly, turning to face him while trying to distance myself.

"Nothing's wrong," he replied, keeping a firm hold of me. "I just have a lot going on this week and I need to be home to take conference calls. This weekend will be busy, too. What I was trying to ask was if you could possibly take off the following week from work? I'd like you to stay at my house that week to see if it pleases you."

I tried not to seem so astonished. I kept my face averted as I formulated a polite reply. I could be mistaken, but his offer sounded like he wanted me to move in with him. I didn't want to say the wrong thing. A lot hinged on my response.

I hadn't thought about being with him beyond when we both had time, like weekends and some weeknights when he was available. I'd assumed we'd date and get to know each other. We had chemistry, and I hadn't wanted to wait for intimacy, but I wasn't ready to live with him. Maybe I was making more out of his offer than he'd meant me to. We'd just be more secure at his house than mine.

He waited for my answer. I mustered my words carefully. "I can check, but I doubt it. I only work part time, on Mondays and Fridays. I'd probably be able to take just one day off, but that would be close to a week, if I left on a Monday night for your place." I spoke as normal as I could make it, but I could hear the hesitancy in my voice. He probably could, too. "I'd have to bring my pets or board them. A shorter visit for a day or so would be better." Plus, I needed my whole paycheck. Telling him I didn't get paid for time off sounded too much like asking for money, so I left that off.

He was surprised and not happy. "One of my people could watch the house and your animals. I don't see why a day should matter."

"What I do at my job may not seem like much compared to what you do, but I take it seriously. It matters to me."

"I see." Danial's expression said otherwise; he didn't understand at all.

"Let me ask, okay? I'll do my best to get the time off. Deal?"

"You're right. Speak to your boss first."

"Are you leaving tonight?" I asked, implying that I wanted him to stay.

"I knew it. You want me just for my body," he teased.

"That's right. And what a lovely body it is." I ran my hand up his chest, to his neck, and brought his lips to mine. We shared a soft, delicate kiss while desire simmered beneath the surface. The kiss became deeper, and I pulled him closer, trying to convince him to stay.

Danial reluctantly pulled away. "I'm sorry. I have to go. But I'm looking forward to our next night together, this one without interruptions. Please, find out if you can take the time off."

He reached into his pocket and handed me a cell phone. "Take this. Use it to call me whenever you want. My number is programmed into the speed dial, under number one." He showed me how to access the speed dial and place a call. It was like my own cell phone, though state of the art. I could probably access the Internet and take pictures, if I studied it enough.

"Does this reach you at your office or home or—?"

"It's my cell. I usually carry it with me. I have a home phone, but I'm hardly ever there." He hugged me. "Call me every night. I want to know you're safe and more about how you occupy your time when I'm not here."

That came out a bit stilted, but I understood what he meant. He wanted to know more about who I was and what I liked to do. Theo's comment that I couldn't share my days with Danial no matter where he was hit home. But we'd work through it.

He kissed me. "Theo told me he gave you the gun. Don't hesitate to use it. They'll be at least four guards at any given time watching, but they won't bother you unless there's a problem. Aran's in charge. He's programmed into speed dial under number three."

"Who is number two?"

"That's Theo's direct line. He's never without his phone, so he'll always answer, day or night. Call him if for any reason you can't contact Aran."

He motioned to a figure out on the lawn. Aran was Theo's height and build, with long reddish brown hair gathered in a tight ponytail. Dressed in camouflage from head to foot, he carried a gun on one hip and a compound bow on his back, along with a quiver of arrows. Unsmiling, he waved to me. I waved back. He must not have Theo's friendly disposition.

"Be safe." Danial kissed me, then drew back. "You'll call me?"

"Promise. Take care."

He smiled, gave me a wink, and then was gone.

* * * *

I asked about taking the following Monday and Friday off. My boss said he could let me be gone for a day but with me working part-time, he really needed me to keep up with workload. I told him I understood and that next Monday would suffice.

I stayed late to get as much done as possible. It was the busy season, with the end of the year wrapping up, and there were a lot of year-end orders to fill. I left that night happy, knowing that I'd get to spend most of the next week with Danial.

The week passed slowly. Every night after dinner, I called Danial and told him about my day. I thought the tales of my simple life would bore him, but he never let on if they did. I learned more about him as he told me of his days. The best news arrived Thursday when he told me that Max was dead, along with anyone from his family who might seek revenge. I breathed a sigh of relief even though I felt guilty about it, and then put it out of my mind.

"Do you think you'll be here tomorrow?"

"It'll be Saturday night before we can see each other. Theo and I need to check into a possible sighting of the vampire who tried to kill me. It was in White Plains. It'll take about five hours to get there."

"Somebody saw him?"

"We got a call from an ally there. He said there'd been a drowning that looked suspicious to him. When he investigated, the body had been exsanguinated."

"Drained."

"Yes. Ryan claims he didn't do it, so it had to have been another vampire. But there are no other vampires who live there."

"I understand. Be careful. Call me if you find out anything."

"I will. You be careful, too."

We said our good-byes and hung up. I called Aran to let him know this, and he said he already knew. As I hung up, it occurred to me that I had Friday night free. I decided to give Kat a call to see if she was free for a movie.

As I waited for her to answer, I dreamed up my own fantasy. In it, she was available and we got together for a movie. We were attacked leaving the theater, and Danial and his men came in like gangbusters to save us. I was so grateful that I decide to move in with Danial and we lived happy ever after.

My reality fell short of my fantasy. Katrina was busy, though we made plans to get together the following weekend.

I decided to stay in and rent a pay-per-view movie. Not a big night next to the ones I'd had lately, but I did need to rest up if I was going to keep up with Danial Saturday night. I envisioned a repeat of the latter half of last Saturday night and things began to stir in the lower part of my body. I reminded myself that I had work tomorrow and another whole twenty-four hours after that.

Besides, he might not want to have sex Saturday night.

I laughed out loud. Yeah right, Danial was a man, so it was safe to say he'd want to have sex. I anticipated it myself, anticipating spending the whole night together. Could my body hold up under that kind of strain? I stretched deliciously and decided to go to bed to get extra sleep.

Friday went like clockwork; I did the day's work and most of what needed to be done Monday. There would still be catch-up work when I got back next Friday, but I didn't mind. A whole week with Danial was worth it.

I drove home, got the mail, and went inside. My dogs weren't waiting for me at the door, as they should have been. Something was terribly wrong.

I dropped my coat and purse, and began searching the house. I found them a few minutes later, cowering by the couch.

"What is it?"

The dogs were scared by thunder or other loud noises, but I'd never seen them like this before. I tried to coax them up, but they were afraid to go outside. I had to get their leashes to drag them out. They did their business as quickly as possible and ran back inside, banging into the door in their scrambling. I ran in after them, following them into my bedroom.

Something was up. Now that I had people just a phone call away, I didn't have to brave this alone. I called Aran, but as the rings continued, I knew the men Danial had set up to guard me had somehow been neutralized. I hung up and dialed Theo.

"Theo!"

"Sar?" His voice was alarmed and loud.

The phone was knocked from my hand as I was shoved backward. I hit the couch and slumped to the floor, the wind knocked out of me. A foot stepped down deliberately on the phone, crushing it to pieces.

A deep voice filled with sarcasm said, "You must be Sarelle."

I looked up from the foot. It belonged to a man in his early twenties. He was about my height, with straight dark hair pulled back in a ponytail so short it was a bob. His eyes were a ruddy color and his complexion was pale, lacking the luster of Danial's skin. He was dressed in a plaid shirt and jeans, and there was a gun at his waist, a semiautomatic. The rage and feeling of danger emanating off him was far scarier than the weapon he carried. Now I knew why my dogs were scared. I cowered myself. I'd never felt so vulnerable before, not even when Max's agent was about to cut me. Something came out of this man that triggered my fear, intensifying it.

I reached inside myself and found some courage. "What do you want?"

I meant it to come out bold, but it was a whisper. The man regarded me but didn't speak. He looked furious.

"Who are you?" I demanded, my voice rising in volume. "I want to know your name so I can tell Danial whose ass to kill."

"Brave words," he said as he glided to me, "for the position you find yourself in." He knelt next to me. "Do you know the manner of evil whose bed you share?"

He phrased the question oddly, and I wondered if it was for effect. They didn't sound natural, more like he read them from a script. What part would I have to play in order to live through this?

"Answer me, girl," he ordered angrily.

I looked him in the eye. "I know the evil I see right in front of me."

Those reddish brown eyes bored into me. I took courage from his lack of a reply and demanded an answer of my own. "What did you do to the guards? Where—?"

"Your werefoxes? I made them change shape against their will and locked them in that form. I imagine it will take them a while to get some distance from me before they can break the spell."

Werefoxes? A lot suddenly became clear: Theo's sunglasses at night, the shapes I had seen near the barn the night Max had attacked. To think they couldn't return to human form...The county allowed shooting foxes for fur and sport. I had a fondness for all animals, especially foxes.

I looked at him with disgust. "Why are you doing this?"

"I owe Danial." His words were stone cold and grated out of him harsh with hatred. "And maybe some of his people as well."

Shit, this was the vampire who'd been stalking Danial. Max was dead, and the other threat Danial had was a woman.

The man leaned toward me, and I pulled back. My shoulders pressed against the couch and I couldn't go any farther. I felt a wave of fear, and lost it a little. "I don't understand any of this."

His hand darted out, and I recoiled, scared he was going to hurt me. Instead, he reached up and retrieved a box of tissues. When he handed it to me, I took one and wiped my eyes.

"My name is Terian. All you need to know about me is that I'm here for Danial. I'll kill you if you get in the way." His deep voice was still angry but it had lost some of its coldness. "If you cooperate, you'll live."

"Okay," I said, watching him carefully. What choice did I have?

He stood and held out his hand. I didn't want to take it but I was afraid to refuse. When I touched him, I let out a gasp and snatched my hand back. His skin was hot as newly sawed metal. I jumped back from him and nearly fell over the couch. Terian gave me a scary smile, showing fangs different from Danial's. He covered them up before I had a chance to see more.

"My skin tells you I'm not a vampire, although Danial and Theo believe me to be. I was careful to hide that from them."

"What are you?" I asked. "You said you did a spell? Are you a warlock or something?" It was ridiculous, but I was in a whole new world now. My survival might depend getting up to speed as fast as I could.

"I'm dhamphir; half human and half vampire." He sighed. "All cursed."

Okay, that was it. I'd been brave enough. Like everyone with limitations, I'd reached mine. I bolted, and though Terian reached out to grab me, he missed. I ran toward my bedroom.

He came after me. "Stop or I'll stop you."

He hadn't yelled it, but I heard a good deal of eagerness in his voice. I froze, and he walked up to me, gliding. He stopped a foot away from me. I could feel heat come off him. I thought for a second about trying for the gun but decided to wait. I'd only get one chance. Better to relax him first, if that was possible.

I turned and faced him. "What do you want me to do?" I asked, trying to sound utterly defeated. "I'll cooperate if you don't hurt me or my pets."

Terian gave me a nod, satisfied. "You are not to contact Danial. I know Theo, and by now, he's got an armada on the way. Danial will come. But they won't be able to make it here until tomorrow night. Neither of them will allow the rescue without supervising it themselves. We're going to be ready for them when they get here."

"We? You and who else?"

He came towards me, and I backed up, until I was up against the wall. He put his arms on either side of me, palms flat against the wall, and leaned close. He pushed with his arms, and I felt the wall start to crumble as his hands passed through it. I screamed and he laughed. Then he pulled one hand out and reached for the fox head I wore. His hand was covered in white dust. His eyes were inches from mine. They were red, really red, like blood, not brown at all. I swallowed hard.

"Do you know what this is? What it means?" he asked scathingly.

"It's custom-made jewelry that serves as protection. It marks me as Danial's...woman."

He laughed. I wanted to curse at him but I was too afraid.

"Really? Try to take it off," he said casually, showing his pointed teeth.

God, he had multiple rows of them, like a shark. I clenched my jaw and forced myself to be calm. "Why?"

"Try to take it off," he repeated, his eyes gleaming, his smile full of malice.

I tried to remember what sort of clasp the choker had. Hook and eye? Maybe a button or tab release? I fumbled with the back but couldn't find a clasp of any kind. How could that be? Danial had put it on easily.

"I don't want to take it off," I said. "You might be trying to get me to do that so you can plead ignorance to Danial. That you didn't know I was his."

"That's all part of its charm."

"What do you mean?"

"I mean," he said with relish, "that you can't remove it. There's a spell on it that discourages its removal so you never want to take it off."

I panicked. This was all too much. I tried to pry it off, but it was so tight around my neck I couldn't get my hands under it. I ran into the bathroom and tried to look at the back, but I couldn't see it. I tried to tear it off with both hands but the links held. Burning hands held mine, pulling them away from my neck.

"Leave it. All you'll do is tear your skin."

I looked at him in the mirror. "Can you remove it?" I asked haltingly.

"Maybe, but most likely not. Only your master can remove your collar—"

"Collar?" I shrieked, half horrified and half enraged. "Master?"

"Yes, what you're wearing is coined a collar by most vampires, though I've never seen one of gold before, or with jewels in it. Most are made of silver. All are the same design. They bear the personal symbol of the vampire the human belongs to, so any other vampire knows that human is off limits."

Danial had told me it was for protection. He'd neglected to say I could never take it off or that I'd wear it until *he* chose to remove it...I felt sick.

"Why are you saying all this to me?" I cried.

"Because you need to hear it," he said. "And I smell another spell at work here." He made a move toward the bedroom.

I blocked him. I couldn't let him find the gun. "Please don't go in there. My dogs are terrified. Let me keep them confined in there. I promise they won't bother you—"

"Danial gave you something, didn't he?" he demanded.

"The necklace—"

"Besides the necklace!" he spat. "Something you might be tempted to wear close to your skin?"

I went into the bedroom and brought him the shirt Danial had given me, handing it to him.

"Ahh," he said in a voice low and broiling with dark delight. "You smell that scent?"

"It's nutmeg and cedar, along with a few others—"

"Indeed, there are a few 'other' ingredients involved in making something like this."

He came toward me. I backed up until I sat in the chair in front of the wood stove. He stood in front of me, the shirt in his hands, glaring down at me. "This is dosed with what I call 'L.F.' It's a sexy smell to be sure, at least to humans. And that, my dear, is who it is made for."

He went to his haunches in front of me, still holding the shirt, clearly enjoying this.

"Sarelle, common vampire practice for making the L.F. involves mixing up a rather complex spell. The nutmeg and cedar might have been the essential oils that were used in this, but those are interchangeable. Any oils could have done. What I smelled wasn't them, but the most important ingredient in this is blood. There has to be several drops of the vampire's blood included in the mixture. The vampire whose blood goes into the spell is the only one who can feed through that spell." He paused. "Do you know why I call it L.F.?"

I was hurt and nauseous, but also angry. I didn't answer.

"It's for Life Force, Sarelle; your life force. Danial has been feeding off you, draining your life energy to sustain him."

I wanted him to shut up, shut his mouth, this was hurting too much to hear. I closed my eyes, but he kept talking.

"With the Life Force spell, a vampire can visit you in your dreams. As you act out fantasies, they feed off your life energy. The victim doesn't notice it like having their blood taken because a little goes a long way for a vampire. Just a taste can sustain a vampire for a week. And sometimes, just for kicks, the vampire decides to mingle his blood with a few other vampires. Then they can feed from the same victim. I saw one girl go from the beauty and fullness of youth to a walking ghost in days." He smiled. "Have any dreams of Danial lately?"

I swung at him, but he caught my hand. His grip was strong as he pushed me back in the chair and let me go. I curled up in the chair, watching through tears as he took the shirt and tossed it into the wood stove. He tossed a match in and the shirt ignited. Some of the smoke vented up the chimney, but I could smell a bitter, oily odor. I watched it burn to nothing with a hollow feeling in my chest.

"Go in with your pets. And don't try to leave."

I retreated to my bedroom, where I curled up in bed and cried some more. Even if some of what Terian said was bullshit, he was telling the truth about the choker not being removable. Given that, why wouldn't the rest be true? How could Danial do this to me?

I wallowed in my misery, crying it all out. A little while later, I dried my tears and thought about what to do. I was too angry to think clearly, so I envisioned wrecking Danial's truck with my sledgehammer; Headlight glass flying everywhere, flattening the tires, ripping up the interior. Then I told myself to let that go. Danial was rich; he could buy a new truck. But I felt more rational, having vented a little.

That rationality brought out an interesting point. I only had Terian's word that most of the terrible things Danial had done were true. He might be lying to get me to turn against Danial, hoping I'd help him get revenge.

I wasn't giving Danial a pass. If he and I lived through this, he had some things to answer for, like the choker. I remembered how thrilled I'd been to put it on. Another tear slid down my cheek. I wiped it away and got up from the bed.

I had to stop feeling sorry for myself and decide what to do. Crying wasn't going to help anyone. I thought briefly about getting the gun and taking my best shot. I wouldn't have to be too accurate. The bullets would explode, and he was only half a vampire, or so he said. But he knew magic—enough to incapacitate the guards. What if he had a protective spell to deflect a bullet? The stump I'd hit in practice had smoldered. I might catch my house on fire if the bullet missed him and exploded in a wall. And what if the gun misfired or it didn't kill him? If I failed, Terian would have the gun.

In giving me the gun, Danial and Theo had given me the means to destroy them both. I didn't know what Theo was, but he was something other than human. Was he a werefox? Most likely. Was Danial that overconfident of me that he'd give me the power to destroy him? I had saved his life, but he didn't seem the type who'd hand that kind of advantage over to someone he'd just met, not without thinking of the possible consequences. Moreover, Theo didn't seem the type to just hand me a gun and trust that I'd never use it against him.

Nothing seemed to fit. I didn't know who to believe. I was betting that everyone had lied to me at least a little, and that pissed me off more than I was afraid. So I did what any brave girl would do. I squared my shoulders and went out to get more information.

Chapter Nine

I stopped with my hand on the doorknob, second-guessing myself. Was this really a good idea, to just go out there and try to talk sense into a killer? Probably not. I took a few minutes to both rid myself of metal fumes and grease, and formulate a plan.

As I put on some sweat pants and a fleece shirt, I noticed that my face was blotchy from crying. I told myself that was good. I wanted to downplay any sexiness or femininity, because if Terian wasn't thinking about it, I didn't want to give him any ideas.

Ghost and Darkness were still frightened, along with Jess and Cavity, who were hiding under the bed. I petted them one by one, then shut the door after me as I went out to keep them safe. I left the gun where it was. Until I knew more about Terian's weaknesses, I wasn't risking blowing my only ace in the hole.

I found him downstairs trying to access Danial's computer. He wasn't having any luck from his annoyed expression and the way he slammed his fingers on the keyboard. Anger came off him like heat, and I could tell he was at his breaking point by his body language. He lifted the laptop as if to throw it.

"Please don't destroy things in my home," I said quietly.

He actually paused and looked at me, then got up from the desk, leaving the laptop there. "Did you have yourself a good cry?" he asked sarcastically.

Asshole. "Yes, I feel better."

His expression softened a bit. I latched onto that. If I could get him to see me as a person with feelings, it would make it harder for him to want to hurt me. At least, that's what I hoped.

"I told you just hours ago that your lover lied to you and has been

94

draining off your energy. How can you feel better so quickly?"

Steel yourself and say it, Sar. "I don't like what you've told me, but I did need to hear it, especially if it's true."

"You doubt what I told you?" he asked, affronted.

"I don't know you at all and you're accusing someone I'm in a relationship with of awful things. Of course I'm going to be loyal to Danial. What proof do you have of the things you said?"

"He doesn't deserve your loyalty."

"Do you have any proof?" I tried to hold his stare but his eyes were hard to look at. The redness was so unnatural and almost glowing in the gloom of the basement. Terian hadn't turned on the overhead lights. The only light on was the one I'd turned on coming downstairs. Could he see in the dark? Was that from being part vampire? Likely. Danial could. He had seen okay that night we'd been attacked. Theo obviously could, too, wearing sunglasses at night.

"You can't remove your necklace because it's not a necklace at all. You don't think that's proof of his treachery?"

"He told me it was for protection. I admit, I thought I could remove it, but I might have agreed to wear it anyway. I wanted to be safe."

"You will never be safe as long as you stay with him," Terian said darkly.

I'd had enough of his haughty talk and innuendoes. Time to cut to the chase. "Tell me what he did to you."

"You don't want to hear it." His tone was more menacing than ever.

"You're right. I don't. But you need to tell me anyway."

That surprised him. For a moment, he just stood there looking oddly at me. "Do you know Danial's password?" he said finally.

"No."

"And you wouldn't tell me if you did."

"Right. But I don't."

He grumbled and went back to the desk. I decided to give him some time, heading upstairs, into the kitchen.

He got up and followed me. Suspicion clouded his voice. "What are you doing? Don't try to call for help—"

"I'm not; I'm making dinner." I caught his eyes. The redness in them still gave me a chill, but I plowed ahead. "Do you eat? Do you want something?"

His expression was priceless. If I hadn't been terrified, I'd have laughed my ass off.

"I...can eat normal food but I usually don't," he said reluctantly.

Maybe he thought I'd poison him. I might have, if I'd known what to use as poison. I didn't want to know what he ate instead of "normal" food, so I hurried to say my next words. "I'm making pasta with meat sauce. It's right from the jar there, and the pasta is from that box. You can watch if you want, to see I'm not adding anything to it."

"Why is the pasta so dark and has flecks on it?"

He'd said he didn't eat regular food but he knew what pasta looked like? Hmmm. "Because it's whole wheat. I might have some regular around here someplace—"

"No," he said hesitantly. "This is suitable."

After that, the night took on a surreal quality. There I was, making a meal for my captor and myself. The act of cooking comforted me as it usually did, at least until I remembered that I'd let it slip to my mom that Danial and I might stop by this weekend. She'd been irritated that we hadn't gone there last weekend and didn't have a lot of patience. She might even convince my stepfather that it was a good idea to drop by to surprise us.

Shit, I had to call them to circumvent that happening. I didn't want them walking into this. Terian wouldn't let them leave once they'd arrived. Chris and he would come to blows. My stepfather was an intimidating man, but he wouldn't stand a chance against a half-vampire.

"Terian, I have to make a call, please."

"No," he said, immediately distrustful.

"I have to call my parents," I said, trying to placate him. "Otherwise, they might show up. They wanted to meet Danial—"

"Ah, so they know you're seeing a vampire? I can't imagine they approve—"

Wise ass. "Of course they don't know, you dolt." Oops, I hadn't meant that to slip. "Sorry. Look, please let me call. You can motion me to hang up anytime. They might be thinking of stopping over tonight and I want to keep them out of this."

"Go ahead," he said slowly, albeit reluctantly.

I called and reported the days' events to my parents, editing out everything since I'd come home. I told them that Danial would not be coming this week after all because of business. They were disappointed but said they could wait another week if I could. Cute.

By the time I hung up, the pasta was done. I dished it out, and handed both plates to Terian. He took them uncomfortably. We went into the dining room, me carrying glasses of water. He sat opposite me in the only other chair. Closing my eyes, I said grace.

"What are you doing?" he asked curiously, yet poignantly. His voice was strained to breaking, as if he were in pain. The moment I heard him, I believed I had a chance to turn this situation around.

"Saying grace." Praying that I'd get through tonight and wasn't acting stupid trying to earn his trust enough to survive the ordeal.

We ate in silence. My mind worked furiously to think of a way to engage him. I needed to find out more information. It turned out that my silence, while I thought, was the best plan of all.

"I'm sorry for what's happened to you," he said quietly.

"I brought it on myself. Literally. I brought Danial inside, sheltered him, and gave him my blood to heal him."

"That's true," he pointed out. "Why didn't you leave him to die where you found him?"

"Did you track him here?" I said, watching him carefully.

"Yes," he said proudly. "I knew he'd come in this direction but the trail ended a good ways from your door. I put a tracking spell on the arrow, and when he tore it out, he left a little of the spell on him. When it touched his skin, it reacted with the poison, leaving me a trail I could follow. But he wasn't stupid. He knew I was after him and somehow washed it off. There was still some on his shirt, though. It would have led me to him, except for the rain that night. It washed away the trail, and it's taken me this long to find out where he'd gone. After checking out your neighbors, I knew they hadn't been the ones to rescue him. It had to be you."

I'd washed Danial's shirt. I hadn't known it at the time, but I'd concealed him better doing that than hiding his truck.

"Water breaks a lot of simpler spells or weakens them. I'd have gotten him that night if you hadn't helped him. Why did you have to help him?"

He was angry again. I had to diffuse the situation quick. "I don't know. I've thought about that before. Mostly because I didn't know what he was at first. I usually try to help something when I find it injured at my doorstep."

"It's a good trait to have." He sounded earnest and almost comforting. "It just didn't work out this time."

"You know, I don't get you. You threaten to hurt me in one breath and console me in the next. You say you want me to help you get Danial back for something he did to you but won't tell me what. Am I supposed to be afraid of you, or trust you? Are you a friend or an enemy?"

"I'm neither," he snapped. "I'm someone not to trifle with."

What a piece of work. "What did he do to you?"

"Danial killed my half-brother, the only family I had left. Alive, anyway."

"Why?"

"Who knows," he said sullenly, "Most likely, Keriam did something to anger him. Or he got in Danial's way. You've seen how ruthless he is."

Danial might be violent but he didn't kill casually, from what I knew of him. He'd used violence with Max only after we'd been attacked, as a last resort. That wasn't the action of someone who killed people on a whim.

"That's not true. Danial doesn't kill arbitrarily."

"You know this for a fact?"

"Yes, I'd—" Stake my life on it. "—say it's a fact."

"The information I have came from a good source."

Ah, now we were getting somewhere. "Who?"

"Keriam's wife, Alexa."

"Would she have any reason to lie?"

"About her husband's killer? They were in love. He doted on her," Terian said fiercely.

The feeling of danger that had subsided during dinner returned like tendrils of bitter cold moving through the room. I shivered, but I wasn't going to let it stop me. I switched tactics. "What did she say happened?"

He ran his hands over his face and back down the sides, as if to wipe

98

away the despair I heard in his voice. "She said they came home from dinner out one night and Danial was waiting for them outside their door. He said he had to speak to Keriam alone. They talked in the den. She heard raised voices and then Keriam yelling, 'No, I won't let you—!' She heard a crash, and when she went to investigate, Danial was gone and Keriam was dead."

"Did she tell that to the police?"

"She said she did, but there were no signs of a struggle. No one believed anyone else had been there. The coroner ruled it as a heart attack."

Why had Terian not believed them? "Were you there? Or is this what she told you?"

"No, I...live apart from them."

I guessed it wasn't by his choice. My mind worked faster trying to come up with something that would point to Alexa as the culprit. If I could cast doubt on Danial being to blame, maybe Terian would let me go. "Did Keriam know Danial socially? Had you ever heard his name mentioned, or met him?"

"No, he never mentioned him. I didn't know anything about him before a month ago. It was Alexa who—"

"So all this is based on her word? You've got no proof otherwise?" I had trouble conceiving that anyone could be so gullible.

"Yes. And no."

I could feel Terian wobbling in his relentlessness. Now was the time to hit him with everything I could. "Then I know it has to be a lie."

"Why?"

"Because I know his business matters the most to him. Danial would never endanger himself or leave a reason for the police to come looking for him. He wants to stay out of the public eye, not draw attention to himself. If your brother ran afoul of Danial, he would have sent Theo to kill him and left no witnesses. I'm betting it was your brother's wife who actually killed him, or arranged to have it done. The only question here is why she chose Danial to pin this on. What does she have to gain by you killing Danial?" I fastened my eyes on him. "There's something between her and Danial. Whatever that was got your brother killed."

"I can ask Danial that when he gets here tomorrow night."

99

"Why don't you let me call and ask him?" I offered quickly.

"No! He'll try to talk his way out of this and trick me into losing my one advantage: you. I want him here in front of me to answer my questions. Alone, without his friends, so I can kill him if I don't believe him."

My mind worked furiously. "Did Alexa tell you Danial was a vampire? Did she give you the poison?"

"No, she just gave me his name. I made the poison when I found out what he was."

"Theo told me a week ago that a woman had been threatening Danial for making her lose her job. Did Alexa lose her job recently?"

"No. She's an engineer for Wilco Chemicals. She's worked there for at least two decades, maybe three."

I was back to square one. To cover my disappointment, I asked, "How did you make the poison?"

"It's my job," he said, as if he was surprised I hadn't guessed. Maybe I should have.

"You're a poisoner?" I said, contemptuously.

"I'm a sorcerer. I learned a long time ago what I was from an old herbalist who found me one night drinking blood..." He trailed off, then cleared his throat. "She helped me come to terms with what I am and taught me all she knew. It wasn't a lot but it was enough to keep me sane. Keriam had been supporting the both of us my whole life, but I wanted to help him. I couldn't get a regular job. The heat of my skin and that feeling of terror I inspire in humans prevented that. What she did for me saved me."

"What happened to your parents?"

The cold blackness seeped back into the room so quickly I let out a gasp. "Stop doing that!" I shouted. Like a miracle, the blackness evaporated and the air grew warmer.

"Sorry. Talking about my mother makes me angry and very sad."

"It's okay," I said gently. "Please tell me. You'll feel better if you do."

"You want to know, Sarelle?" He looked up at me with flaming eyes.

The blackness coiled out of him again, stronger this time. My heart felt as if it was going to stop in my chest. His voice was dark and so cold it hurt to hear it. The dogs howled and the cats screeched.

"Know this. I killed my mother being born. I tore my way out of her and almost killed the midwife attending her. My brother was there to witness it. My mother had told him that I would be different. She told him if she died to take care of me, not to blame me for my nature." The blackness lessened but the air was still thick with heaviness and icy breath. "What else do you want to know? How my brother struggled to care for us, even though he was only eighteen? How people made fun of my red eyes no matter what town we settled in? How he gave up the next twenty years to raise me, even though I didn't give him back nearly the love and support he gave me?"

"He must have been an exceptional man. I'm sorry he died," I said softly.

The blackness faded and the room became warm again.

"I know this isn't anything to do with you."

Something occurred to me as I talked to him, and I pressed my advantage again. I had placed him at twenty-something, but... "How old was your brother?"

"Eighty-six."

"And he was eighteen years older than you?"

"Yes," he replied, somewhat amused. His mood swings were unpredictable. Maybe he hadn't had friends for reasons other than his eyes.

"That makes you...sixty-eight?"

"Actually sixty-seven until December. I don't age," he said with a grimace. "It makes it hard to stay in one place for very long." He gave me a pain-filled look. "One of the hardest things to bear was watching Keriam grow older while I remained young."

Had Keriam felt the same way watching Terian stay young while he grew old? Knowing he wouldn't be around forever to look after his younger brother, that he would die and Terian would have to go on without him? I'd experience that myself if I got serious with Danial. I pushed the thought away quickly.

Terian saw the realization in my face. "You'll see how hard it is yourself, Sarelle. Danial doesn't age either."

"He's still not as old as you," I said acidly.

He laughed. "You're right; Danial is *older* than I."

My anger returned, but this time it was focused on Danial, who'd told me all these lies in return for opening myself to him.

"Danial said he was around fifty—"

"Try five hundred." He watched me closely. "Five hundred years."

I'd had enough for one night. I'd been terrified once too often when I wasn't being outright hassled. I got up, cleared our plates, and loaded everything into the dishwasher. I returned to find Terian still at the table, staring into space.

"Terian, could you please go wherever you're going to stay the night? I want to get some sleep, and the dogs refuse to come out of the bedroom while you're here. I need to let them out before I go to bed."

He stood and faced me. "I'm going to stay here with you so you don't escape."

I'd expected something like that. "Fine, you can sleep in Danial's room in the basement."

"No, Sarelle, I'm sleeping in your room." His words were casual, but I got a chill thinking about sleeping in the same room with him. There was no way I'd get any sleep. And my dogs wouldn't be able to handle it, either.

"Look Terian, I've been really nice about all this, but there is a limit. You are *not* sleeping in my room. You are not even sleeping on the first floor. You are sleeping as far away as I can get you to go."

"I might have come to value your reasoning, and I may even believe you about Danial. I admit it makes sense. But I don't trust you. I want to be within reach of you if Theo or Danial find a way to make it here tonight."

I didn't like the sound of that. *Within reach to do what?* Shudder. I had to reassure him that I wasn't going to try to escape. I had to make him think I was completely under his control.

"You can lock me in my room if you want. You smashed the cell phone that Danial gave me. You must have kept or smashed the guards' phones—not that anyone would be able to answer in fox form. I'll give you the phone from my room and my car keys. But you have to promise to wake me if there's a fire. I'm trusting you not to leave me and my animals locked in to burn."

"If there was a fire, you could go out the window, which you might do if I let you stay up here alone," he said, stonewalling me.

"I'd never leave my pets behind. They're my responsibility and I take that seriously. I can't take them all with me on foot—"

"Okay," he said grudgingly. "But I'll hear you if you try to leave. My hearing is very acute."

"Thank you," I said, relieved. "Goodnight."

I went into my bedroom, unplugged the phone, and gave it to him. He went downstairs with it. I let the dogs out in the fenced side yard, where they did their business. They were restless from being cooped up for so long. I let them run around for a few minutes as I tried to think how best to grab my old cell phone out of my purse.

I heard the kitchen phone ring and called the dogs. They ran inside, slipping and sliding as they hightailed it back to the bedroom, just as the phone cut off in mid-ring. Terian's agitated voice came from the kitchen telling someone that he had me. It had to be either Theo or Danial. Crap, why hadn't I grabbed the phone on the way out here?

Like an answered prayer, I saw a shape slink into the yard under the wooden fence. I thought it was a cat, but when it got closer, I saw it was a fox. It was beautiful, a reddish gold with a snow white tail. It stopped and looked at me, waiting. I snuck a look behind me, where Terian was still talking loudly in the kitchen.

"Here kitty, kitty," I called and slowly walked toward it. When I was almost to it, I saw it held something in its mouth. I reached out and took it. It was a cell phone, in Danial's make and model. The fox immediately fled, running back under the fence. I hurriedly tucked the phone in my waistband, covering it with my loose shirt. I hastened back inside, walking past Terian to my bedroom, and hid the phone under the edge of the mattress.

It was then that I missed Asher and realized she was still in the basement. I felt awful, but I told myself she'd be okay; she was mostly feral and would hide from Terian just as well as she'd hid from me.

My bedroom door opened abruptly. "That was your lover," Terian said irately. "He wanted to negotiate for your release." His smile didn't reach his eyes. "I told him your well-being depended on him being here tomorrow by sunset. He agreed on the stipulation that you remained untouched when he arrived." He studied me. "Who were you calling in the backyard?"

"My cat. One is still outside. That's okay; she's kind of feral anyway."

"You're afraid I'd hurt her. Don't be. I only hurt people who hurt me first."

I let out an inward sigh of relief. "Good. I'm going to bed. You can lock the door."

"Don't try to leave. I'll hear you trying to open a window."

He shut the door and twisted the handle with enough force that the doorframe cracked. His steps descended on the cellar stairs a few seconds later.

I put on pajamas and started the clock radio to cover the noise I'd make when I used the phone. Turning off the light, I lay down and watched the illuminated numbers of the clock. I meant to wait a half-hour before attempting to contact Danial, but I fell asleep.

I woke with a gasp. Looking at the clock, I saw it was four a.m. I let out a curse, and then a thank you for my loud furnace. The fire in the wood stove had gone out and the oil furnace had come on, waking me. Its noise would mask my call much better than the radio.

Retrieving the phone from beneath the mattress, I flipped it open. The battery was still good and I had a signal. I searched the menu, looking for the programmed numbers list. Then it hit me; I could text instead of call. I'd never done it before, but how hard could it be? There was no risk of voices being overheard.

I found Theo's number in the menu and pushed the text option next to it. Typing very slowly, I sent a message, albeit with some misspellings.

Theo, Sar. Guards stuck in fox form. Dhamphir w/red eyes Terian— not vampire. Am OK. Sent by Alexa, her husband Keriam killed? Alexa knows Danial.

I wanted to add, "Get me out of here now!" but I figured that was implied. I pushed SEND, and turned to hide the phone beneath my mattress. In my hurry, I dropped it, and it skittered under the bed, beeping. Snatching it up, I stuck it under the mattress, cursing my clumsiness.

Putting on my robe, I tried the door. With a little jiggling, it opened. I went out and checked the stove. After stirring the coals, I added two big logs, which was enough wood to keep the fire burning until morning. As I closed the stove door, I heard Terian's steps on the basement stairs and the cellar door opening fast. I turned to him. His eyes glowed red in the dimness of the room. There was no light except for the weak glow coming from the hall outside my bedroom. And his eyes.

"What are you doing?" Blackness threaded itself through the air.

"I needed to restart the fire. The furnace came on and woke me. I didn't know if the door would open, but when it did, I decided to—"

"Then why are you holding that poker?" he demanded. "Drop it."

I was holding the poker in front of me like a weapon. I quickly put it back with the other stove tools, then turned back to him empty-handed. "Sorry. Force of habit—"

"Get back to bed. You try anything like that again, I'll know I can't trust you and be forced to spend the rest of the night in your room. I hear you even get out of bed, I'll come up." Menace filled his voice. "Move it."

I nodded and walked into my bedroom. Terian slammed the door. There was a snapping sound as the door bulged in. His footsteps descended the stairs again a few seconds later. Sighing with relief, I crawled back into bed.

I'd done what I could. I'd gotten information to Theo that would get me out of this safely. Unlike Danial, I knew Theo wouldn't let me down.

Chapter Ten

I woke up to the sound of birds singing. It was almost ten in the morning, according to the clock. My eyes moved to my bulging door and narrowed in anger, remembering Terian.

But I was alive and unhurt. I just had to make it through another eight hours.

I got out of bed and slipped on some clothes after washing up in the sink. As I brushed my hair and braided it back, I thought about whether to drop the charade and just wait on the bed with the gun. I could shoot Terian the moment he opened the door.

No. The gun could kill Danial and Theo. I couldn't risk it falling into his hands.

After Terian's display of anger last night, I decided to read a book for a while instead of waking him. A half hour passed, then an hour. By that time, the dogs were whining and pacing, needing to go out. Just like that, I lost my temper and banged on the door with both fists, yelling for Terian. Footsteps sounded on the basement stairs a minute later, and with a wrenching crack, he opened the door.

"Good morning," he said gruffly.

A piece of the splintered doorframe fell off and hit the floor. I glared at it and then at him. He looked stonily back at me.

"Please go downstairs," I said. "The dogs won't come out if you're here."

"No. They and you stay where I can see you. You lied; they aren't afraid of me."

I pushed past him to let the dogs out. "They are."

He followed me to the side door. "That cat you were calling for outside last night was inside. That one." He pointed to the gray and tan calico blur as Asher streaked past me, out the door, followed by both dogs and the other two cats. "She slept with me on the bed all night, purring."

I gaped at him, astonished. Asher never spent any time on my lap, even after knowing me for three years. She came out to be fed and then hid. Why had she chosen to be close to Terian? He had to be lying.

"That's bullshit. She's afraid, they're all—"

My words cut off as I looked down to see Asher twining around his ankles, purring. He smirked at me as he petted her. "See?"

The other animals watched. Ghost and Darkness came forward slowly, sniffing Terian, their tails wagging hesitantly. Asher rolled onto her back as he rubbed her belly, acting for all the world like another cat.

Something to think about. If Asher and the dogs trusted him, there had to be something good in him. Was it a spell? Not on my dogs. He hadn't even given them a treat.

The moment was broken by the ringing of the phone. "Should I answer?"

"Yes. Give it to me if it's Danial or Theo. If it's anyone else, get rid of them."

I picked up the phone. "Hello?"

"Sar, please tell me you're okay." It was Danial. The relief in his voice was overwhelming. "Sar, are you okay? Tell me that bastard hasn't hurt you. He swore he wouldn't—"

Hearing his worry, I felt a rush of feeling for him, despite what he'd done. "I'm okay, but there's someone who wants to talk to you." Terian was already drawing close, motioning for the phone. "I'm going to hand the phone to him."

"Alexa's nephew, you said. Put him on and pick up another line."

He'd gotten the message I'd sent Theo. That was a relief. I handed the phone to Terian and got on other phone in the living room.

Danial's voice was cold as a fieldstone in winter. "Talk."

"My name is Terian. I've got your concubine, Sarelle. I want a meeting alone with you to discuss my brother's death. I heard from a trusted source that you killed him."

"I had nothing to do with your brother's death," Danial's said calmly. "Theo told you all this last night—"

"How can you be so sure?" Terian said sarcastically. "Check your files; see if he's listed in the big one labeled *Victims*."

"Theo's getting the truth from Alexa right now," His tone lost its edge, becoming comforting. "Sar, this will all be over tonight. You won't be hurt. No matter what happens, Terian's agreed to let you go."

Terian's eyes bore into mine. "I have, so long as you get here tonight."

"I'll be there an hour after sundown," Danial growled and hung up.

I put down the phone, and so did Terian. He slumped on the couch with an expression akin to having stepped in dog shit.

I studied him, surprised. "I thought you'd be happy. You got what you wanted. You'll hear from Danial tonight that he didn't kill your brother."

He flopped back on the couch and put his head in his hands. "I know it's what I wanted. But I thought a lot last night about what you said over dinner and I think Alexa lied to me. I believe you, that she has something against Danial. She wanted me to take him out." He paused, then continued haltingly. "And what's probably worse, she knew who and what Danial is when she sent me after him. She did that to make sure I'd never return."

That was pretty awful, considering Alexa was the only family he had left. "Why would she want you dead?"

"Because Keriam left half his estate to me. He'd always worried about me, what would happen when he wasn't around. He knew he was getting older and the time wouldn't be far off. With me dead, she gets it all."

If that had been the plan, Alexa was utterly ruthless. Hopefully, Theo was interrogating her with sharp incentive-inducing implements.

"Wait until you talk to Danial and find out what she was to him. Then you'll know for sure who—"

"Don't act like you're on my side," he said bitterly as he got to his feet. "No one but my brother has ever been. I'll be in the basement. Don't leave the house."

He strode downstairs, slamming the cellar door behind him.

I tried watching TV and then reading, but I couldn't concentrate. I slept for a while, the cats on my lap. At noon, I had lunch alone, forcing myself to eat toast because I wasn't hungry. In the evening, I went to my bedroom and opened the drawer where I'd stashed the gun, trying to decide if I should put it on. A few minutes later, I heard a truck pull into the drive.

I made a dash for the front door and ran into Terian. He immediately grabbed me by the arm. I tried to jerk free, but his grip was solid, and when he squeezed me, I remembered the wall crumbling and stopped struggling. He banged open the door and strode onto the deck with me in tow. The dogs barked in the house, although I didn't know if it was because of the truck's arrival or Terian's blackness. Danial was already out of his truck. He appeared to be alone. Gravel crunched under his boots as he walked to the front bumper looking thoroughly pissed. Terian's rage built as that metaphysical blackness oozed out of him. I shivered.

"Don't worry, sweetheart, this will be over soon," Danial called. He addressed Terian next. "Are you going to let her go so we can get to it?"

"No way," Terian said icily. "She stays right here. She's my only insurance that you won't overwhelm me with brute force."

"I won't need any help to beat you into the ground. Get down here and face me, coward. You wanted me. Here I am."

"Aren't you two going to talk this over?"

"The time for talk is over," Danial said coldly. "Stay out of this, Sar."

His arrogant stance was as irritating as Terian's half-cocked scheme for vengeance, and it pissed me off. "Then whatever you're going to do, do it out in the field. I don't want the deck wrecked or my home to catch on fire."

Danial gave me a surprised look. "I don't have a problem with that. Do you, Terian?"

"No." He strode down the steps, and I stumbled after him, as he half-pulled, half-dragged me to a level spot in the field in front of the barn. He told me to stay back, and I nodded. Terian and Danial faced off and began circling one another.

I tried again. "Please, don't fight. This is a misunderstanding—"

Danial cut me off. "I don't care. I told him I had nothing to do with his brother's death and he didn't believe me." His tone grew more menacing. "To add to his insult, he dared to take you hostage and threaten you. He knows who I am and he still dared that!"

"I would never have hurt her," Terian retorted. "She's got nothing to do with you and me. She's just another of your victims! Tell me the truth, you bastard! Did you kill my brother?"

"I didn't even know your brother. It's Alexa who knows me, both as a companion in her youth and more recently as the person who exposed her private sale of company technology to a rival company. I told her employer and she was fired. She used your brother's heart attack as the catalyst to get payback through you. She's been sending threatening letters to me for a month—"

"You're lying! He was in perfect health!"

Terian swung at Danial, but he gracefully sidestepped and continued goading. "Maybe Alexa slipped a little poison into his nightcap. Maybe she purchased it from someone like you, or snuck it out of your personal stash? You do have a seedy reputation for alchemy, with those potions you concoct for that *Witch's Brew* shop you run online—"

Terian drew a dagger, snarling. Danial sneered, drawing one from his boot. They circled each other, lunging but not landing any strikes.

"This knife has the same poison that almost killed you the last time, vampire," Terian hissed. "Something tells me Sarelle won't let you drain her blood this time."

Danial smiled at him, a fearsome grin baring his fangs. "I want you to know that my knife has been dipped in holy water and blessed by a priest."

Uncertainty flashed across Terian's face. "That won't hurt me any more than it hurts you."

Danial's knife connected, gashing Terian across the cheekbone. It didn't look like a deep cut, but it smoked. An acrid sulfur smell filled the air. Terian let out a loud scream and staggered, dropping his knife.

"You're a fool, Terian. You think because some old witch tells you that you're dhamphir that makes it true? Dhamphirs are myth, something out of legends, and you aren't one. I suspected what you really were when I heard your skin was hot and your eyes were always red, even in daylight. But the knife proves it. You're half-human all right, but your father was no vampire. He was a demon. And any symbol of faith can hurt a demon."

A lot made sudden sense. The red eyes, the burning skin, the evil feeling Terian was able to exude when he wanted to, and his look of pain when I'd prayed.

Terian held his still smoking face, wobbling as if he'd collapse. Danial walked a little closer; his knife at the ready. He kicked Terian's poison-coated knife away.

"I'm glad I got the antidote for this, even though you weren't able to scratch me this time. Where was I? Ah, yes, it's a crushing weight, isn't it? Thinking your mother bedded a vampire was bad enough, but you could always tell yourself that he'd raped her. But not now. Now you have to face that she was a willing partner in the tryst. Because a demon could never force a woman to have sex with him. At least not a pure woman—"

"No!" shouted Terian. "That's a lie!" The oppressive evil feeling poured out of him stronger than I'd ever felt it. I huddled in the dirt, shaking hard.

Danial was unaffected. He continued in that seductive taunting voice. "A pure woman would be *safe*. A demon could never touch her. Maybe your mother had a lust for power. Maybe she was a witch who got tired of asking sweetly for favors from the gods and decided it was time to start demanding. Maybe she just wanted to experience a demon in the flesh—"

Terian looked up, tendrils of smoke still rising from his gashed face. His eyes were glowing red orbs. "You think you've cornered the market on truth? You lied to Sarelle. No matter what you say to me, no matter if you kill me, I've won. She *knows*, Danial, she knows all of it! The collar you gave her, that you were feeding off her through that shirt drenched in the potion made from your blood, your true age, all of it."

Danial suddenly looked up, his eyes darting to mine. The guilt on his face grew with every word Terian uttered. It had been awful to hear the first time, but it was worse to see his face and know it, know he'd deceived me, that everything Terian had said was true.

I looked back to see Terian lunge at Danial, a stake in his hands. Danial never saw it coming. The stake plunged into Danial's chest as he backpedaled. Terian fell on him trying to get it into his heart. I let out a scream and started toward them.

"Stay back!" Terian shouted, glaring at me with his red eyes. I froze.

He sat astride Danial, trying to work the stake deeper into his chest. Danial screeched as blood oozed out of his chest to pool beside his body. He fought Terian but he was badly wounded, his strength fading. He'd been so sure Terian would have no will to fight after hearing the truth. He'd forgotten that truth didn't always make a person powerless when they heard it; it sometimes strengthened their resolve.

"Stop," Danial growled. He had a hold of the stake, but it was slick with blood and slipped through his hands inch by inch. "I didn't kill him. I swear it."

"You've killed plenty of others," Terian snarled, leaning with all his weight on the stake. "You'll kill again if I don't kill you. You'll come after me if I don't do this. I'll never be safe as long as you're alive."

Both of them had forgotten me. I got to my feet, reached for my back holster, and drew the gun. Sprinting to them, I slipped off the safety and pressed the barrel against the middle of Terian's back. He froze when he felt the gun. Danial's eyes looked up in shock.

"I've had enough. Let him go. Now!"

Terian was incredulous and almost did let him go. Danial was too weak to take the opening before Terian resumed pushing the stake home.

When Danial cried out again, I pressed the barrel a little deeper into Terian's back. "You heard me. Stop!"

"He lied to you. He's just using you. He would have killed you as soon as you weren't useful to him anymore."

"I don't believe that. But that's not your business, it's his and mine—"

"How can you do this after everything he's put you through?"

"I think I might love him." God, the worst admission to have let slip. I plowed on. "But even if I don't, I can't watch you execute him in cold blood for something he didn't do. I can't stand here and not try to stop you."

Terian turned to look at me, his face reflecting fury and bitter anger. "You can't love him. He's a killer!"

"I'm sorry," I said softly. Then I shot him in the back with Theo's gun.

Terian jerked and slumped over Danial, who let out another cry of pain. Acrid smoke wafted up from the hole in Terian's back, bad enough to make my eyes water. I wiped my eyes and rolled the body off Danial. He was alive, but Terian had pushed the stake in another inch with the weight of his body.

Trying to ignore all the blood, I straddled Danial and put my hands on the stake. The blood was warm as it smeared my hands.

"Please, Sar," Danial panted, "help me pull it out. I haven't the strength."

I looked at him lying there. Bastard. "Give me one good reason why I shouldn't push it the rest of the way in."

"Because," he panted, "You could have let him kill me...and saved yourself the trouble."

A few weeks ago, he'd told me I didn't have the strength to put a stake through his heart. He'd been right; I didn't stand a chance. It had taken all of Terian's supernatural muscle to do it, something I'd better remember.

I put down the gun. Tightening my hands on the stake, Danial and I wrenched it out. He screamed worse than when Terian had driven it in. The gaping hole in his chest filled with blood. As I watched, it scabbed over and became muscle, and then unbroken skin. Danial looked as bad as he had when I'd first found him, his skin bone white and just as lusterless. His eyes were dull, his breathing ragged.

I moved to his side, not sure what to do next. I'd be damned if I was giving him my blood after all his bullshit. "What now?"

"I'll be okay," he said weakly. "It didn't get deep enough to puncture my heart. But it will take some time for me to regain my strength.

"Should I stay away from you?" I asked.

"Help me inside. I won't hurt you, I promise. It's rest I need, not blood."

I helped him to his feet and then to the house, supporting him. I opened the basement door with the keypad so he wouldn't have to navigate the stairs. As soon as he got inside, he collapsed on the bed. I moved all his paperwork back to his desk. Helping him out of his shirt, I thought to myself that I was always washing blood out of his clothes. As a bonus tonight, I'd be washing blood out of mine, too. I covered him up, gathered the shirt, and went to leave.

"Sar, please come back—"

"No. I'm going to bed. What do you want?"

"Why did you help me, after what he told you?"

"I don't owe you anything after tonight, not even a last word." I had had enough of him for one night, maybe for the rest of my nights. "It makes me sick I had to shoot someone again. I might have been lonely when I was alone, but at least I had peace and quiet."

"Tell me why—"

"Because aside from all the stuff Terian accused you of, you never hurt me. You could have but you didn't. You saved me from Max's men. You came alone tonight to face Terian, when it would have been less risky for you to send in the troops. I know Theo kills for you." He tried to interrupt, but I talked over him. "You lied to me about your age and the collar and God knows what else."

He didn't say anything, and that admission of guilt was somehow worse than if he'd tried to explain.

I turned and looked straight at him. "I care for you. I do believe you care for me, just not enough to tell me the truth. That's why I'm giving you a chance to decide whether to come clean or leave. You aren't protecting me by keeping me in the dark. If you don't tell me all of it, everything, we're through. That means you leave tomorrow night and don't ever come back. You never see me again. Take tonight and think it over."

I got up and walked to the door. I reached for the handle when he said tiredly, "What do you want to know?"

I looked back at him. "Everything you lied about."

"You won't want to hear some of it," he said, his eyes not meeting mine.

"I need to hear all of it. You put a collar on me knowing full well I'd never be able to remove it myself." The disgust was palpable in my voice and I saw him wince, even as his eyes remained downcast.

"I'll tell you whatever you want to know. But let me rest tonight."

"Do you want me to call Theo? Do you need him to bring you...food?"

He still didn't look up. His voice was flat when he answered. "He's busy dealing with Alexa. She's not a real threat without Terian, but we can't have her sniping at our heels either. Theo says she admitted that this was just an attempt to get Terian out of the way, so she could inherit without sharing. It's not clear that she planned this out very well, but Alexa was always opportunistic. From the coroner's report, the heart attack looks like it really was natural. The sample of blood tested concurs. She may have seen an opportunity and taken it. She's been pissed at me since she lost her job, so motive's clear—"

"I don't give a shit about Alexa. Do you want me to call Theo or not?"

"I'll call him. As I said, I just need rest."

"Okay." I turned to leave again, feeling both relieved for him and irritated that I cared.

"Thank you," he said quickly. "What you texted to Theo really helped." More quietly, he added, "And thank you for saving me...again."

I'd fucking saved him twice now yet I still had to push down a thrill hearing that appreciation in his voice. Unbelievable. I gritted my teeth, picked up the clothes, and left.

My hands were covered with his drying blood, so I washed them off in the kitchen sink. Before I knew it, I felt tears sliding down my face. I let it out for a few minutes and then clamped down on my emotions, drying my hands and face. I had to move and move fast.

* * * *

I walked cautiously out to the field, wondering if fox eyes were watching me. Hopefully, they had fled when the fighting had started, as none of them had tried to step in to save their master. I puzzled over that as I approached Terian's body. Maybe they had orders not to or he'd told them to back off, that this was his fight. I didn't know. And right now I didn't care.

Terian lay on his back where I'd rolled him off Danial. There was no smoke anymore, but the gash on his face was an ugly raised welt. I crouched next to him and shook him. He flopped bonelessly. Shit.

"Sarelle?" he said weakly, opening his eyes. They still glowed red, but much fainter. "You shot me—"

I put my finger to his lips and said, "Shh. I aimed to the left of your heart. Danial thinks you're dead. We need to keep it that way."

His eyes widened.

Hoping I'd judged him correctly—or I was going to be the one lying on the ground shortly—I told him what Danial had said about his brother not being murdered.

"You're sure?"

"Yes. Eat." I gave him some raw steak. He'd said he could drink blood, so I reasoned that this had to help. There was blood in raw meat.

He tore into it, devouring the whole slab. Slowly, the gunshot wound closed. By the time he'd finished, it was a nice shiny scar. Pretty remarkable for a hole that had been the size of a cantaloupe. The gash on his cheek, though, was still an angry red color.

He touched his scar. "I usually heal this fast, even when the wound is bad. I always thought it was vampire blood—"

"Feel sorry for yourself when you're safe. Danial's people are coming. There may be foxes around even now. Get up."

He picked up his knife and got to his feet, sheathing it.

"Where's your car?" I asked. "I'll help you get to it."

"I don't have one," he said lamely.

I rolled my eye, and sighed. Why couldn't helping him be quick or easy? "Then how did you get here?"

"I hitched a ride as far as the Pennsylvania border. I walked the rest of the way. It wasn't that far." He shrugged. "I don't tire easily."

It was a hundred and fifty mile hike and he described it as if it was a half-hour walk. Walking out of here the way he'd walked in wasn't going to work this time. I didn't want to do it, but I didn't have a choice. "Take my husband's car. It's the red one in the garage. I assume you can drive?"

He gave me another surprised look.

"I'm a widow," I snapped. "And I'm not giving you the car. I expect it back, with some reimbursement for the miles you'll put on it. But taking the car is the best way. Now come on—"

"Why?" he said, his eyes searching mine.

"Why what?" I said tiredly.

"Why are you helping me, after all that's happened?"

116

"Because you told me some things I'm very glad to know, even if I hated to hear them. This was a misunderstanding, even if Danial doesn't see it that way. And because Asher trusted you. She never trusts anyone."

"You're trusting your cat as a judge of my character? You can't be serious—"

"Even just letting me see she was with you is completely at odds with what I know of her. She's scared of everything, but she felt safe with you. I'm taking that as a sign that I should help you. Now move it, before I change my mind."

He looked at me thoughtfully, and then said, "I'll bring you back the car. And I owe you." He clasped my hand and gave it a brief squeeze.

God, his hands were hot. I tried not to recoil, but it was almost more than I could bear, like boiling water. He saw me jerk and abruptly let go.

"Sorry."

He got into the late model Forester, started the engine, and backed out of the garage. The passenger window rolled down. "I'll contact you when I'm safe and arrange to get you your car back."

"I'd rather you write than call," I said. "Just tell me what parking lot you leave it in and I'll arrange—"

"Don't let him back in your life. You'll end up dead or a slave."

"You have to go. Now."

"Staying with him will kill you."

"It's my decision, and only I can make it."

"That's true," he said with a sad smile. "Good-bye."

He drove off as I closed the garage and walked back to the site of the battle. Except for Danial's blood, a hole in the ground still wafting up a bitter smell of sulfur, and the remaining weapons, there was nothing but flattened grass. I kicked some earth over the blood and into the hole. I reholstered the gun, berating myself for not doing that before helping Danial inside, then picked up the stake and Danial's knife. I tried to wipe them off on the nearby long grass, but that just seemed to smear the blood. I held them away from me so as not to get any on me. My stomach rolled. I could still smell the sulfur odor, which made me nauseous.

Inside, I washed the blood off both weapons, wrapped them in paper towels, and put them in a plastic container. Then I tried to clean the remaining blood off my hands.

Danial's came off easily as it had before, but Terian's seemed impervious to the soap and water. I tried makeup remover that had worked for me in the past on oil paint but had no success. Panicking, I turned the water hot and scrubbed my hands hard with a nailbrush. I scoured my hands raw to get it off, and even then, it left a slight stain. I was concerned but not scared enough to ask Danial about it. He'd gotten Terian's blood on himself and hadn't seemed worried about it.

It was after ten. I let the dogs out, made a cat check, and grabbed a couple cookies from a jar on the counter before I turned off the lights. I was in bed and almost asleep when the phone rang.

"Sar, its Theo. Are you okay? I got a call from Danial saying everything was fine, but the...uh...other guards out there can't find Terian's body. We searched the field and your barn."

Shit, that was close. "I'm fine. The gun worked great. Danial says he's okay, though he nearly got a stake through the chest. I saw Terian was gone when I went back out to get the weapons. I put dirt over the blood—"

"I see that. Thank you, but it wasn't necessary. Damage control is an everyday thing for me."

Was that supposed to be comforting? Maybe it was. "Okay."

"Relax and get some sleep. You're in good hands. I have guards watching that won't succumb to magic like the last ones did."

"Thanks Theo. Are the...other guards okay?"

"Yes, we found everybody. One had been shot a few houses over, but she's okay, it was just a few pellets. She'll be as good as new."

It had been close but no one had actually died during Terian's siege. Part of that was because I'd helped make that happen. I felt a rush of pride and a large dose of relief.

"Sar, are you there?"

"Theo, I'm exhausted and I'm going to sleep in. Do not come in the house and wake me unless it's an emergency."

"Roger that. We'll let you and Danial sleep. Goodnight."

Chapter Eleven

My eyes snapped open and my body tensed as adrenaline spiked through my veins. Another metallic rumbling sounded, then a whoosh of air.

Stupid. I'd heard the furnace.

I'd forgotten to stock the fire before I went to sleep. That was twice in two nights. And just like usual, in late October, the temperature had dropped during the night. I was using up my precious fuel.

Grumbling, I climbed out of bed, stepped over the sleeping dogs, and went out to the wood stove. The heat from the two big dogs and me had kept my small bedroom comfortable, but it was colder outside my room. I checked the thermometer. Fifty-two degrees. I opened the wood stove door, emptied the cold ashes into a steel bucket, and started a new fire. As soon as the flame was steady, I put on my coat and slipped on my boots. A blast of cold air hit me as I opened the front door, shocking me fully awake. As I trudged outside, I saw the first flakes of snow whirling down and remembered that it was Halloween. The snow was only a small dusting blown into patterns by the brisk wind. I scattered the ashes on the gravel driveway in front of the house and dashed back inside. Taking off my boots and coat, I settled down to watch the fire for a few minutes. I couldn't go back to bed until the flame was a nice roaring blaze guaranteed not to go out.

I held my hands in front of the glass door and felt the first faint heat. I put more logs in and the fire blazed. That should do it.

"Is everything okay?"

I let out a squeal and whipped my head around. Danial stood in the shadows near the cellar stairs.

"I heard the front door open, but I didn't hear anyone but you moving around."

"Everything's okay. I just forgot to build up the fire. But its set now and I'm going back to bed."

"Your furnace is on. Why did you get up to start a fire?"

"I have to pay for oil to run the furnace. I can cut wood to burn in the stove. It costs a lot less in terms of money."

"I'll give you money," Danial said. "I want you to be comfortable—"

"I don't want your money," I said, leveling my eyes at him. "It might come with rules that you don't tell me until I'm already bound by them."

He sat beside me. He looked much better, although there was a definite pallor to his skin and he moved stiffly. He was dressed in sweatpants and a T-shirt. I smelled a familiar scent of nutmeg and cedar. He'd probably showered in my guest bathroom after I'd gone to bed.

"I'm glad you're awake. I didn't want to wait until tomorrow night to talk to you." He paused. "I'd like to say a few things."

"Then say them."

"To start, if I'd have told you that I was the only one who could remove the choker, would you have let me put it on you?"

"That depends—"

"On what?"

"On...on whether or not I believed you would remove it if I asked you to."

"Do you want me to remove it now?"

My first thought, insane as it sounded, was no. I had begun to think of the choker as some kind of mystical armor. Wearing it would be safer, no question. But I resented feeling owned

"Sar, yes or no?"

"Yes, please," I whispered. "At least for now."

He motioned for me to sit in front of him, and I scooted over. I felt his hands at the back of my neck, a small sliding sound of metal on metal, and then the choker fell off, into my lap. I reached down and picked it up. It was still as beautiful as when I first saw it, but it was a relief to have it off.

"Are you happy now?" Danial growled softly from behind me.

"No, as a matter of fact I'm not—"

"Did you ever consider the main reason it can't be removed by anyone but me was for your safety? It can't be left behind, lost, or forcibly removed. Any vampire or any supernatural creature who trifles with anyone wearing one of these forfeits their life, no matter what reason or who they are."

"Says who?"

"It's common knowledge," Danial said flatly. "A law, you might say."

"I understand that," I said grudgingly. "But what if you refused to take it off? What if you die? I still think it's beautiful, but that doesn't mean I want to wear it every day for the rest of my life."

"I had hoped you would," Danial said softly. I felt his breath on my neck and wanted so much to relax against him, but I stayed where I was.

"If I died, you'd know. The choker would fall off a few seconds after my heart ceased to beat. If you had waited a few minutes longer yesterday, you'd have been rid of us both." He said the last with bitter sadness.

Comforting him wasn't on my agenda. He still had a couple more things to answer for. "Are you really five hundred years old?"

"No," he said, chuckling. "But I'm about four hundred. I was born in 1604, or close to that. Things were different then. My village didn't have a daily paper; in fact, I think the only book in the entire county was a bible. The local priest had that, and I'm not even sure if it was a real bible. None of us could read or write. I didn't learn more than my own name until after I was made vampire. Years were counted by the turn of seasons and noted by scratched marks on a piece of wood. Sometimes mistakes were made." He leaned closer to my neck and whispered coldly, "And don't think you can play the martyr with me."

I froze, thinking of Terian, but he was on a different tirade.

"You may think you're poor, but you have no idea what true poverty is. I experienced it firsthand through my first two hundred years of life. Just because I have money now doesn't mean I don't appreciate how hard it is to be without it. I care about you. I want to make your life easier. Don't throw the gift back in my face out of some warped sense of righteousness."

Now it was my turn to feel ashamed. "I'm sorry. I didn't mean to offend you. But I want to be clear that I don't expect you to give me money because we…because we're—"

"Intimate?" he supplied with a leer. "Lovers?"

I blushed, glad my back was to him. "Yes," I said curtly.

"It's my feelings for you that make me offer. I understand you're independent and used to taking care of yourself. But I want you to have an easier time of it than you had trying to go it alone. I want to take care of you. It's your right, as befitting your station."

"What station?"

"As my lover." He nibbled the back of my neck, his hands sliding down my arms. "That is, if you still want to be."

Did I ever. God, his lips felt good. I could feel little pricks where his fangs brushed against me...

Focus! "What about the shirt?"

Danial paused what he was doing. "What about it?"

"Did you take some of my life force? Did you deliberately try to seduce me with a spell to get me to feed you?"

He didn't reply. I shifted back from the fire and made to get up, but he pulled me off balance and I went down, falling into his waiting arms. I struggled in vain as he rolled me over on the carpet and straddled me, holding both my arms over my head with one hand, while the other caressed my cheek. I fumed as I looked at him above me, his upper half silhouetted by the fire. His eyes sparkled, his face in shadow.

"Now, Sarelle," he purred, "why would I need to seduce you to get you to feed me?"

He stretched down against me. I felt my body betray my anger as my breasts hardened and my breaths came faster.

"You gave me your blood when I was a stranger, willingly." He leaned in closer as if to kiss me, but remained just out of reach. His dark eyes were locked on mine, filled with desire and familiar arrogance. He bent down to kiss my throat. "You gave yourself to me a night later, with no hesitation."

His lips moved to the side of my throat. He ran a fang down my neck. I writhed, both in desire and a touch of fear.

"That was a dream. I knew it—"

"You knew nothing of the sort," he said, his breath warm against my neck. He drew back and used his free hand to start unbuttoning my nightshirt.

"Stop," I said, my breath tearing out of me.

"Stop what?" he said teasingly. "You want me, just like you have from the first moment you saw me. I can feel your body beneath mine, aching for me. Just as I'm aching for you."

He continued unbuttoning my top.

"Stop screwing around! I need to know if you—"

"It was your fantasy. A predictable one," he said, his hand on the next to last button. He paused to run that hand between my breasts, up to clasp my throat. "But I was never in control of you. I couldn't feed from you—not that I didn't try. You seemed so willing to let me. But I couldn't draw any energy from you and I awoke hungry, almost ravenous."

"Terian was right—"

His hand tightened on my throat. "Why are you so determined to be the victim? Nothing happened that you didn't choose to happen." He gave me a half smile, his eyes growing darker. He brought his hand back to my nightshirt and undid the last button. He pushed my shirt to each side, baring my breasts and my lower body as he gave me a slow savoring look. That nimble hand slid up to grip my neck loosely. I knew he could feel how fast my heart beat. "That you could resist and take control from me in the dream amazed me." His voice was full of wonder and affection. "No one has ever been able to do that. Not with me. Not in three hundred and seventy-five years."

He let go of my throat and slid his hand down to brush my breast with the back of it. He moved lower, touching my mound. I let out a gasp and then a moan as he caressed me.

"Please, Danial," I said, moving beneath him.

"Please what?" His finger slipped inside me. We both could feel how ready I was for him. He slipped out of me and pulled his sweat pants off. He straddled me again in a flash. I could feel the tip of him pushing against me, wanting in.

"You want me inside you, to feel my touch, my kiss." His words were ragged, his breathing fast. He pressed himself against me, and just the tip of him entered. He stayed there, just inside, waiting, watching me.

"Tell me you want me." Danial's voice was so deep with need it was almost a command. "Tell me, Sar," he whispered, brushing his lips with mine. His head dipped lower to my right breast. He took my nipple in his mouth, while his hand cupped my other breast. He sucked hard, his fangs grazing me, and I cried out. He drew his lips away and kissed the side of my neck.

"Tell me, Sar," he whispered between kisses.

"Please, Danial, I want you so badly—"

He bore down as I shoved up against him to bury him inside me. He pushed himself in and out quickly, kissing me passionately. His fangs scratched my mouth and I tasted blood. His tongue slipped in, tasting me, and he moaned, thrusting faster. I felt his body spasm, his orgasm breaking over him as he groaned into my mouth. I was close, too, so close because of what he'd done, and I came with him, screaming his name, clutching him to me as he emptied himself into me.

He uttered a loud, gratified sigh, then gave me a tender kiss. He rolled onto his back, pulling me with him, still inside, growing smaller. We were both sweaty. The room that had seemed so cold an hour before was now like an oven. My heart hammered so fast I felt like it was going to break through my rib cage. I put my ear to Danial's chest, listening for his heart. It was definitely beating faster than it had been in daylight.

"Are you checking to make sure it's beating?" he asked, nuzzling me.

"It was so much slower that morning I woke up with you."

"It's always a little slower in the daytime, especially when I'm resting. But never as fast as yours. Depending on the activity, of course," he added, laughing.

The sex had been great, but everything between us wasn't back to normal. "Why did you lie about your age?" I asked.

"Because I'm so old," he replied. "I saw in your eyes how upsetting it was to think I was several decades older. I was worried you might decide it was too much if you really knew how old I was."

"It does make me feel a little strange," I said gently. "But that alone won't keep me from being with you."

"Good," he said, drawing me close. "I like being with you—"

I gently pushed him away. We weren't done. "Why did you try to feed off me? I'd already given you my blood. Wasn't that enough?"

He cleared his throat in embarrassment. "I'm sorry for that."

"Then why did you do it?"

"It wasn't for the energy. I did it because I liked you and I needed to know if you would welcome me into your arms, given the opportunity. My being vampire doesn't ever go away. I'd hurt you pretty badly taking your blood when I was injured. I thought there might be a good chance you'd tell me to get lost." He sighed. "If you had, I wouldn't have come back to see you again."

"Not likely," I murmured, touching his chest. "You were right; I wanted you from the first. I liked the dream of us making love. I couldn't help thinking about it every time we were together afterward. It's a big part of the reason why I didn't stop you that night you first kissed me. Why I said yes that night." I cracked a grin. "Even if you didn't set out to seduce me, you still managed to."

"But I couldn't feed from you," he said, bemused. "I had to go out and feed after I woke. I had to take blood from five women because I really wanted to drain one, and I don't kill if I can help it. I was that hungry. That's never happened to me before, not being able to feed from a woman through the dream." He paused. "In case it's not obvious, I haven't and won't do that again. I know you want me now, and that's what I wanted to find out. Any dreams you have of me will be your own."

I nuzzled his neck and scented that wonderful smell of rich spices. It wasn't anywhere near as potent as it had been on his shirt, but it was there, just the lightest scent of it on his skin. I wanted an answer about that, too.

"Why do you smell of nutmeg and cedar? Is it some product you use? If it is, I want the brand name, so I can get some for myself."

He laughed. There was pure joy in its rich deep sound. "I'm glad I smell good to you," he said with relish. "But it's not a product. I showered with your regular soap and shampoo. What you smell is my scent, how you perceive me to smell."

Wow. And yum.

"Come below with me," he whispered. "It's going to be day soon and I don't want to end this now."

He was right, I could see it was lighter outside and the stars had disappeared.

"Do you have to sleep during the day? I mean, I know you can't go outside, in daylight, but do you have to actually sleep?" I asked seductively.

"No," he grinned. "I don't have to sleep, at least not the whole day."

"I'll be down shortly, then. Let me get things taken care of up here."

He rose to a sitting position with me still on him. With a quick motion, he helped us both stand. I picked up my discarded nightshirt and put it back on, and he gathered his pants.

"Hurry," he said and went downstairs.

I added some more logs to the fire and let the dogs out. The cats came in from outside, and I fed everyone. I thought about eating myself, but I didn't want to waste the time. It was already seven a.m.

I ventured downstairs to find Danial waiting. Terian had slept down there, but the mess he'd made of Danial's papers had been cleaned up. I didn't want to bring that up, but it was strange being naked where Terian had slept. Had Terian been naked in the bed? He hadn't had any spare clothes with him.

I shoved that thought out of my mind, but I'd paused too long in the doorway and Danial noticed. "He spent the night down here, didn't he?"

"I told him he had to." I raised my eyebrows and crossed to the bed. "He wanted to sleep with me, but I said no."

"He what!" Danial sat bolt upright in bed. If I'd thought I'd seen him angry before, I'd been mistaken. His eyes had a red tint to them. "Did he try anything—?"

"Calm down. Nothing happened. He just wanted to make sure I wouldn't escape."

Danial relaxed back onto the bed. "It's a relief, too, knowing the gun works, even if it didn't kill him outright. He's badly injured and Theo's tracking him. He won't get far."

I nodded. I wasn't lying; just omitting the truth to save a life, not for kicks or personal gain. That made it okay. At least, I told myself it did.

Danial interrupted my thoughts. "If you see him or suspect he's around, notify Theo right away. He'll take care of it."

I had no intention of calling Theo, but I also didn't plan on seeing Terian again. I nodded and kissed him. He grasped me and pushed me away. I was so shocked, I stared at him, which is what he wanted.

"I mean it, Sar. You might think he doesn't care that you shot him. But he'll remember that night for the rest of his life. That scar I gave him will never go away. Never."

I remembered the smoke coming from Terian's face, how the wound had still been red and angry even after the chest wound had healed over. I shuddered.

Danial pulled me close and kissed my forehead. "I don't want to lose you. Watch yourself."

"Okay," I said, a little shaken. "I'll let you or Theo know if he comes back."

He held me for a while. I was drifting off when he said, "Sar?"

I stretched and yawned. "Yes?"

"I'd like to ask a favor," he began nervously.

I knew he'd want to bite me sooner or later. "Shoot."

"Tonight is Halloween, right?"

"That's right."

"Were you able to get the time off from work?"

I gave him a big smile, expecting he would be happy. "Yes."

"Then come home with me for a few days. I'd planned for us to have been there for a few days by now, but..." He trailed off.

Something was up. I leaned up on one arm so I could study him. "That sounds fine, but I'd like to bring my dogs, like we talked about."

"That would be fine. What about the cats?"

"No, not for just a few days. They like to go out until it gets too cold. But I'll need to hire someone to stay here and tend to things—"

"That isn't a problem," he said quickly. Too quickly.

"Danial," I said with half a smile. "What's the catch? You weren't nervous about me coming before."

He looked down at me with an uneasy expression. "I'm throwing a party tonight, on All Hallows Eve. I want you to come with me. I was going to ask you—"

I smiled at him reassuringly. "That sounds fun. Are we carving pumpkins? Bobbing for apples?"

He wasn't smiling. "This is a different kind of party. It's a costume party."

I still didn't see the problem. "I don't have a costume, but I suppose I can fix something quick—"

"I have a costume for you," he said worriedly. "It's already made."

I got nervous. "Then what's the problem? Cut to the chase already."

"This is not a small party. I throw an annual one every year on All Hallows Eve. There will be over two hundred people there."

I'd been to a wedding once with that many people and had been overwhelmed. Moreover, I'd be out in the spotlight this time, not on the sidelines. The parties I usually went to had about five other couples there. But all I'd likely need to do was smile. It would be nice to be at Danial's side, to meet his friends. What would they be like? Would they be vampire or human?

"You'll need to wear the choker. There will be other vampires there besides me."

"Surely no one would try anything at your own party."

"Yes," he said bluntly. "There are one or two who might."

"What kinds of friends are these?" I asked, appalled.

"They're not friends; they're allies. I have very few real friends, especially in my business. And you already know my best one, Theo."

I was wide-awake then, my mind racing for a way to beg off the invitation as I thought of all the things that could go wrong. I wouldn't know anyone and I'd be sure to forget everyone's names. It would be horrible. I might embarrass myself, or worse, Danial. But I knew I was going to say yes before the word left my mouth. If we were going to be together, this was one of the things I'd have to learn how to deal with. It was the price of admission to his life.

"Sure." I tried to make my response light, and for the most part, I succeeded.

"Can you be ready to leave by six this evening?"

"You're cutting it close. The sun will be setting." I said, confused.

"I can be out in daylight. As long as it's weak and I'm completely covered, I can tolerate it for a brief time. We don't have a choice if we're going to be on time."

It was odd to risk his life just to be on time, but Danial was old enough to know his limitations. "I can be ready. But I need to know how many days to pack for. Three? Four?"

"Four." He'd wanted to say five, but he wouldn't push me. Good for him. He was learning more about me all the time.

"Do I pack casual or formal?"

He kissed me quickly and smiled. "Just pack some of your comfortable clothes. I already bought you a few things."

Immediate joy spread through me. How could I not be excited? I hadn't gotten anything new in a long time. It surprised me that he'd have had time to arrange all this. If he'd arranged a gala for all those people, he probably had a coordinator or a personal assistant do it for him.

I checked my watch and saw that it was almost nine. I went to get up, but Danial pulled me back to sprawl next to him. "Where are you running off to?"

He kissed me, long and slow at first, and then more urgently. I tried to push him away, but he just laughed and kissed me again.

"Danial!" I said loudly and with more than a little agitation, "I have to go get ready now that I know we're leaving tonight. I've got so much to accomplish before we leave."

"Yes, you do." He laughed, pulling me against him. "And I know where you can start."

* * * *

I'd donned my costume, a blood red ball gown with black lace edging. The top was a bit loose, so I had to remember not to bend over too far when I greeted someone. I'd come into a vast ballroom, expecting everyone to be dressed like me. But everyone was in normal dressy clothes, suits with shirts, and cocktail dresses. No one was in a costume. I looked desperately for Danial but only saw a sea of unfamiliar faces.

The band started to play, a loud bass beat blaring out of huge speakers. What the hell? I'd expected some violins or something more refined. The lead singer grabbed the mike and screamed, "Let's get this fucking party started!"

I stood still in confusion as everyone around me cheered. The first song started. The lyrics were barely decipherable, something about nothing being free:

Sign upon the dotted line

I'll be yours and you'll be mine
Nothing's free

Danial was suddenly beside me, smiling dangerously, his eyes gleaming. "Dance with me, Sar." It wasn't an invitation; it was a command. I felt a shiver of fear.

I took his hand, and he led me to the dance floor, where other couples already twirled. He moved me expertly around.

"Where's your costume?" I asked. "Why am I the only one in costume?"

"This *is* my costume," he hissed. "And it's time you see who I really am." His voice dropped as he spoke, dissolving into a mocking laugh. He opened his mouth, his fangs dripping blood, his dark eyes dissolving into solid red. I screamed and backed away, but everyone around me had red eyes. I couldn't get away. They just pushed me back at him. Danial drove me to the ground, his teeth in my throat and my blood fountaining up. I tried to close the wound, but my hands slipped in my own blood. I tried to scream again, but I could only gurgle as my vision dimmed.

Chapter Twelve

I woke up with a scream, falling out of the chair I'd been napping in onto the floor. A familiar face grinned down at me.

"Goddamn it, Theo!"

He gave me an innocent look as he helped me up. "You looked so peaceful in that chair, I didn't want to wake you."

"So you thought you'd play me some of The Last Temptation to help me sleep?"

"It's your CD. Aran said he'd never heard Alice Cooper before, so—"

I missed the end of what he said as I looked past Theo's shoulder to see Aran reclining on my couch, the two dogs next to him. All three of them looked at me.

"Some guard dogs you are," I said, shooting them a dark look. Both dogs wagged their tails. Aran scratched Darkness under her chin, and she grinned for him, her eyes closing in pleasure.

"Sorry, Sar," Aran said. He hit the stereo remote and the music stopped.

Had he been the fox who'd brought me the phone? I didn't want to ask. What if he'd run and deserted me instead? That would be embarrassing to call him on.

"We would have had to wake you anyway," Aran continued. "We've got to get on the road. We've got fifty miles to cover tonight. We'll just make it on time if we leave in the next half hour."

Theo anticipated my next question. "Yes, we made provisions for your dogs to come. Cia is going to stay with your cats."

He pronounced the name "See-ah." I wondered if it was a nickname, or a real name. Did they all have odd names? Theopolis sounded vaguely

131

Irish, or maybe Greek.

A short woman walked in from the living room. She was slight, built like a dancer, and dressed as they were in casual clothes. Her eyes were a friendly brown, like melted chocolate and her blond hair was cut in a short bob. She came up to me and shook my hand.

"We've met before," she said shyly.

My eyes widened. "It was you, that night, who—"

"Gave you the phone, yes," she finished. "I only wish I could have done more."

"What you did made all the difference." I gave her a hug impulsively. She tensed, but recovered quickly, and hugged me back. I let her go before I embarrassed us both, and she stepped back. To cover my feeling of self-consciousness, I said to Aran. "Is there anyone else in the living room or kitchen I can't see?"

"No, just us three. Everyone else left with Danial."

"Danial's gone?" I said in surprise and disappointment.

"Don't feel bad, Sarelle," Cia said. "He had to go as soon as he could. There is a lot to prepare. This night is a big deal for him. He needs it to go well."

That sounded ominous and full of hidden meaning. I told myself I could think about that on the way. If I had any more pressure about tonight before leaving, I wouldn't get in the car at all. "Let's put the bags and dogs in the car, and go."

"How many bags do you have?" Theo cracked. "We only have so much room—"

"I have one bag. Stop wisecracking and let's go."

"We'll be fine," Cia said, holding Cavity. "Have a good time."

I didn't hear her; my eyes were focused on my cat. Cia was a werefox, yet the cats seemed to like her. Jess had been twining around her feet and purring this whole time. Both dogs liked Aran, who was also a werefox. Why didn't my animals like Theo? They were more at ease with him, but they were still standoffish.

"Sar, we need to go," Theo said. It was a command, not an effort to coax me along.

I grabbed my one bag. "Let's go, guys."

Both dogs jumped off the couch. We went out the door after Theo, with Aran following us. A Harley was parked next to the black Expedition, a helmet on its seat. Good to see Aran had some taste.

Theo opened the back of the Expedition. Both dogs jumped in on command, lying down as instructed. They were anxious and already panting. I shut the door and got into the front seat. Theo got inside, having put my bag in the back seat.

Aran cranked up the Harley and moved out first. We followed him down the driveway. Turning back, I saw Cia go inside. My house looked so comforting, I longed to get out of the car and go back inside. I could cuddle up with the dogs and watch a movie. Less than a month ago, that kind of evening had summed up my life. So much had changed for me so fast.

Had I been happy? No, I'd been hiding, afraid to face life without Brennan, a world where disaster struck seemingly without purpose or despite prevention. Hiding was easier, but it wasn't living. Tonight was going to be the first of many nights of my new life with Danial.

Aran zoomed off. Theo gunned the engine and followed. We sped through the night. The scenery was mostly farms, though we passed some moderate-sized towns. I didn't recognize any of them, but I'd never been this far to the northeast before.

Theo spun the wheel as Aran swung a hard right. The Expedition hit the curb, the dogs clawing to hold their positions. Theo cursed and swerved back into his lane.

"What was that about?" I snapped. "Don't you know the way home?"

"Did I interrupt your introspective moment?"

"Yeah. My life has changed so much since I met Danial. I'm glad I met him."

He looked at me out of the corner of his eye. "Good for you."

"Have I done something to piss you off in the last few minutes?"

"Sar, just be quiet."

I wanted to snap back at him, but I decided to take his advice and shut up. I was a bundle of nerves. Yelling at him wouldn't help.

We rode in silence for a while, finally coming to a small town called Edgefield. It was decorated for Halloween, unlike most of the towns we'd passed. There were children out with parents, dressed as witches, ghosts, princesses, and pirates. I watched them running around, envying them their youth and candy. I would be wearing a costume myself this evening, maybe I'd get some candy, too.

Theo spoke suddenly. "I'm not pissed at you. I've got a lot on my mind. This party is an annual thing for Danial, the one party that everyone he knows is invited to. Security is always a bitch, especially with the sort that show up. Everyone is in costume, which makes it easy to hide weapons. This year I have two extra things to worry about."

"Well, I'm one," I said mockingly. "What's the other?"

Theo glared at me, showing his teeth. "Don't trivialize this"

He'd had teeth as ordinary as mine, but now his incisors were as long as my finger. Yipe. Thoroughly chastened, I shut up and waited for him to spill it to me.

"The other," he said after a long pause, "is the Ruler of the Vampires for the United States."

The title was said with such reverence and fear that I took his next words very seriously. Something that would scare Theo had to be pretty fucking scary.

"He's come before a few times and always creates a problem. This year it will just be worse." He glanced pointedly at me and then away.

"Because of me? Why would I being there make him act worse?"

"He'll have to meet you as Danial's date. I can exert authority over anyone else, but I can't touch him. He is more powerful than Danial, and as Ruler of a country, his word is law."

"You're worried you can't protect us?" I squeaked out.

"I don't have the power to protect you from him."

His words came out flat. I felt sick and took a deep breath. "Then what's the plan?" I asked shakily.

"Danial will be with you. Don't leave his side for any reason unless I'm with you. I'll be in a position to watch the both of you most of the time. But you can't separate. You'll be safe with him."

"Check. Anything else?"

"You may be required to perform as hostess. Trust Danial. Do whatever he tells you to do. I can't tell you more. Danial's never brought a date to these parties before."

My bad feeling grew. "This sounds like more than a meet and greet,

Theo."

"It's okay, Sar. It'll involve some blood drinking ritual, but it won't hurt you. Danial wouldn't let that happen. Relax."

I thought I might vomit in his lap, but I closed my eyes. Theo gave up on comforting me after he saw how upset I was and drove the rest of the way in silence. Abruptly, he turned down a dirt road that was no more than a break in the underbrush. As we continued down it, the SUV hit a large bump. Theo sped up, now driving on blacktop.

We pulled into a clearing a minute later. Theo drove up to a small well-lit house with a wraparound porch and a rocking chair by the door. When we got out, Ghost and Darkness gratefully raced around to stretch their legs. I grabbed my bag from the back seat and followed Theo onto the porch. He opened the door for me, and I walked in, calling for the dogs. They came in hesitantly, sniffing here and there.

The front door opened to a small rust-colored entryway. I was glad Danial had gotten a few pumpkins. The two chairs were antiques, but comfortable, not the huge, heavy overstuffed ones. A stone bench dominated the room.

Theo cleared his throat and made a point of looking at his watch. I ignored him, taking off my muddy shoes for a quick look around. I'd wondered what kind of place Danial called home, but had imagined something huge and imposing, a place I wouldn't be comfortable in. This home had a lived-in look that said it was more cozy than showcase.

The hallway opened to a small dining room with a table and six chairs. They were delicate but sturdy, the bark of the trees they'd been carved from varnished. A corner hutch contained small woodcarvings instead of china.

The great room had a twenty-foot ceiling and many windows, and it-had been a dark color—

"Sar, we have to get going!" Theo yelled from the entryway.

I jumped and backtracked. "I'm ready. Can I leave the dogs in the great room?"

"Put them wherever; we need to go. Aran will look after them."

He sounded urgent, so I hurried, getting the dogs settled down on their blankets. I reached into my bag and pulled out the red velvet box. Opening it to check that the choker was still inside, I slipped it into my pocket and shoved on my shoes. With a last goodbye to the dogs, I followed Theo back to the Expedition. I gave the house one last look in the mirror as he drove off.

"Is it what you thought it would be?"

"Actually, yes. Danial said he didn't spend much time at home. He wouldn't have a huge house then. But it's much cozier than I expected."

He didn't say anything. I lapsed into silence, my anxiety returning. We drove another twenty minutes, and then pulled into a steep, wide driveway. The Expedition climbed laboriously until we reached the top, entering a well-lit parking lot. There were several cars of all makes and models, and some limos with drivers by them. I saw one huge RV with at least three guards near it. The vampire king's ride?

"Duck down," Theo commanded.

I scooted down in the seat as he drove around to the service entrance. From the size of the building, I imagined we were at a conference center, although I hadn't seen any signs. But I could have missed them in the dark.

He left the engine running, got out, and hustled me towards the door, which opened before we reached it. A woman appeared, dressed in silver. She had long dark hair worn up elaborately, with ringlets cascading down to frame her blue eyes. Her dress was in the style of the early 1860s, with a petticoat and lots of lace. She was beautiful, more than I was.

She noticed my awestruck look and laughed, a low rich sound that made me relax. "Hurry," she said. "The party is going to start in about ten minutes. Most of the guests have arrived and are looking forward to meeting you."

"Can you take her inside, Tatiana? I've got to get ready myself."

"Sure thing, Theo. I'll help her get ready."

Theo went off as Tatiana led me through a maze of corridors. We reached a fair-sized dressing room with a full-length mirror. She sat me in a chair and bustled about, grabbing makeup brushes and hairpins.

"Shouldn't I dress first?" I said in a small voice.

She paused, looked at me, and then burst out laughing. I did, too, nervously.

"You're right. Stand up and take off your clothes."

"All of them?"

"All of them."

I did as she asked. When I stood in front of her with nary a stitch, she looked me over.

"Where's my dress? Shouldn't we be hurrying?"

"I'm going to make you one."

"In ten minutes?"

"More like one." She waved her hand. I was suddenly dressed in a shift. It was light, lacy, and see-through. Hopefully, it was just the first layer.

She held her hands apart, fingers extended, and slowly pushed in just a little with her hands. I felt the shift tighten and conform to my body, the top tightening to push up my breasts and pulling in my waist. She turned behind her and brought out an aquamarine gown from a bag. Next to hers, it was perfect in its simplicity. No hoop skirts or yards of fabric making it difficult for me to move, especially when I was already nervous enough. It had long sleeves, a wide off-the-shoulder neckline, a tucked waist, and full skirt falling to the floor.

When she slipped it over my head, I understood why the girdle was necessary. The heavy cotton gown clung to my body like a second skin. It would have revealed everything I wore beneath. The girdle gave me clean lines.

I admired myself in the mirror. "You're amazing."

"I was kidding about the dress. That takes more than ten minutes of work."

"That's okay, I love it!"

She instructed me to sit down and quickly brushed on some foundation and blush. She darkened my eyebrows and put mascara around my eyes. She added darker eye shadow and a dab of lipstick.

"That's it for the makeup. You're so fair that anymore would be too much," she said, giggling. "We have another minute or so. Let's see what we can do with your hair. Danial wants it left down, but I think we can do a little something more with it."

That was an understatement. I had washed it earlier in the day, but after sleeping in the chair and the ride in the car, it had straightened in spots. Half was curly and half was flat.

Tatiana stood behind me. She put her hands in my hair on either side of my brow, and pulled it up and back. My hair magically lifted, the curl returning. She pulled her fingers all the way down to the ends, and my hair fluffed up the way it had been at the beginning of the night.

"Sorry, but it's not permanent. Hold still." She grabbed some hairspray and gave it a good shellacking. I coughed, but I let her do it. It was better for my hair to be stiff than having it look slept on. Some nights, *au naturale* just wasn't glamorous enough.

"You look lovely." She smiled and put her hand on my shoulder.

"Thank you," I said gratefully. "Can you show me how to do that with my hair? I'd really appreciate it."

I thought she might refuse, but she just said, "Sure. Come back to the club sometime and I'll show you. It's easy to learn."

Then it clicked. I'd heard her name before. "You were there that night," I said, turning from the mirror to look at her, "At the Haunt."

"Yes. I cater events in addition to running that club. I do Danial's Hallows Party every year."

"I knew he had to have help."

I laughed, and she joined in. There was a knock at the door. "Come in," Tatiana called out.

Danial stepped into the room. If I'd thought he was handsome before, I'd been mistaken. He was dressed to match me in a shirt made of a slightly darker shade of teal. It was heavy cotton also, but was cut in a swordsman's style, with ties at the wrists to keep billowing sleeves out of the way of swordplay. Completing the outfit were a pair of black leather pants and a belt of artfully twisted leather. A small gold nugget shone in his left ear. His hair was shockingly different; it had returned to shoulder length. Someone—Tatiana—had done it. It was sultry and windswept, sculptured to set off his beautiful features. I drank in the sight of him and was pleased to see him do the same to me.

"She's ready," Tatiana said. "Good luck to you both out there. I'll check with you throughout the party. Tell me if there is anything that comes up that needs attention."

"Okay," he replied, still looking at me.

She walked out, closing the door behind her.

"You look wonderful," Danial said.

"You look very good yourself."

He smiled back and produced a box from his pocket. "Please wear these."

I opened the velvet box to find a pair of gold nugget stud earrings like the one he was wearing. I put them on and handed him the choker to fasten around my neck. The metal made a soft clink as the ends came together.

"I'll take it off tonight, after the party, if you wish." He ran his hands down my shoulders to enfold me in his arms.

"I trust that you will."

His expression softened and his lips found mine for a second gentle kiss. "Good. We've got to go." He led me out of the room and down a hallway.

"Wait, who are we supposed to be?"

"We're Robin Hood and Maid Marian," he said, his hand resting on a sword at his hip that I suspected was not a prop. The handle was too plain, made functional, something the real Robin of Locksley would have used.

"Didn't Robin Hood use a bow and arrows?"

"He used anything he had to in order to get the job done," Danial said as he hurried me down another corridor. "He was a well-thought-of thief, but I'm better with a sword than a bow any day."

Sweet, but I'd still prefer he had a gun. "Wouldn't it have been easier to play 007? I could have been a Bond girl, and you could have carried all sorts of weapons."

"You're hysterical, Sar. See me laughing?" He rolled his eyes at me. "The idea is to be in costume. I customarily forbid anyone to dress as paid killers."

I gave him an odd look and opened my mouth to reply, but we were suddenly before a pair of doors. I forgot my curiosity as I clutched his arm and pasted a smile on my face. The door opened as if by magic.

There was a sea of faces before us but no one was looking at me. I let out the breath I'd been holding. This wasn't so bad.

"Danial Racklan and his guest, Sarelle," came over the speaker system. Every eye in the place turned to look at the two of us. Danial smiled. I did as well, telling myself to follow his lead.

It was the largest conference room I'd ever been in. There were at least two hundred people, if not more in the vast hall. Exits were along both walls on either side of us. Against the far wall were tables piled with an assortment of food and drink. A long bar ran the length of a portion of one wall to my left with three bartenders. There was loud laughter and joking voices. Either someone played a harp or music was piped in through loudspeakers. The soft sound under the cacophony put me at ease. My courage finally got up off its duff and kicked in. I could do this.

Danial guided me into the closest throng and we were surrounded. He introduced me to the first of his guests, a couple whose names I forgot as soon as they were mentioned. They made small talk about this and that, and then thanked Danial for helping before drifting away.

This interaction was repeated throughout the night by several attendees. Only the manner of job and involvement of the guest varied. Danial was excellent at his job, as the glowing praise attested. The only disturbing thing was how vague some of the guests were about what it was Danial had done for them. *That favor you did me, I appreciate you taking care of it. Let me know if you need anything.* That kind of talk was enough to make my danger signals flare, though I smiled and pretended all was well. There didn't seem to be any supernatural beings there, aside from Danial's guards near every entrance, and that was strange. I filed that away to ask Danial about later.

I looked around several times but didn't see Theo. Danial didn't once let go of my hand, even with only humans around us. The night wore on, and I was starving before long. Finally, we made it all the way across the room to the food. I tried the meat, crackers and cheese, and pasta, leaving the fancier foods alone. Danial didn't eat himself but enjoyed feeding me. I was embarrassed at the way people watched, but I relaxed after the third bite of food, and began having a good time. The large glass of Shiraz helped.

By the time we got to the dessert table, I was stuffed and glad for the girdle. Danial called Tatiana over for a piece of red velvet cake to save for later. When she passed by with it in her hands, I remembered I'd forgotten to compliment her on her good work.

"Thanks again for the dress and for your help getting ready."

"You're welcome. Have a good time." She continued on.

"I love your dress, too. What's that material?"

"Spider webs," she called over her shoulder.

How cool was that? I'd thought the material looked familiar. Maybe she'd make me a dress like that if I asked her.

Danial and I began to make our way back across the room. By that time, I'd become more confident. Another glass of Shiraz helped, coupled with some of the guests leaving. But most of my confidence came from Danial's support.

It felt great to be there on the arm of a handsome man, to be thought of as beautiful. It was better than being a fairytale princess or a woman who'd survived terrible luck to win the jackpot. I felt like I belonged there, because that was how Danial treated me.

As soon as I'd relaxed, Danial encouraged me to speak my views on any subject he and his guests discussed. At first, I was shy, unwilling to say much. But before long, someone raised an issue important to me, and I spoke up, giving my thoughts.

Afterward, I whispered to Danial, "Sorry. I didn't mean to monopolize the conversation back there. But reforestation is important to me."

"Don't apologize," he replied. "I didn't invite you here to be a pretty face who echoed all my answers. I value your opinions, even if I don't always agree with them. Say what you want to. You're my date, not my employee." He gave me a kiss on the cheek. "Come on, we have a lot more people to see."

Our first problem of the night wasn't what I'd expected. A squat little man in a fancy Armani suit came up and thanked Danial. He introduced the young woman on his arm as his wife, but I knew it was a lie. She was a tall, slinky blond with hair as long as mine, although hers was straight and a lot lighter. She was dressed in a flashy sequin belly dancer outfit that outlined her curves. She had on heavy makeup and glitter in her hair. When she slinked over to Danial, her 'husband' became annoyed, but Danial was enticed. He looked at her out of the corner of his eye and smirked. She ignored me completely, and I rolled my eyes. Danial squeezed my hand.

"I want to thank you for what you did for my Arty," she said in a breathy voice.

"You're welcome," Danial said with a charming smile. "Thanks are always appreciated."

Art took this as an excuse to get himself a drink, and Barbie—or whatever her name was—stepped closer to Danial. He gave another squeeze, then let go of my hand. I took a step backward, running into Theo as my temper began to flare.

"Shh," he whispered. "Watch."

"Let me thank you in my own way," Barbie said throatily to Danial, and without preamble, gave him a large open-mouthed kiss.

He took her by the arms and pried her off him, still smiling. "Enough."

"I know what you are," she said, looking into his eyes. "And I'm into it."

"Are you?" he said, and I heard a note of irritation. "How into it?"

She took his question for an invitation and kissed him again. This time, he kissed her back, turning her body so he was facing me, so I could watch him. She was enraptured, but Danial kept his eyes opened to watch me watch him kiss her. He winked at me and suddenly kissed her harder. She recoiled, but he held her to him, still kissing. She frantically pushed at him, and I felt my heart race as I remembered fighting to get free of him when he'd first taken my blood.

He let her go suddenly, and she stumbled back, her eyes full of fear. She put her hand to her mouth and a drop of blood came away. Danial gazed at her with disdain, blood on the edge of his mouth. He rubbed his top lip over the lower one and the blood disappeared. Her eyes narrowed. She stepped toward him, her hand coming up to slap him. He caught it easily, stopping her, still giving her a slight smile.

"Bastard," she hissed. "How dare you—"

"You dared me." I saw a flicker of red in his eyes, which let me know he was very annoyed. He leaned in close to her and said coldly, "Get your lover and leave."

She turned and walked to her date at the bar, and then both hustled out the nearest door. Danial turned back to me and took my hand again.

"What was that all about?" I asked.

"I gave her what she thought she wanted," he said, shooting me a grin. "I was getting thirsty myself."

"There's one every year," Theo grumbled. "I'll head on back."

Danial watched me carefully as Theo walked off. Maybe it happened every year, but he'd done what he had to see how I'd react. I wasn't angry. She'd kissed him, even when he'd made it clear that he didn't want her to. Barbie had known I was his date and hadn't cared. I didn't mind what he'd done under those circumstances.

"Ready to greet more guests?"

I vowed to myself not to kiss him until he'd brushed his teeth. "Lead on."

* * * *

The night wore on. We'd greeted most of the human guests early. Then the dynamic of the crowd changed. There were people other than human among the guests. Most of those we'd talked to had left. At least half, if not most, of the remaining guests were vampires. They watched us from the sides and didn't approach.

They had the same luster to their skin that Danial had and a touch of the same arrogance. Some with the vampires were human, and I felt a chill that several had necklaces like mine. None of them looked unhappy or afraid, just nervous. Terian had been right. All looked to be made of silver and none had jewels. Maybe it was a mark of wealth. I would ask Danial later.

He said goodbye to the last human guest then gave an almost imperceptible nod. The couples came forward one by one, each person bowing slightly to him. None of them spoke to us. The human wearing the choker wasn't always a female with a male vampire. As they came forward, Danial spoke their names to me and mine to them, but I was nervous enough that I remembered only the first two couples.

"Akira and Chi." I wasn't sure which name belonged to whom. They were both Asian and dressed as Samurai or Japanese royalty. I guessed Akira was the male, but they both looked like vampires to me.

"Van and Erik." Those were two men, but neither wore a collar. Both had lustrous skin, dark hair and dark eyes. I didn't know if they gay or brothers. They had on camouflage and belt knives, pretending to be soldiers or hunters.

This went on until all the couples had been introduced. Everyone was polite and respectful, nodding to me after they'd given Danial a slight bow.

A woman hissed softly in pain. Danial and I turned to look. The other vampires turned in unison toward a couple coming through the doors.

"Garrett and Neoline," Danial muttered under his breath. His next words carried. "Nice of you to be on time, Garrett."

A vampire with blue eyes and steel gray hair came to stand before us, an insolent expression on his face. Garrett was dressed as a mountain man. With him was a young blond woman dressed in buckskins. Neoline looked like she'd been treated badly, and I hoped it was just makeup. A deerskin thong about her throat was attached to Garrett's waist. He didn't bow or incline his head; he just looked callously at Danial.

Danial stared down at him, then rolled his eyes. "Do we have to do this again? Last year, you refused to show me respect—until you were on your knees with my sword in your heart. Everyone knows I'm stronger. Just bow and get out."

"I'll not bow to you ever again," Garrett said stonily. "It's you who should bow to me. Fight me and win, but that's the only way I'll acknowledge you as the stronger one."

"I win this year, Garrett, I'll take your life," Danial said harshly. "I'm tired of your insolence."

Garrett snarled. "Let it be to the death then this time."

Danial turned to me and whispered, "Don't worry; this won't take long." He deftly drew his sword from its sheath.

Garrett let go of Neoline and waited with his sword drawn.

A deadly beautiful voice like a tiger's purr rippled across the room. "Enough of this."

Garrett sank to his knees, buckling. He fought all the way down, but in seconds, his forehead pressed against the floor, humbling himself before Danial. The guests watched silently, no one looking surprised. I turned to Danial, then cast my eyes to the door we'd first entered through hours ago. That door had everyone's attention.

A man had shoved them open, and they swung as he walked toward us. He walked like a great cat, with a swagger masking tightly coiled strength ready to unleash in an instant. We all waited, unmoving.

There was no doubt who this was. He had to be the Ruler with a capital R, the unnamed vampire king. He radiated power and strength, and carried himself with absolute authority. But he wasn't what I'd expected. I'd watched too many Dracula movies. I'd expected an older Christopher Lee-type, dressed all in black or a period costume with a long cape. He was nothing like that.

He looked to be about thirty-five, though if he was king, he was likely as old in human years as Danial, if not older. His hair was gold. Not really blond, but a dark rich gold, with none of the brassy shine. It had more of a shimmer. It was shorter than I expected, the loose curls not even reaching his shoulders. He had a slight stubble of that same gold on his face, along with a rakish smile; but I noticed as he came closer that the smile didn't reach his eyes. He wasn't so much handsome as he was rugged, yet there was a grace and sensuality to his features. His eyebrows arched expressively, and his face, while masculine, was more heart-shaped than oval. He was dressed in jeans, a white T-shirt, and a denim jacket, with low-heeled boots.

I did a double take when I saw his eyes. I'd never seen eyes that color before. They were gold as well, lighter than his hair, more metallic. They were so unusual, I found myself staring at him. He took no notice of me, however. He stopped before Danial.

"My apologies, Danial, for being later than I expected."

"Glad you could make it, sir," Danial replied courteously. "We just finished the niceties, so you didn't miss much. You're just in time for the fight."

"How utterly enthralling. Carry on."

"Let him up and I shall."

I couldn't tell if this was a well-rehearsed act and they disliked each other, or if they really got along. Another thing to ask him.

"You should just kill him while you have him at your feet," the vampire king said casually. "Then we could get to what I really came here for—"

"Do I have your permission for that?" Danial said frigidly.

"No," the vampire king said regretfully. "By law, I need to give him a fighting chance."

Garrett was suddenly free, and he bolted to his feet, rushing at Danial with his sword. Danial countered his thrust. Garrett quickly backed up, and the two circled, a second later, clashing again. Steel rang off steel as Danial and Garrett grunted with every powerful thrust and block. I felt a nudge and noticed Theo by my side. He looked anxious, as did the other vampires watching the fight. I snuck a glance at the vampire king. He alone enjoyed it.

Danial was easily the better man with a sword. After a few more parries, he went on the attack. He ran his sword into Garrett's chest with a snarl, the edge going through his back. Garrett dropped his blade, groaning. He sank to his knees as Danial lowered his sword, keeping him on the blade. When Garrett was down, Danial wrenched the blade out. Garrett convulsed, letting out a painful cry. Danial raised his sword again, and with a sweeping motion, separated Garrett's head from his body. Both parts didn't explode into dust or combust into flames. Instead, they lay there oozing blood. I averted my eyes, giving thanks that my dress was still clean.

Danial wiped off his blade on a pocket-handkerchief and resheathed the sword. Tatiana directed her staff in with a cart and bag. They took away Garrett's remains while Tatiana guided Neoline away. The girl went willingly, her eyes unseeing. Her expression hadn't changed since I'd first seen her. What had Garrett done to her while she'd been under his power?

"You know, he'd coated his sword with poison," the vampire king said with relish. "The same poison you had a taste of a few weeks ago."

Danial froze, then turned and faced the Ruler, looking annoyed. "Thank you for warning me."

"You were in no real danger." He sounded jovial. "All your compatriots are about, aren't they? Someone would have saved you, I'm sure—"

"And just who are you supposed to be dressed as?" Danial said mockingly. "A chicken rancher?"

"Hardly. I forgot you don't watch much television. I'm the Devil from Stephen King's *The Stand*."

I knew I'd recognized his getup. He even had a crow feather tucked behind his ear, what Danial had taken for a chicken's feather. I'd picked up enough crow feathers to know the difference.

Danial abruptly squeezed my hand. I looked up to see the vampire king directly in front of me, studying me.

Chapter Thirteen

"Devlin, may I present my lover, Sarelle. Sarelle, this is Devlin Dalcon, Vampire Ruler of the United States—"

"The States, Danial. That was all they were when I first landed on these shores. Introduce me correctly, or allow me to do it myself."

Danial wasn't ruffled by Devlin's sharp tone. "Ruler of the States."

"*Enchante*," Devlin said and kissed my hand. "So this is the woman you have taken up with." He walked around me, examining me like a coyote circling a rabbit. I stayed very still but kept my chin up, unwilling to look scared. "I don't see anything that remarkable about her." His voice was rich but cruel. "Except that she doesn't look as I'd expected." He stopped in front of me. "But that alone is interesting."

Danial didn't reply. The tension was thick, everyone waiting for something to happen. Even the music had ceased. Minutes passed. Devlin didn't move as he studied me with his golden eyes, his expression thoughtful. I stared right back at him, getting annoyed. Had he said I wasn't pretty enough?

"Has she been Oathed to you?"

I felt the first stirrings of real danger in a chill that went down my spine. I bit on the wound in my mouth from the night before. The pain distracted me enough from my fear to keep me still.

"No," Danial said casually. "We met only a—"

"May I taste her then? It's custom."

I started to back away involuntarily, but Danial squeezed my hand. "I'd prefer you not. Sarelle isn't yet used to being tasted," he said slowly. "Though by law, it is your right."

"There is no time like the present for learning," Devlin said with an eager smile. "And I would love to instruct her in this particular art." His eyes flicked from mine to Danial. "Are you going to give me permission?" he taunted.

"You may taste her," Danial said dispassionately. "So long as she gives you her consent."

I licked my lips, the wound throbbing. Devlin took a step closer until there wasn't an inch between us. He gazed down at me through half lidded eyes. Very slowly, the tip of his tongue ran over his upper fangs, and he gave me a rakish grin.

"Will you consent to a little kiss?" he asked mockingly. "Or are you afraid of me?"

I didn't reply, furiously trying to choose what to say. Several questions went through my mind. Was this some sort of test? Would Danial lose face if I refused? Moreover, would refusing Devlin piss him off? Danial had said no one could harm me in any way when I was wearing the choker. No vampire could. What could he do other than kiss me?

"Spineless," Devlin said. He gave me a look of reproval, then moved back as if he might catch something from standing too close. "And a bad hostess to boot."

"I'm not spineless," I grated. "You can't hurt me."

"Yes, that'd be obvious to anyone with intelligence. But as you're still grasping that concept, I'm happy to abstain. I've no wish to sample the flavor of cowardice."

Arrogant prick. "You have my permission for one kiss."

Devlin grinned widely, baring both his upper and lower fangs. "Lovely. Come to me, Sar." He inclined his head. "That is what your friends call you, isn't it?"

Danial inhaled sharply, grasping both my hands. I squeezed his, and he squeezed back. Together, we took a step toward Devlin. He put one hand on my waist and the other on my neck. When he brought his face closer to mine, I closed my eyes as he leaned in and kissed me. He was a good kisser, and if I hadn't been so self-conscious of Danial and everyone watching us, I might have enjoyed it. But the threat in his last words had me trembling, even as I fought to stand still.

He deepened the kiss, opening my mouth with a caress of his

tongue, and when he tasted a hint of blood from my cut, he jerked his head. It was the same move Danial had made last night, though I'd mistaken it for an accident then. Devlin put more force behind his technique, opening the wound deeper, wider. My mouth filled with the taste of blood yet there was no pain. The kiss continued, Devlin's tongue licking my blood as he swallowed, letting out pleasure-filled sounds.

He took his time, but my fear probably stretched thirty seconds into two minutes. Finally, I couldn't stand it and tried to draw back. His hand on my neck tightened, keeping my head from moving. I tasted something sweet but a coppery tang told me it had to be blood. Devlin's blood. The wound in my mouth healed almost instantly. He gave me an extra light peck and drew back. I didn't see any of my blood on his lips, and for that, I was grateful.

"She tastes like summer. I see now why you're so taken with her."

Devlin's eyes were hot with lust as they looked into mine. Before I could say anything, he leaned in fast, pulling me closer. I felt the press of his fangs at my throat. I went utterly still, afraid to move.

"Take care," Danial said evocatively. "You've had your taste, and one's all you're allowed."

Devlin ignored him. "Shall I kiss you again?" he whispered seductively. "I think you want me to."

I felt my face flush. Part of me thought that exact thing.

Devlin sucked gently at my unbroken skin, then pricked me again. "Or do you want me to sink my fangs in instead?"

My heart raced. I forced myself to remain calm, pushing away my desire. "No."

"Bullshit," he said, drawing away so fast I staggered. "You're awash with desire for me. All you're thinking about is me inside you." He raised his brows. "And I don't mean only my fangs."

My mouth fell open, even as I flushed darker.

"Back off," Danial said harshly. "Right now. Or I'll throw you out of this party, Ruler or not."

Devlin produced a card, and with a jaunty smile, slid it between my breasts. "Feel free to call me," he purred. "But don't bother unless you're willing to give me everything I ask for. I'd be delighted to be the first to plunge into your virgin throat—"

150

Danial stepped in front of me, blocking Devlin. "I said now, Dalcon."

Tatiana snatched my hand. "I'll take her to the ladies room if you don't mind. Sarelle seems to have a rip in her dress."

"Yes, take her now," Danial grated, his eyes still on Devlin.

She hustled me away while appearing to walk leisurely. Tears of rage and shame were in my eyes, and as casually as I could, I wiped them away. I did have a rip in my gown, a rather large one in the neckline. I was lucky the gown hadn't fallen down and exposed my undergarments. Devlin had done it as another way to embarrass me.

We entered the bathroom, where Tatiana locked the door. She turned to me with a sympathetic look. "Are you okay? Are you hurt?"

"No." My shock faded, fast replaced by fury. Bad enough to do that to me at all, but in front of everyone...God, what a bastard!

She grabbed Devlin's card out of my cleavage, tossed it in the nearest toilet, and flushed. "But did he drink some of your blood? He looked like he did."

"He opened up a cut. But he healed it, too. With his blood," I added with mounting fury. "It tasted sweet—"

Tatiana made a sour face. "He's not supposed to do that, not without permission."

"Danial gave him permission. I heard him." I wiped a few more tears away in frustration. "And so did I. But I didn't think he'd—"

"Stop crying," Tatiana hissed. "Danial had no choice. He did everything he could to prevent this. You were the one who stupidly gave Dalcon permission. Or do you think your dress ripped on accident?"

She whipped out a needle and thread, and began stitching the tear in clear thread. The edges of the rip were ragged, but there were the smallest remnants of tiny threads.

"You ripped this ahead of time and basted it closed?" I asked. "In case you needed a reason to get me away?"

"Smart girl." She finished her work within a few minutes. "There. That should hold for the rest of the night. We can return now." She held out her hand.

I didn't want to go back out there. I wanted to go home and forget how nasty Devlin had been. Screw him and this party. Everyone else could go to hell, too. Who cared if Danial had tried to protect me. He could have fucking warned me not to give permission for anything.

"Sar, we must return. Come on."

"No. I'm staying in here until that prick leaves."

"Oh, please." She gave me a look. "He'll stay out there until you come out."

"The sun will rise and he'll have to leave. They all will."

"Then he'll come in here before he leaves. You can't hide from him. Yes, he is a prick, but don't think it's personal. He'd feuding with Danial. He's already done all that Danial will stand for tonight, though I wouldn't advise any more discourse with him." She fingered my choker. "You don't have to speak to him or answer when he addresses you. And he can do nothing to you until you tell him he can. Remember that."

Whether the rest was right or not, I couldn't hide in the bathroom all night like a teenage girl at a high school dance. I dusted off my pride and followed her out.

The party was in full swing when we returned. A live band had set up and was playing dance music. Mostly soft rock, but also a little country and older classical music. Couples danced in a variety of ways, while others stood in groups talking. Devlin stood with Danial, both looking irritated.

Devlin nodded to me when I returned. He gave me another sexy grin.

Danial put his arms around me. "Let's dance."

"I'd love to."

When we reached the dance floor, he nodded to the band and the song changed to a slow number. Danial held me close, almost hugging me as he moved us.

"Are you okay?" he murmured into my hair.

"No," I replied.

"Are you hurt?" he asked with concern.

"I was, but he gave me some of his blood to heal the cut."

"Damn him." He inhaled sharply, casting an angry look at Devlin, while stroking my hair. "Forget him and dance with me. The song and the night are almost over."

We danced the rest of the song in silence, then walked back to

Devlin. I braced myself for more of his nastiness.

"Danial, Sarelle, thank you for your hospitality. It was the most pleasurable party I've been to in more than fifty years. But I'm afraid I must leave."

He shook Danial's hand and kissed mine chastely, holding my gaze as he did. I knew better than to recoil from his touch, but I shook slightly with repressed anger.

He bared his fangs in a gleeful smile. "Please forgive my rash words, Sar. I hope to see a good deal more of you, my dear," he said elegantly. "A good evening to you both." He dropped my hand and swaggered off.

I watched him leave, thinking if I never saw him again in my life it would be too soon.

Devlin turned at the door. "Danial, let me know how it goes. Good luck." Then he was gone.

A half hour later, the last guests nodded goodbye and left. I checked the clock. Three a.m. No wonder I was so tired.

"Are you ready to go home?"

"Do your parties always run this late?"

"The annual ones. Human guests arrive at seven p.m. and stay until ten or eleven. Vampires get up about seven and need travel time, so they don't get here until ten or eleven. It is a long night, but it's only once a year." He gave me a half smile. I didn't return it, and his faded. He turned and walked over to Tatiana.

As they spoke, I walked through the double doors. Wandering around for a few moments, I finally found the back entrance. To my relief, Theo was with the car.

"Sar, I think—"

"Save it," I cut him off. "I don't care what you think."

He shut up, and I got into the back seat, curling myself up in a ball.

Danial came out with my clothes. He threw them in the back, got in beside me, and Theo drove off.

I didn't look at Danial, but I felt his eyes on me. Part of me didn't want him to touch me. The other part wanted him to hold me because I was exhausted more than anything else. When he brought me into his lap, I didn't fight him.

Theo dropped us off at Danial's home, and Danial carried me in. He lay me on his bed, turning on a small floor lamp. He left, closing the door.

There was enough light to see that the walls were a dark midnight blue and there were no windows. The ceiling was the most beautiful of all. The entire night sky glowed on the ceiling with all the stars depicted. Seeing the familiar designs of the major constellations and the North Star calmed me.

Danial returned, and I curled into a ball again. He sat next to me, reaching, but I recoiled. His hand stopped for a moment, then suddenly grabbed me and hauled me into his arms. I shrieked and tried to push him away, but he held me close.

"Leave me alone. Don't touch me," I hissed, on the edge of hysteria.

"No," he said calmly. "Tell me what's wrong."

I shrieked, "He sliced me open and insulted me worse than anyone ever has! Everyone acted like it was nothing!"

"I know," he said softly. "I was there."

"How could you let him say those things to me? You gave him permission!"

"I had no choice. We weren't oathed. He knew I didn't want to share you, but he did it because I couldn't stop him. He can taste any human he wants that isn't oathed—"

"You didn't tell me!"

"I told you to beware of other vampires at the party. Theo said he warned you, too. How could you think I'd want you to give permission? I gave you the choker precisely so you'd never have to submit to advances of any kind."

Yes, he had done all of that. I'd been so pissed at Devlin for calling me afraid that I hadn't stopped to think.

"Tell me the truth," he said. "Did you give him permission because you wanted him to kiss you, because you found him attractive?"

I gave him a look of disbelief. "No. I was outraged. How can you ask that?"

"Because seeing him kiss you made me jealous. I'd rather admit that right now, ask you, and hear that it meant nothing than not to speak of it and find out it was what you wanted. That he's what you want."

"I didn't want it or him. What I want is never to see him again. Can that be arranged?"

"Yes," he said in relief. "It can. Now, lie here with me and let me hold you."

I snuggled into him and promptly fell asleep.

* * * *

I opened my eyes, feeling terribly exhausted and disoriented. I looked over in relief to find Danial lying next to me. Then I saw the dress with its tear, and the night flooded back to me. I bolted up and made it into the bathroom just in time to lose my dinner.

The door creaked behind me and Danial said, "Are you okay?"

Even puking my guts out, I still had some pride. "Give me a minute."

I looked like hell. Makeup had run from all the crying I'd done, and then dried that way. Throwing up hadn't helped my complexion. My hair had flattened, and what hadn't had clumped from the hairspray.

I washed my face and hands, then blew my nose. Then I washed my face again. Rechecking, I looked a lot better. At least, the makeup was gone. I couldn't fix anything else until I showered.

"Sar?"

"You can come in."

He was still handsome though exhausted. "I have to sleep longer. You can get up if you like, but you should really sleep, too."

"I have to let out the dogs. They—"

"Aran has already seen to them. I gave him instructions last night. I knew we'd need to rest most of today. Brush your teeth and come back to bed."

There was a knock at the bathroom door. A woman said hesitantly, "Danial?"

"Come in," Danial said with relief.

The door opened, and a plump woman came into the bathroom with an armful of fresh towels. "Here you go, sir," she said cheerily.

"I didn't think you'd be up yet, with the party so late and all," she said, eyeing me. "You should find everything you'll need, Miss."

What I needed was a shower, but with all these people in the bathroom with me, I didn't see that happening. Then I remembered I was a guest and decided not to be rude. Yet. "Thanks."

"This is Mary, my housekeeper. Mary, Sarelle."

"It's good to meet you," she said. "I've heard a lot about you."

"It's good to meet you. Have you seen two large dogs?"

"Aran is out with them. They were up at dawn, and we didn't want them disturbing you. Call me if you need anything." She bustled out, her footsteps retreating.

"I'm sorry for what happened last night," Danial said. "Devlin was out of line. He pushed to the limit of the law by drinking from you, and then crossed it when he gave you his blood. I meant what I said; you won't have to see him again."

"You and Tatiana are making a big deal out of him giving me his blood. More than him taking mine. Explain that to me." He ran his hand through his hair. It was back to shoulder length. "And what happened to your hair? Wasn't it shorter a day ago?"

"Let's take a shower," he said tiredly, "and then we'll talk about it."

I opened my mouth to argue, but decided I wanted a shower more than answers right then. His shower had two showerheads, so there was plenty of room for both of us. The water felt wonderful, and I took my time, though Danial was done in a few minutes. He left, saying he would wait for me in the bedroom. I opened the door a half hour later, wrapped in a warm robe. When I sat on the bed, he began to talk.

"First off, the choker kept you safe, at least from every vampire there except Devlin. Remember the woman I drank from? Anyone at the party was fair game, except those with chokers on. That's a sign that no one is to drink from them or engage them in anything other than conversation. Even that must be initiated by the human. They are off limits." He paused. "Devlin is the absolute Ruler in this country. As such, he can do what he wants, within reason. He can taste anyone he wants at least once, except an oathed human. He wasn't supposed to give you his blood. Blood exchange is forbidden by the collar...choker, except with the vampire who gave the choker in the first place."

Quick save, but not quick enough to cover his slip. Terian had been right. "What's the big deal with the blood? It didn't do anything to me."

"The big deal is that enough blood in a short amount of time will change you. Or kill you."

"So the books and movies are true. Blood exchange is the way vampires are made."

He watched me closely. "Yes and no. Vampires come into being that way, but most of the time, the human dies." He closed his eyes. "I have to laugh when I see all those movies about vampires taking over the world, trying to turn everyone." He opened his eyes and looked at me. "I may have lived a long time, but I have never been able to create another vampire. All my efforts with the blood exchange failed. I finally stopped trying. I couldn't watch another person I loved die."

I didn't feel sorry for him. He'd still lived a long time. "Go on."

"That's why Devlin is Regent, or Ruler, as he prefers to call it. Of all the vampires in America, he is the most powerful one who can pass on vampirism. A vampire cannot be such a Ruler without being able to create new vampires."

"So you can't make me a vampire," I said slowly, feeling both relief and a kind of letdown that made me ashamed enough to blush

"Not without help."

"Help from Devlin," I elaborated.

"You want to become vampire?" he asked with disgust.

Did he think that was what I wanted? Why I was with him? Taken aback, I said, "No."

"I'm sorry for saying that," he said contritely. "I'm touchy about the subject. I get a lot of passes because of what I am, as you saw earlier."

I nodded. "I get that. Please go on"

"My hair was this length when I was turned. It will always return to this length when my body renews itself with blood." He smiled faintly and put his hands behind his head. "I could cut it for you in that style you like, but I'm afraid it doesn't last long. A few days at best."

"Back to the blood," I said, determinedly. "Will I turn into a vampire because of what Devlin did?"

"No, but you might have if I'd drunk from you before he gave you his blood. If I'd taken even a quarter of what I'd taken from you that first time, it might have happened. His blood is very potent."

"What would have happened to me?"

"You would be vampire. Your life as you knew it would be over."

He reached out and grasped my arm, his fingers digging into me, his eyes staring into mine with hopelessness. "We would be over," he said quietly.

"Why? Don't vampires love each other? Is there some law—?"

"If he had turned you last night, he'd have power over your will. He would have laid claim to you, and I wouldn't have been able to stop him. Where he asked you to go, you would go. Whatever he asked you to do, you would do. You saw Garrett. Devlin made him. And even now, a hundred years later, he could bend him to his will."

My stomach flip-flopped, thinking about Devlin having that kind of control over me. I squeaked out, "Why would he bother with me?"

"For the simplest reason of all: because he could. He knows me well, Sar; perhaps too well. Devlin is the vampire who was turned with me that night, all those centuries ago." He paused. "I've never been able to figure out why he has the power to create vampires, and I don't."

His searching tone intrigued me, as did the mention that he was the same age as Devlin. However, that could wait until I'd finished my first list of questions from earlier tonight. "What was Garrett's problem?"

He drew himself up with arrogance, his eyes shining. "You asked me once if I'd killed people. Sometimes I have to, in order to protect myself. And sometimes I have to, to protect my position."

"What position?"

"I rule New York."

Danial was a Ruler, too. I felt a shiver of anticipation. "Then those vampires—"

"—are the ones that make their home in New York. Garrett has been chafing to take my seat from me. He was going to have to die eventually, because he wouldn't give up. Devlin just brought things to a head quicker."

Since he was being so forthright, I decided to press on. "Why is my choker gold with jewels when the others I saw were just silver?"

His expression softened. "I thought you would prefer it a little fancier. Gold brings out the highlights in your hair."

Liking that flattering image, I touched the fox head, stroking it between my thumb and forefinger. "Why did you ask me to come to your party if you knew this might happen?"

"You'd have to meet him, but I could control the time and place. Unfortunately, I couldn't control his actions. Devlin could have asked me to bring you to him for a private meeting, and I would have had to take you. He could also have just shown up at your door some night when I wasn't there. I'd be surprised if he didn't know where you lived. He knows your nickname, and I didn't tell him. I didn't want him to get you alone, or in a position where he could take more blood from you than he did tonight. He authored a good deal of vampire law, so he knows several exploitable loopholes."

I tried not to think of how bad things might have turned out if Devlin had shown up one night Danial wasn't with me. "What is the Oath he spoke of?"

"It's like a marriage between a human and vampire. Take you and I, for example. You pledge to me that you will only be with me sexually and emotionally. You are saying that only I have a right to take your blood, embrace your body, and enjoy your affections."

"I don't understand. Wearing the choker sounds just like that. They're not the same?"

"A human chooses to take the oath and the oath is binding until death," he said flatly. "The unappealing truth is that any vampire can put a collar on any human. He can also take it off whenever he wants. It's a much more casual arrangement. Temporary relationship, temporary protection. Do you understand now? The collar—or choker, as I prefer to call it—is for protection and sex. For the unfortunate, it's a type of slavery. The oath is love, a relationship of equals. It can't be taken by force. It must be given freely."

I detected some inequality there. "But even if someone were to make an Oath to you, you don't give an Oath back?"

"As a general rule, no," he said. "A vampire can't promise to take only one human's blood. The vampire would starve, falling into a coma-like sleep." He paused and smiled. "But for most, being Oathed is viewed as monogamous in all other regards other than blood."

"Who do you...um...?" I had some trouble finding the right words. "Bite" sounded bad.

"Who else is there in my life that I take blood from?" Danial finished for me.

"Yes," I said quickly.

"There are a few women who know what I am. They give me their blood willingly. They like the thrill of being with me. There are a few others I pay. Sometimes I feed from them through that potion that gives me a bit of a person's life force." He didn't sound sure how I would take this information. "I feed from them in their dreams as I act out their fantasies with them." Since I wasn't screaming at him yet, he decided it was okay to go on. "Sometimes, it's like it was last night. I'll be somewhere on business or at a club and a woman will approach me. Sometimes she just wants a kiss. Sometimes more. I give her a kiss or arrange to be with her, and when she begins to kiss me, I—"

"You do that movement," I said.

"Yes, it's the most effective and least painful. I take what I need and heal her. The cut is so small she usually doesn't notice. By the time I stop kissing her, it's healed. The ones who want more than a kiss, I take more blood, enough that they faint. Then I heal them and leave them to think we passed a night together."

"So you really don't...spend the night?"

He laughed. "No, I don't sleep with them. I know several vampires who do, but they're young and newly made." He paused again, introspectively. "It gets old, having sex with the women you take blood from. I won't lie; I did it often in my early days. It seemed exciting and daring in those repressed times. But it turned tiresome, debasing myself trading sex for blood. I have sex only with someone I want to share myself with. Someone who wants to share themselves with me." He pulled me into his arms, and I happily relaxed in his embrace, tucking my head under his chin. "Do you have any more questions?"

"No."

"You only have to ask. I'll always try to be as honest as possible."

I felt guilt crash down on me. I'd bitched at Danial for his lies, but I'd lied to him about Terian.

"What is it?" he asked. "Your scent has changed to one of anxiousness."

I took a deep breath. "I have to tell you something," I said haltingly. "I lied to you, and I can't do it any longer."

His body went rigid. He leaned back to look me in the eye. "About what?"

"I helped Terian escape. I gave him some meat and told him to get gone. He took my SUV. He promised to stay away and to get the car back when he could. I haven't heard from him since."

The silence stretched between us. I felt worse and worse by the moment.

Finally, he said, "Is that everything, Sarelle?"

"Yes. Danial—"

"Stop," he said, putting his palm up. "I've known since it happened."

Chapter Fourteen

I was both relieved he knew and apprehensive about what that meant for us. "How did you know?"

"Theo."

That explained Theo's crappy attitude last night. It hadn't all been nerves about party security.

"Sarelle, werefoxes are animals, and like animals, they don't rely on their eyes to track someone; they rely on their noses. Shoving dirt around didn't cover up your trail. Theo could tell that you were with Terian when he got up and walked to the garage for the car. He also saw you there. My people were at the end of the driveway from the moment I arrived."

"Then why didn't they shoot him when he was staking you?"

"I gave them instructions not to interfere. That was my fight. If I were to fall, they were to kill Terian and make sure you were extracted."

"So you didn't come alone. And Theo wasn't with Alexa."

"I wasn't going to risk your wellbeing on the word of a half-demon, even one I calculated wouldn't be a problem."

"You miscalculated that."

He watched me with a cold expression, his eyes faintly red. "Perhaps honesty is just as unfamiliar to you as nobility is."

I'd been trying to be honest and now we were fighting. "I'm sorry about Terian. I wasn't about to let him kill you, but I couldn't let him get killed for what Alexa did."

"Theo told me your reasons for helping him, but they don't matter."

He suddenly grabbed me by my wrists and yanked me to him. He squeezed tightly.

"Ouch!"

His eyes were burning pools of black where red flames danced. "You are NEVER to do anything like that again. You are not to keep something like that from me! Terian could have killed you out there. I'm not sure why he didn't—"

"He wouldn't."

"Theo saw you come out of the house after helping me inside. He called me when he heard Terian speak. I told him to interfere only if it looked like you were in danger, that you'd probably gone back to make sure that evil thing was dead—"

"He isn't evil."

"Really? He's a half-breed demon, not an angel. What if he reconsiders what you did to save me and comes back while you're alone? Or when you're out walking? He acts on impulse, before he thinks of the consequences."

"So did I the night I saved you."

He bared one fang in a sneer. "Would you rather I hadn't come to save you?" His tone sent a trickle of cold water down my body. He was scarier than Devlin, scarier than Terian's evil tendrils. My sense of danger kicked in as high as it could. Danial controlled himself on the surface, but inside...he was angry enough to kill.

"Answer me, Sar. I thought you needed me that night. I was ready to do whatever I had to in order to save you. Instead, I find out you had your own plan to save the life of a thing that just tried to kill me."

"Why the hell didn't you say something that night? Or the day after?"

"I wanted to see if you would tell me yourself." He loosened his grip on me. "And you did, though you took your time."

"I did what I thought was right. But I did keep it from you, and that wasn't right. I'm sorry. I should have told you the truth."

"I should be the one who apologizes," he said with a sigh, releasing my wrists. "I promised myself I wouldn't lose my temper or scare you if you admitted what you'd done. I'm sorry. My anger comes from my fear of losing you."

"I wanted to tell you, but I couldn't think of a way without you feeling exactly the way you do. I need you to understand that my helping Terian wasn't about you. It had nothing to do with us. I felt it was the right thing to do. I didn't do it to hurt you. If I thought saving him would hurt you, or that he was a threat to you, I wouldn't have done it."

"What matters is that you told me the truth. You saved me from him, both before shooting him and after. I—"

"Don't act like a martyr. I'm not the only one who kept someone in the dark."

"I said I was sorry for that already."

I dropped the steely tone. "I understand you grew up in a time when women didn't have any rights, where you might have made all the decisions without telling your lover anything, but don't try that with me. It's not going to fly."

"No secrets on either side. Agreed?"

"Agreed."

He held out his hand to me. I took it, and he held me close. We lay down on the bed, where he held me, saying nothing. Then he broke the silence. "You should know that it matters a great deal what you said right before you shot him. Even though I was hurt, I was coherent enough to remember those words."

I paused in mid-breath. I waited for him to tip my chin up to look me in the eyes, but he was as hesitant as I was. Neither of us moved.

"Are you in love with me?" he finally asked.

I held him tighter. "Yes. The more time I spend with you, the more I'm falling in love."

He moved back so he could look at me. "Are you afraid to ask the same of me? Even when my answer is obvious from my willingness to ask that question?"

"Are you falling in love with me, Danial?"

"Yes," he said tenderly. "It was infatuation at first, but I admire your strength and courage under fire. Not many women could have done what you have in the last few days." He kissed my forehead. "Get some rest. Tomorrow will be a better day for us."

* * * *

We awakened well after dusk. I felt much better after getting some sleep, especially when I woke in Danial's arms.

When he took my arm to help me get out of bed, I winced. My

wrists revealed slight bruises where Danial had gripped them. They were much lighter than the ones I'd had when he'd first drank my blood, but these hadn't been an accident. And that both scared me and pissed me off. I showed him my wrists so he could see what he'd done.

"Did you mean to do this?"

"I'm sorry, Sarelle," he said remorsefully. "There's no excuse. But believe me, I didn't mean to hurt you."

"If I ask you to let go and you don't, that means you're hurting me."

"It won't happen again, I assure you," he said quietly. "A man doesn't hurt the woman he cares for, for any reason."

We left the bedroom somberly. He switched on the overhead lights, and I finally saw the great room. The walls were a light gray, extending up to a high white ceiling. Two dormers in the outside wall faced the road. They were too high to see out, but I could see the light of the porch to the side of one. There were a lot of windows in the other walls, more than I'd expected from a man who should hate the sun.

I cut my eyes to Danial. "Shouldn't you be igniting?"

"Special glass," he said with a smirk. "Sunlight doesn't penetrate it. And the trees close to the house keep it shady."

A plush tan sectional dominated the room. Danial had gone overboard with seven extra sections. It looked extremely comfortable and inviting. There were a few matching chairs and floor lamps illuminating the edges of the room. Bookshelves along the walls were filled to overflowing. Checking titles, I saw some poetry and thick specialized astronomy books. Otherwise, most of the books had been published in the last twenty years, both fiction and non-fiction paperbacks, not leather-bound first editions or hardbacks.

"Surprised that I read novels?" Danial asked. "Or that I study the stars?"

"No, I know you're intelligent. But I thought you'd have...older books."

He burst out laughing. When he was done, he smiled the first true smile I'd seen in a while, one without sarcasm or double meaning. "Books are a good way to understand the current times. TV is also useful, but it's still new to me. It doesn't substitute for what I feel when I read."

He moved to the wall and selected a book from an upper shelf. "I like mysteries." He handed it to me *Seven*. I'd seen a Brad Pitt movie of the same name, but reading the back cover, I decided it wasn't the same. I handed it back to him, and he handed me another, this one called *Dog is my Copilot*.

"I enjoy true stories, too. I just finished this one."

"I read this. But you don't have any dogs."

"I got it when I met you. I've never had dogs, at least not the same way you do. Dogs were for herding sheep or hunting. They were rarely allowed indoors. I've had cats before, but…not for some time."

There was something he wasn't telling me, but I decided to leave it alone. It sounded like a painful memory. He could gloss it over if he wanted to.

"I like Ghost and Darkness. How long have you had them?"

"About three years. They're like my family—" Speaking of which, I looked around for them, suddenly panicked. With a quick look at Danial, I walked to the entryway to find empty dog beds.

"They're likely outside with Aran or one of the other foxes."

I opened the door and stepped out. "Ghost! Darkness!" When there was no answering bark, I called again.

"They're coming," Danial said.

A moment later, I heard a far-off bark. I called again, and Ghost burst into the yard, followed by Darkness. They raced up to the steps, panting. A small form came running after them, panting hard. It was a fox. It came to the bottom porch steps and bared its teeth to grin at us. Then it took off, racing around the back of the house.

"Who was that? Can you tell?"

"Aran," he said with a wink. "He doesn't like to change in front of anyone. He'll be back when he gets some clothes on."

I was glad he hadn't changed in front of us. Danial asked me if I was hungry.

"Yes. But I didn't see any kitchen here."

"It's off the dining room." He gestured to a door I'd thought was a closet.

I went through it and walked into a small but cozy kitchen. It was yellow with white curtains. Danial watched me as I looked into cabinets

166

and through shelves and checked the refrigerator. I left that for last, unsure what I'd find, wanting to prepare myself. It's one thing to know your lover needs blood to live, but something else to see bags or bottles of it in the refrigerator.

There were only the normal things you'd expect to find in a fridge: milk, eggs, bread, butter, something called polenta, and meat. A lot of meat, actually. An entire ten-pound brisket, whole chickens, black Angus burgers, and four—count 'em four—three-pound packages of bacon. There was more red meat in the freezer, primarily steaks, but also thick-cut bacon. I was about to make a crack over how all that red meat was a healthy diet when I realized a werefox probably needed it.

"This is for your werefoxes?"

"Yes. They like a lot of protein."

"Do they just come in here after their shift to eat? Do they live with you?"

"They have their living quarters elsewhere on the property." He walked back towards the great room, and I followed. "Theo stays over when we're brainstorming a hard case. The room right above mine can be a guestroom when needed. Mostly it's just storage." He gestured to a staircase extending up the wall to the second level. "The other room above the dining room is my office. Would you like to see?"

"Sure."

The guestroom at the top was also gray, with a full-size bed in one corner and a chair in the other. Danial had spoken of storage, but there were no boxes. Then I noticed a few gray plastic containers against one wall. They blended in so well I hadn't seen them at first glance.

"What's in them?"

"They're what are left of my former lives," he said with a touch of sadness.

"Mementos?" I asked delicately.

"Photos and souvenirs of things I saw and did. Memories of people I knew and cared for, long gone."

It struck me with all the strength and sharpness of a slap across the face. Danial would always remain as he was. He wouldn't age but I would. I would grow older and eventually die. Perhaps he would put my sea green dress in one of those boxes someday, to take out and remember me on occasion. Perhaps my necklace would go in there, too. He could take it out and remember how it had set off my hair. I wouldn't need it. I'd be...

He grabbed my hand, and pulled me close to him. "Sar, don't."

I kept looking at those boxes, so innocent and common, the kind many people had for storage. He took my face in his hands and turned my head to look into his eyes. My eyes gravitated back to those boxes.

"Look at me," he said. He turned so his body was in my line of sight, blocking my view of the boxes.

I looked into his eyes. "I am looking at you."

"You're here with me now. We're together. That's all that matters." He kissed me, but I was unresponsive, and he broke it off. He led me to his office. Once I was inside, he closed the door.

I mentally shook myself and looked around. Everything was state of the art. There were two computer stations and two phones. Both desks were piled with folders, papers, pens, and all sorts of Post-It notes. The voice mail lights on both phones were lit.

I found my voice, but it was a bit creaky. "Danial."

"Yes?"

He'd invited me to stay for a few days, but I wasn't sure if I was supposed to amuse myself for some of it. Being the CEO of his own company, he would at least need to be on call. "Should I let you get to work?"

"I'll need about an hour later to work on some pressing matters. Theo will be over then." He led me to the door. "But first, we should go downstairs and get you something to eat."

He led me out of the office and down the stairs. I purposely didn't look in the direction of the boxes, but I felt them there all the same.

"Hello, Danial, Sarelle," Aran said, not smiling.

"Aran," Danial said cordially.

"Did you have a good walk?" I asked, not knowing how else to phrase it.

"We were hunting mice," Aran said, and then gave a slight smile. "They're better than I am, to tell the truth."

I thought about asking him if he'd caught any, but then I'd have to assume he ate them. Ew. "Thanks for watching them."

"We went for a long run."

It must have been a marathon. Both dogs were on their beds, zonked out.

Theo strode in through the front door, slamming it behind him with a bang. He got right to business. "Everything's fine. There are no emergencies so far tonight, but—"

"What about Garrett? Were there any problems?" Danial asked tersely.

"Devlin's people said they would take care of it. They took the body when they left."

"That works out well," he said evenly, but he didn't smile. Neither did Theo.

"What is it?" Aran asked, looking from Theo to Danial. I mimicked him.

"They also took Neoline," Theo said. "Devlin claimed her, and she agreed to go."

I remembered the woman in buckskins. For as much as Devlin was an asshole, maybe he would treat her better. That was a big maybe.

"He'll give her a quick death or transport back to her family, once she gives him what he wants," Danial said. "She'll likely choose death. You know that, Theo. You saw the ghost she's become."

Theo turned on me. "Curious how she got that way, Sarelle? Neoline's family warned her to stay away from Garrett, that he had a reputation for cruelty, that she shouldn't trust him. But Neoline promised herself to him and he made her his slave. He didn't even give her a collar, just tied her hands and dragged her around by that leash."

"If you want to say something, just spit it out."

"It's okay, Theo," Danial said, putting a hand on Theo's shoulder. "She told me about Terian."

"She needs to hear this." Theo turned to face me, still annoyed. "Terian isn't innocent like you think he is. He killed his sister-in-law yesterday, although he covered it up nicely. Another heart attack."

"I'm not surprised. He's capable of it. He thought she'd set him up."

"Yes, he is capable of it. Years ago, he murdered his brother's ex-girlfriend back when they lived together. Terian moved out after that and got his own place. Others connected to him died when he opened that online shop in the late nineties. They all can't be accidents."

"Then why mention them?"

"Because you need to remember that you're dealing with a being you can't treat like a bird with a broken wing. Sure, he's half-human, but that's not the stronger half. He can fight the demon side of him all he wants, but he will never have enough control over himself to rein it to his will."

Remembering Terian's outbursts and how he wrecked my door, I conceded that Theo was probably right. I was weary of the argument. "You can relax," I said tiredly. "I'm not going to help him again, or see him. He can keep the car."

"He's returned your car," Theo said. "Cia said he left it in your garage and walked off down the road."

Stupid Terian. So much for staying away and keeping a low profile. "Then it's finished."

"Maybe. But—"

"No maybes. It's done. You can stay here and talk to Danial about Terian. I'm getting something to eat." I looked over to Danial. "Where's the nearest town?"

"What do you need? There's food in the kitchen."

"What I need," I said, standing up to look at them with my hands on my hips, "is some comfort food. I need pizza. I'm not eating meat or making myself breakfast this late at night. So hand me the keys and clear the way to the door."

Hearing myself and seeing their expression, I almost laughed. I had to laugh or I would start screaming from all the tension. With all the demon and vampire bullshit of the last forty-eight hours, I was frenzied. Being ravenous didn't do anything for my bad mood.

"Sar?" Theo said hesitantly.

"What?" I said, glaring at him.

"There's no pizza place around here."

I was shocked. "How can there be no pizza? I live outside the city, and there's a pizza place within a few minutes."

"There's a Chinese place," Danial said, trying to placate me.

"Where?"

"I'll take her there," Theo said. "You need to answer a call that just came in."

"It can wait."

"No, it can't. Devlin left you a message."

Danial's eyes glanced at me, then at Theo. He turned without a word and went up to his office.

Theo tried to lead me out the door. "C'mon."

I let him think I was going, then hauled back suddenly. He lost my hand, and I ran up the stairs with him hot on my tail. I got to the landing, turned, and burst through the office door. Theo tackled me, and we sprawled on the floor just in time to hear Devlin's voice.

"—per our conversation, you have six months to Oath Sarelle. Your strategy is admirable, but I don't believe you're capable of carrying it to a conclusion. Let me know as soon as something happens. I'll be waiting.

Chapter Fifteen

I pushed Theo off me and climbed to my feet. "Okay, what was all that about?"

"Dalcon is being a jerk," Danial said. He reclined in his chair, looking at me thoughtfully. "You didn't have to be so cryptic about this, Theo. It's no emergency."

"Devlin's a pain in my ass and yours," Theo said. "He's showing too much interest in your affairs of late. You know it has to do with Sarelle."

"That's his misfortune. By law, he can't do anything. He knows that." Danial got to his feet and took my hand. "Let's go."

We went downstairs, got our coats, and headed to the garage, where a fleet of black Expeditions was parked in a row. Danial took the wheel of the nearest one and navigated down the long driveway, where we emerged onto the road and took a right. Within minutes, we arrived at a small town called Alan's Creek and placed our order for dinner—Theo's and mine, that is. Danial told me a little about the town while we waited, but we didn't speak of Devlin's message. I ignored Theo, and he ignored me, checking messages or texting on his cell phone.

On the drive back, I couldn't get my thoughts off Devlin's message. Danial had said it was nothing to worry about, but it still bothered me that Devlin had tried to give Danial a deadline. The underlying threat was obvious; if Danial failed to claim me, then Devlin was going to try his hand at me. King-shit or not, he didn't know what he was in for, trying to bend me to his will.

"We're home."

Theo had opened my door and stood glaring at me. I glared back as I got out.

We went into the dining room. Danial excused himself, saying he'd be back in an hour or so. I thought he was going to work upstairs, but he went to his bedroom and closed the door. Odd, but I was relieved to have time to think about Danial's boxes without him there. The only trouble was Theo.

I ate as fast as I could, then called Cia to check on how she was making out with the cats. She reported that everything was fine.

Hearing her friendly manner gave me the gumption to ask her something that had been bugging me for a few days. "Don't the cats know you're a fox? They don't seem afraid of you."

"You're thinking with your eyes and discounting your nose. It matters more what I smell like than what form I wear. I smell like Cia, not a fox. At first, they were wary, but they relaxed after they saw I wasn't going to hurt them."

I thanked her and said good-bye. After hanging up, I got on my coat and walked outside to sit on the front steps.

It was a nice night, if a little chilly. The stars were shining brightly, as was the moon. The deep forest looked primeval, impenetrable and menacing; like it was waiting for me to look away so it could move closer.

The front door opened, startling me from my dark thoughts. I turned to see Theo.

"Sarelle, I'm sorry about being so nasty to you earlier—"

I focused back on the forest, gritting my teeth. "Apology accepted. Let's leave it at that."

"It wasn't because you helped Terian. I feel like a third wheel, and it's hard for me. Danial's been single since I started working for him. We used to spend a lot of time together. Now he spends most of it with you."

I knew what it felt like to be lonely. "I—"

"I'm happy for you both, especially for Danial. Like you said, let's leave it at that."

"Okay. For the record, you can relax about Terian. He's not coming back."

He nudged me in the back with his foot. When I looked up, disgruntled, he said, "Just because you're done with Terian doesn't mean he's done with you. Come for a walk with me. You can bring the dogs."

I got to my feet. "We'll leave them."

We walked along the drive leading to the road. Snow fell gently, mostly from the wind dislodging it from pine branches. I waited for him to talk, but he was quiet and withdrawn. I thought to ask him about the memory boxes and Danial's former girlfriends but didn't. All my opening lines seemed either jealous or morbid.

"Why did you want me to walk with you?" I finally asked.

"Danial is feeding from another woman through her dreams. It's with her permission and not intimate, but I thought you might not want to be there."

He was suddenly concerned about my feelings? "I don't have a problem with it. We just ate, so it makes sense that he needs to."

"It's easier for him than drinking blood," he said nonchalantly. "What he did last night was more to get that woman to back off than anything else. He wouldn't dare drink yours until at least another day passes to make sure Devlin's blood is out of your system. And he hates wereblood—"

"He told me earlier what Devlin's blood could do to me."

"And about how his own can't change you?" he asked.

"Yes. He said he didn't know why it can't." I paused. "Would Danial be Ruler instead of Devlin, if he had that power?"

"I'm not sure. Danial doesn't have the love of power that Devlin does. He has enough power to rule New York without much opposition, but he doesn't flaunt it like Devlin or other vampires who control a territory. He just settles for being someone most know not to fuck with. For the most part, no one does. If he had the power Devlin does to make vampires, he would be on par with Devlin. There would probably be a clash just because of that."

"I noticed that they seem to be rivals," I said sarcastically.

"They were good friends for many years. At least, that's the way Danial tells it. Although they split up after becoming vampire, they kept in touch through the years. Devlin didn't find out about his ability to make vampires until he was over a century old. Danial had already tried and failed. Devlin wasn't willing to risk his lover. He was sure he would fail. The first time he tried, he succeeded. When he accomplished what Danial couldn't, they had their falling out. They're allies now, but..."

"But no longer friends," I finished for him.

"No. And when one of them has a woman he cares for, the other seems hell bent on breaking them up, one way or another."

I couldn't believe that. "You're saying that Danial would seduce a woman Devlin loved just for the sake of taking her away?"

"He's only done it once, over two hundred years ago. But he started it. Devlin never forgave him and he's been punishing him for it ever since."

No wonder Danial hadn't had a lover in a long time. "That's awful."

Theo stopped walking and faced me. "I tell you this because I want you to be on guard. Devlin will try to seduce you if he can. And what he wants, he usually gets."

I flushed red.

"If you wanted to be with him and not Danial, Danial would have to remove your necklace. So before you're tempted like before, just say no."

That was uncalled for. I was offended. "How can you say that? I'm with Danial—"

"To quote you, 'save it'," he said. "It's my job to keep him safe. I take that seriously. Part of that job now is keeping you safe for him."

"What is it with you two?" I asked irritably, running to catch up as he strode away.

"He's my friend. I was mucking out an existence at the edge of state land, getting shot at by rednecks and eating whatever I could catch. Then the land was sold to developers. Luckily, Danial had contracted with them. It was in the early days of his company, when it was just a one-man operation. Building materials were being stolen. One night when he was doing surveillance, he saw me change. He tracked me down the next night and offered me a job. I took it, and I've been grateful ever since."

That explained his loyalty, at least to some extent. "How long has Danial had his company?"

"I don't know. When I met him, it was already respectable, although it was just him. After he met me and we'd worked together a few years, he told me he wanted the company to grow. I agreed to help. That was ten years ago, and now we're a success."

I couldn't decide what to ask first. Theo's revelation about his past had only opened up more questions. Why had he been scavenging in the wilderness? Had he always been a werefox? Where was his family? But I didn't ask. He was in a good mood and I didn't want him snarling at me again. I had more important things to ask him about.

"If all this effort is being expended to keep me from Devlin, why doesn't Danial just ask me to take the oath now?"

"If you'd have come along with me nicely and not have been an ass, you would have understood that wasn't the case at all."

I did a slow burn, but controlled it well. "Fine Theo. Since I'm so far off the mark, what did that message mean?"

"It meant he wanted to possess you, but he can't just take someone's lover. You have a collar and neither of you want to break that arrangement. The most Dalcon could do is seduce you away. Short of that, he can't do anything. That he gave you his blood when he wasn't supposed to clinches it."

"Clinches what?"

"He wrote the law on chokers, making no one exempt from it, not even the Ruling class. He would be ousted from power if he broke that law again with you. Devlin likes his power too much to give it up. Most of that message was posturing."

"Then why the hell were you so upset about it?"

"You didn't hear the first part," he said quietly. "He said he'd called on Neoline's behalf, to let me know she was dead. It was at her request..." His voice suddenly cracked. Glancing over, I saw him wiping his eyes.

I reached out and touched his shoulder. "I'm sorry."

We stood there for a moment. The snow around us tapered off, making the night darker. We began walking again.

"I liked her a long time ago," he began. "I should be relieved. She wanted to die after Oathing herself to Garrett, but he never gave her the opportunity. Nothing could be done. She'd given him her Oath. She was trapped."

He grabbed my arm, turning me to face him. Snow swirled about us. His gaze was chilling, his eyes no longer blue, but a golden yellow. Animal eyes.

"I'll say this once and only once. If you take the Oath, there is no turning back, no changing your mind. It's not like a marriage. There is no divorce. There's no running away either. You'll be hunted down. Make damn sure it's what you want."

He leaned closer, so close I thought he was going to kiss me. His yellow eyes looked into mine with barely checked rage. I wanted to back up, but didn't dare. He whispered his words just loud enough for me to hear over the rising wind. "Because once you say you're his, he will never let you go."

My mouth fell open. Everything seemed to freeze. I waited for Theo to move, but he remained there. I didn't want to move first.

Think of a comeback quick. "Theo, I appreciate your candor, but—"

"Fuck your appreciation, Sar. And don't ever refer to what I said publicly."

I broke eye contact and looked down. He turned away and strode back to the house. I followed at a distance. Theo left me at the porch without a word.

The dogs were still asleep, but they woke to welcome me home. The familiar act brought me conflicting emotions. I wasn't home; I was in the home of a vampire I didn't even know that well. I thought I loved him and he loved me, but what was I doing? What was I thinking? Was this who I was, the type of person who would take off in the night, ignoring my job, my friends and family, so I could be with an ageless killer who might enslave me?

Overcome, I lay on the floor between the dogs. They snuggled closer with sighs of contentment. Seeing Danial could wait. I just wanted to rest and not have to think about any of this.

* * * *

Some time later, I woke up naked and alone in Danial's bed. There were voices outside the door. I grabbed the quilt, wrapped it around myself, and eased over to the door to see who was there. I looked out the crack, but could only see a part of the great room. No one was in sight.

"Why are you here disturbing us?" It was an innocent question, but the sneer in Danial's voice was unmistakable. "Make it quick—"

"You know why I'm here," said a cool, clear voice dripping with meaning. I knew that voice and feared it. Devlin. "You didn't call, so I

177

stopped by for a visit."

"You gave me six months," Danial said sarcastically. "I hadn't expected that you would show up in twenty-four hours looking for a progress report."

"I'm not here for Sarelle," Devlin said indifferently. "You'd know if I were. I want to know if you've been successful yet."

"Not to my knowledge," he said glumly.

"Do you really believe you can do it?"

"I don't know, Dev. He said it was possible but not probable. That I wasn't you and my blood might not be strong enough to get the job done. I wanted to kill him for being so vague."

Wait a minute! Dev?

"That seems a bit out of character for you," Devlin said solemnly.

Danial laughed. "More like you."

Devlin joined in. "Yes, brother. You were always the nicer one."

That would explain why Danial and Devlin argued and yet were so close. They were brothers but not equal. Devlin had to be older.

Devlin continued. "Knowing that, you're still—?"

"Yes," Danial said hesitantly but hopefully. "I need to try."

"Then good luck. As for your new lady, I'll call you in a month for my 'progress report'," Devlin said, laughing.

"Enough of your jokes. You know if anything happens, I'll let you know."

"I'll be going then. You have places to be and a woman to do." He laughed again, but Danial didn't. This time, Devlin's trailed into silence.

"What about Neoline?" Danial asked gravely.

"What about her?"

"Did she take her own life, or was it by your hand?"

"I offered to end it, but she chose to do it herself. It was quick. She said she wanted peace. She'd endured enough from that bastard. Permitting that kind of treatment wasn't what I intended when I wrote the laws."

"I'll tell Theo," Danial said abruptly. "Thank you for letting her die according to her wishes."

"I'm sorry about Sarelle. About the blood."

"You should be! You would have turned her if I had taken more of her blood." His voice dropped lower, and I heard real killing anger in it. "Don't take Sarelle as a dalliance, brother. I intend to spend the foreseeable future with her."

Devlin issued a rich laugh that would have been beautiful if not for the mocking note in it, making the melodious sound discordant. "I know. That's why I did it." His pleasure rippled, undulating like a snake. "I know how much you always take, just as you know it's my nature to taste anyone you start to love. There was no danger of her turning." His voice turned passionate. "I could taste that it was so. She tasted so good."

Shudder. I was glad I was out of sight.

"I forbid you giving her your blood again. It's against both our wishes and vampire law."

"I won't do it again," Devlin said sincerely. "At least, without an invitation."

"I'll walk you out," Danial said pointedly.

I heard footsteps. With a sigh, I got back into bed and waited for Danial to come back. But he took his time and I fell asleep.

I woke later to find myself in bed with him. We were both naked, spooning.

"Wake up, Sar."

"I'm awake," I said, remembering the conversation I'd overheard.

"I know you overheard us. I'm going to have to teach you better manners. You shouldn't be listening at doors."

"Maybe I wouldn't have to listen at doors if you'd have told me what was going on." I said, turning to glare at him. "Devlin's your brother?"

"Yes, though there have been times when I wished we weren't."

"Why didn't you tell me?" I asked with barely restrained anger.

"What's the difference? Being my brother doesn't excuse him for what he did. He's always been like that, even when we were human. We competed for the woman who later became my wife."

Irked, I began to get up, but he held me tighter. "You'll stay and listen. When was I supposed to tell you? Would it have made it any better for you if you knew he was my brother when he kissed you? Would it have been a good time to tell you when you were upset? Maybe when we were making love?"

"But I'm always the last to know. Do you understand how that makes me feel?"

"You're not the last to know," he said. "No one else knows. Theo suspects, and maybe some others of our respective guards. Most of the vampires we knew in our younger days have long turned to dust. We don't speak of it in public."

"Why not, other than for the obvious reasons?" I said sarcastically.

"Because I have enough people trying to kill me at any given time, I don't need more attention from Devlin's enemies. It's not a blessing to be the brother of the Vampire Ruler of the States, especially one who likes to throw his weight around. I don't want his clout. I just want you," he said, his fangs trailing down my neck with delicate pressure. "Is that enough for you?"

I tried to hold onto my annoyance, but he licked my neck, and I gave in, pulling him closer. He rolled on top of me, resting his weight on his forearms. He pressed himself to me, his lips almost to mine. He froze there, staring at my mouth, then slowly tracked his eyes up to mine.

"Am I enough?" he whispered into my mouth, his eyes so dark and full of wanting.

My heart beat once. "Yes."

I reached one hand up to the back of his neck and entwined my fingers through his hair. It was so soft, like rabbit's fur. He tried to kiss me, but I tightened my fingers and pulled his head back. His eyes widened in surprise. I leaned up, kissing his throat, and whispered against his skin, "For now."

I bit him gently on his throat. His head went back, his eyes closed. I traced down his chest with my mouth, kissing him, but he'd had enough foreplay. He pushed up on his arms, realigning his body against mine, and thrust into me, pinning me to the bed with his weight. He kissed me with abandon, his lips curving against mine, smiling his gratification as he moved himself in and out of me.

Sensations of pleasure built within me. I hugged him to me so I could feel every muscle contract, all moving as one to drive himself as far into me as he could. He moved more quickly, and I could feel the readiness of both our bodies.

He stopped kissing me, even as he moved faster. "Sar?" he rasped, heavy with need.

"Yes."

He kissed me again, deeper this time. With a slight jerk of his head, blood from my wound seasoned our kiss. He'd cut me deeper than he had before, and I was sickened by the taste of my own blood. He swallowed, making soft sighs of satisfaction. That turned me on so much I spasmed around him, jerking in his arms. He held me tightly so my mouth didn't leave his. He came a moment later with a harsh guttural cry.

He continued to kiss and drink from me as he clutched me to him. I had aftershocks, writhing on the bed. I cried out as he hovered above me, holding me, still kissing, still drinking. Too soon, I tasted a bit of his blood, and my mouth began to heal. He gave me only a bit and the wound didn't close completely.

"I loved that," he whispered. "You were wonderful."

"So were you," I said with a satisfied sigh. "That was intense."

We were both tired, and within a few minutes, I fell asleep.

* * * *

I awoke to find Danial still asleep, but I felt rejuvenated.

Remembering our sex, I probed my mouth with my tongue and found it to be mostly healed, though tender. I laid there for a while watching Danial sleep. He looked at peace, an expression he rarely wore when awake. Thinking that prompted me to feel sad. I wouldn't want Devlin for a distant relative, much less my brother.

My eyes traveled around the room and alighted on garment bags hanging from the door hook. Danial had told me last night they contained some he'd purchased for me.

I got up and looked in the first one. There were several pairs of jeans and red long-sleeved T-shirts. They should fit, but I'd need to try on the jeans. I fingered the choker, remembering the ruby eyes he'd put in.

In the second bag were a soft red fleece robe and two long silk shifts, one red and the other black. Those I'd have to try on, too.

I opened the last bag and found underwear. They weren't my usual cotton undergarments, but a black push-up bra with half cups, lace, and ribbons, and a pair of matching sheer panties. There was an identical set in red and another in white. There were also a few pairs of socks. Everything was the right size.

Two more hangers were under the bags. Someone had cleaned our party clothes. The dress was still as beautiful as when I'd worn it, save for it had bad memories. But maybe I'd wear it again.

After a shower, I felt renewed, except for the dull pain in my abdomen. Grumbling to myself, I remembered my period was coming soon. I should be okay for another day yet, long enough to get home. I hadn't seen any female guards and didn't want to get some 'supplies.'

I dried off and decided what to put on. I ended up with the jeans and long-sleeved T, figuring casual was probably best. Maybe we weren't going anywhere tonight either.

I'd come to stay with Danial as a guest and had expected to have sex while I was there. Other than going to the party, and then for Chinese food, all we'd done was sleep and had sex. And argue. Had all the romance already left the building?

Leaving Danial sleeping, I went out to see who else was around. I located my watch and found out it was two in the afternoon. I wandered into the kitchen, where Aran was feeding the dogs pieces of bacon, eating some himself.

"You'll teach them to beg," I said as I went to the fridge.

"They're good dogs," he said. "I'm sharing." They finished the last piece of bacon, and Aran put the pan and dishes in the sink.

I poured myself some cereal. The milk was a trifle out of date but smelled okay. When I poured some chunks in the bowl, I got disgusted.

"Aran," I said politely "Why is there nothing to eat here?"

"What do you mean? There's a lot—"

Time for bluntness. "Can you drive?"

"Sure, but—"

"Are there sufficient guards to keep Danial safe if we leave?"

"Yes, but—"

"No buts. Get your coat."

He followed me, mystified. I made him drive into town and we went grocery shopping. I tried not to buy many perishables, but I craved fruit, dairy, and chocolate. We got some looks as we walked the aisles. Aran might have had on a normal coat and jeans, but his long hair and

182

arrogant bearing made people stare. I thought about asking him to smile more, but I didn't know if that might be worse.

We got apples and bananas, fresh milk and cheese, and crackers and canned soup. Aran lingered over the desserts.

"What's your favorite?" I asked.

"I like pie."

Could he make this any harder by being any vaguer? Breathe. Men were just that way naturally, something I should have remembered. "What kind of pie?"

"Fruit pie."

Deep breaths. "What kind of fruit?"

"Apple is good, pumpkin is better, but key lime is my favorite."

Ah ha. "Go get some extra apples then, about five or six, and some limes, at least four. Pumpkin will have to wait; we only have a few hours."

He looked at me quizzically, and then the light bulb went on. He turned and walked quickly, not saying a word. I called after him, "Get some eggs and butter too."

I went to the baking aisle, got the necessary ingredients and supplies. I knew Danial had mixing bowls in his kitchen, but I hadn't seen anything else when I'd looked through his cabinets.

Aran insisted on paying for the food. "Danial would expect it," he said, as if that explained everything.

"I don't, though."

"You're not taking all this home for you to eat," he elaborated. "And even if you were, he'd probably want to pay for it. He wants you to be comfortable. I know better than to go against his orders."

We drove back to Danial's house, and I set out making the pies. I had just gotten the apples sliced, and Aran was whipping the egg whites, when I heard the front door slam.

"What's all this?" A shadowy figure stood in the door.

Chapter Sixteen

Theo studied the scattered half-done baking. "I said what's all this? There's stuff everywhere."

"She's making pies for us," Aran said happily

Theo quickly stopped bitching and started to help. Soon, we had the apple pie in the oven. The lime pie went in as soon as that came out.

"I'm sorry, guys; we don't have time to do the pumpkin before—"

"Before what?"

Danial stood at the door in his robe, looking very edible. "Before you got up," I said, half apologetically. "I wasn't sure if you'd made plans, and pumpkin pie takes a while to make from scratch."

"I see. Yes, we have plans, I'm afraid."

I turned back to Aran and Theo, who looked a little crestfallen. "It's okay. I'll show you how to cook up the pumpkin and freeze it. Everything else should keep until the next time I come."

"When are you coming back?" Aran asked hopefully. "This weekend?"

He sounded like he was twelve, making me smile.

The silence stretched as everyone awaited my response. I flushed, getting hot. I didn't know what to say. On one hand, I'd enjoyed my visit. This was a beautiful place, but it wasn't my home. On the other hand, I missed my cats and my things. Most of all, I missed the sun on my face. I hadn't realized it until I'd stepped out into it earlier in the afternoon. But it would be cruel to say that in front of Danial. I'd almost said it without thinking.

"When are you thinking of inviting me back?" I asked him, trying to cover up my embarrassment.

He strode over to me and gently touched my face. "I wish you wouldn't leave tomorrow."

Okay, that was too fast. "I'll try to come back next week," I said slowly. "Maybe get here early Monday night and leave on Thursday."

He leaned close and brushed his lips across my cheek. "Sounds good to me."

The timer went off on the oven and we all jumped. I grabbed an oven mitt and pulled the pie out, pleased to see it looked perfect.

"How many did you plan to make?" Danial asked. "I count two."

"Just three; apple and lime are Aran's favorites, next to pumpkin." I turned to Theo and Aran. "You can have the apple now if you like. It's cool enough."

They carried it and two forks into the dining room. I set all the dirty dishes in the dishwasher and got it going. Danial watched me with the warmest look I'd ever seen on his face. Seeing him like that, I believed he loved me. Some looks just can't be faked.

I dried my hands. "Why are you looking at me like that?"

"It's been a long time since I had a woman I loved in my kitchen," he said with effort. "Since I watched a woman I loved bake anything." He came over and held me. "It's been a long time since I saw anyone do something kind without expecting anything back. If I needed another reason to love you, I have it."

He tilted my head up and kissed me. He suddenly lifted me and sat me on the counter.

I broke the kiss, worried that this was his big plan for the night. "Wait."

He tensed, as if bracing himself for something. "What is it?"

"Can we go out?" I asked awkwardly. "I know I'm your guest and I shouldn't be the one suggesting—"

He laughed, his hand going to my cheek. "I'm sorry. No wonder you were uneasy about coming back. We haven't done much except sleep and make love. What would you like to do? Drive somewhere and walk? Movie? Dinner? Shopping?"

Shopping? "Shopping for what?" I asked guardedly. It was too good to be true.

"For whatever you want."

For being four hundred plus, he should know better than to utter those words within hearing distance of a woman. "We can't go shopping," I said. "All the stores are closed."

"It's only the early evening. We should have a few hours yet. There's a mall about twenty minutes from here."

Screw being polite or virtuous, I wasn't going to pass up the opportunity to window shop and try on a few things. It would give me an idea of what Danial liked other than evening gowns.

Then I remembered that he'd already bought me other casual wear. I blushed, feeling greedy when I said, "Sounds good."

"So what would you like to do?"

"Let's do all of them," I said hopefully.

"Okay." He gave me a quick kiss. "Let me get changed."

We headed out alone. Danial said we'd be okay without Theo's company since the mall was so public. I was pleased to have him to myself, even though I refused to think about the last time we'd tried to have a private moment without guards.

I modeled a few sweaters and pants for him. He liked red and black, so I chose those colors, but I also asked him for suggestions. He was honest with his opinions and I appreciated it. I hadn't planned to buy anything, but he told me either I chose a few or he'd tell the saleswoman to wrap them all up. I chose a green sweater and a pair of gray slacks. At my urging, he chose a dark green cotton shirt and a white linen one for himself.

We walked to a nearby seafood restaurant. He ordered wine and actually drank a bit as I ate my shrimp fettuccini.

"I thought you couldn't eat anything?" I whispered. "Can you?"

"I can have a tiny bit. It's better to suffer a little later on than to be noticed."

"I'm sorry," I said, feeling awful. "I didn't think. I should have gotten takeout."

"I'll be fine. I enjoy being out with you." He squeezed my hand. "Go ahead and eat. You need it."

He was right about that. I hadn't noticed how weak I felt until I'd started eating. By the time I was done, I felt normal.

We skipped the movie after dinner. It was late and we'd both had our fill of crowds. Instead, we drove to a secluded park. The weather was cold, and I was glad I'd brought a winter coat. We walked in the frosty night, holding hands as we strolled down a narrow trail leading to a lake. It hadn't frozen yet but there was an edge of ice around the shore. I stepped on some and broke it. I liked the crunch of it breaking. The moon was up, but the clouds obscured it, darkening the night. We walked a little further, and Danial asked if I was cold.

"Yes. But I'm not uncomfortable. Are you? Do you get cold?"

"Yes," he said with a smile. "But it's like your foot falling asleep. It's not as dangerous as it can be for you. It just gets hard to move."

"Are you sure we shouldn't be worried about being out here alone?"

"I have exceptional hearing and I'm armed. But it is getting late, so let's head back."

When we were still some distance from the car, Danial whispered that someone was waiting for us and he would go first. We returned to find a police car sitting next to the Expedition, the engine purring loudly. He rolled down the window as we approached. I clenched Danial's left hand tightly.

"Is there a problem, Officer?" Danial asked.

I shrank behind Danial. The night had been going so well...

"You can't park here after the first week in October," the officer said. "Especially at night. I'll need to see your license and registration, and then you'll have to leave. The park closed a few hours ago."

Danial took out the documents and handed them over. I stayed where I was, waiting for the other shoe to drop.

"Everything seems to be in order." The officer looked curiously at me. "Are you okay?"

"She's just shy," Danial deadpanned. "May we leave now?"

"Yes. Have a good night. I'll follow you as far as the park gates. If you want to come back before Memorial Day, you have to park by the park office, and that's only during daylight hours."

"We understand. Thank you, Officer."

As soon as we were clear of the gates, Danial burst out laughing. "What did you think was going to happen?

"I thought he might be, I don't know, someone who was going to ambush us. I kept waiting for him to pull his gun."

"His heartbeat was too slow. If he'd been lying in wait, he'd have been a lot more nervous."

I squeezed his hand.

As we drove back, the snow came down harder. We managed to make it home with no trouble. By the time we walked in the door, I was exhausted. Soon after, we were asleep, him cradling me in his arms.

* * * *

I was burning. Someone had set me on fire!

The orange and yellow flames licked my body. There was no pain, just an incredible sense of heat. I screamed in terror, and the air I breathed seared my lungs. Steam billowed around me from my burning flesh, cracking, peeling. I screamed repeatedly. I was tied and I couldn't get loose!

"Wake up! Sarelle, wake up!" Danial yelled in panic.

My eyes sprung open. He held me in his arms, his face etched with terror, the sheets tangled around us. "You're okay; it was just a dream. You're safe."

I drew a gasping breath, releasing it in a burst of horror and anguish.

Someone banged on the door. "Danial? Sar?" Theo yelled, impatient and worried. "Everything okay?"

"We're okay. You can come in," Danial said, covering me with the sheet.

Theo burst into the room, a different version of the explosive gun in his hand. At least two men were behind him, guards I didn't know.

"What's wrong? We heard Sarelle screaming."

One of the guards called off what must have been more guards on their way.

"It was a nightmare," I said shakily. "I'm sorry for freaking everybody out."

"As long as you're both okay," Theo said. He turned to his men. "Let's get back outside."

They retreated, shutting the door after them. Danial hugged me close. "What was the nightmare about?"

I started to cry. "I was burning alive. I was tied and couldn't escape—"

"Shh, you're safe. I won't let anything happen to you."

He held me until I stopped crying, then handed me some tissues. When I was myself again, he took me by the shoulders to get me to look at him. "Was this the first nightmare you've had? Have you had any before?"

"Not about burning. The only other nightmare I've had was the night before the party."

I didn't want to tell him that it been about him turning into a monster, but I knew if I didn't tell him, he'd drag it out of me. "It was about you. You ripped out my throat in front of everyone at the Hallows party."

Apparently, he could handle that. He let go of my shoulders and looked inward. "Damn it. I thought this might happen."

"Is something wrong with me?" I asked irrationally. "Am I changing?"

"You're okay; you aren't turning. There are individuals with the power to manipulate dreams. It's possible someone is sending you these nightmares. They're not natural." He held me tighter. "Don't worry. I know someone who can help."

"Could it be Devlin sending them?"

"It could be," he said thoughtfully. "But I doubt it. If he wanted someone to feel like they were burning, he'd just set them on fire."

What a charmer. "Maybe we're overreacting. Maybe it was just a dream."

"Maybe. I'll call a man I know just in case. He can tell us for sure. Get some sleep. I'll be right here."

* * * *

It hit me a few seconds after I awoke that I'd be going home. I turned to Danial still sleeping beside me. It had only been a few days, but I would miss waking up next to him. I reached out and ran my fingers through his hair. He stirred but didn't wake. That simple act gave me a rush of heady pleasure.

Despite all he'd done, all the trouble he'd brought into my life, I knew I was in love with him. He was ruthless; he could be cruel, but he was no serial killer, murdering without provocation. He wasn't the monster Terian had led me to believe.

I watched him for a while, thinking tender thoughts about him. I remembered his words in the kitchen and the look in his eyes as he watched me. His voice had been so hesitant a day ago, when he'd asked me if I loved him. I could easily lose myself for hours just watching him sleep. When he didn't have to be strong, or ready for anything or have all the answers. He could just be relaxed and content and in love.

But I had to leave, and the longer I stayed, the harder it would be. I shook myself and got up.

Mary had taken care of washing my clothes and left them folded on my overnight bag. I packed them and went into the bathroom. After a shower, I dressed in the outfit Danial had bought me last night.

I thought about packing my toiletries but decided to leave them. If I was coming back in a few days, what would be the point? Maybe it would reassure him that I would return. I didn't understand his concern about that. Why wouldn't I come back?

I looked at my face in the mirror for the first time since the party and noticed a difference. My eyes seemed brighter and my complexion was almost radiant. No matter what I thought as I looked in the mirror, there was a smile on my lips, as if I knew a secret no one else did. Being with Danial had changed me. I looked like a woman in love. Yes, I was a walking billboard with flashing lights.

I laughed at myself and went back into the bedroom. Danial opened his eyes and looked at me. He was never groggy, the way I was when I first woke up. He'd shared that his sleep and dreams weren't like mine.

His face broke into a smile. As we had spent more time together, his smiles had become less sarcastic and wry. But when he saw the way I was dressed, he grew grim. "You're dressed already."

"I have to leave. I have work tomorrow."

His eyes were unabashedly sad when they searched mine. "Why are you so eager to leave me?"

I felt a stab of guilt and then a rush of anger. I'd hoped we weren't going to fight when I left, but I'd had an inkling we would. "You know I'm falling for you. I'd like to stay, but—"

"Then stay with me," he said as if that settled it.

I continued more forcefully, "—I need to go home."

"Why? This could be your home."

It sounded so simple, and part of me wanted to give in. But more of me knew this wasn't something I was ready for; not yet, if ever. I missed the sunlight after only a few days. I missed home. It was too soon.

"I'm not ready to move in with you. It's not you; it's me."

"Don't you want to be taken care of?" he asked softly. "Loved?"

I don't know what it cost him to say that, but it cost a lot to hear it. I felt the tears form in my eyes, and my breath tore out of me. But it would be worse in the end if I gave in. I did want to be taken care of. I wanted to be loved. Especially after losing Brennan and being alone. The year after he'd died had felt like fifty. I'd passed happy couples and hated them, remembering what I'd had and lost. I'd felt the ache of missing him and the emotional hole I couldn't fill. I'd tried to fill it with hard work, volunteering, and animal rescue, but even when I exhausted myself, at the end of the day I could still feel the emptiness inside me. I'd erased all trace of Brennan from my life, putting away the pictures and my rings, even his favorite CDs. I thought it would help, but now, standing here in this maelstrom of emotions, I felt just as bad. Just as unsure.

I clamped down on my emotions. Vulnerable or not, I knew who I was. I knew what I could do and what I couldn't. And I couldn't stay with him. I couldn't give up my way of life, not yet.

"I gave you my answer," I said more calmly that I felt. "I'm not saying never. I'm not saying no. I'm just asking for more time to make sure it's the right thing for me. Please understand that."

I left him and went out to the dining room to find Darkness and Ghost. I also found Theo and Aran waiting for me in the kitchen, looking expectantly and more than a little hopefully. I put my bags on the floor by the door. I knew what they wanted. "Let's get started."

In no time, I set them to cutting up two of the smaller pumpkins that I thought might pass for pie pumpkins. Then I showed them how to cook it until it was tender. Aran mashed it and Theo got out the other ingredients, while I made the crust and rolled it out. We only had two pie plates but enough pumpkin for at least four pies. I made extra crust and froze some, showing them how to roll it. We put the two pies in the oven and settled down to wait.

Danial didn't come in during the prep work. I couldn't stand his absence any longer. I told Theo and Aran to watch the pies and went back to the bedroom. He'd showered and was buttoning his shirt when I walked in. He looked as delectable as ever. I stood for a moment watching him. He knew I was there, but he didn't look up.

"I thought you'd left already." He spoke nonchalantly.

"I wouldn't have left without saying goodbye."

He didn't answer. I stepped behind him and held him around the waist, my head against his back. He turned in my arms to hold me as well.

"This is hard for me," he said softly. "I'm not a man who hears no often, especially when it's something I feel strongly about."

I'd have laughed but the pain in his voice was too real. "It's hard for me, too. Don't rush us."

"I won't ask again," he said testily. He tipped my head up to face him. "I tell you now that you're always welcome to stay, but I won't mention it again. When you're ready, you can tell me."

I nodded once. Before I could speak, he kissed me passionately. I instantly melted against him. I had to get going; I had a lot to do before my head hit my pillow at home tonight.

Danial kissed me again, his fingers twining into my hair to pull me closer. Ah, screw it; I had a little time.

* * * *

Danial and I lay on the bed amidst a tangle of sheets. Our discarded clothes lay scattered on the floor. I thought ruefully of my shower and my hair that was only half-dry.

Danial sniffed and said, "What is that smell?"

Shit, something was burning! I grabbed my robe and ran into the kitchen.

The pie was fine, but Aran's hands weren't. They were bright red and smoking. "Didn't you use the oven mitts?" I yelled at him.

Theo ran water over Aran's hands. "The problem isn't that he touched it, but that he didn't want to drop it." He wasn't that upset about the incident. "Grab the other pie; I've got this under control."

I got the other pie out and turned off the oven. It was a little brown, but by no means burned. The problem was the burning flesh smell. I opened a window and turned on the ceiling fan.

"He'll be fine," Danial said from the doorway. "Look for yourself."

As water ran over Aran's hands, the burned skin sloughed off to reveal new skin underneath. Aran grimaced and rubbed his hands together, and I saw the whole mess detach itself and fall into the sink. He washed and dried his hands, then held them up for me to see they were healed. He took the burned skin from the sink and threw it in the garbage. The only evidence that he'd ever been hurt was the lingering smell.

"It's true. We can heal most anything," Theo said.

"Good to know," I said, for lack of anything else to say.

As I left with the dogs, I saw that a snowstorm had dropped six inches of fresh powder. I'd have to plow when I got home. Joy.

Our trip back home seemed to take less time than getting to Danial's house. I chalked it up to how anxious I'd felt on Halloween and how much better I felt with Danial beside me now. We turned into my drive, where I saw that someone had plowed it.

Danial noticed my amazement and said, "I hired one of your neighbors to do it."

I wanted to tell him I didn't need that, but I was grateful. "Thank you."

The dogs were happy to be home and raced around in the snow. It had come down thicker there than at Danial's place. Cia came out to welcome us home. She was happy to see Aran and Theo, but I wasn't sure if it was because she was tired of cat-sitting or she was close to them.

It was good to be home. My wood stove was working faithfully and Jessica was lying on my armchair by the fire. The dogs settled down after I gave them a treat. Danial and Theo waited by the door. It was Theo who spoke.

"We aren't going to leave any guards here tonight. Things aren't hot right now. But I'll be back tomorrow evening with Cia. Danial would like her to stay with you when he's not with you."

I wondered if that was for my peace of mind or his. Either way, I was glad of the company. "Is that okay with her though?"

Danial answered. "She's content to stay."

That meant nothing. I gave an inward sigh, wondering if he'd even bothered to ask her or just told her that she was going to do it. I'd have to ask her myself tomorrow.

Theo glanced at Danial and left with a goodbye over his shoulder to me.

"You'd better get going," I said as I hugged Danial. "You have work to catch up on."

He kissed my forehead. "You're right," he said reluctantly. "Be careful, Sar. And call me every night."

He kissed me a final time. With one last smile, he walked out and closed the door. I watched him walk to the SUV with Theo and waved to him from the window as they drove away.

I sorted my stack of mail. There was a bunch of bills to pay, and letters from my in-laws and a college friend. I didn't see any letters from Terian. Had one come and Cia intercepted it? If so, it was probably just as well.

I got the bare necessities done, ate a bowl of canned soup, and went to bed. For the last few days, I'd been getting up in the late afternoon. Tomorrow morning, five a.m., was going to feel like death.

Chapter Seventeen

Five a.m. was worse than death; it was hell, complete with torture and agony. My eyes felt like sand coated them. I was so nauseous from exhaustion that I almost threw up brushing my teeth. Adding to the fun, I got my period. Oddly, its appearance relieved me. I could believe I was a normal woman. Despite going through a month of unbelievable chaos, I was still on schedule.

I staggered through the employee entrance with only a few seconds to spare. Mark was just ahead of me, clocking in.

"How're you doing?" he said as he punched his timecard. "How was your vacation?" Then he took a good look at me. "You look like shit. What the hell have you been doing?"

I hadn't thought I looked that bad. "I just partied a little too hard."

"Did you have a good time?"

"Sure did."

"That's all that matters then." He swaggered off into the shop.

I went to my office, where there was a huge pile on my desk. There was no way I'd get out of there by five. My boss, Curt, came in to touch base and echoed Mark's sentiments. I repeated my answer. He gave me a concerned look, but that was it. Then he said he needed the blueprints pulled for next week's jobs, all three hundred of them, and I got down to business.

I worked hard to get everything done. At four, I still had a few hours of work left. I called Theo to let him know I'd be working late and told him he could let himself in with Danial's spare key. He said he would before he abruptly ended the call. Jerk. What was his problem?

There wasn't anything I could do about it. I put it out of my mind as I filed blueprints and completed inspection sheets.

By the time it was five, I was alone in the office but not afraid. There were at least five guys still on the shop floor getting in their overtime. At the rate I worked, I'd be done in time to get home before dark.

A noise came from the shadowy cafeteria down the hall. Considering how messy the guys were, I wasn't too concerned. A lot of mice lived off crumbs and discarded food throughout the plant.

I turned to get a folder for a new part. When I turned back, Terian stood before me. I let out shriek and jumped back, crashing into the wall. I managed to catch myself with my hands. The only injury was to my ego.

"How are you, Sarelle?" he said as he extended a hand to straighten me up. He looked much the same as when I'd seen him last, except his hair was cut shorter and layered to fall over his forehead. The back was so short it was almost shaved. There was stubble on his face, although it could have been dirt, and his clothes were filthy. He smiled good-naturedly at me.

I did a double take. "Your eyes are—"

"Contacts. I should have thought of it years ago. And I can regulate my body temperature when I'm calm and concentrate hard."

He'd picked a dark brown color for his eyes, yet a little of the natural red bled through, giving his pupils the look of aged cherry wood. I couldn't believe how much more normal he appeared. He was handsome.

"I look that much better?" he laughed.

Was he trying to flirt? "What are you doing here?"

"Did you get my letters?"

So much for giving Cia the benefit of the doubt. "No. Whatever you wrote to me is probably in Danial's hands right now."

"So he knows I'm alive? Spectacular."

I decided to lay it all on the table. "He knows everything. Theo watched that night I saved you. He saw you take the car—"

"Then they probably know where I'm staying."

He shrugged. I thought he would be more worried, but I had a lot of trouble understanding his reasoning.

"You shouldn't have written to me."

Promise Me

"There were no details in the letters. Just thanks for the car and that I'd been able to locate someone to help me understand my nature."

"What do you mean?"

"I thought I was a dhamphir most of my life. There are no dhamphirs in the United States, maybe not anywhere. I've read several books, but a lot of the information is conflicting. I just managed the best I could most of my life, figuring my eyes and my skin heat were just things I had to live with." He paused. "Danial's insult was the best thing anyone could have said to me. There are more than a few half-demons in this country, and I was able to contact one after I left you. Just the little he's told me so far has made me feel much better. Best of all, I can be around people now without scaring them."

The anger that had always surrounded him was gone, as was the blackness. "I'm happy for you."

"I can learn how to control the evil inside me. I'm already doing it. And I might be able to develop other powers besides strength. This guy out west says he can teach me—"

He was manic—and still holding my hand. I pried it out of his grip. "I have to go."

"Sarelle," he said with confusion, "I thought we were friends."

"You held me prisoner and tried to kill the man I love. I shot you," I said bluntly. "Friends don't do that."

"You saved my life by helping me heal and get away," he blurted. "Friends do that."

I wasn't going to have this conversation with him. "I'm with Danial. I spent the last few days at his house."

"Are you Oathed to him?" he asked coldly.

Like that was any of his business. "No. But he wants me to move in with him. And I may do it. I'm not getting any younger."

I didn't know why I was telling a stranger this. Maybe because I couldn't tell anyone I was close to. It was too much outside the norm for my friends and family. They were all on the far side of normal anyway, leaning toward strange, if not already there.

"Are you going to oath to him?" Terian asked, his eyes searching mine.

"I don't know. Not now. Maybe someday. But all I'm going to do

197

right now is go home."

I gathered my stuff and clocked out. Terian followed me to the parking lot. I unlocked my car and got in, thinking he would take the hint. But he got in the passenger side.

"Do you want me to drop you off somewhere?" I asked pointedly.

"I wanted to talk to you, but there was a werefox at your house with you." He sounded shy, but also perturbed. "Likely, the same one who took my letters."

"For your information, Cia and the guards are there because of you. Danial had a conniption over me saving you after you tried to kill him. I promised him I wouldn't be seeing you again."

"Is that why he hurt you?" he growled as he pushed up my sleeves to reveal the fading bruises on my wrists.

I didn't reply. I just rolled my sleeves back down.

"Sar—"

"Yes. I admitted helping you, but he already knew. He lost his temper and held me a little too hard. He apologized as soon as he saw the bruises and promised it would never happen again."

"Isn't that what abusive boyfriends always say?"

"It isn't like that," I said softly.

"Isn't it? It sounds exactly like that."

"He hasn't threatened to kill me or hurt me like you have," I pointed out, making him look away. "He took bullets for me, cried over me, and fought for me. He took care of me when I was hurt and scared. I'll excuse him an accidental squeeze."

"Sounds like the perfect guy," he said sarcastically.

"And you are? Theo told me you killed Alexa and your brother's girlfriend."

"That's true. My brother's girlfriend came on to me one night several years ago. I turned her down but she persisted. She wanted me because I was supernatural. She said she loved my eyes and heat." His disgust was palpable. "She hung onto me, and I pushed her away when I got angry. She fell and hit her head. My brother found us. He might have forgiven me, but I think he believed I'd done it because of what I was. I moved out after that."

"And how is what Danial did to me any different?"

He ignored my question. "Alexa was a different story. I went after her the night I left here. She'd escaped Theo and was hiding at a local motel. I confronted her and asked if she'd tried to kill me. She admitted that she had, so I killed her."

I didn't care one way or the other. "Please get out."

"I came to see you because you're the only person next to Keriam and the woman who taught me magic who was ever kind to me. Everyone else just looked at me and couldn't get away fast enough. You're different." He reached for my face and I flinched. He took his hand back. "I came to tell you something else."

"Then tell me already; I've got to go." The sun had set. Theo would send someone soon to find out why I was so late. Finding me with Terian wouldn't be good.

"Danial's been trying to buy some unusual stuff from other alchemists. Two have e-mailed me to ask if I could make a particular potion for a large share of the profit. I can, but I'm wondering if I should." He faced me. "I had to be sure it wouldn't hurt you."

Danial had said that Terian ran an online shop selling different spells. I was amazed that there was enough of a market to support him. But the Internet was a big business and people were gullible. Maybe he was good at magic and what he sold worked. How much would people pay for a spell to make themselves handsome or lucky?

"What's the potion? A love spell? An enslavement spell?"

"There are two actually. One is a spell to strengthen virility."

I was shocked. Danial had more virility that anyone I knew. He shouldn't need any help in that department. But he was centuries old, so maybe he did. Or maybe he wanted to impress me by going all night. I cursed his foolish male ego. I could have told him it wasn't necessary. But no man would ask a woman if she thought he needed "help." Even Brennan wouldn't have been so forthcoming.

Just because he'd placed the order didn't mean it was for him. He had several people working for him. One of them might have asked him to order it for them. Even Theo. It didn't make sense, but I'd been around enough men to know that sometimes what they did didn't make sense.

"And the other?"

"The other is to keep warm."

"That's enough to freak you out?"

"It's not the result of those spells that's so troubling. It's the complex nature of them. These are old spells that need blood as an ingredient. The potency one specifically calls for supernatural as well as human blood. Do you understand?"

I gave him a blank look to let him know I didn't.

"There are other spells that would work the same that require no blood and have less prep work. They would also be a fraction of the cost."

I saw what he was getting at. "You're saying he has some reason to want these old spells, and you think it involves me."

"Maybe. He's a monstrous bastard."

I'd finally reached the maximum level of bullshit I was going to take. "There are simple explanations, I'm sure. Danial likely ordered these for someone else. I can't speak for the Viagra spell, but the one to keep warm would be useful for anyone outside in winter. As for his preference for older spells, Danial is old himself. He might trust these more than newer ones. Maybe they don't give the same results." I paused. "Or maybe he got these for himself and me. He knows I have a pretty drafty home."

"If you think it's nothing, I'll make them for him."

I took a deep breath and let out all the tension. "I appreciate you telling me. It means something that you bothered, knowing you might have to expose yourself to Danial. Feel free to make the spells. Or don't, if you don't want to. But stop worrying. No one is going to force me to do anything I'm not ready to do."

I gave him a hug, which he seemed to like a little too much. I told him to leave a message on my cell phone if he wanted to get in touch with me and gave him the number. No one ever checked it but me. I left him standing in the parking lot as I drove away.

The ride home was too short. I dreaded telling Danial about Terian's visit. I had an idea I hadn't shared with Terian of what Danial might want with these potions. He wanted to create vampires. I remembered the conversation he'd had with his brother. *Maybe together, the potions could serve that purpose.* My only question was why he wanted to. Just to know he could?

I pulled into the driveway to find Theo, Cia, and Danial standing in the snow by Danial's Expedition.

What the hell? I put my SUV in the garage and walked up to them. "Why's everyone here?"

"Where have you been?" Danial asked.

"Come inside, and I'll tell you."

As we entered the house and took off out coats, Ghost and Darkness whined for their walk.

"Cia, take care of the dogs. I have to speak to Sar."

I raised my eyebrows. Cia put on her coat back on and left with the dogs.

"Why are you so late?"

I related to him and Theo that Terian had stopped by to say hello. I emphasized that there'd been men working nearby, within hearing distance. I also left out the hug when Danial's eyes went red and Theo swore under his breath. I didn't bring up the question of why Danial would want the potions, just in case they were for him. I expected Danial to be angry, but when I had finished, he looked calm. The red even faded from his eyes. Theo was pissed, though.

"There's no way we can stop that half-breed from dropping in on Sarelle unless we put her under twenty-four-hour guard," Theo said. "But say the word, and it's done."

"Why bother?" I said. "He doesn't want to hurt me. His intentions were just misdirected. And I told him not to come by again."

"Bullshit—"

"I'm beginning to think Sar is right about him," Danial said slowly. "At any rate, she seems able to handle herself with him. Cia will stay with her, but that's the only guard we'll leave here. She already knows to call if Terian is seen around the house or tries to contact her." He came to me and took me in his arms. The feel of him comforted me almost instantly. "I have to go, but I'll come back to stay tomorrow night if that's acceptable."

"You're always welcome here; you don't have to ask." I gave him a sexy look. "You should give me a heads up so I can get some extra sleep the day before."

"Until tomorrow then," he said, kissing my hand.

"Tomorrow," I said, nodding.

I waved goodbye as they drove off, then went out to join Cia and the dogs. I met her coming through the woods and we walked in silence for a while.

"I'm sorry you have to stay with me."

"It's fine," she said in her tiny voice. "I just miss the other foxes."

"Is there someone special?" I asked hesitantly.

"Not really," she said with a sigh. "But it's natural to be with your own kind. Being here reminds me of when I was alone before we joined Danial."

"How did it happen?"

"I can't speak for the others, but I was the only daughter of two werefoxes. They were good parents. They helped me learn how to take care of myself as a fox and a woman." She swallowed hard. "They were murdered one night. A bounty hunter had been after a rampaging werecoyote. He'd killed the coyote, but the scum had given up my parents in an effort to save himself. The bounty hunter thought he'd get a little extra cash and killed them. I came home to see him standing over them with a skinning knife and butcher tools laid out in a row on the floor."

"Why?" I choked out.

"Our pelts are used for various spells and bring a high price. Some creatures consider weremeat a delicacy."

"I'm sorry," I said, sickened.

"I ripped him apart," she said with enmity. "I was arrested for killing him. Theo had met Danial by that time. He found out what had happened to me and arranged for me to be found dead in my cell. With more of his help, a body was found that matched my description exactly."

How clever. With friends like Tatiana, Danial probably could have made someone like Theo appear to be Cia. "And then?"

"I've worked for Danial ever since, doing whatever he asks. And yes, that includes donating blood in an emergency and fighting for him. Mostly, we just guard him when he needs us to."

We kept walking in silence as I digested her words.

"What is it?" she said finally. "You smell curious."

"Foxes aren't very powerful," I said. "I'm surprised he chose you as his bodyguards."

She laughed. "What do you think is appropriately menacing?"

I started laughing myself. "I just meant—"

"I know what you meant." She wiped her eyes. "It's true; foxes aren't as strong as a wolf, but we're good at our job. We don't rely on our werepowers. All of us are trained in light combat and carry weapons with maximum stopping power." She paused. "It might be easier on everyone if we were all like Theo."

"What do you mean? Theo isn't werefox?"

"He's cougar. Or, if you prefer, mountain lion."

Wait a minute. "He told me about how the land where he was scavenging had been sold to developers and—"

"—how Danial saved him? How enough people had seen him and were lining up to get a shot at him? The last mountain lion living in the Northeast?"

"I didn't hear that," I said quietly. "And he never said he was a fox."

"Don't be too hard on him," she said. "I think he didn't tell you everything because he wishes he were a fox. He doesn't like being cougar and won't change if he can help it. He spends a lot of time with us, and I think that makes him happy. Down deep, though, he knows he's not one of us."

"Why doesn't Theo want to be with other cougars the way you want to be with other foxes? Aren't there more like him?"

"Out west there are some, though not many. But it's a moot point. He's committed to serving Danial in return for what Danial did for him."

"You're saying that Danial wouldn't release him? Not even to find a mate?" She looked at me as if I was dense. "Danial told him to go several years ago, when it became apparent that Theo had started to suppress his nature. Theo said no, that he would go when he was ready; not before."

"That sounds cryptic enough to come from him," I remarked. "Let's get inside; I'm freezing."

As we took off our coats and boots, Cia said she would be happy to sleep downstairs if I preferred, or she could curl up in front of the fire. I wanted to see her change into her other form, but I didn't ask her to. She wasn't my plaything to perform for me, so I told her to do whatever made her most comfortable.

She went downstairs. A few minutes later, I heard scratching at the basement door too loud to be a cat. I opened the door and saw her standing on four legs, looking up at me. Her eyes were a golden brown much darker than Theo's. Her coat was a brilliant red-orange, with black socks and a snow-white tipped tail. She stepped out of the cellar stairway and trotted over to the wood stove. She made almost no noise as she walked. I was surprised how delicate and breakable she seemed.

She looked at me and gave a sharp bark.

"What?"

She turned around, looked at herself pointedly, and then back at me expectantly.

"You're gorgeous," I said, smiling.

Cia stuck out her tongue and gave me a fox smile.

I laughed and headed for the door, calling for Ghost and Darkness. I let them out one final time and then turned out the lights. When we came back, Cia was curled up in front of the fire, the cat next to her. The dogs sniffed her curiously, and then continued into the bedroom with me.

"Have a good night," I said.

She put her head down, sliding her tail over her nose. Cavity was already asleep at her side.

I lay in bed awhile, thinking about what Terian had said. Danial seemed to be mellowing out. Maybe I would get my happy ending with him after all.

How naive I was.

Chapter Eighteen

I walked into the kitchen around ten thirty to find Cia dressed and waiting for me.

"Good morning—"

Cavity let out an ear-splitting yowl at my feet.

"Don't let him fool you," Cia said. "I already fed everyone an hour ago."

Ahh, this was nice. I put back the cat food and headed over to my fridge. "Thanks for that."

"Danial will be here after dusk. You need your rest."

I didn't reply, focused instead on the twelve pounds of fresh meat occupying my whole second shelf.

"I hope you don't mind. It tastes better unfrozen."

"I don't. This should work out fine."

I ate quickly, washed the dishes, and let the dogs out. They barked joyfully, rolling in the fresh snow, even eating some. After letting them in, I threw another log on the fire, grateful I didn't have to start one. "Did you have a good night?"

"I love being in front of the wood stove. It reminds me of our home on Danial's land. There's a big fireplace in our common room."

"Where is it? I didn't see it driving in or while I was there."

"You might be more accurate in thinking of it as a barracks. It was an older home Danial converted into a big common room with surrounding bedrooms for each of us. There's only a tiny kitchen converted to a walk-in refrigerator-freezer. We have some nice perks: a Jacuzzi, a gym, and an indoor shooting range."

"I'm sorry you're not able to be there."

"Don't be," she said, catching my mood. "You mean a great deal to

Danial, and he means a lot to us. I'm happy to stay here to keep you safe."

"Are you going to stay the night?"

"Probably not, now that Danial's staying over. But he'll tell me when he gets here."

After I showered and got dressed, she helped me get a load of wood into the basement from the woodpile. We also shoveled the new snow from last night off the deck.

"Should I plow out the drive? I usually don't unless I have to work or there's over five inches."

"Danial's vehicles are all four-wheel drive, so you don't have to bother."

It was a moot point a minute later. My neighbor arrived and cleared the driveway with a few deft movements of his plow truck. I waved to him as I went out to fill my birdfeeders. He waved back and drove off. I walked back on the iced over gravel, reminding myself to thank Danial again later for hiring him.

"Is there anything you need help with?" Cia said abruptly.

There was a lot of stuff I should do, but nothing I felt like doing. "No thanks."

"Then will you teach me how to make pie?"

She was so shy, and yet so eager, I let out a laugh.

She looked up in alarm. When she caught my eye, she laughed herself. "Is that a yes?"

"Sure. What kind do you want to learn to make?"

"The ones you made before, to start with."

"It's Aran, isn't it?" I said softly. "You like him."

She turned red all the way to her ears.

I patted her on the shoulder. "He'll literally be eating out of your hand in no time. Let's get started."

I checked my shelves. "We have most of the ingredients." I shot her a smile. "And we can wing the rest."

She bit her lip in unease. "Won't it come out badly if we do that?"

"No, Grasshopper. Let's get started."

We spent the rest of the morning and most of the early afternoon baking the pies. Cia was a quick study, asking questions and making notes on a piece of paper. Inspired by her willingness to try, I even made an extra pumpkin pie for Theo. Who knew, maybe it would improve his disposition. From what Cia had told me, he didn't have anyone who would make him a pie anytime soon. That struck me as terribly sad. He was the closest thing Danial had to family and I wanted him to be friendly towards me like he'd been in the beginning.

As the pies were cooling, I copied out my recipes for all three pies, and handed them to her.

"Thanks, Sar. I really appreciate this."

"I'm glad to help." I winked at her. "It's the way to a man's heart."

Cia either didn't know the saying or just thought I was being strange because she changed the subject. "You're sure this is all there is to it? I expected it to be harder."

"That's it," I said, drying my hands. "Just follow the recipe and you'll be fine. Familiarity with the utensils is the hardest thing to master. Self-confidence is a close second. And you'll need good bakeware."

"I'm sure I can borrow Danial's—"

"While you can make do with two pie plates and a set of measuring spoons, it's much easier to have a bunch. In fact, I'll give you some of my extra ones."

"Sar, I couldn't—"

"You can and you will," I said firmly. "Come with me."

I went with her to the cellar. Near the old furnace was a rack filled with dusty bakeware, extra dishes, and kitchen gadgets. I gave her a bunch of spoons, some extra bowls, measuring cups, and other things, like a pastry cutter and a few bread pans. "This should get you started."

"Why do you have all this down here instead of in the kitchen?"

I didn't answer her immediately and she stayed silent watching me. Finally, I said, "My husband liked me to bake for him. I baked almost every week. I haven't baked in a long time."

"Since he died."

It wasn't a question, but I nodded anyway.

"I'm sorry, Sar." Her voice was heavy with empathy.

"It's okay." The concern in her eyes was almost more than I could bear. "Let's go upstairs."

When we were back the kitchen, I packed the items up for her.

"Sar, you don't have to—"

"Cia, really, it's okay. I'm okay. It was just hard being down there, looking at that stuff. I haven't done it since Brennan died. But it's time I did. I want you to have all this. It was made to be used, not collected. And I think you'll put it to good use."

She abruptly hugged me. "I will."

I hugged her back, glad she'd reached out to me. "Good. Help me pack. The moon's already up."

We finished packing just in time for Danial and Aran to arrive. Cia went out to greet them, getting Aran's attention right away with the pies she carried. I smiled, thinking new love was a grand thing.

Another man got out of the passenger side of Danial's SUV. Tall and a little heavy, he had a gray beard. Danial wasn't short by any stretch of the imagination, but this guy was taller. They both walked up to the house while Aran helped Cia load up the car with her bakeware.

"Sarelle?" Danial called, shaking off the snow from his boots. The gentleman came in also, closing the door behind him.

I went to meet them. "Hi."

"This is Doctor Stephen Camlyn. Stephen, this is Sarelle."

Stephen nodded hello. "Danial told me of the nightmare you had. There may be some spell on you. I need to check and see. If there's anything of a magical nature, I'll be able to remove it."

"What do I have to do?"

"I'll touch you in specific areas with this," he said, pulling out a metal stick, either silver or stainless steel. Maybe it was supposed to be a wand. "You'll tell me if you feel any pain or weakness. It's pretty simple."

I looked over at Danial. "Right now?"

"Time is of the essence. Did you have another nightmare last night? Cia said she heard you cry out."

"Yes," I said reluctantly.

"What was the nature of the dream?" Stephen asked.

"I was in an old building that was deserted. I walked down long corridors that were quiet, but after a few steps, I thought I heard footsteps behind me. Every time I stopped, they seem to stop, so I couldn't be sure. Every time it was getting closer. The last time I stopped, I finally heard the other footsteps stop directly behind me. I went to run and felt hands cover my mouth. I woke up bathed in sweat."

Danial came to me and put his arms around me. "This is why I said right now. Stephen, what do you think?"

"She most likely has at least two, maybe more, curses on her."

My eyes went wide. "Curses?"

He saw my expression and smiled. "Don't worry; I can get them off. I just need to know what type they are. Lead us into the bedroom so we can begin."

I followed them into my bedroom, glad Danial had a hold of me because my legs were unsteady and I fought not to hyperventilate. A few moments later, I stood naked and flushing while Stephen went through various areas on my body. I felt like a cat that had ticks she couldn't see feeding on her and no way to pull them off. I tried not to squirm.

The procedure took a while. Stephen found four curses in total and removed them all. He would hold his hand over the area where I'd felt pain or weakness and say a phrase in a language I didn't understood. Then he would lift his wand and I would feel something come through my skin. He'd hold the curse in the form of a small swirl of foul-colored smoke. With a few more words, the smoke dissipated, leaving a charred odor in the air. He did it three times.

"Burning, Stalking, and Drowning; pretty basic," Stephen said. "They won't kill you, but they'd make you exhausted, and eventually weaken you to the point where you wouldn't be able to leave your bed."

The fourth curse was different. It rose into his hand from my chest. I felt as if he took my heart out with the curse. Danial had to hold me down while Stephen drew it out. I didn't scream, but it was a near thing. Even looking at it was hard. While the others had been small and transparent, this was a dense oily shadow and had touches of yellow smoke mixed into its blackness. I felt sick that it had been in my body.

"A death curse," Stephen said slowly, rotating it so he could see it better. "You were right to call me." His eyes met Danial's. "Someone placed it on her, most likely the one responsible for putting all of them on."

The smoke continued to move in his hand and the oily substance threatened to spill out of it. I felt like it was reaching for me, wanting to get back inside and finish the job. I shuddered. Danial moved to me, putting his hands on my shoulders. Stephen destroyed it as he had the others. When it was gone, I felt much better.

"Who would want to hurt me?" I asked, shaken.

"Anyone could have put these on you," Stephen said. "They only had to touch your skin. You would have felt weaker right away, but it's possible you might not have noticed."

"You'll be okay now," Danial said softly. "I'm going to step outside and make a call to Devlin. It's his duty as Vampire Ruler to find and punish whoever did this. Will you be okay?"

"Go ahead, call him," I said angrily. "I don't want this happening again."

He nodded and left. As the bedroom door swung closed, I belatedly noticed someone had repaired the frame and lock.

My fury left me and I was suddenly tired. I'd felt that way a lot in the past few weeks, and more and more frequently as we handled one crisis on top of another. Either I needed to reconcile myself to handling these things in stride or I should tell Danial that it was over between us. There wasn't another course.

A sudden chill made me shiver. Stephen had opened the window to let out the charred odor from the destroyed curses. I began to put my clothes on, but he stopped me.

"Wait. I want to check you over and take some blood, if you don't mind. In addition to my mystical healing skills, I'm a regular doctor. I spend a lot more of my time seeing patients with normal illnesses and injuries. And Danial asked me to make sure that you're completely healthy before I leave today."

"Why? I had a physical this past May—"

"You're human and Danial isn't. You're intimate with him. I want to check your blood levels to make sure he's not taking too much, and that your body is physically able to handle losing it. Not to mention that the death curse might have begun its work."

I started to voice my protest, but he held up his hand. "Let me finish. I removed the curse and it can't hurt you anymore. But its purpose was to weaken various systems in your body so they all began to fail. Eventually, you'd die. By the time you started feeling it, it would already

210

be too late."

"I'm having my period right now."

"That isn't a problem. I'm not going to perform a pelvic exam. Just lie back on the bed and relax. Tell me if there's any pain."

I did as he asked to the best of my ability. As he said a few words, my skin began to glow and tingle. I was glad he didn't use his wand, or whatever it was, because that would be too much like something out of Harry Potter and the Vampire's Curse.

"Do I have to believe in this for it to work?"

"No. Lie still."

I laid there, my body faintly shining. Stephen looked me over carefully and said another word. The light dimmed and went out.

"Your systems seem to be fine," he said, relieved. "You're weaker than you should be, but you'll rebound with rest and good food. Don't skip any meals, and make sure to eat plenty of protein."

He again said a few words, then held his hand over my abdomen and moved lower. I felt warmth and a little pressure but no pain.

"You're fine inside. Get dressed; you're all set." He moved back from me, the pressure and warmth ceasing.

I got dressed quickly. By the time I'd finished, he was ready with a few needles.

"Make a fist with your left hand."

I extended my arm to him. "Couldn't you do this as easily as waving your wand?"

He chuckled. "It's better if I see your blood cells under a microscope. I'll call you in a few days or so to let you know the results."

"Will you let Danial know as well?"

"I respect patient-client confidentiality in my practice. But I'll let him know if you want me to."

It was good to have a doctor who cut to the chase. "You have my permission to let him know all the results, so long as I'm notified of them first."

Stephen nodded and put the vials in his bag. "I can certainly do that. Be aware that vampire hearing is acute. Danial is likely aware of all that was discussed today, even not being in the room. But as you wanted him with you during the exam, I didn't mention it until now."

"That's not a problem," I said easily. "I just want to know any lab results first."

"That can be done. I'll call Danial in a few days with the results and ask for you, if that's all right."

"Yes."

When we walked out of the bedroom, Danial was sitting in a chair by the window, looking out at the snow-covered field, the phone at his ear. He nodded to Stephen.

Aran and Cia headed out a few moments later with Stephen. I hoped to get to hear about Aran's reaction to the pies, but she'd be back tomorrow. I'd ask her then.

Danial was still on the phone when I returned to the house, although he wasn't talking. He just looked pissed off. He held up a finger, asking me to give him a moment.

I nodded, went into my bedroom, and drew a bath. I used the expensive bath oil I saved for special occasions. If there was ever a reason to indulge, being saved from a curse had to be close to number one.

Danial strode in, glowering. He tossed the cell phone across the room. It bounced against the wall but didn't break, and landed on the bed. "I can't get through to Devlin. His man said he's busy."

"Did you leave a message?" I asked tentatively.

"Yes," he said with anger. "But this is important. You could have died. You would have died if I hadn't been paranoid or you hadn't told me about the dreams."

"Thank you for that." I stepped closer and put my arms around him. "I thought you were overreacting. If you hadn't pushed so hard and brought the doctor, I'd still be cursed."

The red tint vanished from his eyes to be replaced with tenderness. "I'll always do my best to protect you. But I'm keeping you from your bath."

"Will you join me?" I took my clothes off and posed suggestively. "Well?"

"Not tonight. You're weak and should rest. But I'll keep you company, if you want."

I got into the tub quickly, thinking I'd been rejected and telling myself that was a stupid thing to feel.

I saw it a tiny black dot in the water. I reached just as it began to sink and scooped it up with my hand. It took a few careful tries, but I finally got it.

"What are you doing?" Danial asked, looking at me quizzically.

"Watch," I said softly.

I emptied my hand by spreading my fingers. Water spilled back into the tub and I could see the dot resting on my palm.

"What is that, sand?" He crouched down by the tub. "A dead bug? Do you want me to throw it away?"

The dot lay unmoving, but I knew it would come back to life if I just gave it a chance. "No, it's a spider. And he's alive."

"He's not moving. He must be dead by now. Here, hand it to me." He moved to take it from me.

I put my free hand on his arm. "No, he's alive. Give him a chance." Suddenly, the tiny ball sprouted eight arms and a tiny head. He tried to crawl forward, but he was waterlogged. I put him carefully on the edge of the tile beyond the rim of the tub and made sure he was crawling in the right direction. I felt a sudden and profound joy to see him alive and moving.

"See?" I said.

Danial didn't reply. There was such shock on his face, I dropped my eyes.

"You were right," he whispered.

I knew what I'd done wasn't usual behavior for someone finding a spider in the bathwater. I waited for him to make some comment about so many spiders in the world and they died all the time, so why bother saving one? But he stayed silent.

I turned red and tried to explain myself. "I've had to save him before when I bathe. He has a web in the corner, but he wanders out of it every so often. Sometimes he falls back in the water unless I get him going in the right direction—"

"Why did you save him?"

"Because I can't sit here and watch something die without trying to help," I said simply. "Plus, I've been told its bad luck."

"Why not just move him somewhere else? Outdoors?"

"He lives here," I said, embarrassed again. "It's not for me to move him. He might not be able to survive where I relocate him."

"Why do you save him over and over?"

"Because I can't let him die when it's within my power to help him."

Only my immediate family and Brennan had ever seen this odd side of me and I felt awkward for sharing it with Danial. I began to speak quickly, trying to make light of what I'd done. "I know he's just a spider. Not many people would bother to scoop him out the first time; or if they did, they'd toss him in the garbage, not caring that he might still be alive." I gave a half laugh. "You probably think I'm a little crazy."

"I don't think you're crazy."

His voice cracked a little. I looked into his eyes, expecting to find amusement or uncertainty, but all I saw was his love for me. I looked away. It was too raw.

He abruptly tilted my head so I was looking at him again. "Don't be afraid to share things like this with me. Your compassion is something I love about you. It's why you helped me that night you found me unconscious. Why you concealed me and risked your life to bring me back from the edge of death. And why you shot Terian when he was trying to kill me."

"I couldn't let you die, not if I could save you."

He brushed his eyes with the back of his hand, then moved from his crouch to kneel on one knee. He took my hand in his, and I looked at him, suddenly uneasy.

"Sarelle, you know by now that I'm in love with you. I know you aren't ready to move in with me. I'm not asking you to, not until there comes a time that you want to, or you're ready." He paused, steeling himself for something. "I told you that I no longer have sex with the women I sustain myself with. But that wasn't entirely the whole story. I haven't been physically intimate with any woman for a long time. It seemed pointless. Any woman who found out what I was...well, they only wanted me just to live out a fantasy. Or they wanted to be vampire. Once they found out I had no power to make them that, they said what they had to go through to be with me wasn't worth it."

His voice was rough with how much that had hurt. I reached out to

214

him, covering his hand with mine. "That's not true. You are worth it."

"You are so different, Sar. You want me for me, for the man I am. And you've done a lot, accepted a lot, to try to make it work between us."

My view of Danial blurred from the tears in my eyes. "I want us to be together."

"I want that, too. Because of all you are, all that you feel, all you make me believe is possible again." He kissed my hand gently. "I want you to Oath to me. I want your word you'll be with me and no one else. Not for the rest of your life."

Chapter Nineteen

I swallowed hard, my eyes still locked with Danial's as my brain worked overtime. I wasn't ready to move in with him, let alone give him my word that I'd be his for the rest of my life.

"Sar?"

Time to wing it. "I told you about how Brennan died, but I glossed over how my life fell apart. I was getting by when I met you—"

"I was getting by, too. After spending time with you, I remembered what it was like to care for someone. It wasn't enough anymore to get by. I wanted to live again." He kissed my hand. "We could have a good life together."

I took a deep breath. "I do want to share your life, no question about it. I'll consider giving you my promise, but it won't be for a while; not until we've spent more time together."

He cleared his throat. "That's what I'd hoped you'd say. If you didn't want more than what we have now, I needed to know. I didn't want to get hurt hoping for something that was never going to happen."

I squeezed his hand. "I do want more, but I can't rush into this."

"I'm not asking you to. Forget Devlin's posturing. I want your word only when you're ready to give it. Take as much time as you need to know that it's...that I'm what you want. I can wait." He got to his feet. "Come out when you're ready. I'll wait for you in the living room."

"You're leaving?" I said, confused. "Why?"

"Because you've said you'll consider being my Oathed One. You need time to relax, and also recuperate," he said with a smoky look. "I either leave now to respect the latter or stay to celebrate the former. Loving you, the choice is easy."

He strode out, leaving me surprised and very touched.

* * * *

Later, we watched a sci-fi movie with poor acting and terrible dialogue about a mutant fish that could come out of water and attack on land. We had a great time laughing and pointing at the bad special effects.

"Did she really just say what I thought she said?"

"That they'd be safer in the water."

As the credits rolled, Danial leaned back and sighed. "That was the worst movie I've ever seen. I think a few brain cells died in the watching."

I nuzzled him. "At least your cells will regenerate. Mine will stay dead."

I meant it as a joke, but the silence stretched between us.

"I didn't mean it the way it sounded."

"I know you didn't," he said softly.

I tried to gloss over the awkwardness. "Let's go to bed."

He helped me to my feet. "I'll be downstairs. Join me when you're ready."

I let out the dogs, stoked the fire, and turned off the lights. After slipping into a silky nightgown and brushing my hair, I ventured downstairs. Danial slipped his arm around me as I curled up next to him.

"We need to get some blackout curtains for your bedroom. I'll purchase some next week."

"Good idea." It would be nice to wake up with him beside me in my own bed. Before I could think anything else, I was asleep.

* * * *

I woke up early the next morning, gave Danial a kiss while he slept, and went upstairs.

After eating, I checked the weather channel. Heavy snow was the forecast for the middle of the week, which was normal weather for the first week of November. Another month and it would be Christmas. I would be spending it with a man I loved again. I remembered my last Christmas. My family had been there for me, but all their attention only

217

made it harder when I returned to an empty house. I'd started to put up my tree, but had taken it down. I hadn't been willing to go through the farce of trying to celebrate. I'd ended the night crying, thinking about Brennan.

It was at that moment when I finally let the last of my grief go. I'd always cherish his memory, but I had another man who loved me now, someone I loved. And that was okay, because I'd been right when I'd told myself it was time to move on.

I was able to rejoin Danial in bed by mid-afternoon. We slept until he woke at dark, saying that he'd heard tires. We both got dressed and went to the door.

"Be safe, okay? Call me every night."

He kissed me goodbye before he walked to the waiting Expedition. He turned back when he reached it. As he waved, I committed his image to memory: his glossy hair with a slight curl, dark eyes now a little sad, and the line of his jaw strong and graceful, as if an artist had brought him to life with brushstrokes.

Then he suddenly turned and ran back to me, looking sheepish. "I forgot to confirm that you were coming to stay again this week. Tuesday night?"

"I'll be there about seven," I said with a smile.

He gave me a quick kiss and jogged back. A few moments later, he was gone.

The rest of Sunday passed uneventfully. I worked hard stacking wood and baking pies—banana cream this time—for Theo and Company. Right after dinner, I gave up on the chore list and went to bed early.

After work on Monday, I stopped by Flora's to check on her. As always, she was glad to see me. She brought me into her kitchen, telling me to sit down as she settled her twig-like frame into the opposite chair. "Tell me all about him."

I blushed. "How did you know?"

She took my hand in her wrinkled, frail one. "Because you look happy the way you haven't in a long time. Now tell me everything."

I told her about Danial, leaving out the paranormal aspects. "He makes me happy. But I'm worried about moving too fast."

"You said he proposed. Men don't do that unless they're sure they're in love."

"I want to believe that."

"Then why don't you? He's not out to get your money." She chuckled.

I gritted my teeth a little. "I know that. I'm not ready to get married, or to live with him."

"Aren't you? If you're missing him after being apart only a day, I'd say you were. And it's obvious you love him."

"What about my job? I can't commute that far."

"That's not a reason to refuse him."

"What about my house? I don't want to give that up." Even if Danial wanted to live with me, it was impractical. Where would the guards live? A dozen foxes roaming around the property would be noticed, to say nothing of a huge cougar. "It's too soon."

"I'm going to tell you something," she said sharply. "I've never told anyone this, so pay attention. I loved my husbands, both of them. But neither of them was the love of my life."

"Who was?"

"A man I met when I was recently divorced. He showered me with presents and asked me to elope after knowing me a few months. I said no, because I felt it was too soon."

"Why didn't you go?"

"He was married. That wasn't done in those days. He left her shortly after that. She remarried a year later."

I was hanging on every word, incredulous that I'd known Flora for ten years and had never heard any of this. "What happened? Did he write? Did you go to him?"

"I never heard from him again," she said sadly. "I don't know what happened to him. But I always regretted not taking the opportunity."

"Maybe that was better. You got remarried, had a son, and lived a great life. You've done everything you set your mind to—"

"Not everything. Maybe not the most important thing. That's my point. Many people go into and out of your life, but only a handful stay. Make sure you have no regrets about the ones that disappear. Make damn sure."

Tara Fox Hall

I still pondered her words as I walked the dogs later that night. Maybe she was right. Times were tough, but I was a hard worker. I could probably get a job closer to Danial's place. Or I could help him with his business. From the state of his office, he and Theo could use a little help.

By the time I'd arrived home, I'd decided to throw caution to the wind and see Danial. I'd tell him how I felt and let him help me figure out what to do.

* * * *

Finding Danial's house was harder than I'd expected. I could only remember that Alan was part of the name of the town nearest to Danial's house, but not how it had been spelled. When I searched on MapQuest, that information wasn't enough. I tried looking up Racklan, Allantown, and Alanville on the Internet, but got nothing. I almost called Danial and asked him to send a car and driver, then didn't. I wanted to make it to Danial's by myself. I tried cross-referencing various Chinese restaurants in the same town beginning with Alan in the name within an hour from my address and scored a hit almost immediately.

"Alan's Creek" I said triumphantly. It was forty minutes to an hour from my place, depending on the route. That sounded about right. I could backtrack it to Danial's from the Chinese place.

I printed out the map to the restaurant. The hardest part would be finding the unmarked dirt road leading to his house. I didn't even know the name of the nearest street or road on which Danial's place was located. It was rural, with no other houses for miles. But there should be tire tracks in the snow; I would look for them.

I left the cats with food and water and turned up the heat, then climbed into the car with the dogs.

My plan to find his place worked like a charm. I got to the restaurant easily and ordered shrimp fried rice and dumplings to take with me for dinner. I also got an order of chicken for Theo; then for the hard part. I closed my eyes and remembered the route Danial had driven when we'd left the restaurant.

After one wrong turn and a quick correction, I determined that I was on the right track. But when I got to the road leading to Danial's driveway, I couldn't find the turnoff. The snow coating the ground made everything blend into white, disguising any tracks. Making matters worse, there were no streetlights. I drove up and down four times before I saw a car brake hard and pull off the main road, entering the trees ahead of me. It had to be Danial's driveway, although the car wasn't familiar.

I pulled over and turned off the lights, kicking myself. Danial had asked me to come Tuesday, not tonight, because he had company. Maybe even Devlin. I shivered, feeling stupid for showing up without calling first.

Screw it. I'd gone through too much to get there not to go through with it. Danial had asked me to live with him. I had every right to drop in, announced or not.

I turned into Danial's driveway. A few minutes went by before I felt a bump as the wheels drove onto the blacktop. Soon, I drove into the clearing in front of Danial's house.

Someone had plowed and shoveled it. The porch light was the only one on and the car I'd followed was parked beneath it, unoccupied. I didn't want to block it in so I drove around the side and parked near the garage. I got out and heard voices I didn't recognize. Closing the door to keep the dogs in and the dome light off, I crouched behind the car.

The porch door opened and two men came out, Danial following. He wasn't dressed casually, like usual. Instead, he had on a suit, and his shoulder length hair had been put back in a loose ponytail. The men were also dressed in expensive suits.

"It was good doing business with you again," said the taller and older of the two strangers.

"Thanks, Tony," Danial said.

"We should have made it to your party," the other said. "Sorry 'bout that. Hope to make it up to you with the present." He laughed loudly.

"I appreciate the thoughtfulness, gentlemen," Danial said politely, but then flashed them a leer. "Call me if any other problems pop up."

"Donaldson's dead," Tony said. "That'll take care of our problems."

"I apologize again for the delay," Danial said. "I had difficulties the first time out."

"Not a problem. We know you always finish what you start."

Their voices were calm and businesslike, but I knew they were discussing a murder. Danial had killed someone for money.

As I stood in shock, it got better. Tony yelled back to Danial as he and the other man backed away, "When you're done with the girl, send her home, compliments of Thane. Take as long as you want."

Danial flashed him a ruthless smile, which abruptly vanished as the car drove off. Then he turned around and went inside. A moment later, a light went on in the great room.

I let the dogs out and praised them for not having barked. I hadn't wanted the two men to know I'd seen them. But, by God, someone else was going to know what I'd witnessed.

I didn't bother grabbing my things. Odds were I would be driving back home after I had this out with Danial.

Theo was waiting on the porch, his arms folded over his chest. "What are you doing here?"

I thought about trying to bribe him with the chicken No, he wasn't going to go for it. "Get out of my way," I growled.

"You're not going in there right now."

My fury boiled up past reasoning. I went to shove by him, but he grabbed me. The dogs immediately barked and growled at him.

"Let me go!"

His fingers locked on my arm. "You're not going in there."

I was going in and he wasn't going to stop me. "Get him!"

My dogs weren't trained to attack, but they took my command to heart. Ghost grabbed one of Theo's arms and Darkness the other. Theo swore and struggled against them. Material ripped. Darkness spit out a piece of shirt and grabbed Theo's arm again. I had only a few seconds before he realized they wouldn't really hurt him.

I raced inside. The kitchen was empty and so was the great room. I stood breathing hard, looking at Danial's closed bedroom door. I didn't want to open it to see what was going on inside. I wanted to let Theo stop me.

But I'd come too far to see Danial. I was going to see him before I left.

I reached for the handle and threw the door open. A beautiful woman lay on Danial's bed, her dark hair falling over the pillow. Her eyes were unfocused, filled with desire. She was partially undressed; the top of her evening gown open to expose her breasts. She squinted up at me to see who'd interrupted and loosened her grip on Danial. He held her in his arms, one hand clutching her neck, lifting it, the other under her breast, his thumb over her heart. He was feeding, moaning pleasurably as he had when he'd fed off me, his eyes closed.

I let out a gasp. He opened his eyes. "Sar?"

I moved back quickly and shut the door, then headed toward the porch, cursing my own stupidity. Theo blocked my way, his sleeves in tatters though his arms were unmarked. The dogs sat in the spots their beds had been, wagging their tails.

"Are you happy now you've seen he's feeding?" Theo spat at me. "I hope it was everything you imagined it would be."

I had wanted to see, and I'd gotten an eyeful. "You could've told me, jackass."

The bedroom door opened and Danial emerged, disheveled. "What are you doing here?"

"I came to see you."

"How did you get here?" he asked quickly.

"I drove," I muttered.

Theo had to add his input. "How did you find the house?"

"You think I can't remember enough details to figure out how to find the way on my own?" I left out that I'd still be driving if I hadn't seen Tony's car.

"Is there something wrong?" he asked as he came closer. "Are you okay?"

"I needed to see you," I said softly. I put my head in my hands, trying not to think of him with another woman in his bed. "I wanted to talk to you."

"Stay here with her, Theo. I'll be right back."

After he closed the door, the only sounds were the dogs panting and Theo cursing under his breath. I decided to slip out with the dogs for a quick walk so I wouldn't have to be there when Danial came out with that other woman.

Theo stopped me as I was opening the front door. "Nice try. Go back in and sit down."

"I'm just going for a walk—"

"Stay and face it now or get back in your car and leave," he said cruelly. "I told you there were some things he couldn't change for you. Get a grip."

I considered that a moment, and then walked back into the great room. Theo followed me in and leaned against the wall. I watched him with my eyes lowered. He'd taken off his shirt and had on only a tight T-shirt and his loose jeans, revealing the kind of muscles you only get from training hard with heavy weights. I wasn't surprised he was fit, but my appreciation for his physique was new. Theo was handsome…

"I can't believe you sicced your dogs on me. Son of a bitch, Sar."

At least, aside from his temperament and all the swearing he did. "I'm sorry," I said, making sure I didn't sound sorry. "Are you hurt?"

"You can see I'm not. But don't do that again. Next time I won't be so gentle with them. Or you."

Next time I wouldn't be getting him chicken, either. I ignored him.

The bedroom door opened and the dark-haired woman came out, her strapless sequined dress now covering her breasts. She held a gauze pad to her neck, her blue-eyed gaze unchallenging but very interested. Her wavy hair fell almost to her waist. She had to be younger than twenty-five. I gritted my teeth. "Hi."

"Hi," she said awkwardly with an up and down look.

Danial appeared behind her in the doorway. She turned and gave him a brief hug, which he returned, and then a kiss. He pulled away from her instantly. "Thank you, Angelica."

"Always my pleasure," she said with a lascivious smile.

Danial turned from her. His gaze rested on me briefly, then went to Theo. "Take Angelica home."

Theo pushed off the wall and followed Angelica to the front door, giving me a grumpy look as he opened it for her. Then the door shut, and Danial and I were alone.

I didn't know whether to be relieved or upset, or what to say. He took the initiative. "You would have had to see something like that sooner or later. I do regret you walked in on us unknowing."

"I wasn't prepared for how it made me feel."

"You couldn't feed me…sustain me alone, I told you that. You'd die. If you lived here with me, I couldn't send you away every time I needed to drink. This isn't anything more than sustenance." He paused. "You'll need to come to terms with this if you Oath to me."

"Is it only women, or—"

"Yes, unless it's an emergency. Blood is blood. But it's easiest to get from women. They're content with what I'm comfortable giving them and don't push to take it further." He made a face. "The men who would find this act titillating wouldn't be content with me just taking blood. And that's as much as I'm going to speak of that, my dear."

Cold went through me. If I lived with Danial, this was how it was going to be, watching other women come to him. "How often?"

"I feed from her on average once a month. She's one of five women. One of them comes every few days, depending on my activity level."

I began to reply, but he talked over me. "Right now, she thinks it's exciting and wonderful, and so do the others." He became weary. "In another few years, she'll marry, and I'll have to find someone new to replace her. I don't love her."

That was why other women had passed on being with Danial. Could I handle this? I wasn't sure. I pushed that uncertainty away as I remembered the look on Angelica's face while Danial fed. "Doesn't what you do to her hurt?"

"My saliva anesthetizes pain," he reminded. "Most women don't notice a shallow bite or cut, especially if I heal it after." His voice dropped an octave. "When I bit you the first time, I wasn't careful and bit too hard. That's why you felt pain. This isn't that."

No shit. Danial had never bitten me except in the dream we'd shared. I realized then that I wanted him to. I was jealous of Angelica for those sounds he made with her. "Angelica wants you. She isn't just here for thrills."

"I know that. I can smell her excitement when I touch her. It gives her blood a certain flavor. But there's no reason for you to be jealous. I don't want more from her than what we are now: donor and benefactor."

"I'm not jealous," I lied. "But it's the bed where we made love. It's our bed."

"I'd like it to be our bed, but right now it's just my bed." He turned tender. "You are my only lover. Don't begrudge them their fantasies when you have the reality."

"That's why I came tonight," I said forcefully, drowning his words. "I wanted to tell you that I've decided to try living with you."

He stepped closer, confused. "Why now? You said you needed time."

"What I need is to have you beside me when I wake up." I swallowed hard. "Most of all, I need that look in your eyes that hits me so hard I can't bear it. The look that says you see all of me, and what you see is so precious that nothing else matters." I swallowed hard. "I lost an opportunity a year ago by chance. I don't want to lose another out of fear."

He pulled me into his arms, and the tears sliding down my face soaked into his shirt. "Of all the nights to come to me, you would have to pick tonight," he said ruefully. He unclipped his cell from his belt and dialed a number.

"Mary, come and change the sheets on my bed."

He picked me up suddenly and carried me into the bathroom, kicking the door shut behind us. He sat me on the toilet seat, started the shower running, and began unbuttoning his shirt. "Take off your clothes."

"Moving kind of fast, aren't—"

"Not to be critical, sweetheart, but you must have come here right from work. You smell of metal fumes and burnt oil."

Good going, Sar. I'd taken care of the pets, researched the route, hell, even stopped for chicken, and forgotten the most important thing: showering. Ugh. No wonder Angelica had looked at me with such interest; she was surprised someone like me was Danial's girl. I took off my clothes and stepped under the spray, Danial slipping in a few minutes behind me. The water felt heavenly as it washed away the day's grime. I let it wash away all my reservations, too.

No sooner had I finished with my hair than he was in front of me. "Kiss me, Sar."

"Did you...um...?" I couldn't deal with tasting someone else's blood on his tongue. I didn't like tasting my own blood.

"Of course, before I came in. That's why it took me a moment. Kiss me."

I reached up to put my arms around his neck, kissing him gently. His

226

arms went around my waist, crushing me to him as he devoured me, his body stirring to life. He shut off the shower and scooped me up in his arms, then carried me into the bedroom. Fresh sheets adorned the bed, shining. He laid me down on them, leaning over to kiss me again. I responded, pulling his head down to crush his lips to mine. He cupped my breasts with his hands and gently squeezed, bringing a whimper to my lips. I reached down and caressed him, stroking gently.

He abruptly pushed himself up, bearing his weight on his arms. His eyes were black with desire. "Do you know how much I wanted you to say those words?" he asked huskily. He moved his legs so he was between mine. "I hoped you would come to me like this, deciding you wanted a life with me, not able to wait another day to tell me. God, I've wanted it so much."

All the trouble I'd taken to come to him was suddenly nothing, hearing that satisfaction. He kissed my neck, his teeth grazing gently.

"There is only one thing I want more right now, and that's to be inside you in all ways." He thrust the full length of himself into me and bit hard into my neck.

I cried out, but he held me tightly as he kept thrusting, feeding at my throat. I groaned, my body awash in pleasurable sensations even as I felt the pressure of his mouth sucking hard. My heart throbbed so fast the beats seemed to run together. God, what he was doing felt good!

I pulled his head closer as I arched my back toward him. He drove into me as hard and as fast as he could, making muffled sounds of pleasure, as if what my body and blood was doing to him was like nothing he'd felt before. I came screaming his name, pleading for him not to stop. He came with me, arching his head back with a loud cry, only to sink his fangs into the other side of my neck. I spasmed again as his teeth penetrated my skin.

He moved back, withdrawing from me. I let out a sigh of pleasure, going limp in his arms. He kissed me gently, licking both wounds as he hugged me to him.

"God, that was good," he said. "Sar? Are you okay?"

I snuggled closer, tired. That had been the best sex of my life.

"Shit," he swore. He got up and rushed into the bathroom.

I lay there thinking how good I felt. I hoped I wasn't bleeding too much on the clean sheets, but I wasn't worried about it. Happily, Danial returned with gauze and got me to hold it against my neck while he held more against the other side. We stayed that way for some time. Finally, he checked my throat and removed the gauze.

"Sar, talk to me."

"That was incredible," I said softly. "Just incredible."

"Do you feel okay?" he asked urgently.

"I feel wonderful," I said, languidly stretching. That made me a little dizzy, so I lay still again, blinking.

"What did you have for dinner? You didn't eat anything, did you?"

"I had to get here to...talk to you." I slurred my words.

"We need to get you something to eat. I took too much."

"It's okay," I reassured him with a yawn. "I picked up some food. It's in the car. Chicken for Theo—"

"Stay here and don't move. I'll be back."

He was back in a few minutes with a huge bowl of steaming shrimp and rice. I was absurdly touched that he'd nuked it in the microwave. After a few bites, I came back to myself enough to take the spoon from him.

I ate the whole bowl, the entire quart. By the time I was half done, I felt better. When I'd finished, I was okay enough to sit up without dizziness. I went into the bathroom against his protests and looked into the mirror. He followed me in, his arms protectively around me.

"I look so pale."

"It's my love bites," he murmured. "Give it an hour or so and the redness will fade." He touched one gently. "Did it hurt?"

The twin bites below my choker were angry against my white skin, but there was no pain, not even at his touch. "No."

"They may leave a scar, but we can remove it if that happens."

"I'm surprised you bit me. Instead of the kiss, I mean."

He smiled. "Truth be told, though the blood is the same, it feels better to bite. My teeth are intended to puncture not slice open a cut. At least, that's what some scholars theorize."

What scholars? First things first. "Can I see?" I said curiously.

He obediently bared his teeth for me. He was right; they were made for sinking into flesh and holding. Interestingly enough, he didn't have only the upper incisors as fangs: his bottom canines were longer, although not as long as the top ones. I ran my index finger over one, pressing down and it pricked me. A drop of blood welled from my finger.

"Careful, sweetheart. The front and outside edges are sharpest." He pressed it to his lips and kissed it, his eyes holding mine. When he released my finger, the wound was healed.

"It took a long time to get used to speaking with my fangs," he continued. "I still cut myself accidentally sometimes. But the cut always heals fast, and it's usually shallow."

I examined the bite marks again. Each mark didn't have two wounds, but four.

"Come to bed," he said seductively. "Come to our bed."

He scooped me up yet again and settled me under the covers. I fell asleep almost instantly cuddled up against him.

* * * *

I woke up the next morning feeling groggy, unaware of the time. Leaving Danial still asleep, I padded to the bathroom to see how I looked.

Whoa. My reflection was spectacular. My skin was almost white, making my green eyes darker and my hair more light brown than blonde. My pallor set off my choker, and the gold glowed, the ruby eyes winking. The bites stood out on either side, the skin red and purple. The bites themselves had scabbed over, though the deeper one had opened during the night and seeped blood. I thought about cleaning it but didn't know if I should. What if it opened again? I'd lost enough blood last night...

I put on some clothes and located my watch on the floor. It was seven in the evening. I'd slept for almost nine hours. I put on a robe and went out to kitchen in search of my dumplings and dogs. Cia was in the kitchen reading the paper.

"Evening," she said, and did a double-take. Her eyes widened as she took in my appearance, her mouth open.

I was self-conscious, the "lovebites" like huge hickies on my neck. But covering them with gauze wouldn't fool anybody living there.

"Something wrong?"

"I'm sorry for staring. I've never seen a double mark before." She came over and inspected the wounds. "Are you in any pain?"

"No," I said, blushing. "But they are certainly eye catching."

"As they should be," a melodious but ruthless voice said.

I turned to see Devlin standing in the doorway, his golden eyes fixed on me.

Chapter Twenty

"Had a busy night, did you?" Devlin leaned one arm upon the door nonchalantly. "You should've invited me, Sar. I would have been glad to come." He bared one fang in a smile. "And you'd have been delighted when I did."

I expected his brazen language, but blushed anyway.

"Leave," Cia growled as she maneuvered quickly in front of me. "Now."

"Or what?" he said casually. "You'll make me?"

Cia grabbed for her cell phone on the table, but he was faster, slamming his hand on it so it broke into pieces. We both jumped and backed up.

He held up one finger when Cia took a breath to say something. His lips wrinkled back to expose his fangs. "Don't. And you try for the phone, I'll snap your neck."

Cia backed me up almost to the counter, her eyes fixed on him.

His face smoothed. "Stop running away." His features then curved into a sardonic smile, focusing on me. "My God, you'd think I was brandishing an ax or something. Do you find my appearance that frightening?"

"No." On the surface, he was normal, dressed in jeans and a cotton shirt, his gold hair falling to his shoulders matching the stubble on his jaw. But his tawny eyes were cold. He might be as gorgeous as Danial was, but there was nothing of his brother's softer side in him.

"Good. Come over here."

"No way." I wasn't going to fall for his manipulation this time.

He gave an elaborate sigh. "Then I guess I shall have to come to you." He stalked toward me, deliberately moving slowly and sensuously.

"Danial!" I yelled.

"He can't hear you. His bedroom is soundproof."

Cia growled, baring her distending teeth. Her nails were an inch long and curved like claws.

"Get out of the way, little fox."

She didn't move. "Run, Sar."

I made a dash for the kitchen door, but Devlin lunged to block me. I backed up with a gasp. He was almost within reach.

"You're unarmed, fox," he said in an offhand manner. "How long do you think you can last against me?"

"Long enough for help to come."

With a growl, she launched herself at him. Their bodies collided, falling against the counter. I lost my balance but pulled myself up fast and ran for the door, glancing back once I cleared it.

Devlin had Cia's arms behind her back and drove her to her knees. She fought back until there was a wet crunch, then a thud of something heavy hitting the floor. I bolted only three steps before a hand fastened on the back of my neck. As Devlin turned me to face him, I saw Cia on the kitchen floor, unmoving, her head at a crooked angle.

He flipped my hair out of the way to examine the bites on my neck. I tried to pull away, but he held me easily.

"Now, Sar," he said seductively, "don't jerk so much. You'll open those lovely bites my brother gave you. Ah," he said, leaning closer so his nose touched mine. "You've already opened this one."

He caressed my neck, and I felt wetness on my skin from the deeper bite.

"The bites are technically supposed to be the same depth, but on the whole, he did nice work marking you. I wished he'd have asked for my help. I would have healed this—"

"I want only him to bite me," I said with anger. "I'm his, not yours!"

He purred, "Stop, Sar, you're turning me on." He held up his hand, my blood on his index finger. He put it to his lips and tasted it, looking into my eyes as he did. "Hey, if you want to bleed, I'm all for it."

He leaned in close enough to kiss me. "And I must apologize. You see, I asked Ryan to get a spell for you, since by law, I couldn't interfere myself. Nothing bad, just something to make you weak so Danial would know you weren't strong enough to be his companion." His lips were nearly on mine, but then he shifted, moving closer so he whispered in my ear. "But the idiot had to get a death curse. He's in my dungeon at Hayden, counting his last hours. Don't worry; he'll be tortured by my best man—"

Fear squeezed my heart, making it hard to breathe. "Don't hurt me—"

He let out a peal of laughter, moving back to face me. "As if I wanted you hurt." His golden eyes narrowed. "If I'd wanted you dead, you'd be dead. I'm here because we both know you want me here."

"I don't!"

He gave me a seductive smile. "Don't you?"

He pulled my head back, his hands in my hair. He leaned in and kissed my bleeding neck. He groaned as a shudder of pleasure went through him. I struggled, but I couldn't get free.

"Stop fighting," he murmured. "All you need to say is that you want me, and I'll take you home with me." He kissed up my neck, brushing me lightly with his fangs. "I'll give you anything you ask for. Just tell me you want me and not him. That's all you have to say. Say the words for me, darling—"

"No! I love him, not you—"

"Look at me," he purred. "Look at me and tell me you'd prefer my brother." He bared his fangs slightly. "I'm what you really want. I'm your fantasy come to life." He leaned in and gave me a perfect kiss. "And it only gets better. There is nothing I haven't done, nothing I balk at doing." He kissed me again, sensuously, and then drew back, his eyes like molten gold. "Those things you think about in the dark at night and don't dare utter to him for fear he'd recoil, we'll do them. We'll do them all. And I promise, they'll be better in the flesh with me than they were in your dreams." He trailed kisses up my face as Danial had done. "Give in to me."

In that instant, I remembered Theo's talk of how Devlin had seduced Danial's lovers away from him. Rage filled me, because this was all bullshit. "Let me go, you bastard! You don't care about me."

"But I do," he crooned, sounding hurt. "I dream of great feats in your defense. But you don't need a man to save you, do you?" He turned pleased. "You're more than capable of saving the day all by yourself. I love that."

"You can't love me. You don't know me."

"I know enough about you to be ensnared. What else have I been saying with every word and with no right? I know I shouldn't be here," he whispered conspiratorially. "But I couldn't stay away, laws be damned."

I was intrigued by his passion, even if I didn't believe a word he said. "Why not?"

"He told me how you saved him; how you let him drink you down like water," he said lustily. "Just imagining that is enough to put me into a tailspin." He pressed a little harder with his fangs, breathing hard. "I want to bury myself in your soft flesh, Sweet Sar. Tell me you want me." He nibbled lightly. "Tell me you want me to bite you—"

Of course. I took a deep breath, got his earlobe between my teeth, and bit down hard.

He jerked back, ripping his ear out of my mouth. "You bitch!"

I tried to knee him, but he blocked me. I shoved him hard, and he staggered. The moment I was free, I raced for Danial's room.

Devlin had me as my hand closed on the doorknob, yanking me to him. "You are going to pay for that. A bite for a bite." He leaned closer, his breath on my neck making my skin crawl. I tensed, bracing myself for the thrust of his fangs.

The bedroom door burst open. "Let her go, Devlin."

"What if—"

Danial cut him off with a punch to the jaw, knocking him to his knees. Before he could get to his feet, Danial smashed an end table over his back. The thick wood cracked, two legs breaking off, and Devlin collapsed with a grunt. Danial kicked him in the side with enough force to lift him off the ground, and then rolled him over. He straddled Devlin, a table leg in his hands. He leaned on it, and Devlin let out a hiss as it sunk into him.

"Feel that, brother?" Danial snarled, his words dipped in acid. "I can stake you right here and now. You attacked a woman clearly marked as my own."

"But you won't," he said, laughing. "You don't have it in you—"

Danial leaned hard on the leg, and it sunk farther into him.

Devlin's face contorted, breathing with effort. But he remained resolute even in pain. "Who will you call...when you eventually take too much blood from her? When she's dying and your blood is useless?" He smiled widely. "You'll call me."

Danial went still over him. I held my breath.

"I saw how pale she is. You just can't let her recover," Devlin snorted. "There's only one way this can end—"

Danial pushed the stake in another half inch. Devlin screamed and writhed.

"There's been too many years of this," Danial said with hate and disgust. "Too many years and too many women I've lost to you. I always assumed the woman was to blame; that she was weak and didn't love me. For the others, that might have been true, but it's not with Sar. She doesn't want you, and you know it!"

"I know it's true now," he hissed at him. "But given enough time—"

"You saw the bite marks on her, my emblem on her choker. Say it!"

"I saw them. I know she's about to give herself to you, if she hasn't already."

"Then you owe me for trying to taste her."

"I owe you," Devlin said grudgingly. "And I pay my debts. What do you want?"

"Get Tony and Thane to back off. I don't care how. Get them to accept money instead. I want out of our arrangement."

"Consider it done," he said arrogantly. "Now get off me before you piss me off."

I hoped Danial would slam the stake home and end him. Instead, he jerked it out, throwing it aside as they both got to their feet. Devlin's shirt was ruined, but he appeared uninjured. Danial gestured for him to leave with him and they walked out of sight.

I went into the bedroom and slammed the door, pissed. The door didn't latch and swung partly open.

"Don't you think it's time you let this go? I've apologized a hundred times for what I did with Annabelle." Danial exposed real sorrow, real regret.

Who was Annabelle?

"You're right. I'm sorry. It's gone on long enough between us." Devlin paused. "I hope she makes you happy, the way Anna and I were."

I suddenly knew who Annabelle had to be. She had to be the woman Danial had seduced away from Devlin centuries ago.

Screw that Devlin sounded like he'd died along with her. I wasn't letting him just walk out of there. I strode out as Danial opened the front door. Devlin turned to him just in time to put his face in line with my fist. My punch wasn't nearly as strong as Danial's had been, but the solid steel rod I held in my hand helped. The blow was strong enough to knock Devlin off balance and down the stairs.

I tossed the metal rod to Danial and went into the kitchen. Cia lay where she had fallen. I checked for a heartbeat and found one, steady and strong.

Theo came through the door and kneeled beside me. "I saw Devlin fall down the stairs. What happened?"

I told him the story.

"Devlin's his brother?"

"Yes. What can we do for her?"

"I need to straighten her neck." He had me hold her still as best as I could while he grasped her head and yanked quickly. There was a horrible bone-grating-on-bone sound, but Cia's neck looked more like it should.

"We wait," he said. "In a few minutes, she'll be okay. I need to speak to Danial. Wait here."

He returned with Danial a few minutes later. Cia hadn't changed position or opened her eyes, so I was worried. Theo saw my expression. "Don't worry. She'll be okay. This isn't the first time he's done something like this."

"What?" I said furiously.

"He snapped her neck, but he didn't kill her. All he did was incapacitate her. She couldn't heal this without help, but as soon as we straightened out the break, she began recovering. It's not a big deal for a were, trust me."

"It had to hurt. She was fighting him."

"It hurt, but she'll be okay." He actually patted me on the shoulder, in one of his nicer moods.

A few moments later, Cia opened her eyes and sat up. "Sar, are you okay? What happened?"

I soothed her as best I could. "It's over now. Devlin's gone. I'm fine."

"You're not fine," Theo said. "You're bleeding again."

I reached up and felt the wetness on my neck. The same deeper bite. But it wasn't bad, just a few drops. "It's no big deal."

"It is. Go take care of it. I'll get Cia to bed. Her motor function is going to be impaired for a little while." He lifted her with one arm to help her stand and they walked outside.

Danial brought me into the bathroom to attend my bite. "I should heal this one," he said, apprehensive. "It's deep. But I can't risk poisoning you with my blood. Not after I took so much from you last night."

"Can't just your saliva help? There's some of what makes you a vampire in that, right?"

"It helps, but it takes blood for major healing. A scratch could be healed with saliva, but a wound this deep needs blood to heal it."

The phone rang. He answered it, then turned to me and mouthed, "Stephen."

I took the phone. "Hello?"

"I was calling to tell you the results of that blood work I did for you. Your blood levels look fine. All the numbers are within normal limits; platelets, red blood cells, white blood cells. "

"I'm glad to hear it," I said, relieved.

"Ask Danial to get on the line, if you've no objections."

"Get another line," I said to Danial.

A moment later, I heard him pick up. "I'm here. What is it?"

"I'm going to write her a prescription for vitamins. She needs more iron, but all her vitals could use a little help. I'll call it in to the Alan's Creek pharmacy tonight. You can pick it up in an hour."

"I'll have someone pick it up," Danial said. "Anything else?"

"She should come in for a checkup in a month."

"You just looked me over a few days ago—"

"November thirtieth, at three in the afternoon?"

Stephen was concerned, and if he was, I probably should be, too.

"Okay," I said, grabbing a pencil and paper to jot down the information.

"Danial, I need a few words for you, too. Sar needs time to heal before you take anymore of her blood. Don't drink from her until she comes in to see me in a month—"

"I drank from her last night. It was a large amount."

"Look, both of you," Stephen said, exasperated, "I'll call in another prescription, something to help counteract the blood loss. But don't do this again for at least a month. You're risking her life if you do."

"I understand," Danial said apologetically. "I won't."

"By the way, Danial, your tests were negative. I'll retest you again in a month." He paused. "I'm sorry." He said good-bye and hung up.

"What was that about?" I asked when Danial came back.

"Nothing," he said, running his hands over his face.

"It didn't sound like nothing."

"You remember the potions I bought, the ones Terian made?" He sighed. "You said he mentioned them to you."

"Yes."

"They might have side effects; at least, that's what I've been told. Stephen is making sure I'm okay. I've given him permission to let you know about it, which is why he didn't ask to speak to me alone." He abruptly grinned.

"What?" I said, smiling back at him.

"I can't believe you punched Devlin." He laughed. "Seriously, Sarelle, you probably shouldn't have."

"He apologized to you, not to me. Not to Cia."

"Cia was doing her job. She knew what might happen if she went against him."

"Why are you afraid of him? You just bested him—"

"I beat him because he was focused on you and he didn't think I was going to attack—not like I did. I never have before, ever. I was lucky to catch him off guard. But he'll remember this day forever. I won't be able to turn the tables on him so easily again."

I wanted to say, "then perhaps you should have staked him," but it was his brother, so I kept my mouth shut.

"Besides, getting him to agree that I can stop killing for Thane and Tony is enough of a relief."

"I'll bet it is," I said sarcastically. "I understand now why you said it would be in bad taste to dress as assassins for your party. Why dress up as an assassin when you are one in real life?"

"It's true that I've killed people for money before. I was a mercenary back when that was an acceptable profession. But I'm done with that."

"You killed someone in the last few days for money. That doesn't sound like you're done."

"I'd already agreed to do it, so I had to finish the job. This isn't a movie, where if you suddenly decide you should have better morals, you just tell the people who hired you sorry, no deal. I've wanted that part of my life to be done with for a long time. Now it can be, with Dev's intercession." He looked at me earnestly, willing me to believe him.

"No more killing for hire?" I said. "Promise me now."

"No more, I promise you."

I changed the subject. "What's the name of your company? I tried to locate it on the Internet, but couldn't find anything under 'Racklan'."

He smiled. "Solutions Inc. I thought you knew."

I'd expected something more edgy and otherworldly, but he did work mostly in the corporate world. It made sense.

"There's no address linked to the company, just a P.O. Box."

Theo strolled in. "Danial, you should know that Devlin took out two of the border guards we had around the house. He left his Hummer where the blacktop starts and circled around to come at the house from the side. Ivan and Demetri are okay. Devlin also snapped their necks, but they're recovering."

"He did it because he wasn't here for an all-out attack. He was here to see if he could get Sar to submit to him. At least, that's what I think. But instead of kissing him, she punched him in the face." He snorted. "You should've seen it."

"I did it for Cia."

Theo looked amazed and proud. "So that's why he fell down the stairs." He cleared his throat. "Thank you for both the pies and the chicken. I'm surprised you bothered getting me anything. You know you don't like me, really."

I smiled sweetly at him. "I like you just fine when you aren't being an ass."

He laughed and walked out.

I focused again on Danial. "How does this work?"

He brushed the hair back from my face. "What?"

"I want to try living here with you because I think I'm ready. But I need help meshing our lives together, especially with my job. I want us to have time together, but I don't want you to feel like I'm overwhelming you by being around all the time."

"That's not going to happen. I want you around. And you can work or not work, though it would be easier if you didn't."

He wasn't getting it. "What about when you have to go out of town for a night or a few days? Would you want me with you or not? Would you be offended if I elected to stay here? Would you refuse if I wanted to go?"

He considered that. "I'd leave it up to you."

"What about when you need blood? I can handle knowing that you need other women, but not seeing it each time and not having them in our bed. Because it is our bed now."

"That's an easier answer. There's another bedroom in the basement. It was reserved for visitors who didn't want to stay in the exposed upper room, on the second floor. I'll take any of my blood donors there. Come with me."

I took his hand, and he led me down to the basement. It was finished but spartan, having only a large wood wardrobe, a king-size bed, and a nightstand with some leather-bound first editions of poetry. I touched one gently.

"These were yours when you were mortal?"

"Yes. They were gifts from Devlin." He opened the wardrobe. "These were mine over the years."

I looked at the men's clothes in many styles. There were mostly suits, but mixed in with those were ruffled shirts, breeches, and sword belts. Some swords of different styles were in the drawers, along with other period dress I recognized but didn't know the name for.

"I only saved a few. I had Tatiana enchant some of the older items so they'd last."

"Do you wear them?"

"Not anymore. I keep them to remember."

"Remember what?"

"I try to change as the world changes. Too many of us don't. It used to be just an annoyance, in the old days, because man didn't advance that fast. Vampires could choose not to change for years. But with each decade that passed, new ideas came into play. In the last hundred years, the advances have been phenomenal. Sometimes it also gets too much for me, how complicated the world has become. And I want to be who I was then, not who I am now. And in that way lies certain death. So I try not to dwell on my past. It's easier."

I hugged him to me and told him I understood.

Chapter Twenty-One

The following night, Danial took me ballroom dancing to celebrate us living together. We danced for hours, his skill and natural grace making me feel like a princess as we floated across the dance floor.

The night after, Demetri and Lander moved the wardrobe up from the basement while I took a quick trip home to get most of my warm clothes for winter. It took the rest of the evening, but I managed to organize and pack them away into the wardrobe.

I'd originally refused Danial's offer to use it, telling him I could bring a dresser from home. "You shouldn't have to pack away your stuff. It's already in the basement—"

"I want you to use it. I'll put my memory boxes down there, too." He kissed my forehead. "My life is with you now."

The gesture was sweet but too one-sided. As a concession, I moved his handful of poetry books to a small wooden shelf I'd brought from home, adding a few books I hadn't read yet. I hung it within reach of the left side of the bed, the one I usually ended up sleeping on.

As I stood back to admire my work, it hit me; I had a side of the bed again. My emotions swelled and I sat down to think, fingering a shirt of Danial's I'd found left in the wardrobe. It was red cotton and of an unfamiliar style, like something a poet might wear but without the ruffles.

He came in and took it from me. "I was looking for that. Thanks."

"What is it?"

"A swordsman's shirt. It's close to the one I wore when I was mortal, except for the color. I had this one made for me."

"Would you mind keeping it out? I'd like to see you wear it sometime."

Promise Me

"Of course." He handed it to me. "Put it in the wardrobe for now."

* * * *

A few days later, I was talking to the werefoxes while we waited for a pan of brownies to bake. Suri, the hip-looking Asian with chunky-cut hair, was explaining to me that there was no correlation between the moon and changing form.

"There's never been any correlation. But I think some people use it as an excuse to get violent. It is fun to run around in the moonlight."

"But why do people believe so strongly that werewolves—sorry, werecreatures—had to change on the full moon if they don't?"

"Simple superstition and observation. What night would be the easiest to spot a man changing to a fox and back? A night that was the brightest one in the month."

"That was the night everyone learned to avoid changing on if they were really a were," Janice added, laughing.

"It's also the night wannabes roam around looking to become one." Lander sighed. "Groupies."

We all laughed.

"What do they do?" I asked. "Yell out, 'please come and bite me'?"

"No, but some do lay there naked in the moonlight, waiting for something exciting to happen."

I laughed. "And does it?"

"Those who want to get some, usually do. I'm a giver." He grinned at me.

I flushed, dropping my eyes from his. Suri grabbed his arm and whispered something in his ear. Lander didn't say a word the rest of the night. In fact, he moved as far away as he could and didn't even look at me.

"What did you say to him?" I asked her later.

"I reminded him to look at your neck so he'd remember who he was talking to. He's just young. Forgive him his hormones."

Lander had been bold, but I'd just been caught off guard, not insulted. Still, it was better not to set a precedent. "Thanks."

"Thanks for the brownies. Call out if you need anything." She walked out, the front door slamming behind her a few minutes later.

243

I turned off the light and went to bed, grateful that she'd said something. But I also felt alone in the midst of these people, like a queen bee with many minions but no real friends.

* * * *

The next morning, I wandered out to the kitchen and was immediately besieged. Lander had been waiting for me.

"Uh...I...uh want to apologize for flirting with you last night. I didn't mean it."

I laughed. "You did mean it. But it's okay. Don't worry about it."

His face didn't change. "So you accept my apology?"

"Yes." I looked at him curiously, not understanding his problem.

"Thank you, Sarelle. It won't happen again." He left quickly, the front door slamming behind him.

Hormones, indeed.

I sat down and had breakfast, making sure to take the vitamins that Dr. Camlyn had prescribed for me. I had to take two of the huge pills whenever I first ate that day. I'd also taken the solution for counteracting blood loss the night before. It had come in a packet and was as thick as glue. It tasted awful, but I'd made myself swallow it because I trusted Dr. Camlyn.

* * * *

When I reached down to touch Danial awake the next morning, I recoiled in shock. His skin was warm like mine.

He'd taken at least one potion, and maybe the other, too. Remembering Terian's words about how dangerous they were caused me concern. But it was his body and Stephen tested him for irregularities.

He pulled me closer and opened his eyes. "Do you like it?"

"I liked how you were. You don't have to change for me. But yes, I like this, too."

He kissed me, his hands sliding lower. "Show me."

I sighed reluctantly. "We can't."

He froze. "Why not?"

"It's Saturday. My parental units are waiting for us. We have to leave soon if we're going to be there on time."

I could feel him wanting to swear but he didn't. "Give me five minutes."

When we were nearly there, he dropped a bombshell.

"I have to be out of town all next week. Would you like to come with me this time? You'd have to miss work Monday and Friday. I'll be leaving early Sunday night and getting back early Friday night."

"Can I meet you wherever you're staying and drive back before work?" I asked hopefully. "I can't miss a week of work right after asking to rearrange my work hours."

"I'm going to Akron, then Switzerland and New York City, so no. But I can arrange for you to meet me at the airport while we're refueling. How does a trip to Switzerland sound?"

"Great, but we have to make it through tonight first," I joked, parking the car. "C'mon."

* * * *

"You think it went okay?" he asked on the drive home. "I think they liked me."

"I think it went fine. They liked you a lot. But maybe you should've waited for the second meeting with them to break the news that we'd moved in together."

"We're adults," he said smoothly. "We're old enough to know what we want. Why hide?"

"I wasn't hiding," I said defensively. "But it sounds fast even to me, who's happily living it. And no, before you ask, I'm not having second thoughts."

"Good. Let's get home. Next week is going to be busy."

* * * *

The next two days were a whirlwind. Danial left for the airport with Ivan and Demetri after he woke up Sunday night. He called me from his hotel in Akron at one a.m. to say that he'd arrived safely. I worked Monday from ten to seven and then came back to Danial's home to shower quickly. Theo grabbed my bags as I threw on a jacket.

"Are you coming with us?" I asked as he drove to the airport. "Or are Demetri and Ivan?"

"Do you want me to?" he said with a smirk.

"Yes."

He blushed and looked away.

Stupid as it was, knowing I'd embarrassed him made me embarrassed. "I feel safer when you're with us. The other guards are strong, but you...um..."

"Cia said she told you about me. I'm okay with it." He stared at the road. "Did Lander apologize to you?"

"Yes. Did you say something to him?"

"I reminded him none too gently that he wasn't at the local bar and you weren't available."

Why was he upset? Lander's joking hadn't been any more flirtatious that his own back when Danial and I had first gotten together. "You didn't have to—"

"It would lead to problems if I'd let it slide," he said, his eyes still locked on the road. "Even if he likes you, he should know better than to speak to you about his feelings. Danial would do worse if he found out."

Maybe he was right. Even if Lander's comments had just been teasing, they had made me a little uncomfortable. "Thank you then," I said almost inaudibly.

We were quiet for a minute. Then Theo said, "Yes, I am coming. Overseas trips can be hairy, especially with you along."

I had a sinking feeling. "What is the danger overseas?"

"Danial's out of both his and Devlin's territory. He has enemies in the European Union, though none where we are going."

"Should I stay home?"

"We'll be fine. I'll let you know if there's anything to be worried about."

* * * *

The moment we entered the lobby, I was wowed by the opulence. It had to be a four-star hotel. The ceiling was forty feet high, with a mural of cherubs and angels. The crystal chandeliers were huge, their lights sparkling like diamonds. The lobby was larger than my house, with leather couches and silk upholstered furniture. There was even a baby grand, though no one was playing it. I turned round and round, taking it all in.

"Come, Sar. It's nearly dawn."

Danial led me to our room, Theo trailing us and the bellhop following with the bags. It was a suite, a living room with two bedrooms to either side. Theo dropped the bags and went into one, saying he had to make a call. I followed Danial into the other.

"We'll unpack in the morning. Come."

We undressed and got into bed. I lay in his arms after he'd fallen asleep, still trying to get used to his skin being so warm. Some time later, I fell asleep.

I dreamed of being at the zoo. A lion roared at me from its cage. I wanted to set it free but didn't dare. It was huge and ferocious. It eyes were a light golden and hungry, so hungry.

I woke up as Danial was stirring. The clock on the nightstand said six, the time there. Europe was what, seven hours ahead? How long had we slept?

He groaned. "What time is it?

"Six. Are you okay?" I asked, touching his shoulder.

"Crossing the ocean and adapting to the different time zones is always hard. But I'll be fine." He stretched. "I have a meeting at eight. It will probably last a couple hours. Then I'll need to go out and get something to eat." He went to the door and reemerged with our bags. "You should stay here and order room service. I'll be back before dawn."

"And tomorrow night?" I pressed.

"Tomorrow night, Theo and I have to go out for another meeting. It should be routine, but it'll take at least a few hours. You can wait up for me tonight if you want. But I want you to have fun tomorrow afternoon, so don't stay up too late."

"Where am I going?"

"There's a concierge downstairs. Call him in the morning and go wherever you like for the day. He'll arrange it all. Bill it to the room."

"Are you sure? The Euro is worth almost two of our dollars."

"Sar, what I told your parents is true. I have resources. A good portion of what I make is spent on security, chartered planes, and secure hotel rooms, but there's enough that you don't need to worry about how much something costs. Just have fun."

He began to get dressed. I put on a robe and went out to the living room to look out the window. The lights were beautiful against the night sky.

I heard a noise and turned, expecting it to be Danial. Instead, a woman stood there. She was about my size, with long light brown hair. She was more slender than me, like Cia, but there was strength to her that Cia didn't have. She was also in a robe.

I realized with a start that she'd come out of Theo's room. She looked at me; I looked at her, and we both flushed. Then we burst out laughing.

"Hi, I'm Sarelle," I said, extending my hand.

"Good to meet you. My name is Tawny," she said throatily.

Theo, you dog, I thought to myself with a smile. *Good for you.*

He came out looking very relaxed. We both turned to him, and he flushed, which made Tawny and me laugh again. Danial came out and saw us, but he was cool and just said hi to Tawny.

"We've got to go," Theo said to Danial. "We'll be late."

Danial kissed me. "Stay here. I'll be back before dawn."

He left the room. Theo went after him after saying something similar to Tawny.

As the door shut behind them, I turned to see Tawny perusing the room service menu. "What shall we order?"

"Breakfast for me."

"Steak and eggs for me," she said. "I'll order."

As she hung up the phone, I said, "I heard a lion roaring last night."

She grinned. "Technically, you might have heard two, but most likely you heard me." She touched my neck. "Do your scars hurt?"

"They did when they were fresh, but not since they've healed."

"I was bitten once, but the bastard who did it, tore me. It hurt a lot."

"Why did he do it?"

"He thought I wouldn't resist him. He had other thoughts after I clawed him up."

"Was he someone powerful here? I know there's a hierarchy."

"Theo tells me you've had a few run-ins with him yourself. Chap by the name of Devlin?"

"I know him," I said with a sigh. "I'm glad you clawed him."

The food came and we ate. Then Tawny and I decided to go back to bed.

"I want to be awake and ready for Theo," she said with a lascivious grin.

It was true how different the women in Europe were. Womankind might be better off if all women were so honest with themselves about their needs.

I couldn't sleep, so I read for a while and finally I drifted off. I awoke early the next morning to find Danial beside me, positively shining with the luster that meant he'd fed and fed well. I kissed his cheek gently so as not to wake him and went to take a shower. Tawny didn't make an appearance, and I left her a note asking her to find me in the hotel restaurant when she was ready to go.

To my surprise, I met Theo coming up in the elevator with a doughnut in his mouth, a large bag in his hand. He saw me and coughed, removing the doughnut.

"Bringing her breakfast in bed?"

"Uh...yes," he said, a flush creeping up his cheeks. "She likes the cream filled ones."

I'll bet. I blushed myself. "Sorry, I shouldn't have said anything—"

He was all business. "Are you heading down to the restaurant?"

"Yes."

He walked past me towards the room. "I'll go with you. Danial didn't want you leaving the hotel unescorted, and the hotel restaurant isn't open for another half-hour. We can go to the café down the street. The food's better there anyway. Let me leave these inside the door"

"What about Tawny?"

"She's sleeping. She won't miss me until she wakes up." He turned serious. "And my job is guarding you and Danial. He's less at risk in his room than you are wandering the streets alone. Let's go."

I rolled my eyes, but followed him.

A few minutes later, we were at a sidewalk café, eating more delectable pastries.

"These are good." I finished my second one. "Do you and Danial come to this area often?"

"We go all over, depending on the clients we need to see. When we come to Switzerland, we stay here."

"Is that because Tawny lives nearby?" I jested.

"She lives in France," he said uncomfortably. "But she knew I was coming here, so she arranged to be in town."

"Are you serious?"

He gave me a confused look, then nodded, his face smoothing. "Sorry, I didn't understand what you were asking. You want to know if she and I are an item. And the answer is it isn't any of your business."

"Sorry," I said softly. "I didn't mean to pry."

He only sipped his coffee. The longer I sat there, the more uncomfortable I felt. I finally got to my feet. "I'm heading back. You'll probably need your rest."

"Where do you get off making comments about my sex life?" he said angrily. "We aren't friends. You're my best friend's girl. Show some respect."

I couldn't get out the words fast enough, I was so angry. "When I have to hear it so much I'm dreaming of lions, I'm allowed to comment on it. And I wasn't making a crack; I was trying to be thoughtful. You're going to be up all night guarding Danial, and I don't want something to happen to him because you're too slow on the draw, Jerk."

I stalked back to the hotel. Theo tried to catch me in the elevator, but I closed the doors before he got there. When the door opened on my floor, he was in front of it, waiting for me. I tried to walk past him, but he stepped into me, pushing me back into the elevator. He jabbed the STOP button.

"Listen," he said gruffly. "I didn't mean to snap at you."

"Whatever. Tell Tawny I'll be waiting for her in the lobby near the concierge."

"Don't worry about Danial. I've been protecting him for the last ten years. I know how to do my job—"

"Then go do it and get out of my way."

He moved back, and I abruptly hit the button, closing the doors.

* * * *

Tawny appeared an hour later. She looked like the cat that ate the canary, a goose, and about seven swans.

"Good night?"

"The best ever," she said, shivering a little.

I reevaluated my opinion of Theo and then told myself it wasn't appropriate to be thinking of him like that. "Let's go."

We went to see the concierge, who arranged a tour of the closest chocolate factory. We were picked up by a limo and taken to the Lindt factory within minutes. The hour-long tour was interesting, but the chocolate tasting was the best part.

After we returned, we had lunch at a small coffeehouse around the corner. As we waited for the bill, she excused herself to visit the bathroom.

Sitting there, I noticed a man on the sidewalk looking in the window at the baked goods on display. He noticed me watching and smiled. I looked away, not wanting him to get the idea that I was interested. A moment later, I heard Tawny's chair pushed back as the stranger sat down across from me.

"You were watching me?" he said. His hazel eyes were penetrating.

"Sorry," I said, giving him an apologetic smile, "I was just looking out the window. I didn't mean to make you think anything of it."

"I think maybe you're interested but don't want to admit it," he teased.

"You're mistaken," I said flatly. "I'm engaged."

"Yes, you are. You're engaging and I'm engaged by you. Why don't we go back to my hotel—?"

"Excuse me, but what do you think you're doing?"

Tawny stood there glaring at him, hands folded across her chest.

"I'm seeing if your friend is interested. She claims not to be, but—"

"She's not," she said. "Leave."

"Now, wait just a minute," the man said with slight irritation.

Tawny grabbed a hold of the man and propelled him toward the door. He broke free, gave her a glare, then stalked out of the shop, not looking back.

She came back to the table. "We should go back to the hotel. We both need sleep. Come on."

We walked back to the hotel. Caught up in Tawny's lust for lovemaking with Theo, my own ramped up into overdrive. I decided to turn in early, to be rested and "ready" for Danial when he returned. He and I were in a foreign city; we were in love and we hadn't been together like that for days. Fantasizing, I undressed and got into bed naked. Just as I was falling asleep, there was a knock at the door.

"Come in," I said sexily, baring one shoulder.

Theo opened the door.

I pulled the covers around me quickly, self-conscious. "Hi."

"Danial is checking out one more lead and then he'll get something to eat. He said he'd be here about ten or eleven."

"Okay. Thanks for the heads up."

He nodded and closed the door.

A few minutes later, throaty growls began issuing from the other room. Thirty minutes later, those had morphed into loud ear-splitting roaring.

I had to go somewhere else. While I was happy for them—especially Theo—it was only nine. I couldn't listen to that for another two hours. The concierge had mentioned they had a Jacuzzi. Now was a perfect time to try it out, provided it wasn't too busy.

I went to the closet, pulled out my swimsuit, and put it on. Grabbing a room key and towel, I locked the door and took the elevator down, walked along a dark hallway, and went into the Jacuzzi room. There was no one there.

Intense and complete joy!

Laying my towel down, I settled into the hot water. It felt so good. I laid my watch on the edge so I could keep an eye on the time and pinned up my hair so it wouldn't get wet.

Resting my head back on the edge, I closed my eyes. I stayed like that for the longest while, thinking of nothing, just letting the water soothe me. When I opened my eyes next, I looked into a pair of familiar hazel ones above me.

Chapter Twenty-Two

I let out a scream, splashing water as I moved to the center of the Jacuzzi.

"Sorry. I didn't mean to scare you," he said seductively.

My danger sense went through the roof. "Please leave," I said, glaring at the man from the coffee shop. "I thought I'd made it clear I'm not interested."

"I'm interested. That's what matters."

It was time to leave. I went to the other side of the Jacuzzi, but he moved to intercept me. I went back to the center.

"Stay right there," he said, making it an order. "We'll have a nice time together—"

He was suddenly lifted from his feet by a hand wrapped around his neck.

"She told you to leave. Leave now."

I froze in the water. The cold voice didn't belong to Danial or Theo.

The man from the coffee shop dropped and stumbled to one knee. He regained his feet, grabbed his robe, and ran for the door without a backward look.

"I apologize for that male. His actions were deplorable."

My rescuer came out of the dark, his face in shadows. He was small for a man, only a little taller than me, but stocky. He tossed his robe off, revealing swim trunks below a thickly muscled chest. As he walked closer, I was able to see him better. His hair was light brown and short, no longer than an inch. His blue eyes crinkled at the corners. Kind eyes.

I relaxed a little. "Thanks."

He slowly walked into the tub. Reflexively, I moved away, cautious.

"Please," he said, holding up a hand. "You don't have to leave." He bared his teeth, revealing vampire canines.

I put my arms up on the edge to push myself out of the water, definitely leaving.

"Why do you fear? I know what your choker means, as well as those scars you wear so beautifully. I won't come any closer than I am right now." He tipped back his head and sat in the water. "You are safe with me. Be silent and calm."

I watched him for another few minutes before I relaxed, deciding he'd meant what he'd said. Minutes passed and we didn't speak. There was a lot I wanted to ask, like who the hell he was, but his request for me to be silent made me think the less I knew, the better. It was better to wait a few minutes and then casually leave.

Several minutes later, I pushed myself up and out of the tub, reluctantly leaving the hot water. I put my watch on and then my robe, draping the towel around my neck. "Thank you. Goodnight."

He picked his head up, his blue eyes meeting mine. "You are heading back to your room, yes? You should not roam alone without an escort, Lady."

I didn't see where that was any of his business, but he'd saved me from the jerk from the coffee shop. "Yes."

"It is good to see some of the old traditions still alive. Too many humans feel the Oath is not worth taking today, that wearing the choker demeans them. It warms this old heart to see that there are still some beautiful women who are not afraid to truly give themselves to a man." He paused. "Go. My man will shadow you until you reach the lobby."

* * * *

As I showered off in the room, I bitched at myself for impulsively going off alone when I should have stayed there. The suite was silent enough now.

I dressed in the red silk sheath, unpinned my hair, and lay down to wait. Danial came in a few moments later, exhausted. When he saw me waiting for him, he perked right up.

"Give me a few minutes to shower."

A few minutes later, he was back, a towel wrapped around him, his wet hair falling to his shoulders. Then he was in my arms, his lips burning as he passionately kissed me. He molded my body to his, and I let out a moan, feeling him moving so insistently against me. He slid the straps of my sheath down as his fangs brushed my scars.

I wrapped my hand tightly around him, making him gasp. I stroked him, rubbing with my thumb, and he responded by taking my breast in his mouth. It was then my turn to stiffen and gasp. His hands caressed up and down my body.

He suddenly reached down and pushed up my sheath as he sat me on top of him. The silk whispered over my hips as he pulled my legs apart to straddle him.

"Tell me you want me," he whispered. "Tell me I'm all you want."

"Yes."

He entered as I moved my hips to meet him. He was so warm, I felt as if I were melting. We didn't last long. I came first, screaming my pleasure. As it ebbed, he kissed me again, then rolled us over to resume thrusting. A moment later, the warm rush of him filled me as he cried out his release.

He rolled off and pulled me to him, spooning me. "You're all I want, too," he said lovingly. "Rest with me."

I awoke some time later to find him kissing my face.

"Did you have a good time today?" he said affectionately.

"I had a great time."

I began describing it, getting to the part about Hazel Eyes, when he stopped me. "I have something for you. I forgot when I saw you in bed, waiting for me." He got up and came back with a bag. "Open it."

"What's this?"

"Open it," he said with a wide smile.

I opened the small bag. Inside was a box; more precisely, a square velvet box. I knew what boxes this size and shape usually contained.

I drew it out and carefully opened it. Inside was a diamond ring, a half carat set in white gold. Three strands of gold were woven over and under the diamond, as if magic held it in place.

"It's a tension setting. I had it designed for you. I tried to choose something that wouldn't hamper you, no matter what the activity. Do you like it?"

"I love it!" I said excitedly, giving him a big kiss.

He beamed and put it on my ring finger. I watched it wink in the light for a few minutes, stunned. I'd never expected to have another diamond ring on that hand.

"Why'd you give this to me?" I asked. "Are you asking me to marry you?"

"No, but you've been so accepting of my customs that I wanted to do this for you. You have friends and family that will want to know I'm serious about you. You can't tell them about the Oath or what the choker means. They'll understand this. When you Oath to me, I'll give you a gold band to wear, if that's what you want. And I'll honor you under the Oath the way a married man honors his wife."

Now was as good a time as any to ask him. It wasn't going to get any easier. "Do you want me to keep my scars? I know they mean something more than bite marks."

"Coupled with the choker, they are the sign of an Oathed human," he said just as carefully. "If you want me to remove them, I will. I know we are not Oathed yet and—"

"I'll keep them for you," I said softly.

He looked at me for a moment, then said with heat and passion, "I love you, Sar."

I opened my mouth to say it back, but he cut me off with a kiss. Then he was inside me again, but this time he was tender, gentle, as he hadn't been before. He made love slowly and it went on until I thought I might go crazy with sensation. The length of him sliding inside, the muscles of his chest contracting, his lips kissing my neck, his hands cupping my breasts...

The orgasm broke over us like a wave, my voice joining his. We held each other tightly as we both spasmed a little.

As our breathing slowly returned to normal, I remembered Hazel Eyes. "I need to tell you something."

For once, he didn't seem wary of what I might say. "What is it, dear heart?"

I told him everything. He was angry over what Hazel Eyes had said to me, but when I mentioned the vampire, he became worried. "What did he look like?"

I described the vampire.

Danial shook his head. "That description fits more than a dozen vampires I know. Did he say a name?"

"No. He told me to be silent. I left as soon as I could."

"What did he do? Tell me everything again, word for word."

I repeated my story.

"He must have been old, at least as old as me," he said. "But I don't know anyone that old fitting his description who would be here now." He hugged me to him "I'm glad you weren't harmed by that jerk and for the intercession on your behalf. But no more leaving the room alone while we're traveling—"

"I won't."

"Good."

* * * *

When Danial and I woke, it was time to go. We checked out, and Theo drove us to the airport.

As Danial and I boarded the plane, I looked back to see Tawny and Theo saying good-bye. He hugged her, and a tear on her cheek shined in the nearby hanger lights. It was clearly more than good sex to her. Maybe that was why he refused to go out west when Danial had asked him to go. I wanted to ask her why she didn't come back to the States with us, but I knew enough to mind my own business.

* * * *

The next weeks passed quickly. With a lot of effort, Danial and I made it work. Yet there were a couple of setbacks.

One came when he tasted me the first time since I'd moved in with him. We'd begun to kiss and he'd done that move, cutting me. With a cry, I jerked back, hitting my head on the wall.

"What's wrong?" he asked, shocked.

"It hurt," I said, scared.

"It shouldn't," he said nervously. "I made only a little cut."

His nervousness frightened me. "Try biting me instead."

We resumed our love play. When I relaxed enough, he bit shallowly. I shrieked this time, and he immediately withdrew his fangs, holding his mouth over the wound. I knew by the pain going away that he'd given me blood to heal the wounds.

I began to cry. Giving him my blood was important to both of us. If he couldn't do it without pain, he wouldn't enjoy it—and neither would I.

"Shh, don't cry," he said, hugging me. "We have one more thing we can try."

He made love to me. When I came, he bit shallowly again. There was some pain, but it was hardly noticeable in the deliciousness of the orgasm.

"I'll only take your blood like this from now on. I don't want you to hurt sharing blood with me."

"Why is this happening?" I asked. "Why now?"

"It happens sometimes. If a vampire bites the same person repeatedly that person can develop a resistance to the numbing component in vampire saliva. But the blood always works. I'll always be able to heal you and take the pain away. Don't worry, okay?"

The weeks went past and Danial refused to bite me again, saying he wanted to wait until Doctor Camlyn pronounced me healthy. I knew he loved me and was concerned, but I suspected that he was worried I'd leave him now.

The second and more insidious problem in living with Danial was my indolence.

The first few weeks were heaven, and I basked in my free time; reading for hours, baking complex desserts or watching the entire trilogy of the Lord of the Rings in one sitting. But soon, I began to feel like a true concubine must have felt; tasked with only one real duty. When something broke, I didn't have to fix it. Nor did I have to worry about anything serious, because now that was Danial's job. I'd always been self-reliant. Relying on someone else for everything that mattered felt alien. Was this really how I wanted to spend the rest of my life? Was this all I wanted to achieve?

I avoided thinking about that, telling myself I didn't have to decide anytime soon. Danial had said I could take my time to give myself to him as long as I chose to show the world that I was his. It was a given that he expected my oath eventually. He was very proud, and I knew it pricked him that I wasn't truly his yet.

Promise Me

Then there were the women, his donors. They were never in our bed and I didn't usually see them. Angelica was the one I wanted to avoid the most. Unfortunately, she didn't feel that way.

I was reading in the great room one December night. Engrossed in my book, I didn't hear her ascend from the basement stairs until she was in front of me.

"Hello, Sarelle." Her voice was sexy and threaded with lust.

I looked up. Like the last time, she held a gauze pad to her neck and wore a low-cut dress and spike heels. But I couldn't expect her to wear a fleece sweatshirt, could I? No, that would only be appropriate for cold weather, like the snowstorm raging outside.

"Since we've already met, I wanted to be polite. How are you?"

I tried not to be petty. Sure, she was a bitch, but most decorous women were to women unlike themselves. She was only there for an hour a month when Danial needed her blood. I held my tongue, closed my book with a snap and made sure the light caught my ring sparkling on my finger. "Hello, Angelica."

"I hope you don't mind sharing your man with me," she said lightly. Her smile slipped a little, revealing the envy underneath.

"I'm thankful for what you and the others give him," I said, trying to keep my smile in place.

"I'm surprised you're so understanding. I might not be."

"Don't worry about it. I understand you completely," I said coldly. "So does Danial."

He called out for her from downstairs. With a smirk, she went back down. One of the SUVs started out back.

Danial came upstairs. "I'm sorry she said that. I don't have to see her again if—"

I put my book down. "Don't be sorry. What she said was true for her. What I told her was true for me."

"You aren't upset?"

"This is part of being with you." I wasn't really upset, just irked. "You were open about it. I trust you."

"Frankly, I thought you'd ask me before now to switch to animal or packaged blood. I thought we'd have our first fight over that. I've been worried about it all month."

I laughed a little, which only confused him.

"I wouldn't want to eat only cake made from fat-free chocolate substitute or drink water instead of wine. This is your life and you only get to eat one thing, so you should get the best. You told me fresh tastes best. I just prefer not to watch or meet your donors."

He took my hand. "I know you're still worried about the potions. I've told you, I only have enough of both for the rest of this month. Then we'll decide whether to get more. You're the one I'm worried about."

"Why? My doctor's appointment went well. My blood levels were okay. Camlyn said if I kept taking the vitamins, I'd be fine. I'm just sorry you're no closer to your goal."

"What goal?" he asked uneasily.

"Making vampires, or understanding why you can't and Devlin can."

"It's more of a hobby than a goal," he said with a shrug. "Speaking of Devlin, that was him on the phone." He paused. "Ryan is dead. Devlin killed him tonight. There will be no more curses."

I would rather hear that Devlin had been killed. The curses had been his doing really, not Ryan's. "That's thoughtful of him. He's not planning on visiting, is he?"

"No. He's forbidden from coming here. But forget about him. Why don't we go out tonight? See a movie or go dancing?"

"Was there anything you had in mind?"

"Not really. But we haven't gone out for a while, and you haven't come with me on any more trips. I enjoy taking you out."

"Whatever you'd like, I'm up for a movie or dancing."

"I vote for dancing. Say the Haunt?"

"Give me a half hour. I have a surprise for you."

We had a great time. Tatiana was overjoyed to see us, giving each of us a hug before escorting us to the table we'd sat at a month and a half ago. We danced and talked, sharing how self-conscious we'd been that night.

"So you liked my surprise?" I teased.

"I love the dress," he said, getting to his feet and extending his hand. "Red becomes you. Dance with me."

The strains of Lady in Red began. Blushing, I joined him on the floor. As we danced, he sang some of the words to me. At the end of the song, he held me close to whisper, "My lady in red, I love you."

Driving home that night, I almost told him that I was ready to give him my Oath. But I wanted it to be special, not tell him as we were driving home. So I only told him I loved him and he told me the same.

Later that night, as I prepared for bed, I wondered if I was afraid to commit. I'd put off forwarding my mail or bringing my cats there to live, telling myself it was too soon. It seemed too fast to commit my life to someone after only two months, but how long would be enough? I was happy living with Danial. My old life seemed a black hole of loneliness in comparison. What was I waiting for?

* * * *

Danial announced the night before Christmas Eve that Aran had asked Cia to be his mate and they would be moving back to the communal bunker. "The date for the ceremony is New Year's."

"I'm happy for them."

"Don't worry. Suri volunteered to watch over your house for the winter."

Later that night, I decided that was the sign I'd been waiting for. Christmas Eve would be the perfect time to break the news.

* * * *

Christmas Eve visiting my parents went better than expected.

I'd spoken to my mother every few days but I'd wanted to tell her about the ring face to face. When we came in, I made sure to display it prominently.

"Sarelle, you have a ring!" She almost elbowed Danial into the TV trying to get to me fast enough. "It's beautiful.

"He asked me to marry him." I winced at the lie, and then told myself it was close to truth.

Chris broke out the scotch to celebrate, and we all had a toast. I clinked my glass with Danial's, seeing their happy faces and listening to them making plans.

"Happy?" he whispered.

"Very."

* * * *

Later that night, he and I sat by the blinking Christmas tree in the great room. Suri and the other foxes had helped me put it up earlier that day. I'd brought some lights from home, but others I'd made with the help of Ivan, Janice, and Demetri: popcorn strings, cookie ornaments, pinecones, and various nuts and feathers.

Theo had declined to help, saying he had work to do. He'd come in with a golden star when we were almost done, and I'd seen the pleasure in his face when he'd put it on top. By the time I'd turned to ask him about it, he was already gone.

He'd been distant to me ever since I'd moved in. The few times we'd needed to talk, he'd been polite but short. I wondered if seeing Danial and me so much in love hurt, if he remembered Tawny and missed her.

"You look tense," Danial said. "I can fix that. Slide your feet this way."

He proceeded to give me a foot massage. I writhed in pleasure and uttered moans as he eased all my tensions with the deft manipulation from his strong hands.

"Is there anything you aren't good at?" I asked, sighing with contentment.

"Not many things," he said immodestly.

I laughed. He tickled my foot, and I shrieked. Ghost and Darkness looked up, decided it was nothing important, and laid their heads down again.

"I have something for you," he said. "Look under the tree."

"Really, Danial, you give me too much as it is—"

"Shh," he said holding his finger to my lips. "I'll get it."

He got up and retrieved a gift bag from the tree's base. "Open it."

I opened the package and took out a beautiful black velvet robe. As I slipped it on over my nightgown, I felt something in the pocket. It was red velvet box, containing a pair of stunning gold earrings. I fingered the choker at my neck with the same symbol: the gold fox head, ruby eyes glinting.

"They're beautiful," I said, giving him a kiss. "Thank you."

"Put them on."

I removed my gold nugget earrings and slipped on the others.

"They look lovely. See for yourself."

Looking at myself in the bathroom mirror, I thought it might be too much. Between the scars, the choker, and the fox earrings, I felt like I had a sign on my forehead that said "Danial's" in huge letters. The ruby eyes winked at me in the light and I moved my head to make them flash and sparkle. "They're beautiful."

"I'm glad you like them," he called from the great room.

I paused before the mirror. This was it, the moment I'd planned on telling him I would swear to be his. Like before, my uncertainties arose. I couldn't ever leave him if I did. Ever. Was I that sure?

Words my friend Kat had spoken earlier that week over our holiday celebration lunch came back to me. *Why haven't you told him you'll marry him? Are you crazy? You love him; he loves you, he's rich and he's gorgeous! How can you even have to think about it?*

I went to the bedroom door. Danial waited for me, the strong lines of his face relaxed in a happy smile as he studied the tree. His freshly cut hair feathered back except for a loose wave that fell over his forehead. I loved him so much my chest ached.

It was then or never. It was the perfect moment. Kat was right; things weren't going to get any better. If I didn't do this, I'd wonder the rest of my life what it could have been like with him, what I missed out on by not taking the chance.

I walked to the couch and bent over, kissing him on his lips. "They are beautiful. Thank you."

"I'm glad you like them." He reached for me. "Sit with me."

I took hold of his hand and gently pushed it back toward him. That got his attention.

"Sar?" he said, alarm and wariness clouding his features.

"I have something for you, too."

I went to my knees beside the couch. He watched me, riveted.

God, I so wanted to do this perfectly, like I'd mentally rehearsed all afternoon. "I'm yours, Danial Racklan, for tonight and the rest of my life. I, Sarelle McGarran, promise myself to you."

He helped me to my feet, hugging me tightly. "I, Danial Racklan, accept your Oath to me, Sarelle McGarran. From this day forward, you are mine to love, protect, and honor. What we have joined together no one may put asunder."

I hugged him, shell-shocked. I'd wanted him to understand that I wanted to give him my Oath, not do the actual Oath there and then. "Don't we need witnesses?" I whispered.

"No," he said happily. "You offer your word to bind yourself to me, and I accept. That's all there is." He scooped me up in a quick motion. "Except for the consummation."

He carried me into the bedroom and began removing his clothes. I removed mine, apprehensive. "What do I have to do?" I asked nervously.

"Nothing you haven't done before with me. Come here, sweetheart."

I went to him, my heart racing. He took my face in his hands and brought my lips to his gently, his fingers caressing me. When I tried to kiss him harder, he drew his lips aside and hugged me.

"Patience," he whispered. "We have the rest of our lives stretching out before us. But there will never be another night like this one." He kissed me again, chastely. "I want to remember you exactly as you are now, the way your hair shimmers, the love in your eyes as you look at me." He ran his hands backwards, brushing it from my face. "I forgot how good happiness felt. I want you to remember this night as one of the best of your life, the way I will remember it." He kissed me gently. "Tell me again you're mine, that you want to be."

"I'm yours," I said huskily. "I want you more than anything."

He let out a soft sigh, then his solemn expression curved into an eager smile. He eased us down on the bed and kissed down my throat, his fangs bringing moans with each light prick as he pressed his hips to me. I kissed him harder, shifting my hips under him to receive his first ardent thrust. Moments later, I slid into climax, Danial right behind me.

He kissed me again, then withdrew and cradled me close. For the first time, we didn't speak afterward, even to declare our love. Maybe for the first time, neither of us felt we needed to say the words.

* * * *

Danial drank from me that night during sex, reopening both scars and making the shallow one deeper. He did it very gently and tenderly, his love for me in every kiss and touch. Our sex had always been good, but that night, he made me feel cherished.

As we were drifting off near dawn, he asked "Where would you like to go?

"Go?"

"I understand it's traditional to go on a honeymoon for a week or two after marrying. Where would you most like to go?"

I thought of all the exotic locations that could be mine. "I'd like to stay here."

He looked at me with puzzlement. "Here?"

"I'd like you to stay here with you beside me. That's where I most want to be."

He traced my cheek with his hand, nodding. "Then that's what we'll do. Get some sleep."

I fell asleep in his arms, dreaming of my new life and all that was possible.

Funny. Back then I had no idea of how fast a life can change. But I was about to find out.

Chapter Twenty-Three

I woke up feeling completely happy. God, how had my life gotten so good? I'd been depressed and lonely three months ago, wondering if I'd ever find love again. My definition of an exciting night had been a pay-per-view movie and a bowl of popcorn. Now, I was living a life of luxury, wealthy by most persons' standards, and I had a wonderful successful man who loved me. It didn't get any better than this.

I cuddled up next to Danial and fell back to sleep. The next thing I knew, he was kissing me awake.

"Why are you dressed?" I asked sleepily.

"I've cancelled this week's appointments. After tonight's trip, I'm yours completely, no interruptions."

I kissed him back. "I'm all yours, too."

He sat down beside me and took my hand. "Would you consider quitting your job?"

I was immediately uneasy. "I don't want you to support me. That isn't why I Oathed to you."

He brought me into his arms. "I never thought it was, sweetheart. But I'm uncomfortable with you commuting so far, even two days a week. Some of it is selfishness on my part. I don't want anyone else having claim on your time. I want you to be able to go with me when I travel if you want to and stay up with me without worrying about work the next day. We don't need the money."

"It's not that. I can't just hang out here showing off my choker," I said flatly.

"Still feisty." He paused. "I survived this long because I love what I do. I want the same for you. Knowing you, I don't expect you to sit around long. I would like you to spend your days doing something you feel passionate about."

"Such as?"

"There are several charities you could volunteer your time to. Or perhaps we could build you a greenhouse? I know you love plants and gardening. Or take a few classes online if they interest you. Take your time to decide; there's no rush."

"I agree the commute is too long," I said, some of my anxiousness alleviated. "I thought about quitting, but I'm not sure I can. When I needed a job, my friends helped me out. Even though it's not my dream job, I can't just quit and leave them with no one doing safety work."

"They'll hire someone else," he said. "I'm sure you're replaceable."

I gave him a narrow look. "Am I?"

"I only meant that there are others who could do the safety work," he added quickly, turning serious. "Tell them you'll stay until they find someone else, if that eases your mind. Just know they are not the only ones who need you. Theo and I could use your help here."

Excitement flooded me. "You've never mentioned wanting my help with your business," I said, confused yet eager.

"I wanted to wait until you were sure you wanted your life to be with me," Danial replied, taking me in his arms. "Solutions, Inc is a dream I worked hard to make reality. It takes a large part of my waking hours. I'd like to include you in that dream, to share it with you."

"What would I do?"

"You could help with what you wanted to; be it computer work, other office work, or helping us solve some of the mystery cases we handle."

"Theo's okay with that? I don't want to step on his toes."

"He will be, once he sees your capability," Danial said with pride. "Would you be interested?"

I nodded eagerly, then turned trepidatious. "It sounds exciting, but what about the dangerous aspects? Aren't you going to worry if I've got people out to kill me?"

Danial's arms tightened around me. "You'd be working from home, Sar, not going on stakeouts. You're irreplaceable, and I want you as safe as possible." He kissed up my neck, pricking me gently. "You've made me believe in love again after more than sixty years—"

"Had it been so long?" I whispered.

"Yes," he said, turning cool. "But don't think on that. We're together now and we're going to be happy. Now get some sleep. I'll be back soon."

* * * *

I awoke an hour later, my muscles tensed, my heart racing. Breathing deeply and slowly, I tried to calm down.

I'd had another nightmare of Danial. We'd been making love in our bedroom. When I'd climaxed, he'd bitten me, making me swoon. As the minutes passed, he'd kept drinking. The pleasure had turned to pain, then agony. I'd beaten him, but he'd been a leech at my throat, immovable...

I hadn't had a bad dream of him since before the Hallows party months ago. Why was I having them now?

I ran my hand through my unbound hair, twirling the ends around my fingers. Maybe my fear of commitment, of losing someone I loved again?

The bedside clock read eight p.m. Danial would be gone for hours yet.

I pushed aside the covers. I wasn't going to be able to go back to sleep, and staying there trying was pointless. I'd take a walk to see Cia and announce my good news.

* * * *

After dressing in warm clothes, I walked to the kitchen. I expected Cia or one of the other guards to be there, but no one was. I tried the study next, looking for Theo, but no luck.

From the window near Theo's desk, I saw furtive movement. I opened the window, grimacing in the blast of cold night air. "Theo, is that you?"

Although I called out a few times, I didn't get any reply. Discouraged, I shut the window and went downstairs.

The dogs had heard my voice and were wide awake, waiting for me in the mudroom. "Sure," I said with a shrug. "You can come."

We walked into the cold night. There was a dusting of snow on the path to the fox barracks, and more than a few footprints from patrolling guards. The dogs jumped around and played while I thought more on my nightmare.

It must only be that I was going to give notice at work. I'd read somewhere that changing jobs was one of the most stressful events there was, next to losing a spouse.

"Good evening."

I looked up, startled. A man stood before me, one I didn't recognize. "Hi."

The dogs ran over to greet him, tails wagging. I relaxed visibly.

He patted them. "Out for a walk? You shouldn't be out here alone. Theo would be irritated."

"Where is he, by the way? I was heading to the barracks and wanted to let him know where I was going."

"He's target practicing in the forest. I'll take you to him."

Something about that made me uneasy. "He's practicing at night?"

He laughed. "He can see in the dark, like all werefoxes. Odds are if he needs to shoot someone, it'll be during the night hours." He extended a hand. "I'm Jake."

His grip was so tight it clutched my hand instead of held it. I disentangled myself from him as soon as I could. "I haven't met you before."

"I'm a new hire. This is a dangerous business," he said seriously. "You have to be on your toes all the time."

A shot rang out, making me jump. A few more echoed in succession.

"Come on," he said, beginning to walk. "Let's get going. I need to get back to my post."

I followed him into the forest, Ghost and Darkness coming in closer. There was a narrow gravel trail there. I could see that feet had come down it recently, a lot of feet.

Shots sounded again, sometimes one, and sometimes a volley. I couldn't be sure where they were coming from. We were in a grove of huge pines.

He pushed aside a heavy fir branch covered with snow. "Just a little farther."

I followed him into a clearing. Men watched as a central figure emptied his gun at targets on the far side of the field. It had to be Theo. I opened my mouth to yell a welcome, but it died in my throat.

Ivan sagged in front of one of the targets. He'd been tied to it. The earth and snow at his feet was red with blood. His blood. But his eyes were awake and aware, the gag in his mouth turning his screams of pain to muffled whimpers.

"Prop him up," the shooter said harshly, reloading. "I'm just getting started."

Jake gave me a shove. "Look what I found, Turk."

Turk finished reloading and turned to us. "Well, well, the grand dame." He walked over, his gait almost hitching. "Anyone see you take her?"

"No. She was out walking alone, can you believe it?"

"Get him," I commanded the dogs. "Get him!"

Turk walked up to me and shook his head slightly. Holding my eyes, he reached his hand toward the dogs. To my amazement, their tails wagged as he petted them.

"We're werevultures," he said. "Our avian scent tells them we're harmless. Unless you've trained your dogs to attack birds, you're out of luck."

"You touch me and they'll attack you no matter what you smell like," I said. "Who are you? Why are you here? Where's Theo?"

"I haven't found Theo," Jake rasped from behind me. "I'll go back out. He's got to be here. We've got the only two guards that were near the house."

"And the rest of the guards?"

"In their barracks, still carrying on over their Christmas presents and eggnog. You were right; this was a good night to attack." He grinned and jogged back the way we'd come.

Turk turned to me. "You're a nice bonus. We'll not only get some revenge, we'll get some ransom money out of this."

I turned and ran for the forest, the dogs bounding beside me. Wings buffeted my face as a pair of huge birds descended on the dogs and me, landing in front of us to bar the way. I recoiled at the blood on their beaks and claws. The dogs gave them a confused look and retreated close to me, whining.

270

"Let me go!"

Turk laughed behind me. "Not before we have what we came for—"

The left bird exploded in a cloud of bloody feathers, followed by the right bird.

Turk grabbed hold of me, drawing me close as a shield. "That you, Theo?"

Theo strode into the clearing, his gun smoking. "Get out now or you're dead."

"You've got balls to threaten me," Turk laughed. "I'm ranked and you're shit."

"Let her go," Theo growled.

"Kill him," Turk ordered.

Bullets thwacked the ground where Theo had stood just before he darted into the trees. The other birdmen went after him, guns blazing. Turk backed to the far side of the clearing behind the targets and a still struggling Ivan. My dogs followed us at a distance, whining. Gunfire echoed, then receded.

"You just sit tight," he muttered. "He thinks he's hot stuff, but he's wrong."

"Who are you?" I demanded. "Why do you want revenge?"

I heard a "psst" and then Turk's arms abruptly fell away as his body crumpled to the snow, disbelief and pain on his face.

Theo stepped out of the trees behind us. "Cover your ears and step back."

I grabbed the dogs and moved away.

He put his gun to Turk's temple and shot him. The round took off most of the side of his face and head. The following rounds obliterated his head.

Theo reloaded his gun with a fresh magazine and turned to me. "Are you okay?"

I wanted badly to rush into his arms. Instead, I took a deep breath and tried to stop shaking. "I think so."

"Some of Garrett's old guards," he said, nudging Turk with his shoe. "They were asked to leave the state." He reholstered his gun and held out his hand. "Come on, let's get you back inside."

I cast a look down to the far end of the field. "What about Ivan?"

He kept walking. "He didn't even get off a shot to alert me that we'd been invaded. If it hadn't been for Tatiana, we'd all have been bird meat. He can chew his way loose."

He had a point. With a last look toward Ivan, I followed him back through the trees.

"How did Tatiana know?"

"She's got a spell on the land that makes it appear as forest to anyone looking down from above. Part of that spell includes monitoring any penetration from above by a large object, alive or not." He looked at me, then away. "Danial doesn't like surprises. Neither do I."

"What did he mean about being ranked?"

"Jesus, can't you ever just be quiet—"

He broke off with a jerk, his face grimacing. He stumbled, and I saw Jake behind him, holding a gun.

"She's not the only one who talks too much," Jake said evilly.

Theo drew his gun and fired, but Jake had vanished into the trees.

My eyes darted. "Where is he?"

"Run for the house," he said urgently. "Now!"

Jake suddenly charged him from the shadows, slamming into his side, knocking the gun from his hand as they grappled in the snow. The dogs barked furiously, darting in and snapping at both figures, their hackles up.

Jake tried to bring his gun to fire pointblank into Theo's heart, but Theo knocked it aside in time to have it discharge into the ground. The report made me jump. Theo kneed Jake, who rolled onto his side, and Theo went for his gun. But as he reached for it, he let out a gasp of pain.

"You're nothing, jackass," Jake grated, his hand on the hilt of a knife buried in Theo's back. "Turk was the tenth best killer around." He twisted the knife, making Theo grunt. "You killed all my friends, bastard! Feel that burning? It's poison—"

His words ended in a gurgle as a bullet exploded his throat, showering Theo in brain matter. Jake's headless corpse toppled back to rest on his head, his momentum pulling Theo with him.

I went to my knees, trying to stop Theo from falling. It took all of my strength, but I braced him on his hands and knees.

"Hold me steady," he panted, laying the smoking gun down. "I've got to get it out or I'll die."

I steeled myself. "I can pull it out."

"Don't touch it. The poison might kill you." He took a deep breath, then reached around and up, sliding the knife out with a wash of blood. He dropped it and sagged in my arms, toppling me over backward.

I lay there in the snow, his head on my chest, trying to breath. God, he was heavy. "Are you okay?"

"I will be," he said weakly. He rolled off me with a groan, reaching for his jacket pocket. He tried feebly to get inside it, but the flap was buttoned.

I opened it and took out a vial of liquid. "Here."

He took it from me with grateful eyes and swallowed it. A moment later, he let out a sigh and visibly relaxed. "I can feel it working. Thank God, he used common poison."

Common poison? "Want me to help you up?"

"In a minute." He wiped his face with his hands, smearing snow over it. "The cold helps the pain."

I picked up his gun and handed it to him. "What did he mean about being ranked?"

He looked up and rolled his eyes. "There's a hierarchy for vampires and there's one for people like me who guard them."

"He said killer, not guard," I murmured.

"It's part of the job to kill," he said coldly, getting to his feet. "I'd think you'd be grateful for that by now. Or maybe you'd rather be killed than kill anyone."

"I'm not afraid to kill." I glared up at him. "That doesn't mean I enjoy it."

"That assassin of Max's? You defended yourself, that's all. And these would have done more than ransom you." He turned bitter. "Garrett didn't fuck up Neoline all by himself. He had his men help." He turned arrogant. "You should be thanking me for saving you."

I looked down at Jake's corpse, remembering how quick he'd been. What might have happened to me if Theo hadn't shown up when he had?

"You're trembling," he said. He put his arm around me, patting me awkwardly. "Don't be afraid; they're dead."

I hadn't had a gun. If Jake had finished Theo, I'd have been helpless. My shaking intensified. I hugged Theo hard with both arms, trying not to cry.

His arms tightened around me. "Hey, I'm sorry for saying what I did—"

"I'm okay," I said shakily into his throat. "It's just adrenaline."

"Shh," he said gently. "I'm right here. No one's going to hurt you. Just breathe."

I held him until my breathing went back to normal. The solidness of him was comforting. Safe. I felt safe.

"We should go back," he whispered. "You must be cold."

I smiled, ready to say that he was holding me way too close for me to be cold. But when I looked up and met his concerned storm-cloud blue eyes, my throat was so dry I couldn't talk. I moved back, feeling awkward. "Yes, we should get back. Danial will be home soon."

He nodded. "Please don't mention this to him."

I gave him an incredulous look. "You want me to lie?"

He cleared his throat, embarrassed. "I meant don't say anything tonight. I'll tell him later. But I don't want to ruin the first night of your honeymoon. He's waited a long time to love someone."

"He told you."

"Of course, he told me. He's my friend and he's ecstatic."

"Won't Ivan say something?"

"And risk being fired for watching porn when he was supposed to be standing guard? Not likely." He reholstered his gun. "And as fights go, this was just a scuffle."

I looked at him, then away. "Okay."

"If you'd have stayed indoors, I'd have taken care of them with no problem."

"Sure you would have."

He snorted. "Come on, let's get you back inside. I've got a lot of work to do."

I nodded. We walked away through the trees.

* * * *

After I'd washed away the blood on my hands and thrown my clothes into the washer, I crawled into bed. Danial was still not back.

I went over the events of the night, how scared I'd been and how safe I'd felt with Theo. How I'd felt when he'd held me and said he wouldn't let anything hurt me...

I brushed my thoughts of Theo aside, feeling guilty to be thinking of him on what was the first night of my honeymoon with Danial. I was still rattled by Garrett's men attacking, that's what it was...

"Sar," Cia called from outside the door. "Are you all set? I understand from Ivan there was some excitement earlier."

"I'm fine," I said diffidently. "Theo's out there, right?"

"He's patrolling outside with a group, checking that all of Garrett's men were killed. He'll be out there watching personally the rest of the night, until every inch of the forest is searched."

I stretched out, all the tension leaving my body. "I'm fine. But please tell him thanks for me."

"For what?" she said curiously.

"For being himself," I said with a smile.

"Okay," she said more curiously. "Goodnight."

I lay there silently, considering Danial's offer. It would be challenging work to join Theo and him. Despite his confidence in me, there would be a lot I'd need to learn. But I already knew I was going to tell Danial to count me in.

I'd found the promise of a new life. Now it was time to start living it.

About the Author

Tara Fox Hall's writing credits include nonfiction, horror, suspense, action-adventure, erotica, and contemporary and historical paranormal romance. She is the author of the paranormal action-adventure *Lash* series and the vampire romantic suspense *Promise Me* series. Tara divides her free time unequally between writing novels and short stories, chainsawing firewood, caring for stray animals, sewing cat and dog beds for donation to animal shelters, and target practice.

www.tarafoxhall.com

Other works by the author with Melange Books, LLC

Return To Me
Surrender to Me
The Origin of Fear in Spellbound 2011 Anthology
Kink in Wicked Christmas Wishes Anthology
The Oath in Wicked Christmas Wishes Anthology

www.ingramcontent.com/pod-product-compliance
Lightning Source LLC
Chambersburg PA
CBHW020817260626
47169CB00003B/713